I HATE BEING RIGHT.

"All of their weapons are active and they're trying to target us," Klisiewicz reported. "They're maneuvering to get in below and behind us."

"Let's not show them our ass," Stano said. "Keep us facing them, helm."

"Be ready to reroute shield pow̲e̲ ̲.̲.̲.̲ ̲.̲ ̲K̲ ̲.̲ atami warned, casting a q̲u̲ ̲.̲ ̲.̲ ̲.̲ ̲ who offered a knowin̲ ̲.̲ ̲.̲ ̲.̲ ̲ ̲.̲ ̲ ̲.̲ ̲ this is liable to get."

"All set," Stan̲ ̲.̲ ̲.̲ ̲.̲ ̲.̲ ̲.̲ ̲.̲ ̲.̲ ̲ seat of her own on the b̲ ̲.̲ ̲.̲ ̲.̲ ̲.̲ ̲ago taken up the practice of mannin̲ ̲.̲ ̲.̲ ̲.̲ ̲various stations on a rotating schedule, in order to remain proficient in each position's function. During emergency situations such as this, her ability to operate any of the workstations allowed her to free up the person at that console for other duties. In this case, she was able to relieve the officer normally assigned to the engineering station so that she could return belowdecks to assist Commander Yataro and the rest of the *Endeavour*'s engineering staff.

"They've entered firing range!" Klisiewicz called out. "Locking weapons!"

Without waiting for an order, Neelakanta banked the ship to starboard, and Khatami saw the image of the rings on the viewscreen tilt upward as the *Endeavour* dove toward them. It took only seconds for the display to become clouded with dust and debris, the starship maneuvering through the field as its deflectors pushed aside or simply vaporized most of the fragments and other detritus.

Klisiewicz shouted, "Incoming!"

Read more adventures of the starships
Endeavour and *Sagittarius* in the saga of

STAR TREK®
VANGUARD

STAR TREK®
SEEKERS

POINT OF DIVERGENCE

DAYTON WARD & KEVIN DILMORE

Story by
**Dayton Ward & Kevin Dilmore
and David Mack**

Based upon *Star Trek*
created by Gene Roddenberry

POCKET BOOKS
New York   London   Toronto   Sydney   New Delhi

Pocket Books
A Division of Simon & Schuster, Inc.
1230 Avenue of the Americas
New York, NY 10020

This book is a work of fiction. Any references to historical events, real people, or real places are used fictitiously. Other names, characters, places, and events are products of the authors' imaginations, and any resemblance to actual events or places or persons, living or dead, is entirely coincidental.

First Pocket Books paperback edition September 2014

POCKET and colophon are registered trademarks of Simon & Schuster, Inc.

For information about special discounts for bulk purchases, please contact Simon & Schuster Special Sales at 1-866-506-1949 or business@simonandschuster.com.

The Simon & Schuster Speakers Bureau can bring authors to your live event. For more information or to book an event, contact the Simon & Schuster Speakers Bureau at 1-866-248-3049 or visit our website at www.simonspeakers.com.

Cover art and design by Rob Caswell

Manufactured in the United States of America

10 9 8 7 6 5 4 3 2 1

ISBN 978-1-4767-5726-1
ISBN 978-1-4767-5727-8 (ebook)

Historian's Note

This story takes place in August 2269, a couple of months after the *Starship Enterprise* returns from a rescue mission at Camus II (*Star Trek*, "Turnabout Intruder") and approximately six months after the destruction of Starbase 47 (*Star Trek Vanguard—Storming Heaven*). *Point of Divergence* carries forward from the events of the first *Star Trek: Seekers* novel, *Second Nature*.

POINT OF DIVERGENCE

1

Kang seethed.

Sitting in the high-backed command chair at the center of the *Imperial Klingon Cruiser Voh'tahk*'s bridge, the captain clasped his hands together before his chest, his fingers flexing as their nails pressed against skin, as though ready to draw blood of their own volition. His jaw clenched, he felt the rhythmic cadence of his teeth grinding against one another as he beheld the cursed green ball of water centered on the main viewscreen, all the while imagining the world consumed by fire.

"Report," he snapped. "Where is the Federation cruiser, Mahzh?"

Standing at his tactical console, the *Voh'tahk*'s senior weapons officer turned to face the captain. "The *Endeavour* is maintaining standard orbit, currently on the opposite side of the planet from our present position. Their orbit will bring them over the *Homghor*'s crash site momentarily, and the location of their own downed vessel soon after that. Their weapons and shields are active, and their sensors are scanning both crash locations."

It had been less than a *rep* since the *I.K.S. Homghor*, the bird-of-prey that had accompanied his own vessel to this star system, had plummeted to the surface of the world displayed on the main viewscreen, after falling victim to the weapons of a Federation scout ship, the

U.S.S. Sagittarius. Driven by rage and a thirst for vengeance, Kang had brought the *Voh'tahk*'s own armaments to bear, crippling the smaller Starfleet vessel and driving it down through the planet's atmosphere. The *Homghor* had crash-landed on the world's largest landmass, while the Starfleet scout ship had come to rest on a smaller adjacent island. The *U.S.S. Endeavour* had arrived soon afterward, despite his demands for the Federation warship to give the planet a wide berth. Its captain had rebuked his admonition, choosing instead to offer her own warnings should hostilities ensue. This had served to stoke Kang's temper, and it was requiring every iota of his will to maintain his composure.

"Helm, maintain our present orbit," he ordered, before glancing once more to Mahzh. "And what of the *Sagittarius*?" He still was irritated that he had not been given the opportunity to destroy the bothersome ship before it fell from orbit.

The weapons officer replied, "It fared far better than the *Homghor*, Captain. Its crew was able to effect a partially controlled descent, though sensor readings indicate that the vessel is unable to regain flight."

"Are you detecting any *Homghor* survivors?"

Mahzh nodded. "The only Klingon life sign I can find is Doctor Tormog, Captain. There also is some background interference that is clouding our sensor scans, but I'm detecting several other life-forms, and the readings are somewhat consistent with the Tomol biosigns forwarded to us by Tormog and the reconnaissance party." He paused, and Kang saw him scowl. "There are some . . . variations, as well."

"The transformation Tormog described?" Kang sensed movement to his right and looked up to see his wife, Mara, the *Voh'tahk*'s first officer, moving from her station toward him.

"It would seem that Captain Durak did not heed the doctor's advice," she said. "Tormog warned us not to transport any of the subjects to our ships. At least, not after the transformation had taken place."

Kang grunted in reluctant agreement, his irritation further fueled by the knowledge that the petulant scientist, Tormog, was correct in his judgment regarding the hazardous nature of this planet's inhabitants, the Tomol. Kang had been skeptical of the doctor's claims and the reports he had submitted detailing his observations of these people, which initial accounts had concluded was a primitive society that would bow without resistance to Klingon conquest. Instead, Tormog had described the startling metamorphosis to which the Tomol's bodies were subjected upon reaching maturity, and if they did not choose to end their own life as part of a bizarre, elaborate suicide ritual. It all had sounded more like the imaginative fabrication of a gifted storyteller or the deluded ravings of someone consumed by mental illness. Now, however, the evidence confronting Kang, in the form of the odd life readings on the surface and the deaths of Captain Durak and the crew of the *Homghor*, not only exonerated Tormog but also presented the captain with an unusual challenge.

It had been the doctor's intention to capture and place into stasis one or more subjects who were not yet old enough to exhibit early symptoms of this inexplicable transmutation, and that seemed still to be a viable plan, but surely there was greater glory in capturing one of these ridiculous *pujwI'* not in their natural state but rather after their changing into this far more powerful and dangerous life-form. That, to Kang, was a battle-worth fighting. Perhaps Captain Durak had felt the same way, but even if that were true, it appeared that the *Homghor*'s commander and crew had tragically underestimated their adversary.

Kang had no intention of making that error.

"You're still thinking of attacking them, aren't you?" Mara asked, her voice low enough that only Kang could hear. Before he could offer even the first word of protest, her eyes narrowed and she leaned closer. "I see it in your face. You want to do it now, before reinforcements arrive."

Scowling in disapproval, Kang glanced around the bridge to see if any of his crew might have overheard his wife's blunt statements, but the other officers appeared focused on their duties. "Reinforcements do not concern me. I have considered an attack, but I know that now is not the time." He paused, releasing a small sigh of exasperation. "Loath as I am to admit it, Earthers have a propensity for extracting answers to even the most imposing of questions. It's possible they know more about these Tomol than even Doctor Tormog was able to learn. We must determine whether this is true, and that imperative outweighs any personal agenda I may hold."

His desire to exact vengeance against the *Sagittarius* for the loss of the *Homghor* had been interrupted by the *Endeavour*'s untimely arrival. The *Constitution*-class cruiser and his own vessel were well matched to face off in battle, but Kang long ago had learned the harsh lesson that a ship is only as effective as its commander and the crew who followed him. While he had no doubts about his own abilities, he knew almost nothing about the Starfleet ship's captain. Of course, Kang also was aware that the propaganda the empire liked to distribute about Earthers and their distaste for battle was as inaccurate as it was short-sighted. If humans had proved anything in the generations since the empire had become aware of their existence, it was their tenacity and guile. Kang's own experience against human ship commanders had reinforced this belief, which was further supported upon the *Endeavour*'s arrival and its female Earther captain's quick, unflinching warning that she would unleash her vessel's weapons at the first sign of hostile action on his part. As he replayed the brief exchange in his mind, he found himself both angered and yet impressed by her brash declaration. In some ways, he realized, Captain Khatami seemed to embody many of the same qualities he admired in his own wife.

You would be wise to keep such observations to yourself, Captain, lest Mara carve them from your brain with her own blade.

The rage he had felt after his first and so far only conversation with the *Endeavour*'s commanding officer had ebbed, though he still harbored resentment at the Starfleet captain's arrogant demeanor and threats against him and his ship. His first instinct had been to release the full fury of the *Voh'tahk*'s weapons against the *Endeavour*, but that impulse had subsided thanks in large part to Mara. In the rather pointed manner he tolerated only from her, his wife had reminded him of the larger issues in play here. His orders with respect to this assignment were clear: either secure one or more of the Tomol specimens for study, or do whatever was required to see to it that neither they nor their planet fell into enemy hands. However, the matter had become complicated now that fire had been exchanged with Starfleet forces. With both the Federation and the empire having demonstrated an interest in the planet, things no longer could be decided over something as simple as who had gotten here first.

And we have the meddlesome Organians to thank for that.

Though the Federation and the empire had for the past few years maintained what diplomats might call "strained relations," Kang knew that the High Council had no reservations about going to war with the Earthers and their allies if the opportunity presented itself. This, despite the ever-present threat from the powerful, noncorporeal Organians, who two years earlier had imposed something of a cease-fire on both sides and then done precious little to enforce their edict. Although the empire and the Federation had observed the terms of the so-called peace treaty, there still remained the occasional testing of the accord's limits. For example, none of the Organians had shown themselves during any subsequent incidents involving Starfleet and imperial vessels, including the skirmish that had just taken place here above Arethusa. Though there remained the possibility of the intrusive aliens making an appearance here, Kang doubted such an event would come to pass. Based on all that the Organians had seemingly allowed to transpire since imposing their will, he felt confident that they would not show themselves unless and until the empire and the Federation declared open hostilities.

Should that happen, Kang wanted to be sure it was for the right reasons and of utmost benefit to the empire. At present, the current situation did not seem to justify such extreme steps, at least not while there still was a chance to complete his mission. Though collecting Tomol specimens for transport back to the homeworld now was problematic, there still was the matter of the strange, still unexplained power source emanating from beneath the surface of the planet's largest landmass.

"Mara," he said, "have you examined the sensor data regarding those power readings?"

She nodded. "They are like nothing I have ever seen before and are not consistent with anything on record in our computer memory banks."

What were its origins? What sort of apparatus was behind it, and how did it work? Was it something that could be exploited for the glory of the empire? Was there a connection to the Tomol, and perhaps even to the peculiar condition they exhibited? These were questions for which Tormog had not provided answers, and now they taunted Kang.

Leaning closer, Mara said, "I know what you are thinking, and the readings do not even conform to what we know of the Shedai."

"You're certain?"

She nodded. "I am. The energy signatures are not at all similar."

That was disappointing. Upon learning of Tormog's

discovery, Kang, like his wife, at first thought the Tomol and the mysterious power source might be related to the extinct race of powerful aliens who once had ruled this region of space. The Shedai, by all reports, had commanded an impressive level of technology unseen before or since. Thought to be a long dead species, representatives from the supposedly defunct civilization began revealing themselves soon after Federation scientists and Starfleet officers began seeking and examining artifacts and ruins on the worlds they once inhabited. To say that the Shedai were displeased at being disturbed in this manner was something of an understatement, and though the full circumstances of their threat potential remained unknown to all but a few select individuals, the truth was that the entire quadrant had come within a hairsbreadth of utter annihilation. Kang himself had become aware of the situation only after its resolution some months earlier, and even he did not know all of the details. So far as he had been able to determine, those Klingons who did possess such greater knowledge had been "relocated for security reasons."

This region, which imperial star charts still called the Gonmog Sector but which the Federation had labeled the Taurus Reach, was essentially a wedge separating Klingon territory from that claimed by the Federation as well as the Tholian Assembly, and until recently had held only marginal interest for the empire. All three parties had seemed to treat the area as something of an unofficial neutral zone, preferring instead to expand their boundaries in other directions.

That status quo had been maintained until just a few

years ago, when the Federation established a sizable presence in the region, and Starfleet had wasted no time sending their warships to scout numerous star systems in the hopes of finding resource-rich worlds to exploit. At least, that was what the Klingon High Council had believed, until it was learned that Starfleet had uncovered what at the time was thought to be an unparalleled alien technology. Worried that the empire's most formidable adversary might well have discovered some new weapon with which to threaten imperial interests and security, the council had ordered an increased Klingon presence into the sector. There had been infrequent skirmishes with Starfleet forces during the handful of years Starfleet—along with the Klingons and the Tholians—carried out its search for the alien technology. It was not until the full scope of the Shedai's power and potential revealed itself that such confrontations began to escalate in both frequency and intensity.

Now, however, the Shedai appeared to be gone for good, following a massive battle against Starfleet forces that had resulted in the destruction of the space station they had placed in this region, Starbase 47. Some members of the High Council had put forth the notion that the Federation might withdraw from the sector, perhaps cowed by their experiences here, but Kang knew better. If the Earthers and their allies were consistent about anything, it was their annoying curiosity about everything. With the Shedai seemingly vanquished, this expanse of space was ripe for conquest, and the Klingon Empire had no intention of allowing the Federation or anyone else unfettered claim to the vast resources to be found here. Confrontation between the two powers was almost sure to result.

The council may yet get their war, after all.

"Have you prepared a team for transport to the surface?" Kang asked.

Mara nodded. "They await your command, Captain." She crossed her arms. "Given what's happened to the *Homghor* and that they failed to capture appropriate test subjects, perhaps I should lead the landing force."

Shifting in his chair, Kang considered her suggestion. He was not worried for Mara's safety. She was more than capable of defending herself, and she was correct that with the loss of the *Homghor*, her duties as the *Voh'tahk*'s science officer would require her to take the lead on any specimens his crew managed to capture from among the planet's native population. Still, with so little known about these life-forms, he was concerned with sending anyone—his wife included—to the surface without sufficient information to guarantee success.

As though reading his thoughts, Mara added, "Remember, simply collecting random specimens isn't enough. We need to determine which among their population are at a point in their development that the transition to this other life-form might soon occur. If the metamorphosis is imminent, we can place one or more subjects into stasis as Tormog planned to do."

Kang nodded in agreement, recalling their earlier, private conversation where Mara had made these same points. At the time, Tormog was the one tasked with selecting at least one Tomol specimen for transport to either the *Voh'tahk* or the *Homghor*. With Tormog still on the surface and attempting to continue his mission and despite the loss of the *Homghor*, it now fell to Kang—along with Mara and the rest of his crew—to complete the scientist's work. The captured Tomol would be interred in stasis pods for transport to Qo'noS, where they would be studied and their transformation observed under controlled laboratory conditions. He was skeptical of any sort of regulated experiment yielding useful results, particularly if Tormog's account of the *Homghor*'s fate was in any way truthful, but there was only one way to be certain. The presence of the other Starfleet vessel complicated matters, of course, but Kang was ready to deal with that as well.

"Very well," he said. "Prepare to lead the landing group. Find the Klingon life sign Mahzh detected and verify that there are no others, then proceed with the primary mission." For a moment, he entertained the notion of leading the expedition himself, but with the *Endeavour* in proximity, his place was here on the bridge of his own vessel. For the sake of maintaining military bearing while in the presence of his subordinates as well as avoiding any risks of her later making him pay for any perceived slight—however pleasurable such punishment might end up being—Kang resisted an urge to advise Mara to exercise care while down on the planet. Instead, he merely offered the traditional sentiment whenever a challenging or dangerous task was about to be undertaken. "*Qapla'!*"

"Captain," called out his communications officer, Kyris, and when Kang rotated his chair to face her, he saw that the younger Klingon's features were clouded with confusion. "We are receiving a transmission from the planet surface. It's being sent on one of our frequencies, but there does not appear to be any targeted recipient. Instead, it is broadcasting to anyone who can hear it."

"One of our communicators? Is it Tormog, or possibly a survivor?"

Kyris shook her head. "I do not know, Captain." She paused, studying information on one of her console's smaller display screens that Kang could not see, before adding, "The transmission appears to have concluded." Without waiting for further direction, she tapped several controls and the bridge's intercom system flared to life with a low-pitched buzz that was normal background noise for a ship-to-surface frequency, followed by a feminine voice Kang did not recognize.

"This message is for the people on the sky-ships above us," it said, the words spoken in a deliberate, measured cadence that Kang took to be a product of the communications system's universal translation protocols. *"I don't know where you've come from, what you want, or why you've involved us in whatever fight you seem to be waging. But know this: you are* not *welcome on Arethusa, either of you. My name is Nimur, and I rule this world. Tell your people, and anyone else who might be foolish enough to come here: if you trespass on our soil again, you will do so at your own peril. Because as of now, Arethusa, and every living thing that dwells upon it—including your stranded comrades—are now* mine. *This will be your only warning."*

A sharp crackle echoed over the speakers and Kang turned to Kyris, who shook her head.

"That's the entire message, Captain. Shall I attempt to reestablish a connection?"

Kang waved away the suggestion. "I suspect this Nimur will understand but one form of communication." His first instinct was to order his weapons officer to target the source of the transmission and open fire, but movement near one of the sensor stations made him turn to see Mara leaning over the console, her attention fixed on a pair of computer displays.

"I'm making sure to collect detailed scans of the altered forms," she said, without looking up from her work. "The data may be useful later."

"Do so quickly," Kang replied, his eyes once more fixed on the blue-green world on the viewscreen. Despite his orders to obtain Tomol specimens for study, he was beginning to wonder if the effort would prove more costly than any benefits the empire might realize. As he continued to contemplate releasing the full fury of the *Voh'tahk*'s weapons on the intemperate life-form who dared threaten him, Kang was struck by a new thought.

"The transmission. Was it heard by the *Endeavour*?"

"Yes, Captain," Kyris replied. "They received it just as we did. If the other Starfleet ship on the surface survived its landing, it may have heard it as well."

Her report gave Kang pause. What might the Starfleet captain, Khatami, be thinking at this moment? In all likelihood, her thoughts mirrored his own.

This situation has just become a great deal more complicated.

2

Captain Atish Khatami stood before the main viewscreen on the bridge of the *U.S.S. Endeavour*, arms folded across her chest as she studied the image of the brilliant emerald green world listed in Starfleet data banks simply as Nereus II, but what she now knew its indigenous population called Arethusa. Thanks to the starship's current orbital path, the planet's rings cut a diagonal swath across the image, painting a picture of unfettered serenity that Khatami on any other day would find beautiful.

Today doesn't look to be that day.

"Alert the transporter room," she said. "Tell them not to beam down the landing party, and get Lieutenant Klisiewicz back up here." Her plan had been to dispatch a team led by the *Endeavour*'s senior science officer and second officer, Stephen Klisiewicz, to assist the crew of the *U.S.S. Sagittarius* with repairs to their ship, which had suffered severe damage following a battle with two Klingon vessels and a crash landing on an island near the planet's primary landmass. That would have to wait, at least until she had time to consider this change to an already odd, rapidly evolving situation. "Where are we on defenses?"

"Shields at maximum, Captain," replied her Arcturian helm officer, Lieutenant Neelakanta. "All weapons armed and on standby. All hands have reported to battle stations."

The terse communication from the planet's surface— ostensibly from one of Arethusa's indigenous inhabitants— still rang in her mind. Who was this Nimur individual, and what power did she command that supported the threat just leveled against the *Endeavour* and any other vessel that dared to trespass on the planet below?

I may have to throw out some warnings of my own.

She turned from the viewscreen. "Mister Estrada, can you track the source of that transmission?"

Seated at the communications console near the rear of the bridge, Lieutenant Hector Estrada inserted a slim, silver Feinberg receiver into his right ear, and the veteran officer's brow furrowed as though he was dividing his attention between Khatami and the rush of information being fed to him. "It originated near the Klingon ship's crash site, but I'm not picking up anything now. They've either deactivated or incapacitated the communicator."

"And we're sure the message couldn't have come from Kang's ship?" asked Lieutenant Commander Katherine Stano, the *Endeavour*'s first officer. Seeing Khatami's skeptical expression, she added, "We know they don't want us here. Could they be trying to get rid of us without a fight?"

It was an interesting possibility, but Khatami shook her head. "From what I know of Kang, he's not one for subterfuge. When he's ready for us to be gone, he'll tell us himself, or he'll just start shooting." The D-7 battle cruiser had been waiting for them upon the *Endeavour*'s arrival and still lurked in nearby space, ready to unleash the full power of its arsenal at the slightest provocation, just as it had against the *Sagittarius*. The warship had already sent the *Archer*-class scout plummeting to the surface of Are-thusa, and Khatami held no doubts that Kang was more than happy to visit a similar fate on the *Endeavour*.

Focus, Captain, Khatami reminded herself. *One po-tential act of war at a time, all right?* Almost without thinking about it, she pulled on the hem of her green wraparound uniform tunic, feeling for some reason as though the garment was hugging her just a bit too tightly. Was it nervousness? She dismissed the thought, even as she caught herself about to rub her palms on her trousers.

Okay, maybe it's a little bit nervousness.

"Iacovino," she said, "can you tell me if there are any Klingon survivors at the crash site?"

Working at the science station, Ensign Kayla Iacovino did not look up from the console's hooded viewer, which was providing her data from the *Endeavour*'s sensors. "I'm picking up one Klingon reading, Captain, along with numerous other life-forms. One of those looks to have been tagged by a Klingon subspace transponder, and that signal's coming through loud and clear." Assigned to bridge duty while Klisiewicz headed up the landing party, the junior officer seemed to have wasted no time settling into what Khatami knew was a demanding role, given the present circumstances. With what appeared to be prac-ticed ease, Iacovino moved her right hand from the viewer and across one bank of controls on the console, her fingers playing across the colored buttons as though possessed of their own will.

"There's definitely some similarity to the other Tomol life readings we scanned at the major population center, but these are different. They look to be in some kind of continual growth or flux." For the first time, Iacovino pulled herself away from the viewer, and Khatami saw the uncertainty in the ensign's eyes. "Whatever's happening to them, it's like nothing I've ever seen before."

"Keep tracking that transponder," Khatami said. "The Klingons obviously tagged that individual for a reason."

"Captain," said Estrada, "we're being hailed by Captain Terrell. Audio only."

Moving to her command chair, Khatami pressed the control on its right armrest to open its intercom channel. "Khatami here, Clark."

"Welcome to Arethusa," replied the *Sagittarius*'s commanding officer, his voice sounding small and distant as it piped through the bridge speakers, no doubt a consequence of the low-power frequency that was the best the *Sagittarius*'s damaged communications systems could manage. *"And sorry about the reception waiting for you up there. Hope you haven't been banged up too badly."*

"Not yet, anyway," Khatami replied. "If it's any consolation, I wish I could trade places with you."

The sound of Terrell's dry, tired chuckle drifted through the open frequency, and Khatami pictured the burly captain's wide grin. *"Okay, I'll call that bluff."* After another laugh, he added, *"Are you sending down that repair party? I have to tell you that we're all pretty tired of looking at each other's ugly faces down here."*

"No serious injuries?"

"Thankfully," Terrell said. *"Pretty much just bruises and lacerations, nothing we can't deal with on our own, but the ship itself is in pretty bad shape. You know they're going to bill me for the repairs."*

Khatami smiled. "I'll start a collection." Clark Terrell was known for his easygoing demeanor even in the most stressful situations. To have survived the harrowing plunge from orbit and his ship's near-catastrophic landing on the planet while maintaining his sense of humor was a testament to the captain's character. "So, can you tell me what the hell this is all about? You were supposed to survey this planet, not get into a shooting match with two Klingon ships."

"It certainly wasn't what we had in mind when we got here," replied Terrell. *"You've probably read the initial survey reports about this system. For the most part, that data's correct, in that Arethusa's native population is fairly primitive. They're centuries away from reaching the technological thresholds for us to even consider first contact. That said, there's definitely more going on down here than meets the eye."* He paused, then asked, *"This frequency's encrypted, right?"*

Khatami said, "Of course."

The sound of Terrell drawing a deep breath carried over the speakers before he said, *"We're still trying to figure out everything, but we think these people, the Tomol, once were controlled by the Shedai, and their ancestors were genetically altered for some unknown reason. The Tomol's physiology is such that they evolve into something very different once they reach a certain age, maturity, or whatever."*

"Some kind of metamorphosis?" Khatami asked.

"You got it."

"What?" Stano said, scowling in disbelief. Then, as though realizing her words were loud enough to be picked up by the open comm frequency, she cleared her throat. "Captain Terrell, this is Lieutenant Commander Stano, *Endeavour* XO. You're certain about this change the natives undergo?"

"Like a heart attack," Terrell replied. *"A few of these things nearly tore our rover to shreds with my landing party inside it, and they've already shown they can morph at will into other life-forms to suit their environment, including maneuvering underwater."*

"I'd call that being certain," Khatami said. "Clark, what about those power readings we scanned as coming from somewhere beneath the main landmass? They're not consistent with what we know of Shedai technology."

Terrell said, *"Nope. You're not going to believe this, but it's coming from a Preserver artifact."*

"Preservers?" Khatami repeated.

Stano said, "Klisiewicz is going to love that."

"My landing party found it in an underground cavern not far from the Tomol village," Terrell continued. *"Based on their scans, it's a near match for a similar object the* Enterprise *discovered last year."*

Khatami recalled the report she had read months ago, submitted by the *Enterprise*'s science officer after that starship had surveyed a world that was uninhabited except for a small colony identified as representing several groups of early humans taken centuries ago from Earth's North American continent and deposited by a mysterious ancient race known only as "the Preservers." Little was known about the enigmatic and supposedly defunct civilization, believed to have been at one time a dominant force in the galaxy, which had made a practice of transplanting small segments of humanoid cultures from their home planets to other worlds, in many cases acting to safeguard those selected beings while the rest of their civilization faced extinction due to natural or other means. Such was the case with the humans on "Amerind," as it had been named in Federation planetary databases.

"You think the Tomol are another race rescued by the Preservers? A representative sample relocated in order to protect them from some unknown calamity affecting their home world, and this planet is another repository?"

Terrell replied, *"That's our theory for the time being. However, while the Preservers seemed content to leave the people on that other planet alone to live in peace, there's definitely something else in place here. The Tomol as a society observe a strict set of rituals with respect to their physiological changes. Once the change takes hold, they turn into wild, uncontrollable creatures. They're a danger to everyone and everything around them. According to their ancient legends, while they were under Shedai rule, this affliction swept across their civilization and all but destroyed their home world."*

"And we think the Shedai are responsible for that?" Khatami asked.

"So far as we can tell from the research we were able to do before everything went to hell. The Tomol living here have a way of dealing with the problem, though. When they reach a certain age, and before the transformation can take hold, they sacrifice themselves as part of an elaborate ceremony."

Her eyes widening in disbelief, Stano asked, "They just kill themselves?"

"Not just kill themselves," said the *Sagittarius* captain. *"They throw themselves into a giant fire pit, before this change can take place. That's the way it's been for as far back as they can remember. Every Tomol is conditioned from early childhood to understand and respect the laws and rituals. Only on rare occasions has someone flouted convention, but it's just our luck that it had to happen while we were snooping around."*

Crossing her arms, Khatami blew out her breath. "I think I see now why the Klingons are so interested in this planet."

"Exactly," Terrell said. *"They know about the Tomol, and this change they undergo. They obviously think it's something they can reproduce or exploit in some other manner, and they were trying to capture specimens to take back to the empire for study."*

Turning to the navigator's station, where Lieutenant McCormack manned the console, Khatami asked, "Where's that battle cruiser?"

Consulting her instruments, the young navigator replied, "It's assumed a geosynchronous orbit over the bird-of-prey crash site, Captain. Its weapons remain armed, but we're not being targeted, and its sensors look to be trained on the surface."

"Any sign they might be looking to beam down, or beam something back to their ship?" The idea that Kang might attempt snatching hostages from the *Sagittarius* crew or even other members of the indigenous population had not moved far from her thoughts. Contrary to the supposed wisdom of older Starfleet officers with experience against the empire, Klingons could and would take prisoners if there was a tactical advantage to be exploited.

McCormack shook her head. "Nothing so far, Captain. They seem happy enough to observe from orbit. For now, anyway."

Moving to stand beside Khatami, Stano asked, "Do you think Kang will try anything if we send down our landing party?"

"Not if he's smart," the captain replied. Despite the warning she had given the Klingon commander with respect to consequences for any hostile acts, Khatami knew that Kang felt slighted not only by the *Sagittarius*'s attack on the bird-of-prey but also by her own attitude toward him during their last tense communication. He would not go quietly, and neither did Khatami expect him to sit idle while she and her people ventured to the surface.

Khatami returned her attention to the open communications channel. "Clark, you need to be aware that you might have other company down there. The Klingons are likely going to be sending a team to their ship's crash site to retrieve survivors, but they might decide to hop over and pay you a visit."

Though she anticipated his concerns over this bit of news, Terrell's reply was not at all what Khatami was expecting. *"Wait. There are survivors? Are you sure? Klingons or Tomol?"*

Frowning at the odd question, Khatami said, "We picked up a single Klingon life reading, along with what looks to be about a dozen Tomol." Then she realized a possible reason for Terrell's confusion. "Wait, you didn't hear Nimur's message."

"Nimur?" Terrell was all but shouting now. *"She's still alive? Are you still scanning those life-forms? Do you know where they are?"*

Stano replied, "We're tracking a Klingon transponder tagged to one of the Tomol survivors, and they're still at the crash site."

"Listen to me, both of you. Target the wreckage and destroy whatever's left, then lay a full phaser barrage on the location of that transponder. Do it right now."

Taken aback by her colleague's blunt demand, Khatami leaned closer to her chair's comm panel. "Clark, you're talking about firing on members of the native population without cause."

"And firing on that Klingon ship won't make Kang happy," Stano added. "If we—"

"Damn it!" Terrell barked. *"Forget Kang. Whatever these things are, they're extremely dangerous, and we can't afford to let a single one of them off this planet. Why do you think we shot down that bird-of-prey? I thought they might die in the crash, but if they survived, then they may be even more powerful than we thought. For all I know, they can turn into something that can survive in space, but I'm not eager to find out. Look, I'll explain everything later, and our sensor and tricorder data will back me up, but we don't have time now for debate."*

Hearing the normally unflappable Terrell all but begging Khatami to take action was disconcerting, to say the least. Was he suffering some kind of concussion or other injury that could be impairing his judgment? Was he truly in any shape to be in command? "Clark, are you sure?"

Even as she asked the question, she motioned to Neelakanta, who was sitting at his helm station and, like everyone else on the bridge, was listening to the bizarre conversation with wide eyes and a shocked expression. "Lieutenant, adjust our orbit and move us into firing position."

"Yeah, I'm damned sure. You can put the responsibility for this call on me, but you need to blast that whole area, Atish. Now!"

"The second we start moving," Stano warned, "Kang's going to be all over us."

Khatami nodded, retaking her seat in the command chair. "Then we'll deal with him, too. McCormack, lock phasers and photon torpedoes on the bird-of-prey crash site and prepare to fire on my command."

In front of her, Lieutenant Marielise McCormack, the *Endeavour*'s navigator, replied without turning from her console, "Aye, Captain."

Her eyes fixed on the planet centered on the main viewscreen, Khatami watched as it appeared to rotate clockwise, its rings moving in a downward arc as the *Endeavour* adjusted its trajectory. She knew Kang and his crew would be aware of her ship's every move, and they would know the instant her weapons homed in on their target. She guessed the Klingon commander would take no more than five seconds before he responded.

As it happened, Kang did not take even that long.

From the science station, Ensign Iacovino called out, "Captain, the Klingon cruiser is adjusting its orbit. It looks like they're maneuvering to intercept us."

"Warn them off, Estrada," Khatami ordered, keeping her focus on the screen.

McCormack reported, "Weapons locked on target, Captain. Standing by."

"The *Voh'tahk* isn't responding to our hails," Estrada added.

Hunched over the hooded viewer at her station, Iacovino said, "They're coming right at us. They'll be in firing range in less than two minutes."

It's about to get pretty lively around here.

Releasing a small sigh of resignation, Khatami gave the order.

"Fire."

3

Nimur burned inside.

Perched on the rim of a smoking crater, she looked down at her soot-smeared form and realized that it offered only the merest hint of the fires growing within her. The heat billowed from her core and ignited her senses. She heard the pulse of the smallest insects and the slight breeze rustling the leaves of the tallest trees. Everything was visible to her, from the ultraviolet radiation of the high sun above to the blood coursing through the veins beneath her own skin.

She surged with the thrill of potential offered by the seemingly endless inferno roiling inside her. Since surrendering to the Change and directing but a fraction of the energy she now possessed toward transforming several of her fellow Tomol—people she once had called friends—into beings such as she had become, it was obvious to Nimur that fate had seen fit to charge her with altering the destiny of her entire race. Those fortunate few in whom she had been able to trigger the Change now knew the truth, and so too would the rest of her people in time. And why? Because she had refused to blindly submit to the ancient imperative forced upon them by the Shepherds and give herself over to the Cleansing. Upon reaching the age when the Change began to manifest itself within her, and as their predecessors had done for uncounted generations, Priestess Ysan and other village leaders had implored Nimur to cast herself into the pit of eternal fire before the transformation could claim her. They had described this ritual as a noble act of communal salvation, but Nimur now dismissed the law for what it was: the greatest lie ever foisted upon her people.

Standing before her fellow Tomol—some of them having fully embraced the Change thanks to her—Nimur felt a surge of pride radiating from those who now looked to her for leadership. Several of her new followers had gathered around her along the edges of the crater that in a very real sense was of her own making. It had been created from the destruction of the sky-ship commandeered from the alien captors who called themselves "Klingons"; she and a handful of her followers had defiantly ridden the wounded craft from far above the clouds down to the surface of Arethusa. Now it served as a landmark, a monument that would represent the very moment at which all things would become different for all the Tomol people. Reaching out with her mind's heightened senses, Nimur grasped the uncertain storm of emotions clouding her followers' thoughts. She understood their confusion, their anxiety, and their fear—but also their determination as they struggled to comprehend the possibilities the future now held for them.

Nimur also perceived embers of inextinguishable disdain smoldering within those among the group who had not yet embraced the Change. True enlightenment would continue to elude them until their time came, but for now she conceded that she would have to find some way to bridge the gap separating them from understanding. She studied them, sensing their distrust and fear as exhibited by their harsh blue auras, with none flaring with greater brilliance than that radiated by Kerlo, her mate and the father of her infant daughter.

His disapproval and regret taunted her, and Nimur found herself wrestling with a tempest of conflicting emotions as she writhed between love and contempt. She felt the pull of temptation as she imagined unleashing every iota of her newfound power upon Kerlo, along with everyone else who stood between the stagnation to which her people had been consigned and what she now truly believed was their destiny.

Why do you not act? The question nagged at Nimur. Was it love, for Kerlo as well as those she once had called friends and family? Perhaps, though such thoughts seemed to grow more muddied as time passed. Was it a by-product of the weakness her body was trying to purge as she moved ever deeper into the unrelenting embrace of the Change?

An interesting question, indeed.

She turned her attention to the device she still clutched in her hand, studying its contours and blinking lights as she attempted to extract function from its form. How was such a small device able to capture her voice and propel it beyond the clouds to the sky people who hovered among the stars above Arethusa in their ships? Nimur supposed that the details did not matter as much as the result, in which the sky people had heard her proclaim the planet and its people as now being under her rule and that their trespasses were no longer welcome. As she pondered the declaration she had made, she felt the flames of determination stoking within her, driven by the clarity the Change had given her to see the path along which she would lead her people to the birthright they had been denied for so long. In this, Nimur vowed she would not fail, regardless of the sky people and any efforts they made to stop her.

And what of your own people? How much dissidence will you tolerate from them?

"So, Nimur," a voice shouted. Nimur recognized it as Kerlo's breaking the silence that had blanketed the air since she had finished speaking to the sky people. "Is this the truth you would have us accept? The great power you promised to share with us? Or do you now intend to keep it to yourself, in order to rule over us all?"

His words were like knives piercing her skin, and she felt anger well up from within her. "Stop, Kerlo! Silence your tongue. Do you not understand the threat that weighs on all of us?" She gestured toward the sky. "Above our world are ships that sail among the stars, and they carry people unlike any you have ever seen and power you could not hope to understand."

"I understand more than you think, Nimur."

As Kerlo spoke, Nimur heard a pain in his voice that she believed was veiled to all but her. "You always have thought me to be simple, but—"

"Unless you were with me aboard the sky-ship, *none* of you can understand what I have seen." Nimur pointed toward the bottom of the crater. "If not for the Change, we would not be standing here now. We would be dead, burned to ash in this hole. These strangers wish to ruin our world and take us from it. I will not permit that. I will say what our future holds because I have the power to guide us toward that destiny and to protect us all from them."

Kerlo said, "Or, Nimur, perhaps it is these strangers who will protect us from you."

Though impatience and frustration darkened her emotions, through that thickening cloud she sensed a new flicker of awareness sparking in her mind. Something ominous lurked just beyond her grasp, and she realized it was coming not from within her but from a point far away. Not here on Arethusa, but above, among the stars. The sensation was not unlike seeing kindling used to start a fire, flaring to life as the first sparks from metal against stone touched it. Then it blazed into a white-hot ball of fire, all but blinding her consciousness, but what was it? Instinct made Nimur look toward the sky.

"Wait!" she shouted to the Tomol gathered around the crater. "Now you will witness for yourselves the power the sky people wield, and you will know what I mean when I say I will save you all from harm!"

Blue-white light streaked down from the clouds as the gathered Tomol watched in helpless terror. Cries of fear and shock filled the air around Nimur as Kerlo and the others scrambled away from the scene of destruction. The light streaks rained down upon the wreckage, engulfing it in a shroud of energy Nimur could feel playing across her exposed skin.

There is more coming. Looking to the sky, she raised her hands and closed her eyes, reaching outward with her enhanced senses, searching for the light and trying to perceive its form and power. Something was there, but it eluded her attempts to influence it, and Nimur abruptly tasted a metallic tang and her body trembled as if shocked by lightning. Panic flooded her mind as she began to comprehend the horror carried by the light from the sky.

I am not enough for this.

She did not fear for herself, as she sensed her newfound abilities and inner strength would be sufficient to withstand whatever the sky people might rain down upon them, but she was less certain about those to whom she had so recently brought the Change. They still were growing and had not yet reached her levels of strength and clarity. There were also those Tomol who had not yet become Changed; there could be no doubt that their lives were in mortal danger.

"No!"

Channeling the power roiling inside her and longing for release, Nimur made a sweeping gesture toward those gathered near the crater, all of whom remained transfixed as they watched her. The energy flowed through her body, coursing the length of her outstretched arms and leaping from her fingers, warping the very air before her as it spread. It swept across the collected Tomol, Changed and otherwise, picking them up and flinging them in every direction away from the crater. Screams and shouts reached her ears as she fixed her attention on each of her fellows, guiding them past trees and through the surrounding brush. As the distance separating her from her charges increased, she sensed her control over them waning and she guided them to the ground. Nimur could only hope they now were far enough away to escape the otherworldly torment she knew was coming.

Alone and sensing the attack was almost upon her,

Nimur flung herself down to the center of the crater. She clasped her hands and shoved them skyward toward the light, releasing the energies she had been holding at bay. Light and flame erupted from her hands, the intensity dwarfing even the most powerful of the Wardens' fire lances as it thrust into the sky. The pulse ripped through the air, closing the distance within moments until a brilliant white-hot flash and a deafening, thunderous roar announced its meeting its target just above the tallest of the trees.

An invisible wave of tremendous force smashed Nimur into the glassy crust of the crater. She squeezed her eyes shut and cried out in shock as the concussive bubble of heat, light, and fury washed over her, its wrath unleashed into the bowl of earth beneath her and sweeping across the surrounding landscape. Reeling from the unrelenting bombardment, Nimur willed her thoughts to push past the assault and seek additional threats. Every trace of her being knew without doubt that what she had just endured was but a fraction of the energy and danger she had sensed.

There is more.

Another bolt of blue-white lightning slammed down upon her, this time the sky-ship's devastating assault evoking pain that tore through her body and her mind unlike anything she could ever have imagined. Again Nimur screamed into the face of the maelstrom, directing all of her emerging powers to bear, but it was not enough to keep her from sliding from the light and into the silent and all-consuming darkness.

4

"Bring us about and take us out of orbit!" Khatami shouted over the Red Alert klaxon that had begun wailing across the bridge. "Full power to forward shields! Stand by all weapons and ready for evasive!"

Gripping the arms of her command chair, she watched the image on the viewscreen shift as Arethusa fell out of the frame and the *Endeavour* altered its trajectory to leave the planet behind in a bid to gain maneuvering room. It had been only seconds since the last round of phaser strikes was dispatched to the planet's surface, engulfing the Klingon bird-of-prey's crash site and the surrounding area in the weapons' hellish effects. Khatami still had not had time to process all of the possible ramifications of what she had done at Terrell's urging.

Later!

On the bridge's main viewscreen, a computer-generated schematic showed the points of impact and the resulting destruction wrought on the target and the neighboring terrain. Despite repeated hails to the *Voh'tahk* apprising them of the situation and the rationale for her decision to fire on the wrecked ship, Captain Kang had refused to acknowledge the communication, let alone offer a reply. Instead, the Klingon commander's response had come in the form of his ship altering course and arming its weapons as it began moving to intercept the *Endeavour*.

"I think you made him mad," said Katherine Stano from the engineering station at the rear of the bridge and just over Khatami's left shoulder.

Khatami released a small, humorless chuckle. "Looks that way." Even without the detailed briefing Clark Terrell had promised, it was apparent to her that the Klingons had at least some idea of the Tomol's true nature and likely were attempting to study or exploit the isolated race for military benefit. Now that Khatami had interfered with whatever mission Kang had been assigned with respect to this planet and its people, the Klingon was obviously not in a talkative mood.

"We've broken orbit," Neelakanta reported from his helm console.

"Set a course for the rings," Khatami ordered. "Increase speed to full impulse." Scanner readings had revealed that the rings encircling Arethusa were composed of dense particulate matter as well as a mixture of planetary debris and ice.

Lieutenant Stephen Klisiewicz, who had returned from the transporter room in order to take over from Ensign Iacovino at the science station, said, "This soup won't be enough to hide us from their sensors, Captain."

"I know," Khatami replied. Finding a hiding place for a ship of the *Endeavour*'s size was a tall order on the best of days. "But it might foul their targeting scanners just enough to give us an edge. Helm, get us through to the other side as fast as you can."

"Aye, Captain," replied Neelakanta as he set to work.

Despite artificial gravity and inertial dampening systems, which were as commonplace aboard ship as the air she breathed, Khatami always imagined she could sense the vessel banking and turning as it took up its new course. Far below them, the starship's massive impulse engines were increasing power at a steady rate, their low, omnipresent hum rising in pitch with each passing second as Lieutenant Neelakanta guided the *Endeavour* into open space. Khatami glanced down to the astrogator positioned between the helm officer and McCormack and noted the ship's position relative to the *Voh'tahk*. The rate at which the Klingon battle cruiser was closing the distance between the two ships was increasing, and the astrogator's estimate tallied with Khatami's guess that the enemy vessel would be in firing range in less than thirty seconds.

I hate being right.

"All of their weapons are active and they're trying to target us," Klisiewicz reported. "They're maneuvering to get in below and behind us."

"Let's not show them our ass," Stano said. "Keep us facing them, helm."

"Be ready to reroute shield power on the fly," Khatami warned, casting a quick glance to the first officer, who offered a knowing nod. "There's no telling how crazy this is liable to get."

"All set," Stano replied. As she had no console or seat of her own on the bridge, Stano had long ago taken up the practice of manning the various stations on a rotating schedule, in order to remain proficient in each position's function. During emergency situations such as this, her ability to operate any of the workstations allowed her to free up the person at that console for other duties. In this case, she was able to relieve the officer normally assigned to the engineering station so that she could return below-decks to assist Commander Yataro and the rest of the *Endeavour*'s engineering staff.

"They've entered firing range!" Klisiewicz called out. "Locking weapons!"

Without waiting for an order, Neelakanta banked the ship to starboard, and Khatami saw the image of the rings on the viewscreen tilt upward as the *Endeavour* dove toward them. It took only seconds for the display to become clouded with dust and debris, the starship maneuvering through the field as its deflectors pushed aside or simply vaporized most of the fragments and other detritus.

Klisiewicz shouted, "Incoming!"

Her eyes fixed on the viewscreen, Khatami felt the ship shudder around her as the first salvo struck the deflector shields. A single alarm sounded at one of the forward stations, but the officer manning that console silenced it. The Red Alert indicator positioned at the center of the combined helm and navigation console was flashing, but McCormack had muted its warning tone, as well.

"Moderate strike on port aft shields," Stano reported. "Nothing too bad. This time, anyway."

Khatami asked, "Where's the *Voh'tahk*?"

"Still behind us, and closing fast," Klisiewicz replied. "They've just entered the rings at full impulse. They're firing in our general direction, but I think you were right, and the rings may be screwing with their targeting systems." Lifting his head from the sensor viewer, he frowned.

"They're decreasing speed but maintaining their pursuit course."

"From what I know of Kang," Stano said, "he won't break off now."

"No," Khatami agreed, "but he's not a fool, either." Her own knowledge of the Klingon captain was limited to what was recorded in official Starfleet intelligence files and the reports from other starship captains who had encountered him, most recently James Kirk of the *Enterprise*. By all accounts, Kang was an accomplished tactician and fierce warrior who had served his empire with distinction for longer than Khatami had been alive. He was a formidable adversary.

But he doesn't have your ship and your crew, she chided herself, *so do your job.*

Dividing her attention between the muddled image on the viewscreen and the astrogator as she monitored the distance separating the *Endeavour* and the *Voh'tahk*, she checked the estimated time remaining until the starship cleared the rings. The battle cruiser would be on them within seconds of leaving the field.

"Get us out of this, helm."

In front of her, Neelakanta was hunched over his console, fingers moving almost too fast to follow as he pushed the *Endeavour* through the planet's rings. Seconds later the screen cleared as the ship returned to open space, and the helm officer rolled the ship to port. The astrogator readout showed Khatami what the lieutenant was doing, illustrating the starship's position outside the rings relative to the advancing *Voh'tahk*, which was continuing to plunge through the field at full impulse. Neelakanta, using the ship's maneuvering thrusters, had pivoted the *Endeavour* so that it now faced the rings and was pushing the starship forward once again. On the viewscreen, the image shifted to show the *Voh'tahk* punching through the rings, the forward torpedo launcher at the front of the cruiser's bulbous primary hull glowing red as it prepared to fire. The aspect already was changing as the Arcturian pilot guided the *Endeavour* on a slanting attack run just as the Klingon ship fired a pair of torpedoes, the glowing spheres of crimson energy hurtling across the void.

"Brace for impact!" was all Khatami had time to shout before the torpedoes slammed against the starship's deflectors. The defensive fields absorbed the brunt of the impact, but Khatami still felt the ship shuddering around her, the *Endeavour* having again avoided a direct strike thanks to Neelakanta's expert piloting.

"Phasers and torpedoes," Khatami ordered. "Concentrate on their forward shields as we pass. Full spread, fire!"

Next to Neelakanta, McCormack jabbed at the firing controls, and the bridge's overhead lighting flickered in response to the weapons systems' power demands. The energy from the *Endeavour*'s massive phaser batteries pulsed through the deck plates beneath Khatami's feet, and the image on the screen was tinted blue as twin streaks of focused energy lanced across open space, flanked by a quartet of photon torpedoes. The phaser beams hammered against the *Voh'tahk*'s forward shields, followed an instant later by the torpedoes, and the area immediately forward of the Klingon cruiser erupted in a brilliant yellow-orange maelstrom as the conflicting energies clashed.

"One torpedo made it through!" Klisiewicz shouted.

"I'm picking up an impact on their primary hull. There's damage to their forward torpedo launcher."

Neelakanta reported, "They're coming about." His hands were almost a blur as he worked the helm console. "Continuing evasive."

"They're firing again!" McCormack warned.

The ship trembled once more from the impact of another weapons strike even as the navigator fired another volley of phasers and torpedoes, and Khatami saw that McCormack was targeting the weakened area of the Klingon ship's shields. On the screen, more impacts flared against the enemy vessel's deflectors and Khatami thought she saw at least one strike against the *Voh'tahk*'s hull, but then the other ship had passed, continuing on its own course after emerging from the rings.

"Damage report." Khatami turned her chair to see Estrada bent over his console, his right hand pressing the Feinberg receiver to his ear as he collected reports from the ship's key departments.

"So far, nothing critical, Captain," replied the communications officer. "A few circuit overloads, but that's about it."

Stano added, "Engineering reports we're at eighty-six percent shield capacity."

"What about the Klingons?"

"Another of our torpedoes punched through during that last pass," Klisiewicz said, his attention fixed on his sensor viewer. "Possible damage to the secondary hull, near their engineering section. I'm picking up fluctuations in their main power plant."

McCormack called out, "They're not done yet, Captain." She gestured toward the astrogator, and Khatami saw the icon representing the Klingon cruiser changing course, back again toward the *Endeavour.*

"Their forward torpedo launcher is out of it," Klisiewicz said, "but their disruptors are still live." Then, a moment later, he pulled himself away from the viewer. "Hang on. Something's up." Khatami waited while the lieutenant consulted his station's various displays before turning to face her. "Their primary power systems just went off-line. Backup supplies are kicking in, but the power drop is huge." Pausing to check another of the readouts, he added, "Weapons are down. Life support and other systems are still functioning, but everything's drawing from their impulse engines."

"Captain," Neelakanta said, "they're changing course and moving off." Without Khatami having to ask, the helm officer tapped a control to change the main viewscreen's image, which now displayed the *Voh'tahk*'s stern as the battle cruiser arced away from Arethusa toward open space.

Rising from her chair, Khatami stepped around the helm console, her attention on the screen. "Track their course. They can't be going too far, not without warp drive, but I want an eye on them as long as they're within sensor range." Kang's most logical strategy would be to withdraw to something resembling a safe harbor and attempt to make repairs. Were the circumstances reversed, Khatami would be worried about pursuit and her enemy attempting to capitalize on her ship's compromised condition, and while the thought did cross her mind, at the moment she had other, more pressing concerns.

"They look to be moving deeper into the system,"

Klisiewicz reported. "From what I can tell, the damage to their warp drive isn't too extensive. They may well be able to fix it without calling for help."

At communications, Estrada said, "Well, they're calling somebody." When Khatami turned toward him, the veteran lieutenant frowned. "I'm picking up an encrypted burst transmission, broadcasting on several of the frequencies we know the Klingons use."

"Are you able to translate it?" Stano asked, moving from the engineering station toward him.

Estrada shook his head. "It's not a code we've broken." He shrugged. "At least, not yet. I've already got the computer crunching on it, and we should know at least something soon."

"It's not hard to figure out what the message says." Khatami leaned against the helm console and folded her arms. "Apprising higher command of their current situation and that they've been in a fight, and calling for reinforcements."

"How close can help be?" Stano asked, reaching up to push aside a lock of light brown hair that had fallen across her left eye. "We're out here in the middle of nowhere."

Khatami shrugged. "We got here easily enough. Besides, it's obvious the Klingons are interested in this planet and the people living here, so it's a safe bet Kang has some kind of support hiding somewhere within shouting distance. We're not finished dealing with Klingons today, not by a long shot." She cast a glance toward the viewscreen, which once again featured an image of the beautiful planet Arethusa. "I think it's past time we found out why." That she had fired on members of the world's native population still weighed on her, and it would be up to the *Sagittarius*'s captain to ease her worries.

After directing Stano to oversee and keep her updated on damage control efforts that already were under way throughout the ship—and giving silent thanks to whichever deities or other omniscient beings who may have observed the brief skirmish and seen fit to safeguard her vessel and crew—Khatami ordered Estrada to reestablish contact with Clark Terrell on the planet's surface. With visual communications still not an option until his people had time to make those repairs, Khatami sat in her command chair and listened to the tired voice of her fellow ship commander.

"Everybody okay up there?"

Khatami could not hold back a small smile. "We're fine, Clark. Now that the excitement's over for a little while, we're getting ready to send you some help." She already had instructed Stano to notify the engineering and medical teams originally detailed to the landing party to finalize their preparations and stand by for transport to the planet's surface.

"We've got the welcome mat out. Tell your people to take off their boots before coming inside. We just had the floors done."

Happy to hear her friend's calm, composed demeanor returning, Khatami directed the conversation to more serious matters. "Okay, Clark, I need to know what's going on. What's the story with these Tomol? Are they . . . ?" She cut herself off before she could ask whether this planet's inhabitants might be members of the Shedai race, or some other species that had benefited from that supposedly defunct race's advanced technology. Some things were still prohibited from being discussed on an open communications channel, after all.

"*They're not related to our old friends,*" Terrell replied, picking up on the unasked question. "*This is something different. Whatever you do, don't beam up any of them. The Klingons did that, and, well . . . you saw how that worked out for them.*" In clipped, abbreviated fashion, the *Sagittarius*'s captain gave Khatami and her bridge crew a summary of his people's findings during their survey of Arethusa, during which Khatami, Stano, and Estrada shared more than a few looks of amazement and incredulity. Klisiewicz, who had listened to most of Terrell's report, at one point returned to his station and immersed himself in his instruments, pausing to cast troubled glances toward his captain as he worked. Then, just as Khatami was about to ask what she was sure would be an ever-growing number of questions, Klisiewicz turned from his console.

"Captain, that transponder the Klingons used to tag one of the Tomol? It's still active." He frowned, shaking his head. "It took me a few minutes to separate it from the background radiation and other residual energy readings at the bird-of-prey crash site, but it's there."

"*What was that?*" Terrell asked over the open communications link. "*The transponder?*"

Klisiewicz nodded. "It's still transmitting a signal, and I'm picking up at least a half dozen life signs in the vicinity of the crash site, but they're moving away from that location."

"That's impossible," Stano said, making no attempt to mask her disbelief. "We leveled that whole area."

"*You haven't seen what these things can do,*" Terrell snapped. "*The longer we stay here, the more danger we're in, and like I already told you, we can't afford to let even a single one off this planet.*"

5

His heavy footfalls echoing on the duranium deck plates, Kang made his way down the narrow service corridor leading to the *Voh'tahk*'s engineering spaces. Crowding the passageway were engineers and other technicians, each engrossed in whatever repair task he or she had been assigned. One of the subordinates noted his approach and rose to his feet, assuming a position of rigid attention and offering a formal salute.

"Captain," the junior officer said, all but shouting as his voice reverberated off the corridor's slanted metal bulkheads. The other members of the crew abandoned their work, coming to attention in deference to their commanding officer.

"Return to your duties," Kang snapped, not breaking stride as he continued down the hallway. He had little interest in protocol and other useless points of military etiquette while real tasks waited to be accomplished. "Where is Konvraq?" he asked. The *Voh'tahk*'s engineering officer had to be scurrying about somewhere down here.

"Lieutenant Konvraq is in the main compartment, Captain," replied another subordinate, one whose name Kang did not recall. "He is overseeing repairs on the main propulsion control systems."

Without acknowledging the report, Kang arrived at a reinforced pressure hatch at the end of the corridor, which slid aside at his approach. No sooner did the portal begin to open than he heard the sounds of activity from the chamber beyond. He stepped into the ship's main engineering room, observing members of his crew working alone or in small groups all around the compartment. Several conversations were under way, overlapping one another to the point that Kang could not make out more than a few words from any one exchange. In one corner, two Klingons were employing a laser welder to make repairs to one of the conduits supplying coolant to the ship's mammoth propulsion system.

"Captain," a voice called, shouting to be heard above the commotion permeating the room, and Kang turned to see an older Klingon, Konvraq, walking toward him. Unlike nearly everyone else aboard the ship, the chief engineer wore that time-honored badge of age and wisdom: gray hair, which was clipped close to his scalp. The top of his head was smooth, save for the very narrow ridges that began at the bridge of his nose and proceeded up and over his skull and down his neck. Unlike Kang, Mara, and most of the *Voh'tahk*'s crew, Konvraq along with a handful of other officers was *HemQuch*, Klingons who had retained their cranial ridges over the years since the virus that had swept through the empire more than a century earlier. Kang's parents had been so afflicted, as had Mara's, resulting in their status within Klingon society as members of the *QuchHa'* caste. Unlike many *HemQuch*, Konvraq never seemed to care about such distinctions, and it was but one of the many qualities Kang had always liked about the veteran officer.

"What brings you to my lair?" the engineer asked,

offering a wry grin. "Surely the commander of this, the empire's finest warship, has better things with which to occupy his time?"

Despite his overall foul disposition, Kang could not help but smile at the other man's attempt at whimsical discourse. "You always seem to know how best to elevate my mood, my friend. It is perhaps this reason above all others that I haven't killed you before now."

"That, and my skills as an engineer." Konvraq punctuated the reply with a bout of raucous laughter that bounced off the bulkheads and made his subordinates all pause in their work to regard him. A sharp gaze from Kang made them see the merit of returning to their respective tasks.

"Speaking of your vaunted expertise," the captain asked, "what is the status of your repairs?"

Konvraq motioned for Kang to follow him across the expansive chamber. "Well, all is not lost. I am happy to report that the damage to the propulsion system can be repaired without requiring the ship to be towed to a maintenance facility."

"That's fortunate," Kang replied, "as there are no such facilities in this sector." If circumstances forced him to do so, he would order the *Voh'tahk*'s destruction rather than risk its capture by the Starfleet vessel. With reinforcements already en route to the Nereus system, he and his crew would simply take their chances on the planet's surface until a rescue ship arrived. Faced with that dishonor, Kang would see to it that the *Endeavour* and its captain paid for the disgrace he soon would have to endure. "Do you have a revised repair estimate?"

Konvraq nodded. "The work will require most of the

day. I have a crew outside the hull, attempting to repair damage to the forward torpedo launcher, and another team inside the launch system itself. It suffered a direct hit from one of the Starfleet vessel's torpedoes. It's a miracle the entire forward hull section was not destroyed by exploding munitions."

"What about our shields?" Kang asked. "We experienced several lapses in protection during the battle."

"The generators suffered an overload," replied the engineer, "but damage was not extensive. I expect those will be among the first repairs we complete."

In truth, Kang was prepared to resume the fight without the shields as long as the ship's weapons were at his disposal, though he knew that emotion rather than reason guided that line of thinking. Facing off once more against the Starfleet cruiser would require his own vessel to be at its peak operating condition. Even without shields, the power from their generators could still be of use to other, more vital areas of the ship.

"Your eyes betray what is in your heart," Konvraq said, and Kang saw a small, knowing grin lightening the other Klingon's features. "You would charge headlong into battle at a moment's notice. Do your years of experience offer nothing of counsel to you?"

Aside from his wife, there was no one aboard the *Voh'tahk* who would dare speak to him in this manner, and Kang likely would have killed anyone else who did so. Konvraq, however, had long ago earned the right to offer his unvarnished thoughts to his captain. The engineer had been a trusted friend and ally, whom Kang had known since his first shipboard assignment as a freshly minted officer from the military academy. Though their career paths had separated them for a time, fate and circumstance had seen to it that Konvraq was available for duties as a chief engineer when Kang was assigned command of this battle cruiser. Kang had always appreciated his friend's forthright, direct manner, never hesitating to offer his honest opinions whenever asked, and often without being so prompted.

"Of course a more prudent approach is called for," Kang said, glancing around the engineering compartment to confirm that all of Konvraq's men were once again engrossed in their repair tasks and other work, leaving their superior officers to their private conversation. "At least for the moment. But this Starfleet captain may force me to act more quickly and brashly if I am to complete our mission."

The Earther ship commander with an almost Klingon-sounding name, Khatami, had impressed him with her bravery and guile during their previous conversation and the recently concluded battle. She was not to be underestimated, of that Kang was certain. If she had been a Klingon, she surely would have pressed her attack upon learning that his vessel was so badly wounded and in need of retreat. Instead, and in typical Starfleet fashion, she had allowed the *Voh'tahk* to withdraw. Indeed, Kang was surprised that he had not yet received a customary message from Khatami, offering to render aid. The very thought made Kang snarl with disgust.

Even as his crew hurried to complete repairs to the damaged *Voh'tahk*, he knew that Khatami would soon learn the secret of Arethusa and its people, and why the empire had taken such an interest in them. However, she was hampered—for the moment, at least—by concerns over her companion ship, which remained marooned on the planet surface. Khatami would not abandon any survivors from that crash, in keeping with the finest traditions of Earthers who expended so much energy protecting and nurturing the weakest among them. Still, the resources at her disposal would allow her to see to that effort while also investigating the Tomol. That, of course, presented a number of problems, particularly with the *Voh'tahk* all but drifting helpless out here, well away from the planet and unable to face off against the Starfleet ship.

"Make haste with your repairs," he said. "Time runs short."

Konvraq nodded, his expression hardening as though he understood that the time for friendly banter had passed. "We will double our efforts, Captain. What are your intentions?"

"To complete our mission," Kang replied. "We must secure Tomol specimens for study. If we cannot do that, then we must prevent the Starfleet ship from doing the same, by any means necessary."

And Captain Khatami awaits, he reminded himself. *As does my vengeance.*

6

Pushing upward through the darkness toward the light, Nimur forced open her eyes, holding up a hand to shield her vision from the almost painful brightness that washed over everything. The blurred colors separated and solidified around her as she became aware of her surroundings.

I live.

She was on her back, lying flat at the bottom of the pit created by the fire weapons from the sky-ships. Every molecule of her being radiated agony. An acrid smell of burning embers and soot permeated everything, including the soil beneath her and even her own skin. Choking from a dry mouth, Nimur placed a hand to her chest only to discover her clothing gone, scorched from existence by the fire weapons. Forcing away the pain that accompanied the slightest movement, she planted her left hand on the ground in an effort to push herself to a sitting position, only to realize that her right arm did not respond to her commands. Casting her eyes down upon her blackened body, she beheld the charred stump that was all that remained of her right arm. The pain surged, almost blinding her with its ferocity as she fell back to the dirt.

Gritting her teeth and howling through the renewed torment, she made another attempt to raise herself, this time discovering that her right leg ended at her knee, the stump begrimed with dirt and ash. Fury swelled from her depths and she collapsed once more to the ground. She screamed skyward, hurling her rage to the clouds.

No!

The sound of her own breathing as she drew air deep into her lungs had a calming effect, and within moments Nimur realized the pain was already beginning to fade. Was she slipping into unconsciousness, or perhaps beginning the slide toward death itself? No, she decided. This was something else. Each breath coaxed fire from deep within her. A tingling gripped her, emanating from her core to the tips of her remaining extremities, and in its wake her nerves no longer registered the distress that had been levied upon her entire being.

Turn your thoughts within. Make yourself whole.

Nimur at first did not understand what this suggestion could mean. How could the power she wielded be used solely upon herself? She sensed a peace within her mind, a path to follow toward the answers she sought. Closing her eyes, she cleared her mind and then imagined her flesh and bones divesting themselves of the wounds visited upon them.

Reclaim what was taken from you.

A new pain flowed over her, soaking through her skin and coursing through her veins, the heat growing with every beat of her heart. Each breath was like fire in her lungs. Her vision swam but Nimur willed it to steady, turning her focus inward and seeing herself whole once again, the wrath of the sky-ship's weapons now nothing more than a memory. Releasing a cry of triumph, she pushed herself to her feet, turning her face to the sun and allowing its warmth to caress her skin. She opened her eyes and looked down, beholding with wonder her restored body. No evidence remained of the torment to which she had been subjected. The flawless skin of her nude body gleamed in the sunlight.

I am reborn.

Thrusting her fists skyward, she glared at the clouds, defying them to reveal to her those who had attempted to subdue her. "I live! You have failed!"

They would always fail. Of this, Nimur was certain.

Now aware that she no longer was alone, she turned to where her senses told her others of her kind approached, and she saw several Tomol running from the crater's rim, attempting to flee. Almost without her conscious bidding, her thoughts leaped from her mind as she envisioned those who sought fleeting safety snared by a web only she could see. Climbing from the crater, Nimur saw her captives suspended in the air and held in place by an invisible hand that answered her unspoken commands.

"You fear me," she said, her voice carrying on the breeze to the Tomol's ears. "You fear what you cannot comprehend, or what you refuse to comprehend."

"I don't fear you, Nimur," said a lone voice.

Nimur realized the dissenter was Kintaren, one of her closest friends. A fleeting thought to the unseen force holding her was enough to release her, and Kintaren dropped to the ground. "You say you do not fear me. Perhaps you should."

Stumbling as she regained her footing, Kintaren faced Nimur. Seeing her nakedness for the first time, she removed the heavy garment she wore over her other clothing and offered it to Nimur. "I have not feared you since my parents became your guardians many sun-turns ago, after your parents stepped into the Cleansing fire as you should have done."

Nimur wrapped the garment around her body. "Yes, the Cleansing, as you have been led to believe. Why did you come back here? Were you hoping to find me dead?"

"I came to see what had happened to my sister," Kintaren replied.

"No longer. At least, I am no longer only your sister." Nimur held out her arms. "Have you not seen what I can do? I defied the sky people and the death they rained down upon me. I am Changed, Kintaren! This is what we were meant to be. It is our birthright, and I have reclaimed it, and now it is time to see that all Tomol regain what has been taken from them, what has been kept from us for ages by the Shepherds. The Change is our destiny, Kintaren."

Her sister and friend shook her head. "When the Change visits me, I will be Cleansed, as it is written."

Flames of irritation licked at Nimur's patience. "The Cleansing is a lie, perpetrated by the Shepherds to hold us captive to this world. Only by accepting the Change can you know the truth. It is the only way. Those who cannot accept that will die, either at the hands of the sky people, or as a consequence of ignorance or weakness, or simply because I wish it."

Kintaren's eyes narrowed. "You won't kill me, Nimur. You do not want to kill me, or any of our people."

"I have already killed," Nimur warned. "It was effortless."

"You were threatened. You acted on instinct in response to perceived danger. If you had wanted me or all of us dead, you would have killed us by now, or simply let the fire from the sky-ships burn us to nothingness. We are no threat to you, so what stops you from acting?"

Confusion clouded Nimur's thoughts. *Why save Kintaren and the others? Why not kill them all now and be freed of their constant doubts and fears and anger?*

"I see the battle you fight with yourself," Kintaren said. "Let us go, Nimur."

"No," Nimur said. Beyond Kintaren, the other Tomol she held still hovered in the air. In addition to her sister, several others had not yet been visited by the Change. She saw the flames in the eyes of the muscled metalworker Shem and his mate, Larn; the lithe and wiry weaver Ayan; brothers Bhar and Tane, identical but for the latter being just a sun-turn younger and a head shorter; the teacher Jorn; and Kintaren. Nervousness gripped them, and Nimur could sense their anxiety continuing to increase. As for the Changed, they were looking to her for direction, as it was she who had brought about their transformation.

Nimur pointed to the group. "You have been taught from your earliest days to fear the Change as the end of your life. You have been told to believe that it is the height of selfishness to want the Change, and that it is your duty to leap willingly into the Well of Flames in order to avoid succumbing to its grip. All that you know is false. The Change is not a curse; it is a gift, and it is not the end of our lives but instead the very beginning. This understanding is not mine alone. It belongs to each of you, but only if you have the courage to accept what fate has seen fit to bestow upon us." She saw within Tane and Jorn the same as was evident in Kintaren: their auras communicated the onset of maturity and the summoning of the Change. Nimur might not be able to turn all of the Tomol to her cause—at least, not all at once, and not in the immediate future—but these three? They were ready.

"In time you will understand." Extending her hand, Nimur closed her eyes and searched through the darkness until she almost could touch the three auras. They were there, so very close, just beyond her reach. She enticed them closer.

"Nimur, no!" Kintaren shouted. "Do not do this! We don't want the Change! Nimur, *stop*!"

Ignoring the protests, Nimur opened her mind to the auras. She imagined herself guiding her energy into each of their thoughts, winding it into flesh and muscle before infusing it into their very beings.

When she opened her eyes, she saw Tane, Jorn, and Kintaren looking back at her. Like those of the others and even Nimur herself, their eyes burned red.

Changed.

7

"A few coats of paint, and she should be good to go. Right?"

Standing just outside the main airlock hatch leading into the port side of the *U.S.S. Sagittarius* saucer section's main deck, Lieutenant Stephen Klisiewicz waited as the vessel's commander, Captain Clark Terrell, and its chief engineer, Master Chief Petty Officer Michael Ilucci, descended toward him.

"If that's the only thing keeping you from buying," Terrell said, offering his trademark wide smile, "I'll get my people on it right now."

"That wasn't part of the deal," Ilucci countered, wiping his dirty hands with an equally soiled rag. "We're selling it as is. Take it or leave it. Well, that's if you pass the credit check. Do that, and you can take her home today."

Klisiewicz frowned, playing his part. "What? No test drive?"

"Maybe later," the master chief replied, "after my round of golf. Getting a tee time on this course is a pain in the ass." Like the rest of the *Sagittarius* crew and very much unlike Klisiewicz and the *Endeavour* landing party, Ilucci and Terrell were dressed in olive drab jumpsuits rather than the standard Starfleet duty uniforms worn aboard ships of the line. Klisiewicz knew from experience with long-range scout ships in general, and the *Sagittarius* in particular, that the more relaxed uniforms were a practical choice for the crew. They featured no rank insignia, just a patch on the right shoulder bearing the *Sagittarius*'s ship emblem and the wearer's last name stitched in black lettering above the jumpsuit's left breast pocket. Klisiewicz himself had worn the uniform on rare occasions, but not since joining the *Endeavour*, where Captain Khatami tended to prefer regular duty attire except for those members of the engineering and maintenance departments where the utilitarian coveralls were more appropriate.

As for Ilucci, Terrell, and the rest of the *Sagittarius* crew, their jumpsuits definitely had seen better days. Each was soiled or torn in various places, and the flap of the cargo pocket on Ilucci's right thigh was missing. The top of his left boot had been scored all the way through the black finish so that his sock was visible, which Klisiewicz noted was not regulation black but a rather harsh shade of orange.

That could come in handy if we can't find the distress flares.

"How are your people doing, Captain?" Klisiewicz asked. "I know some of them were banged up pretty good, and there's also the radiation exposure you all suffered." He had read the brief report Terrell had transmitted to the *Endeavour* while he and the rest of the landing party prepared for transport to the surface. The *Sagittarius* had been forced to use an asteroid to shield them from the sensors of the two Klingon vessels, but the same radioactive mineral deposits it contained and that had served to mask the scout ship's energy signature also had threatened to poison its crew. The *Sagittarius*'s chief medical officer, Doctor Lisa Babitz, had subjected everyone to a stringent protocol of antiradiation medications, but there had been concerns that the treatment might prove insufficient to combat the effects of prolonged exposure.

"Looks like we're all going to live," Terrell said. "Doctor Leone's already taken care of all the cuts and bruises, and boosted our antiradiation meds. He still wants to give us all a good going-over on the *Endeavour*." He eyed Ilucci. "That goes double for you and Threx." Klisiewicz knew that the two engineers had been in the bowels of the scout ship during its wild fall from orbit, and Leone wanted to rule out further and potentially dangerous exposure to radiation or any other hazardous materials that might have contaminated the compartment during the crash. In this, the *Endeavour*'s CMO was erring on the side of caution with every member of the *Sagittarius* crew.

"Awesome," Ilucci said. "I haven't had a good double going-over since our last shore leave."

Behind the jocularity expressed by Terrell and Ilucci, Klisiewicz could hear the fatigue in both men's voices. They along with the rest of their crew looked tired, which was understandable considering the plight they and their ship had endured. Still, from where Klisiewicz stood, they looked a damned sight better than the *Sagittarius* itself, which had suffered momentous damage, first from the weapons of the Klingon battle cruiser and then as a consequence of its rough landing after plummeting from orbit to Arethusa's surface. Only the skilled piloting of the ship's helm officer, Ensign Nizsk, and some timely mechanical miracles provided by Master Chief Ilucci had spared the *Sagittarius* from a disastrous crash.

Still, the scout ship had not come through the incident unscathed. That much was obvious from just a casual visual inspection. His first look at the ship had revealed to Klisiewicz an array of scorch marks and other damage from its firefight with the two Klingon ships as well as a host of dented and scarred hull plates from its plunge from orbit and through the planet's atmosphere before Ensign Nizsk had effected the *Sagittarius*'s harrowing landing. Even his untrained eye told Klisiewicz that substantial repair work was required in order to make the compact vessel spaceworthy once again, and even then in the barest sense. The list of damaged systems was as long as his arm, and even if the *Sagittarius* lifted from its current resting place, it still would require a tow or other means of transport to a Starfleet shipyard or starbase repair facility.

Having reached his apparent fill of their friendly chit-chat, Terrell said, "I'll start sending our people up a few at a time, so we can keep going with the repairs. Thanks for your help, Lieutenant. We appreciate it. With your chief engineer and his team helping us, we should have the old girl ready for liftoff in no time." Terrell and Ilucci had prioritized which repair tasks were essential for getting the ship off the ground. To that end, the *Endeavour*'s chief engineer and his team wasted no time climbing into the depths of the grounded scout ship and already were hard at work with the *Sagittarius*'s crew to accelerate the repairs.

"Don't thank me, Captain," Klisiewicz replied. "Commander Yataro and his people are doing the heavy lifting with that." He looked to Ilucci. "Whatever you need from our stores, Master Chief, you just say the word and it's yours, assuming Yataro didn't already bring it with him." He gestured to where the *Masao*, one of the *Endeavour*'s shuttlecraft, sat nearby. Anticipating numerous needs on the part of the *Sagittarius*'s engineers in order to complete repair efforts, Commander Yataro had ordered the small transport craft loaded with all manner of tools and other equipment.

"Much appreciated, Lieutenant," Ilucci replied. "I don't suppose that goes for beer, too?"

Despite their current situation, Klisiewicz could not help but chuckle at the other man's easy humor. "I'll see what I can do." It amazed him that Ilucci, and Terrell, for that matter, were able to maintain their composure with the stresses of the moment, coupled with the knowledge that somewhere on this planet—distant and yet not too far away—a threat loomed.

It's what leaders are supposed to do, Klisiewicz reminded himself. *You should probably take notes.* Captain Khatami was able to foster that same sort of control even during the most trying circumstances, as had her predecessor, Zhao Sheng. That man had been an emotional rock right up until the moment he was killed in what felt like a lifetime ago. Had it really been three years since Zhao had perished on Erilon at the hands of the Shedai? Where had all the time gone? It still amazed Klisiewicz to think of everything that had transpired since the *Endeavour*'s initial posting to the Taurus Reach and Starbase 47, to undertake what at the time was believed to be an extended exploration and research effort into the remnants of a lost race, the Shedai.

The mission had ended up being nothing of the kind,

and the cost for that misjudgment was still being measured not only in lives lost but also the dangers—known and perhaps as yet undiscovered—that might still lurk within the Taurus Reach. This, of course, was just one reason for Starfleet's continued exploration of the region; even with the Shedai supposedly gone forever, the possibility of finding some vestige of their once powerful and quite malevolent civilization remained a pressing concern. Many within Starfleet's command hierarchy believed the destruction of the Shedai at the Battle of Vanguard and the apparent annihilation of any leftover artifacts and other embodiments of their advanced technology meant the threat was gone for good. Even Admiral Heihachiro Nogura, a skeptic if Klisiewicz had ever met one, seemed to be doing his best to bury all knowledge and evidence of Starfleet's activities in the Taurus Reach and the consequences they provoked. Though some aspects of the affair were public knowledge, a great deal of information remained classified. A friend of Klisiewicz's at Starfleet Command had told him that all the data and surviving artifacts of Shedai technology and culture discovered on worlds throughout the Taurus Reach during Operation Vanguard were being held under the tightest security conditions at one of Starfleet's high-security storage facilities.

Buried. Maybe forever, Klisiewicz mused. *What a waste*.

And now this planet, Arethusa, seemed to be a potential treasure trove of its own. If what the *Sagittarius* survey party had said about their discovery was true, then this world might well provide answers to one of the most fascinating unsolved mysteries Starfleet had yet encountered: who were the Preservers, and why had they seen fit to seed planets throughout this part of the galaxy with specimens of humanoids from other worlds? It was a question Klisiewicz had asked from the moment he first had read about the *U.S.S. Enterprise*'s encounter with a Preserver artifact on a planet many light-years from here. What, if anything, had been the ancient civilization's ultimate objective? All signs pointed to the Preservers having been a benevolent race, and it was unlikely any of them or their descendants still lived. Whatever answers were to be found, it would be up to people like Klisiewicz and others with the drive to follow any clues wherever they might lead.

Ming would've loved this.

Klisiewicz could not help but think of his friend, Lieutenant Ming Xiong, an archaeology and anthropology officer assigned to Starbase 47 and a driving force in Operation Vanguard's mission to uncover the mysteries of the Shedai. From the beginning of the project, Xiong had been its moral compass, never ceasing in his efforts to champion peaceful applications for the Shedai information and technology Starfleet had found in the Taurus Reach. He and Klisiewicz had enjoyed more than one philosophical discussion on the topic, both agreeing that any application of knowledge learned from the Shedai should be used for the betterment of the galaxy, rather than as another instrument of war. Despite the ever-increasing threat of conflict among the Federation, the Klingons, and the Tholians over control over the secrets and prizes to be found in the Taurus Reach, Xiong had held fast to his convictions up until the moment of his death during the Battle of Vanguard. Though the man was gone, his influence had not faded, and it was this mind-set that now motivated Klisiewicz as he, the *Endeavour*, and the *Sagittarius* embarked on a new mission of exploration.

I'll make you proud, my friend. Of course, such things would, for the time at least, take a backseat to more pressing matters, such as the repairs to the wounded *Sagittarius*.

Footsteps from inside the ship caught his attention and he, along with Terrell and Ilucci, turned to see Lieutenant Commander Yataro, the *Endeavour*'s chief engineer, emerging from the *Sagittarius*'s airlock. His Starfleet black trousers and red tunic seemed almost too large for his thin, gangly frame, though his physique was typical of his species. A Lirin, Yataro was a humanoid in the broad sense, with a long, thin neck atop which sat a bulbous head that was almost triangular in shape. As he stepped down from the hatch's threshold, the late-afternoon sunlight gave his lavender skin a bright, almost oily sheen. He possessed a small, thin mouth near the base of his narrow chin, and a pair of slits angling out and downward from the center of his face acted as his olfactory organs. Widening as it rose from his chin, his skull culminated in a wide, pronounced brow. His eyes were large, dark orbs, which in the bright light appeared dark blue.

"Captain Terrell," Yataro began, holding up his right hand so that his long, thin fingers seemed to part in an almost Vulcan gesture of greeting, "it is a pleasure to meet you, sir."

"The pleasure's mine, Commander," Terrell replied.

"I'm sorry I wasn't able to greet you when you first beamed down, but by the time I got free from helping in the cargo bay, you were already hard at work."

Yataro nodded. "Time would seem to be of the essence." Shifting his stance so that he faced Ilucci, he said, "Master Chief Petty Officer, I require your assistance in the engineering compartment. There are a few . . . unusual modifications to the master systems control station with which I am having some difficulty."

Smiling, Ilucci said, "Yeah, we had to do some jury-rigging to keep that thing together, sir. Chalk it up to not wanting things to blow up and kill us." He shrugged. "It happens."

"Yes," the Lirin replied, unfazed by the master chief's attempt at levity. "Nevertheless, several of the alterations pose their own risks if they are allowed to remain in place. It is my judgment that they should be rectified and the console returned to proper Starfleet specifications before this vessel can be deemed safe for flight."

"It worked well enough to keep us from crashing," Ilucci retorted.

"Master Chief . . ." Terrell said, his tone quiet, though Klisiewicz caught the hint of warning.

"I'm sure it's no big deal," the science officer said, earning him a harsh look from Ilucci and an unreadable expression from Yataro. "Commander, the master chief and his people are usually required by circumstances to improvise solutions to problems using whatever's available. Remember, the *Sagittarius* doesn't benefit from having ship's stores like the *Endeavour*. Sometimes they just have to make do."

Ilucci grunted. "Yeah. What he said."

"No offense was intended," Yataro said, unperturbed by the exchange. "I merely was pointing out the deficiency, and that we have an opportunity to correct it."

"Deficiency?" Ilucci's eyes looked as though they might pop from his head, at which point Terrell held up a hand.

"That's enough, I think." Eyeing his chief engineer, the captain said, "Go show him whatever it is you've done in there. Let's get this mess sorted out. I don't like sitting here any longer than I have to, not with Klingons up there somewhere and who knows what else wandering around down here."

Having resumed his somewhat spirited yet useless cleaning of his hands with the rag, Ilucci nodded, his expression communicating that the message—and its unspoken addendum—had been received and understood. "I'm on it, Skipper." Turning to Yataro, he gestured toward the airlock. "If you'll accompany me, Commander, we'll kick this party up a notch." When the Lirin paused, looking first to Klisiewicz and then Terrell with an expression of apparent confusion, the master chief added, "I meant we'll get serious about finishing these repairs." As Yataro moved toward the hatch, Ilucci made a show of rolling his eyes and mouthing the silent plea, "Shoot me now," before following the commander into the belly of the ship.

"God help anyone who's stuck in there with them," Klisiewicz said.

Terrell asked, "Is he always like that?"

"Pretty much, yeah." Yataro was a recent addition to

the *Endeavour* crew, replacing the starship's previous chief engineer, Lieutenant Commander Bersh glov Mog, who along with most of the ship's engineering staff had died during the Battle of Vanguard. Klisieiwicz missed the burly Tellarite, who had been one of his closest friends aboard ship. As for Yataro, there was no denying his competency as an engineer, but where Mog's personality had been warm and jovial, the Lirin tended to be composed and businesslike in nearly all of his personal interactions.

You'll get used to him.

His communicator chose that moment to beep, and Klisiewicz retrieved it from his waistband at the small of his back, the unit chirping when he flipped open its antenna grid. "Klisiewicz here."

"*This is Khatami,*" replied the voice of the *Endeavour*'s captain. "*What's your status, Lieutenant?*"

"Repairs are proceeding, Captain," said the science officer. "Yataro and his team are already working with the *Sagittarius*'s people. The ship really took a beating, but the commander and Master Chief Ilucci think they can get her flying again in short order."

"*That's good. We're continuing to track the Tomol, including the one tagged with the Klingon transponder. They were moving away from the bird-of-prey crash site, but they doubled back and now are holding steady in that vicinity. We're also picking up other Tomol life signs moving toward them. These are the . . . regular Tomol, I suppose, if that's what we're calling them, as opposed to the ones from the crash site. We're not sure what's up with that.*"

Klisiewicz frowned. According to the information collected by the *Sagittarius*'s reconnaissance party, the Tomol carried with them the potential to undergo the same metamorphosis that had affected the one calling herself Nimur, though it appeared that some other, possibly artificial factors had come into play, allowing for an acceleration in this transformation in at least a few of the others. Was it something Nimur herself was controlling, or was it the consequence of another outside force?

That's what you're here to find out, Science Officer.

Terrell said, "From what we've learned, the Tomol have rituals and procedures for dealing with any of their people who go through the Change. They may be trying to capture Nimur themselves, in accordance with their society's laws."

"I don't care about any of that right now," Khatami replied. *"If what you told me is true, Clark, then this Nimur and her followers are going to be looking for another way off the planet."*

"Right," Terrell said, "and even as banged up as we are, we're the only game in town."

"Even if the ship's not able to fly, I'm more concerned about what they can do to you and your people. I'm not wild about leaving you down there, Clark."

"We've got time," Terrell countered. "They're still on the other side of the big island, right?" Then he frowned. "Of course, they were able to change their forms to chase after our rover even when it went underwater, so I guess they could swim here, or what if they're able to change into something that lets them fly?"

Klisiewicz said, "I think we'll want to be somewhere else when that happens."

"*Exactly,*" Khatami said. "*The more I think about this, the more I'm leaning toward beaming you all out of there and scuttling the* Sagittarius." It had been a plan she had discussed with Commander Stano and the landing party prior to his leaving the ship, and though Klisiewicz had been instructed to discuss the matter with Terrell, the opportunity to do so had not yet presented itself.

"Let's not get ahead of ourselves," said the *Sagittarius*'s captain. "We've still got time to get her up and running. I damned sure don't want to leave her for . . . well, whatever the hell those things are, but I'm not ready to cut and run."

There was a pause, and Klisiewicz was sure he could hear his captain's teeth grinding as she considered Terrell's position. Finally, Khatami said, "*All right, for now, but I'm sending down some reinforcements, just in case things go bad before we can get you out of there.*"

"Agreed," Terrell replied. "Thanks for everything, Atish."

"*Don't thank me until your ship is back up here. Khatami out.*"

"Time to get back to work," Terrell said, reaching for a handhold set into the bulkhead next to the airlock and pulling himself up into the *Sagittarius*.

"How much time do you think we have, Captain?" Klisiewicz asked as he fell in behind the older officer.

Terrell snorted. "However much it is, something tells me it won't be enough."

8

"Hey, really, are we sure they put us down in the right spot?"

Anthony Leone's eyes, usually moving and looking at anything and everything around him as a matter of course, felt as though they might pop from his head as he freed the strap of his medical tricorder from the protruding branch of a nearby tree. The branch was only the latest obstacle he had confronted while tromping through a stretch of Arethusa's native forest.

"I have to believe the transporter chief knows what he's doing, Doctor," replied Nurse Holly Amos, the youngest member of the *Endeavour*'s medical staff, as she followed Leone through the forest.

"You've got a lot to learn about transporter chiefs." Leone ducked under another, thicker branch as he followed one of the two security officers who had accompanied him and Amos to the surface, the man's bright red tunic contrasting with the softer greens and browns of the indigenous flora. The guards were a condition set by Captain Khatami as part of her agreement to let Leone beam down to the surface, as was the landing party's arrival in a secluded area half a kilometer from the Tomol village. Given the captain's decision that none of the Tomol were to be brought aboard the ship, here was the only place he would be able to conduct the firsthand examination of a native Tomol and obtain useful information about the enigmatic race that could not be achieved via long-range scans.

In truth, the security escort did not bother Leone as much as the fact that Khatami knew him well enough to stipulate it. She harbored no doubts that he would not have hesitated to transport down to the Tomol village at the first opportunity, without regard for the risk such an action engendered. Of course he was aware of the danger from the transformed Tomol and would rather be lying in a beach hammock on some distant resort planet, or even taking fire from the Klingon battle cruiser still lurking in nearby space. But there was work to be done, and he would have preferred to complete it in short order and without the need to expose any other members of the *Endeavour* crew to undue hazards. He was motivated as much by not wanting to see anyone hurt as by a purely selfish desire to avoid additional surgery or other treatment in sickbay for anyone injured during such an excursion.

But Leone knew the captain was right, hence the security detail. As for Amos? He had an angle for that, too. Her youthful appearance and slim, almost petite stature might come in handy when dealing with the Tomol villagers, who might feel somewhat more at ease in the presence of someone who looked to be of similar age to them and appeared nonthreatening. Leone thought it a rather inspired idea on his part, and Amos had enthusiastically agreed to accompany him.

Looking over his shoulder, Leone saw the nurse doing an excellent job of keeping up with the pace set by the lead security officer, Ensign Derek Zapien, with the other security officer, Ensign Carlton McMurray, bringing up the rear. The doctor was certain there was even a spring in her step, and when she saw him looking back at her, she smiled. In response, Leone rolled his eyes.

"What are you so happy about?"

"This is my first real landing party, Doctor," Amos replied, reaching up to brush off a leaf that had landed atop her dark-haired head as she stepped over an exposed tree root. "The last time I got out of sickbay, it was because someone fell off the climbing wall in the ship's gymnasium."

"That's what he deserved for not using the safety harness." Leone shook his head. "A ship full of state-of-the-art exercise equipment, everything with its own set of safety features and protocols, but no! Let's not bother with any of that when you can wake up your doctor in the middle of the night to knit your broken leg." He recalled the incident, along with the decision he had almost made to confine the wayward young engineer in a full body cast for a month.

Ahead of him, Ensign Zapien stopped, and Leone saw that they were approaching a clearing. A short distance from the tree line, huts and other small, simple structures were visible. "Just a reminder, people," he said to the rest of the landing party, "not everyone in the village has seen offworlders, so don't be surprised when we get some funny looks and standoffish behaviors. Let's hope this doesn't take long."

He gestured for Zapien to lead on, and the four officers emerged from the cover of the forest. As they approached the village, Leone wondered whether the site might be deserted, as there appeared to be no one visible. Then he caught a glimpse of a Tomol child peeking his head from around the side of a hut. Their gazes met for a moment, but then the boy ducked back behind the hut, out of sight.

As Leone started moving in that direction, Zapien called after him. "Doctor, you should stay with the group."

Leone turned and frowned at the ensign. "It's a kid. He's probably just nervous." The physician returned to his pace and called out ahead of him. "Hello? Where'd you go? We're not going to hurt you. We're here to . . ."

Rounding the back side of the hut, Leone froze as the sharpened tip of a wooden spear pressed against his belly. Naturally, the weapon's wielder was the child he had just seen. The young Tomol gripped the spear with both hands, poking Leone with it.

"Who are you?"

"I'm Doctor Leone, and I'm here to help you." He heard footsteps behind him and noted the boy's reaction as he shifted his stance to look around the doctor at the new arrivals. A quick glance over his shoulder told him it was Amos and their escorts, with the two security guards having brandished their phasers. Leone returned his attention to the boy when he felt the spear jab him in the gut once more.

"Whoa, hey," he said, raising his arms. "These are my friends, okay?" He gestured to his clothing. "See? Same clothes, right?"

"What do you want here?" asked the boy.

Keeping his hands raised, Leone replied, "We're just making sure everyone here is all right. We're looking for your leader, Seta?" He had been briefed by Khatami on the young Tomol priestess, based on the limited information collected by the *Sagittarius* crew. "Is she here?"

"Brinto!"

The new voice sounded from ahead, and Leone saw a slim figure wrapped in a brightly colored garment standing in the doorway of one of the larger huts. "Brinto, bring them."

"See?" Leone said as the boy stepped backward, removing the spear tip from his belly. "Just here to talk. Not trying to cause a problem." He looked behind him and saw the rest of the landing party standing there. "Thanks for the backup, guys." Gesturing to the security officers' phasers, he added, "Can we put those away? You'll make the natives restless."

"With all due respect, Doctor," said McMurray, "that's sort of the point."

Leone conceded that. "Okay, but you're making me restless, too."

"We'll be discreet," Zapien said.

"Fine," Leone grunted in resignation as he set off to follow the boy, Brinto. Walking farther into the village, he now saw that the Tomol waiting for them was a female, not really much older than Brinto, with the same teal skin and silvery hair that characterized her people. Her cloak was composed of numerous brilliantly colored feathers and obviously was too big for her. She was nervous, Leone noticed, fidgeting under the weight of the cloak, which he assumed served a ceremonial rather than functional purpose.

"I am Seta," she said, and despite what he had been told about the Tomol leader, Leone was surprised by just how *young* she looked. This girl, who looked no older than fourteen, had been thrust into her role by circumstance after one of the transformed Tomol, Nimur, had killed her predecessor. "I knew there would be more of you. Are you from the sky-ships, too?"

Leone nodded. "Yes. I am Leone. I'm a doctor." Looking past her, he saw that at least three other Tomol were standing in the hut. When she appeared not to understand his meaning, he added, "A healer of the sick."

Seta nodded, then gestured to Amos. "You are a healer, as well?"

The nurse replied, "Of a sort. I help Doctor Leone."

"And what of your companions?" Seta asked.

Glancing to Zapien and McMurray, Leone replied, "They protect us from harm."

The young Tomol said, "Like our Wardens?"

"That's right," the doctor replied, recalling the information he had been given about the Tomol society collected by the *Sagittarius* landing party. "I understand that you are now the leader of your people, and that you've met and talked with others of my people. I hope you'll trust us just as you trusted them, as we're not here to hurt you." When she said nothing for a moment, Leone realized she was staring at him. "What's wrong?"

"Your face." Seta reached forward, but then caught herself. "Your skin has creases. Are you sick?"

Amos snorted, and when Leone looked at her, the nurse's cheeks flushed with embarrassment. "She's never seen anyone as old as you, Doctor."

"I'm not *that* old," Leone snapped. Returning to the matter at hand, he said to Seta, "I've come so that I can better understand your people so that maybe I can find a way to help the others, the ones who . . ."

"You mean the Changed," Seta said. "We know little about what happens to us when we come of age. We know only what the wordstone tells us, and that we must accept the Cleansing when the Change is upon us."

"That's why we're here," Leone replied, considering his words based on what he had learned from the landing party's survey report and what the young Tomol was saying. "We think the wordstone might have knowledge it hasn't yet shared with you. If that's true, then we think we may be able to help you with those who've Changed, and hopefully the rest of you."

For a moment, he saw Seta's stony expression soften just enough for a glimpse of the child behind it. Her eyes revealed vulnerability, along with a sense of relief and gratitude, and he thought she might even offer a smile. Then the moment passed, and Seta straightened her posture, as though remembering that despite her young age, she still was the leader of her people.

"Your assistance is welcome."

Leaving Zapien and McMurray outside to stand watch—a duty Seta also assigned to young Brinto—Leone and Amos followed Seta into the hut, which was sparsely decorated and furnished. Several narrow beds were arrayed around the walls of the primitive structure, which lacked windows or a fireplace. A table was positioned at the room's center, atop which sat a bowl filled with what Leone guessed were native fruits. Illumination was provided by a pair of lamps on the table, allowing him to see the three other Tomol females occupying the hut.

None of them appeared to be much older than Seta, and one was decidedly younger. Each was dressed in unremarkable hand-woven clothing.

"How do you intend to help us?" Seta asked.

A good question, Leone admitted to himself. "First, I have to understand more about you and your people. This Change you undergo, it happens when you reach a certain age, which means that it has something to do with what goes on inside your body." Lifting his tricorder from where it rested along his hip, he showed the device to her. "This lets me see that. May I use it? I promise it will not cause any pain."

"The other sky people had boxes like that," Seta replied. "They provided great knowledge. You may proceed."

Gesturing to Amos to follow his lead with the other three Tomol women, Leone activated the tricorder and removed the diagnostic scanner from the unit's storage compartment. Without being asked, Seta removed her heavy cloak, and the doctor was struck by how slight the girl appeared without it—and how young. Waving the scanner over her, Leone watched her eyes follow his motions and noted her concerned expression.

"Will you be able to see everything with that?" she asked.

Leone replied, "I don't know about everything, but I'll have many more answers about your people than I have now."

"Will it tell you when?"

His eyes narrowing, Leone looked up from his tricorder. "When what?"

"When the Change will take me."

Of course she'd ask that.

"Once I understand more about your people and how your bodies work, I should be able to do that." From what he already had been told about Tomol physiology by Doctor Lisa Babitz, the *Sagittarius*'s chief medical officer, he was convinced that Seta was still at least a few years away from whatever natural growth and aging effects might trigger the Change. Halting his tricorder scan, he asked, "But are you sure you really want to know?"

Seta seemed to ponder the question before offering a brief nod. "I want to know only for the sake of my people. I am not fully prepared for my duties as priestess. Ysan did not have the opportunity to teach me all there is to know before Nimur took her from us. I have spent very little time in the Caves of the Shepherds, and I have not mastered the Shepherds' wordstone. If the Change is going to take me soon, I will need to find someone who can carry on as priestess."

"I'm sure you'll have plenty of time," Leone said, unsure how else to proceed with this line of discussion. He knew from the *Sagittarius* reports that the Shepherds were what the Tomol called the Preservers, and that the wordstone was the obelisk the scout ship's landing party had found in the underground caverns. Lieutenant Klisiewicz was convinced that the artifact was a treasure trove of information, most of which likely remained unknown to the Tomol, or that those like Priestess Ysan, who may well have possessed greater information, were dead as a consequence of Nimur's actions. "What do you know about the Shepherds?"

"They are the ones who brought us here to Suba and left us with the laws so we can continue to live here safely and preserve our people."

"So the Shepherds didn't just leave you here all alone," Leone said. "I mean, they gave you what you need to survive here."

Seta nodded. "Yes, Leone. All that we need is within the wordstone. It answers our questions when we have them. According to what Priestess Ysan taught me, it can even give us the power to stop the Changed, should a time come when one does not submit to the Cleansing."

"Times like now?" Leone asked.

"Like now, yes. I know that Nimur can be stopped, or rather that she could have been stopped by a Holy Sister such as Ysan, someone who had completed her education and training." She cast her gaze down to the hands she held clasped at her waist. "I am only a disciple. I know so little of how to consult the wordstone."

Leone felt sorry for the girl, who seemed far too young to have such responsibility forced upon her. "It sounds like you know more about it than anyone else around here."

"I do," Seta replied. "As I said to the others from your sky-ships, it now falls to me to lead our people." She paused. "It is frustrating to hold such responsibility and yet have no ability to carry out what is expected of me. With Ysan gone, I am the Holy Sister, the only person permitted by the Shepherds to draw upon the wordstone's knowledge and power, but I am uncertain how to do that. I do not know if I am ready, but your friends said they would help me learn the things I had not been taught by Ysan."

Something about what she was saying made Leone pause, and he lowered the tricorder and his scanner. "You're the only one able to use the wordstone? So that means you'd be the only one who could call on whatever might be needed to stop any of your people who underwent the Change."

Seta replied, "In accordance with the Shepherds' will, yes."

"And all of your people know this," Leone said, not liking where his thinking was beginning to take him.

"They do," Seta said. "That is as it has been for as long as we have been here."

Amos, having completed her scans of the other Tomol women, walked back to rejoin Leone. "So that means *Nimur* knows you're the only one capable of putting an end to the Changed," she said.

"Exactly," Leone agreed. "Even though you think you might not know anything, you at least know enough to get us to help you. That makes you a target," he told Seta. Reaching for his communicator, he flipped open its antenna grid. "Leone to *Endeavour*. Stand by to beam up the landing party, along with one addition."

"Doctor?" Amos prompted. "Are you sure this is a good idea?" She made a show of looking first to Seta and then back again to Leone. "There are *prime* considerations, after all."

Leone gestured for them to move to the hut entrance so that they could collect Zapien and McMurray before finding a place to transport back to the ship without being observed by the entire village. Yes, there were Prime Directive issues to consider, but it was obvious to Leone that the Tomol in their current state were a textbook example of a culture arrested by an outside influence, rather than one making normal technological and sociological strides.

Besides, the Klingons already screwed up everything, anyway.

"We've got bigger problems right now. We can deal with that other stuff later." Taking Seta by the hand, he said, "I think you're in danger, and I want to keep you safe. By doing that, I think we can help keep all of your people safe. We won't keep you away from your people any longer than absolutely necessary. Do you trust me?"

"I trust you, Leone," the girl replied, clutching his hand.

Nodding in satisfaction, Leone smiled. "All right, then." Realizing what the young Tomol was about to experience, he added, "You're about to see some things that will be hard to believe, Seta, but by coming with me, you're working to help your people."

As they exited the hut, Amos said, "I don't think Captain Khatami's going to be happy."

Leone waved away her concerns. "Relax. She loves it when I do stuff like this."

9

"Tony, I really *hate* it when you do stuff like this."

Atish Khatami stood at the briefing room table, her palms planted flatly upon it as she leaned into Doctor Leone's personal space. They were alone in the room, so Khatami felt no qualms about demonstrating her disapproval to her chief medical officer, who happened also to be her friend and closest thing on the ship to a confidant. She knew better than to expect anything resembling a straightforward apology, but also that Leone would not attempt to deflect blame or responsibility for a decision. Despite this well-established dynamic between them, the doctor still fidgeted in his seat, indicating to Khatami that her point was being made.

"I understand that you gave me orders about this," Leone said, "but I basically made a tactical decision based on new information. Shouldn't I get a little credit for that?"

"Maybe you missed the crater on the surface that resulted from the last time one of the natives was invited into space," Khatami said.

"That was different," Leone replied. "For one, those Klingon idiots beamed aboard a mess of Tomol who'd already Changed. Seta's nowhere near that point in her development."

"How can you be sure?"

"Because I'm a doctor, and that's what doctors do." Leaning forward, Leone rested his elbows on the table. "Seta's not just a valuable resource to us. She's the one who can get us access to the Preserver pyramid. She's the key to getting this Nimur and the rest of the Changed under control. Nimur has to know that. Until we can get a real handle on this thing, the safest place for her is here."

"And you're confident that the *Endeavour* is in no danger from her?" Khatami asked.

Leone nodded. "As confident as I can be with the information we've got. I'm going to do every test and scan I can think of, but right now I'm pretty damn sure she's not about to explode into something we can't handle." He held up his hands as he continued speaking, moving them about in front of his face, which was his habit when he was launching into a lengthy explanation. "The initial readings on her DNA show nucleosides that *could* be influenced by the right catalyst to initiate phosphorylation, and once that starts there's no way to tell whether translocations will occur or how rapidly that might happen or whether the resulting new functions are toxic or superior and . . . I've lost you."

"Is it that obvious?" Khatami asked.

"Your jaw went a little slack, there."

"Well, you could pretend you're not talking to a geneticist."

That evoked a chuckle from the doctor. "Right, sorry. The basic thing about DNA, no matter where we find it, is that it can be altered or mutated by an outside source. That source can be something as simple as sunlight or as damaging as radiation or ingesting a chemical compound. Then, you've got genetic resequencing, which is a strict no-no in the Federation but is practiced on at least a few planets in the known galaxy. Above that, we've got that whole next-level thing going on with races like our friends the Shedai, which we think has something to do with what's going on down below. Anyway, as DNA forms, it spirals up and around and it locks itself up pretty tight. Its propensity is to stabilize and thrive. It's not sitting there just looking to get mutated."

"Okay," Khatami said. "And I sense a 'but' coming."

"*But*," Leone stressed, "the Tomol's DNA *is* different. We performed in-depth scans on four individuals on the surface, and in each of them we found the same series of orphan receptors. They're just hanging out there waiting to connect to . . . *something*."

Khatami nodded. "And we don't know what."

"Right. I can't be sure exactly what will happen to a Tomol whose genes start to receive whatever chemical or signal is intended to start that reaction, but the strands appear primed to unravel in a uniform way once introduced to the right conditions."

Despite the doctor's attempts to simplify the topic for her benefit, Khatami felt her head starting to hurt. "So every one of those people is a bomb with a fuse."

"Pretty much, only the fuse stays unlit until they reach a certain point in their natural development. That will be different from person to person, and for Seta that point isn't going to be for a while yet."

"What about the other effects this Change brings about?" Khatami asked, settling back into her chair. "The reports from the *Sagittarius* people indicate that this Nimur is mentally unbalanced, or becoming that way."

"There's no way to know if this is a normal reaction to the Change, or something unique to her. From what we can tell, this sort of thing rarely if ever happens, because the Tomol have instituted all their laws and rituals that see to it that anyone who's caught up in the beginnings of the transformation throws himself or herself into that fire pit." Leone sighed. "I don't recommend this place as a vacation destination, if anyone's wondering."

Ignoring the comment, Khatami said, "If her transformation is typical, we could be looking at an epidemic resulting in hundreds of demigods, all of them capable of destroying a starship with their bare hands." Before she could continue that line of thinking, the briefing room doors parted to admit Lieutenant Stephen Klisiewicz, who entered at a hurried pace.

"I'm sorry, Captain," he said by way of greeting. "I broke away as quickly as I could." Moving to an empty chair on Leone's side of the table, he added, "We've got a lot happening down there."

Khatami nodded in understanding. Her crew had been working nonstop almost since the *Endeavour*'s arrival at Arethusa. "Anything new?"

"We're still working through the data collected by Commander Theriault and her landing party from their interactions with the Tomol and the Preserver artifact. There are definite similarities to this object and the one the *Enterprise* found on that planet with the transplanted humans from Earth. In that case, the Preserver obelisk's primary function was to act as a defense against asteroids that might threaten the planet. Given the presence of a similar structure here and based on what's already been translated from the glyphs it contains, it's obvious that the obelisk down below has been there for a very, *very* long time and it's there for some specific purpose regarding the Tomol. We're still trying to determine the scope of its abilities."

Leone said, "Seta seems to think it's the only thing that can stop the mutated Tomol from doing . . . whatever it is they're going to do."

"Can she help?" Khatami asked. "I know she thinks she's not yet ready or trained to deal with this sort of thing, but surely she has some basic knowledge we can use as a starting point."

The science officer nodded. "That's what I'm hoping. If we can get inside the obelisk, our existing knowledge of Preserver technology should help us to connect at least some of the dots. The *Sagittarius* crew has already done a bit of this, and I'm confident we can carry it further, but I think we'd have better luck going down to the site and examining the obelisk firsthand."

"Why did I know you were going to say that?" Khatami asked, forcing herself to suppress a knowing smile. It made sense for the science officer to want direct interaction with the object of his study, and there were limits to what could be accomplished aboard ship, particularly with the Preserver obelisk and most of its surrounding underground cavern shielded from the *Endeavour*'s sensors. "How soon can you be ready to go?"

"A few hours, I think," Klisiewicz replied. "I'm having the computer run comparative analysis of the data collected by the *Sagittarius* landing party and information from our memory banks on the obelisk the *Enterprise* found. I figure even if the particulars aren't identical, there may be some commonality we can use to gain access."

Leone said, "That works out just about right. I should be done with my tests on Seta by then, and she's already said she's willing to let us help her to understand the thing."

"Perfect," Khatami said, tapping the table with one fingernail before pushing herself from her chair, the action signaling to her officers that the meeting was concluded. "Keep me informed as to your progress."

Rising from his own seat, Klisiewicz said, "Aye, aye, Captain."

"That goes double for you, Doctor. Keep a close eye on our guest."

Leone nodded. "If she decides to blow up the ship," he said, "you'll be the first to know."

Alone in his quarters, Stephen Klisiewicz leaned forward in the high-backed chair positioned before the desk. Holding a cup of coffee in one hand, he used the other to activate his workstation's computer interface terminal. "Computer, status of data analysis task."

"*Working,*" replied the monotone, feminine voice of the *Endeavour*'s main computer. "*The object scanned below planet's surface is four times larger than the similar artifact discovered by the* U.S.S. Enterprise *on stardate 4842.5. Comparative analysis of external markings on both objects confirms language similarity, including identical instances of symbols that indicate common words and phrases. However, there are a significant number of distinct differences in the character sets of both objects. Without further information pertaining to the larger object's functional purpose, direct translation of all symbols is not possible at this time."*

Klisiewicz leaned back in his chair and reached up to rub the bridge of his nose before running one hand through his dark hair. "Well, that was predictable," he muttered. He had assigned the starship's artificial intelligence to collate the sensor data collected by the *Sagittarius* landing party during their investigation of the Preserver pyramid beneath the surface of Arethusa and cross-check it against information in the data banks pertaining to the similar, smaller object discovered by the *U.S.S. Enterprise* on the planet Amerind. He also had instructed the computer to include in its analysis the data collected by the *Endeavour*'s sensors of the obelisk below and the surrounding area. He knew that latter component likely would prove less than helpful, given the interference from mineral deposits in the rock and soil beneath the Preserver artifact. "Computer, are you able to create a translation protocol for the tonal language depicted on the larger obelisk?"

"Negative. Insufficient information."

"Of course not." Cradling his coffee in both hands, he absently tapped the cup with his fingers. There was no denying that the Preserver obelisks were astounding pieces of engineering, complex and yet designed with the intention of being easily accessed and utilized by people lacking advanced technological knowledge, so deciphering how to access the inner workings of the structure here on Arethusa should be possible, if time-consuming. The artifact likely possessed all the answers he sought, though none of the Tomol seemed to know what questions to pose, and Klisiewicz had not yet learned how to ask them himself. "What about its power source?" he asked, more to himself than anything else. Then, for the computer's benefit, he said, "Show me the schematic of the Arethusa obelisk, in relation to its present location." In response to the query, the image on his workstation monitor shifted to depict a graphic representation of the object, including those areas of its foundation that extended into the bedrock beneath it. He noted what looked to be a tunnel extending from the bottom of the structure deep into the bedrock. "How far does that conduit extend from the bottom of the obelisk into the bedrock?"

"Two thousand, seven hundred thirty-seven kilometers."

"All the way down to the planet's outer core," Klisiewicz said, again to himself. "So it's drawing energy from thermal heat, and the reserves of that energy would be enormous. It has to be four thousand degrees down there."

"Four thousand, two hundred six point seven degrees Celsius," the computer answered.

Rolling his eyes, Klisiewicz took a sip of his coffee, which he noted was growing cold. "Whatever. Based on the sensor readings for power generation and usage, and extrapolating from geothermal energy available to it based on its present configuration, compute a percentage of the structure's maximum power output against its current usage levels."

"Working." The computer seemed to ponder his request for an additional moment, and Klisiewicz sat in silence while finishing his coffee. Then it replied, *"Current energy operations are estimated at six point four percent of total capacity."*

"Six point four percent? That's all?" If the computer's calculations were correct, and he had no reason to suspect otherwise, then the obelisk was barely dipping its proverbial toe into the pool of energy available to it. Given what the structure already seemed to be doing, Klisiewicz was hard-pressed to imagine what it might be capable of if circumstances required it to max out its power usage. "Computer, compare this obelisk's output potential to the one on Amerind. How much more powerful is this one?"

After another pause, the computer answered, *"If utilized in similar fashion, the maximum power output of this object is twelve times greater in capacity. Insufficient data exists to determine uses for energy at these levels."*

He did not need that information. The obelisk found by the *Enterprise* had been capable of altering the trajectory of a massive asteroid moving at incredible speed on a collision course with Amerind. The structure here, possessing twelve times that level of energy, Klisiewicz realized, could destroy every ship in Starfleet in a single attack.

Or a planet. Or this *planet.*

"Damn," he said. However, as he considered that horrific scenario, Klisiewicz decided it simply did not fit with what was known about the Preservers. With that in mind, was the obelisk here intended to act in some defensive capacity, and if so, for what? If its builders had designed it as a weapon against the Tomol in the event their transformation presented some as yet unknown threat, then that implied they wanted to take no chances that the Changed might be able to escape the planet.

Or maybe they had no idea how big a stick they might need, so they opted for overkill.

"And who does that look like?" he said aloud, posing the question to his otherwise empty quarters. While their histories suggested wildly diverging paths, in general terms the Preservers seemed to have much in common with the Shedai, who also once had a propensity for "going all in," as Doctor Leone had put it. Indeed, considering what the *Sagittarius* crew had learned during their own investigation of the Preserver pyramid and the possibility that the Shedai somehow were involved in the Tomol being here on Arethusa, perhaps this was a connection that required further exploration.

"Computer, disengage and deactivate," he said, copying the results of the analysis to a microtape, which he ejected from the workstation. Rising from his chair, he carried the tape across his quarters to the shelf above his bed. Among the few mementoes displayed there—a photograph of his parents on their wedding day, a figurine from his first visit to Alpha Centauri, and a leather-bound copy of *The Teachings of Surak*—was a century-old hand scanner. The device, a distant precursor to Starfleet's current model of tricorder, had been a gift from his friend Lieutenant Ming Xiong. They had met as a consequence of their both being assigned to Starbase 47, Klisiewicz with the *Endeavour* while Xiong had served as the station's archaeology and anthropology officer.

To Klisiewicz, the scanner represented more than a

fascinating era of exploration long ago consigned to the pages of history. Xiong had given it to him not long before his death, describing it as a token of appreciation from one science officer to another as an acknowledgment of service together, and as a gesture of friendship between the two men. Klisiewicz recalled their brief and what ultimately had been their final meeting, and that Xiong had been troubled by the potential for abuse of the Shedai technology they had labored to understand, by enemies of the Federation as well as misguided individuals within Starfleet's ranks. Xiong had described it as sensing a turning of the tide and said that steps had to be taken to safeguard the information that had been collected at such great cost.

Perhaps it was this distress that had motivated Xiong to give the scanner to Klisiewicz and then to explain that it was only a century old on the outside.

Opening the device's gunmetal gray casing revealed a thoroughly contemporary and completely self-contained computer interface. He caressed the internal module, imagining he could sense the power and potential held within its data banks, which had been filled to capacity with every scrap of known information about the Shedai, collected by Ming Xiong during his time assigned to Operation Vanguard.

After the destruction of Starbase 47 and the termination of Project Vanguard, Starfleet had ordered all data and materials classified and archived under heavy security. The computer memory banks of each of the starships involved at any point with the project had been scrubbed of all but the most innocuous information pertaining to the Shedai and the Taurus Reach. As far as Starfleet was concerned, the project was a taboo subject, never to be spoken of again. Possessing the data Klisiewicz now held in his hands would be sufficient to end his Starfleet career and see him sentenced to life imprisonment at a top-security penal facility.

But you knew a time like this would come, didn't you, Ming?

Despite his realization that the project would soon be ended and all of its data buried, Xiong was firm in his belief that the knowledge he had gathered was not itself inherently good or evil and thus should not be feared, as it had been by many in Starfleet Command's highest echelons. Despite anticipating this reaction, Xiong was convinced that even with the apparent destruction of the Shedai, there remained all manner of other worlds and civilizations to be explored in the Taurus Reach, any number of which could have been impacted by the once all-powerful race. The information he and his colleagues had gathered might one day be of use when encountering such planets and their peoples. With that in mind, he had entrusted a copy of the data to Klisiewicz. The computer interface contained within the scanner was stand-alone, capable of operating without interfacing with another system, such as the *Endeavour*'s main computer. This was by design on Xiong's part, to avoid anyone else learning of the data archive's existence, but knowing that a need might arise for Klisiewicz or someone he trusted to access the invaluable information.

Like now, for instance.

He opened the compact device's display screen and

entered a decryption sequence to its keypad. As the access protocols were enabled, he slid the microtape from his workstation into a slot on the unit's side. He then entered a command for the diminutive computer to compare the information on the microtape against its internal database.

Somewhere within that small yet vast storehouse of knowledge, Klisiewicz knew there had to be answers. They were just waiting for the right questions to be asked.

I guess we'll see about that.

10

It was quiet, and everything looked peaceful to Katherine Stano, or at least as peaceful as one could expect from an area recently subjected to orbital bombardment.

"You guys sure were thorough," said Lieutenant Commander Vanessa Theriault, first officer of the *Sagittarius*, as she moved to stand next to Stano, and together they studied what had been the crash site for the Klingon bird-of-prey. Theriault, like her fellow *Sagittarius* crew members, wore a soiled and torn drab green jumpsuit, whereas Stano was dressed in a gold tunic and black trousers. Aboard ship, the first officer tended to prefer the skant uniform variant, opting to change to more appropriate attire for landing party excursions.

Stano nodded. "We do our best," she said, her tone somber as she regarded the scene of destruction. The entire area was a wasteland, with massive craters pockmarking the landscape. Trees had been felled or simply blown apart, and whatever other vegetation might once have been here was gone or scorched beyond all recognition. Thin plumes of white-gray smoke rose from a few small, residual fires. Those few boulders that remained visible had been shattered into smaller pieces and strewn about the site, some now lying at the bottom of the wide shallow craters along with portions of destroyed trees and other debris Stano could not identify. When they had arrived, the area had been as silent as a tomb, which to her seemed an apt description considering what had happened here. However, she now heard the faint telltale sounds of indigenous animal and insect life beginning to reassert themselves in the jungle around them. Lieutenant Klisiewicz had briefed the landing party on what to expect from the local nonsentient inhabitants, and while they had spotted nothing that might pose a significant threat, at least some of the noises she was hearing gave Stano pause.

I don't think I'll want to be spending the night down here.

"I can't believe anything survived this," Theriault said. "You're sure about that?"

"Yeah," Stano replied. "Our sensors detected a half dozen Tomol life-forms and—incredibly—a single Klingon."

Theriault frowned. "According to our sensor logs, there was one Klingon aboard the bird-of-prey when we shot it down. How he survived, I have no idea."

"I don't think it's the same Klingon," Stano said, describing to her fellow first officer how a scan of the area following the bombardment had picked up a single Klingon life sign in the general vicinity, and explaining why she thought it unlikely he or she had been aboard the bird-of-prey. According to Theriault and Captain Terrell, other Klingons were operating on the planet's surface, and several of them had been killed by Nimur, the Tomol who had undergone what her people called the Change and who now seemed to be organizing others of her kind. What she and her new followers might do was anyone's guess, but with the *Sagittarius* still marooned on the planet pending the completion of its repairs, the scout ship made for a viable target.

The chirp of her communicator interrupted Stano's thoughts, and she activated it. "Stano here."

"*Lieutenant Lerax here, Commander,*" replied the voice of the *Endeavour*'s chief of security, who at present was leading the security detail that had accompanied Stano to the surface. "*We have detected the approach of several Tomol and a single Klingon. They are coming on foot, from the approximate direction of their main village, and their life readings do not appear to match the ones you warned us about.*"

Tensing despite the Edoan officer's report, Stano felt her hand moving for the phaser pistol resting on her right hip. She stopped short of brandishing the weapon but did allow her palm to rest on its handgrip. Visitors from the Tomol village.

"Remember what we told you about their Wardens, or guards, or whatever they are," Theriault said. "They have procedures and weapons in the event one of their kind undergoes the Change, and they've been working to capture or contain Nimur from the beginning."

"Right," Stano replied. "If that's the case, then I'm happy for the extra help." Still, until she had a better handle on the evolving situation, she was not about to take any chances. Raising the communicator back to her lips, she said, "Lerax, you're sure this isn't Nimur's group?"

"*Affirmative. We're still tracking the Klingon transponder, and that group of life-forms is remaining stationary.*"

Sensor readings from the *Endeavour* had shown that

following their retreat from the bird-of-prey crash site, Nimur and her small band of followers had moved deeper into the lush forest dominating this area of the island, heading for the base of a nearby mountain range that sensors revealed held an array of caves and tunnels. The scans had not been able to penetrate far enough to determine if any of the subterranean passageways led back to the Tomol village or the Preserver artifact beneath it, but Stano certainly was not ruling it out.

"Have your team spread out to meet them, Lieutenant. We're on our way."

"Acknowledged. Lerax out."

Sidestepping fallen, scorched trees, rocks, and other detritus, Stano and Theriault made their way across the devastated area. Standing near the edge of the forest at the clearing's north end was Lieutenant Lerax. Tall and lanky like most members of his race, the Edoan's bright orange skin clashed with his red tunic. Like his shirt, his black trousers were customized to fit his unusual physiology, which included three lower extremities and a third arm extending from his chest. His legs formed a tripod supporting his body, ending in oversized feet that were without boots or other footwear, allowing him greater traction and balance.

"Commander," Lerax said, nodding to Stano. To Theriault, he offered, "Greetings, Commander Theriault. It is a pleasure to make your acquaintance."

"Same here," Theriault replied. "You're new to the *Endeavour*, right?"

"That is correct. I was assigned to the ship during its most recent repair and maintenance layover." Lerax, along with several others, had been posted to the *Endeavour* following the Battle of Vanguard, during which the ship had taken severe damage and lost a number of its crew, including most of the men and women working in the vessel's main engineering compartments during the fight. Stano and other survivors had lost many good friends that day, and upon the arrival of Lerax and other new personnel there had been some natural resentment to newcomers coming to replace those who had been lost. It was unfair, of course, and thankfully such feelings had been short-lived as everyone settled into their roles, with the new additions quickly becoming part of what Captain Khatami sometimes called "the *Endeavour* family."

Gesturing to the tricorder Lerax held in his left hand, Stano asked, "What have you got?"

"Seven Tomol life-forms, Commander, and one Klingon, though our readings indicate the individual in question has suffered injuries. I sent a team out to meet them, and they are being escorted here now. Two of them were armed, but they surrendered their weapons to my people, and we confirmed that their life readings did not match those of Nimur or other Changed Tomol."

"Small favors," Theriault said.

"Let's get your medic over here," Stano said. "Let him have a look at the Klingon. I'll notify the captain and let her decide whether to beam him up to the *Endeavour* or notify Captain Kang." She released a small sigh. "That should make for an entertaining conversation."

Movement from the trees made her look up to see two members of Lerax's security contingent, each wearing a red Starfleet tunic and wielding a phaser rifle, walking out of the forest. Behind them were the band of Tomol and the one Klingon. Another pair of *Endeavour* security officers trailed the group, also brandishing phaser rifles. Each Tomol was dressed in an assortment of what looked to be leggings and shirts woven from some form of leather or other animal hide, most with sleeves short enough to leave bare the blue-green skin of their arms. Humanoid in appearance, they ranged in height from shorter than Stano to taller than Lerax, most sporting long manes of straight silver hair, with gold-yellow spots tracing from the sides of their faces and down their necks to disappear beneath their clothing. As for the Klingon, to Stano he looked like he had been in a brutal bar fight and come out on the losing end. Pink blood, dried and darkened, crusted around a gash over his left eye and matted the hair on that side of his head. He held his left arm tucked close against his side, and he walked with a pronounced limp. Stano saw that he appeared to carry no disruptor pistol or even a knife, but Klingons had a nasty habit of producing weapons from anywhere, and nowhere.

"That's Tormog," Theriault said, moving to stand once more next to Stano. "He was leading the Klingon group studying the Tomol and the one tasked with selecting specimens for transport back to the empire for study." In a lower voice, she added, "He's an irritating, opportunistic bastard. Don't trust him for a second."

"Don't worry." Stano recalled the name from the reports she had read. Tormog was a scientist and not a member of the warrior caste, which meant that military leaders like Kang had little use or tolerance for him. One might think that Kang, at least, would be somewhat supportive of the doctor, given their similar status as *QuchHa'*, or members of the Klingon race descended from those who had suffered from the viral infection that had ravaged the empire more than a century ago. Tormog, like Kang, lacked the pronounced forehead ridges that were a prominent trait in Klingons who had avoided the virus and its effects, and his physique was comparable to a human male's, though Stano knew the scientist still possessed a strength and stamina rivaled by only the most robust, physically fit humans.

As the security escort and their charges came to a halt, one of the Tomol, a male, stepped to the front of the group, his gaze fixed on Stano.

"You are of the sky-ships."

Stano nodded. "Yes. My name is Katherine Stano. Are you the leader of your people?"

The Tomol seemed to consider her question for a moment before replying, "I am not a leader of anyone, but I suppose I speak for this group." He looked to Theriault. "You are the one they call 'Vanessa,' yes?"

Theriault nodded. "That's right. If you know my name, then you know my people and I are your friends. Or at least we wish to be."

"So I have heard." The Tomol turned back toward the group and pointed to Tormog. "This person is from another sky-ship, and he is injured."

Waving over one of Lerax's security officers, Ensign Kerry Zane, who also was doing double duty as the team's medic, Stano said to Tormog, "We'll see what we can do."

Zane, whose imposing, muscled physique looked as though it might burst from his uniform at any moment, reached up to stroke the thick mustache that was as blond as his receding hairline. He appeared uncertain as he studied his new charge before turning to Stano. "I'm not sure how much good I'll be, Commander. I don't know Klingon anatomy."

"Just do the best you can," Stano said.

The Klingon released a growl of contempt. "I do not require your aid, human."

Stano replied, "But I require yours, so I'd like to make sure you're not about to die or anything, at least, not until we've got this situation under control." As Lerax and Zane escorted Tormog to a fallen tree trunk and had him sit so that he could be examined, Stano returned her attention to the Tomol. "May I ask what you are called?"

"I am Kerlo." He paused for a moment, his gaze dropping to the ground as though weighing what next to say, and when he looked up again Stano saw pain and shame in his eyes. "Nimur is . . . *was* . . . my mate."

"You're kidding," Theriault said.

Apparently not understanding what had been said, Kerlo continued, "The Nimur I loved, the mother of my child, is gone. All that remains is the abomination she has become. This is a sad day for my people, foretold to us through the generations, just as we were warned against allowing it to happen." He stopped again, his eyes lowering once more in sadness and disgrace. "My Nimur has always been of strong mind and spirit, but I never thought she would forsake us . . . forsake me . . . this way."

The sorrow in the Tomol's words was palpable, and Stano pitied him and the child of whom he spoke. "I . . . I don't know what to say."

"Despite her unwillingness to abide by our most sacred traditions," Kerlo said, "she did not ask for what has happened to her. Still, the others she has turned must be stopped before they destroy all of our people, and yours."

"Can they be stopped?" Stano asked. "I'm told you have weapons that may combat someone who has undergone the Change?"

"They are a formidable enemy," said Tormog from where he sat on the felled tree, and Stano saw the Klingon pushing aside Zane and the ensign's efforts to examine him. "They control things with their minds. They change shape at will. They are like gods."

"Don't you Klingons like to brag that you killed all your gods?" Theriault asked. The question earned her a menacing glare from Tormog, which she ignored. To Stano, she said, "We know the Tomol possess at least some knowledge about the Change, along with weapons and maybe other tools to deal with anyone who endures it."

Kerlo said, "You speak of our Wardens. It is true that they wield the lances given to us by the Shepherds."

"Are these lances the most powerful weapons you have?" Stano asked.

Frowning, Kerlo replied, "I have only ever seen the lances. If the Shepherds provided other, more powerful weapons, I have never heard of them."

"Maybe down in the caves," Stano said. "Or something."

"The Shepherds provided many tools," Kerlo continued, "as well as knowledge enshrined in the many glyphs they left us in the underground passages. Only a fraction of those teachings are understood by our people, and I've often wondered what secrets they hold."

"The Preservers," Stano said. If there was a secret to dealing with Nimur and her followers, it stood to reason that the ancient race, along with depositing the Tomol here and setting up the civilization by which they had lived for uncounted generations, would have put in place contingencies for when things did not go according to plan. It would be consistent with their known methods, such as what Captain Kirk and the *Enterprise* had found on that planet where the Preservers had relocated the group of Native Americans. "We need to get Klisiewicz down into those caves. If anybody's going to figure out those symbols in short order, it's him."

"Typical humans," Tormog said again. "Always talking when you should be acting."

Growing annoyed, Stano turned to Zane. "It's obvious he's going to live. Can you do something about that hole under his nose?" Waving off the ensign as he began to reply, she fixed her gaze on the Klingon. "Given how much success you've had with these people, Doctor, what do you suggest we do?"

"A strategic retreat would seem to be in order," Tormog replied. "It is obvious these primitive people do not possess the weapons or the stomach to battle the creatures they one day will become. We must regroup if we are to devise an appropriate plan of attack."

"Retreat?" Theriault asked, her tone one of derision. "I didn't think that was even a word in the Klingon vocabulary." Tormog again scowled at her, but she made a point of turning away from him to face Stano. "He's obviously stalling, hoping Kang will come so they can have another shot at capturing specimens to take back with them."

"That would be a mistake," Kerlo said.

Stano nodded, recalling the destroyed bird-of-prey. "Yeah, we saw what happens when the Klingons tried it. Besides, we're not leaving you down here to deal with them on your own." She gestured toward Tormog. "Like it or not, we're involved now, and we have to try to fix what the Klingons broke."

"The question is whether we've got the juice to do anything against Nimur," Theriault said. "You've seen what she and her followers can do."

Stano said, "But the Changed aren't invulnerable. We killed at least a half dozen of them when we glassed the bird-of-prey."

"Not yet, anyway," Theriault countered, "but while some of her followers may still be weak enough that the Wardens' lances can handle them, Nimur has grown so powerful that she can absorb a full barrage from several of them and just smile. Our hand phasers were slightly more effective, and maybe concentrated fire from a bunch of them will put her down, but I'd rather bet on something with more stopping power." She gestured to some of the security officers Stano had brought with her from the *Endeavour* and the phaser rifles they carried. "You've got the idea."

"Right," Stano replied, thankful once again that she had opted for Lieutenant Lerax and his team to carry the larger, more powerful weaponry. "How's your armory on the *Sagittarius*?"

Theriault shrugged. "No worse than the rest of the ship. We've got eight rifles in a weapons locker and extra power packs for all of them."

"That's a good start," said Stano, "but if nobody has any objections, I'd rather be somewhere else when Nimur comes back."

"Anywhere in particular?"

Stano released a humorless chuckle. "Some place less dangerous. I hear the Neutral Zone's nice this time of year."

11

"I feel so different than I did before," Kintaren said as they moved through the forest with Nimur in the lead. "I understand why you wanted to share this gift."

Nimur nodded. "We must share it with all our people." Pausing her march through the trees, she turned to regard her fellow Tomol, each of their auras now awash with the heat of the Change. She sensed the power pulsing through their bodies, strengthening bone and muscle and heightening their senses. They radiated with untested strength, and she felt them reaching both into and beyond their own minds, testing limits that continued to expand.

"Where are we going?" Kintaren asked. "To the village?"

"No," Nimur replied. "We first must attend to intruders in our midst. I feel them and sense how they do not belong."

Kintaren frowned. "I do not understand."

"You will, in time." Nimur knew that her sister and the other Changed, still coming to terms with their new existence, did not yet comprehend all that was available to them. She sensed their uncertainty and apprehension, though a few among the group, like Larn and Ayan, were beginning to grasp the potential they now wielded. Very soon, Nimur knew, they all would realize the promise of their birthright.

Closing her eyes, she pushed her awareness beyond her being. Her body shifted in rhythm with the branches swaying in the breeze. She sensed the movement of animals over the ground or through the trees or the sky itself. Though distant, she felt the heartbeats of all the people in her village. Even farther she felt the pulse of still more life, though what she sensed was not Tomol. It was at once familiar and alien, so much that Nimur was easily able to identify these energies as strangers such as those she already had encountered in the caves. And yet, even in this, these new sensations were different. They were near where the sky-ship had fallen from the stars and where Nimur had defied the fury unleashed by those still lurking above the clouds to destroy her.

Then she became aware of another concentration of intruders, a larger group even more distant, perhaps beyond Suba's boundaries. Something there resisted her attempts to understand it. Why was that? Moments passed before Nimur realized that her difficulties lay in the fact that whatever she was trying to feel was not alive.

"Nimur?" Kintaren prompted. "What is it?"

"I am not certain." Something was . . . *there*. It was large, and cold, and unyielding. It was not natural, of this Nimur was sure. It did not run in the forest or swim in the sea or soar among the clouds, and yet she sensed the object was perhaps capable of all those things.

Another sky-ship?

Could it be? How was that possible? How many such constructs floated among the stars? There was no way to know, of course. Pushing her thoughts farther, she felt the energies swirling within and around the object, and they were similar to that of the sky-ship on which she had found herself, with the ones who called themselves Kling-ons. This sensation was different, softer and more fo-cused. Auras of blue and yellow and white were prevalent, as opposed to the harsher crimson and black that charac-terized the Klingon ship. What was it doing here? Search-ing for her? Perhaps.

"I see the strangers," Nimur said. "I see their sky-ship." From the air, the intruders seemed to carry all of the ad-vantages in any confrontation, but a sky-ship here on the ground carried with it great potential, if it could be cap-tured. Though she could see it in her mind's eye, she was uncertain of its precise location. Could she use the energy it emitted as a means of finding it? Once more, she probed outward, allowing her thoughts to float as though on the wind until they found the song she remembered when she had spoken with the other sky-ships. There indeed was a similar song being sung toward the clouds, but then Nimur was aware of another, weaker song also in the air. This was different, she decided. It did not seem intended for a vessel high above Arethusa but instead for a place here on Suba.

It seemed intended for her.

"What is this?" she cried, raising her arms as she sensed something within her that was not of her own flesh and blood. Something *alien*. How had it come to be there, and how long had it been inside her?

"Nimur?" Kintaren asked, her tone one of concern.

There, her mind screamed as her gaze penetrated the skin and muscle of her left arm. Embedded within her flesh was a tiny object, forged from metal but in a manner far beyond anything created by one of her people, and featuring tiny barbs that must have been present to ensure the object remained anchored to the flesh of its unsuspecting host.

And it sings. To the sky-ships.

Snarling with newfound rage, Nimur clawed at her flesh, the nails of her right hand digging into her left arm. She sensed no pain at the wounds she was inflicting upon herself, so focused was her anger. Fingers pushed through muscle tissue until she sensed the object before digging it out from beneath her skin and holding it up to examine it.

"What is that?" asked Kintaren.

"It is a means for the sky people to find us," Nimur said, before crushing the object between her fingers. "No more."

Watching in fascination, Kintaren asked, "What do we do now?"

The answer was obvious, at least to Nimur. The intruders must be dealt with; they carried weapons that were more powerful than the Wardens' fire lances. They could not be allowed to impose their will upon the Tomol, and certainly not upon her.

We must attack.

12

Years spent in hospitals, sickbays, and trauma wards had made Anthony Leone all but immune to having his work disrupted by the occasional outburst from a patient. Somewhat less typical was the giggle fit he now heard erupting from somewhere outside his office.

As he sat at his desk, his computer terminal highlighting the physiological scans he and Nurse Amos had made of Seta and the other Tomol villagers, the sounds of at least two people laughing drifted to him from what he knew had to be the sickbay's patient ward. There could be only one explanation, of course, a hunch he confirmed upon entering the room to find Seta sitting cross-legged on one of the beds, a mess tray balanced in her lap. Nurse Amos sat next to her, smiling as she watched the Tomol priestess eating something.

"I've never tasted anything like this before!"

Amos nodded, a motion so frenetic Leone thought she might hurt her neck. "Great, huh?" She pointed to the tray. "Now, take one and dip one end into the red stuff."

Intrigued and a bit puzzled by what was taking place in his sickbay, Leone stepped farther into the room. "Hello, ladies."

"Hello, Doctor," Amos said before gesturing to Seta. "We're having a snack."

Now able to see what the tray held, Leone raised one eyebrow. "French fries and ketchup?"

"They are wonderful, Leone," Seta said, holding up a fry, a blob of ketchup on one end. "Do you like them?"

"I like them well enough. I don't know how well they're suited for a cultural exchange, though." He said the last part while casting a glance at Amos.

The nurse replied, "I scanned for allergies. There's no danger, Doctor."

"Sure, she won't fall over dead during lunch," Leone countered, "but if we're trying to come up with ways to increase a race's long-term chances for survival, I'm thinking fried foods isn't the way to go."

He heard the doors beyond the patient ward and leading to the corridor outside sickbay part and turned to see Lieutenant Klisiewicz enter the room. The science officer was carrying a computer data card and wore a tricorder slung over his left shoulder.

"Hello, Doctor," he said, his gaze moving to Seta. "I came down to meet our guest." Stepping closer to her bed, he offered, "Hello. My name is Stephen."

The girl brushed her fingers against the front of her clothing before extending her hand. "Nurse Holly explained that you touch hands when you meet someone for the first time."

Klisiewicz smiled as he took her hand in his. "Yes, we do."

"Do you take care of people, like Leone and Holly?"

Shaking his head, the lieutenant replied, "Not the same way. I'm a scientist. I study more than just people." He paused, then added, "I guess you could say I study everything."

Amos explained, "He's in charge of anything we want to learn about, especially when it comes to visiting someone new to us like you and your people."

"Do you meet new kinds of people all the time?" Seta asked.

Klisiewicz smiled again. "Not as often as we'd like, so when we do, I'm very interested in finding out as much as I can about them." He indicated Leone with a nod. "The doctor tells me you know more about your people than anyone else on Suba."

The girl straightened her posture, obviously recognizing that she had been identified as the leader she was. "I am the Holy Sister of our village. I am supposed to know more than anyone, but my training is not complete." Her expression fell as she spoke, and Leone noted the hint of guilt in her eyes.

"It's okay, Seta," Leone said. "We know you're trying your best, and we promised we'd help you." He pointed to Klisiewicz. "Stephen's pretty good at that, actually."

This seemed to mollify the young priestess. "My training with Ysan was really just beginning. She told me some of our first stories, such as how our people came to Suba long ago."

Leone noted Klisiewicz eyeing him before the science officer said to her, "I know some of the stories already, but I'd like to hear them from you."

"I do not know," Seta said, casting her eyes toward the tray that still occupied her lap. "This knowledge is supposed to be only for the Holy Sisters. I am not certain what I am allowed to share. There is so much to understand, and Ysan had so much more to teach me."

"Maybe I can help," Klisiewicz said, moving to stand next to her and propping himself against the bed. "I already know some things, so maybe we can help each other."

Confusion seemed to cloud Seta's features. "I do not understand. How can you know our stories?"

"I've been reading some reports," Klisiewicz said, then seemed to catch himself. "I guess you could call them stories, too, from our friends who were with you in the caves. The ones you showed the ob . . . your wordstone, and what you told them about it."

Seta's expression went from uncertainty to worry. "What? You know what happened at the wordstone? Vanessa *told* you?" She shifted her position on the bed, and Amos was barely able to catch the tray in her lap as Seta pulled her legs up to her and hugged her knees. "She promised me that she would share no secrets! She lied to me!"

"No, Seta," Leone said as Amos sat next to her on the bed and placed a hand on her arm. "That's not what he meant. It's all right."

"I have violated the trust of the Shepherds!" Seta said, closing her eyes and tucking her chin against her knees. "I have failed my people!" Tears were running down her cheeks as she rocked back and forth on the bed. Amos moved closer and put an arm around the girl's shoulders.

"It's okay," the nurse offered. "You haven't failed anyone. Our friend told us your story because she wants to help you but can't do it by herself. Now we know your story, too, and we all can help you."

Klisiewicz had moved from the bed and now was

standing near the door leading from the patient ward. "I'm sorry," he said, his eyes wide with concern. "I didn't mean to upset her. I was just . . ."

"It's okay," Leone said, walking toward him and gesturing for him to follow. "Let Amos take this for a minute." Once they were out of the room and crossing sickbay toward his office, he added, "She and Seta seem to have hit it off, but Seta's had to take in a lot pretty quickly. Amos will get her calmed down, and it'll be okay."

The science officer nodded. "I hope so." As Leone led the way into his office, he said, "Since I'm here, can we talk about your preliminary reports on the Tomol genetic structure?"

"Sure." Leone gestured to the chair in front of his desk as he moved around to his own seat. "What's up?"

By way of reply, Klisiewicz reached for the computer workstation on Leone's desk and swiveled it so both men could see its screen, then inserted the data card he had been carrying into the terminal's input slot and pressed the control to activate it. "I see you've been studying the same material, along with the information Doctor Babitz gave us. Her analysis shows that the Shedai markers in the Tomol DNA aren't simply additions to the existing genetic structure but are replacements. Key elements of the original segments are missing. If this was a computer program, it's like saying whole subroutines have been deleted and replaced with similar functions that do different things within the program's same basic framework."

"I know bodies, Lieutenant," Leone said, "not computers."

Klisiewicz tapped the computer screen. "But the principles are the same. Our bodies follow the instructions contained in our DNA and we get ears and cognitive thinking and immune systems and everything that makes us up. Computers work in a similar fashion. A program is executed and commands are issued and the computer carries out the instructions. Now, if a subroutine or a section of code gets removed from a program, it doesn't perform correctly and you get errors. You can go back in and either replace the missing code or else substitute something else, but if you do that and you don't account for all the variables and scenarios that can occur during the execution, you end up with different errors or other unexpected results. But you can't just not run the program, because it's a critical process. So you find a way to bypass the problem areas in order to get to a result you can live with."

"So you're saying . . . ?"

"I'm saying I think we're going about this the wrong way. We've been operating under the assumption that the Change that afflicts the Tomol is something the Shedai introduced, but from what I'm seeing, I don't think that's the case, and I think the glyphs on the Preserver obelisk are bearing this out. The Tomol were always beings who evolved this way, or at least that's how they were when the Shedai found them, and the Shedai tried to conquer and exploit them, just like the Klingons are trying to do now. They came in, messed with the Tomol's DNA in an attempt to control the Change and maybe enhance or expand the scope of the transformation for their own purposes, and they screwed up. Maybe they took things too far and the Tomol began to grow beyond their ability to control, so they went back in and tried to fix it, and ended up making things worse, leading to what we have now."

"I think I can feel my brain melting," Leone said, resting his elbows on his desk. "That's a lot of gaps you just filled with speculation. Why would the Shedai even do that?"

"Why did the Shedai do any of the things they did?"

"Okay, point taken, but how did you get here with your thinking?" When he saw the look of uneasiness on Klisiewicz's face, Leone added, "The reason I ask is that the more I study the DNA, the more I see that the markers that obviously are Shedai in origin don't seem to be the actual triggers for the Change. They've added some pieces to the puzzle, sure, but once you start to unravel the whole thing, most of it looks like it was already there. I didn't catch it at first, and I know what to look for. What tipped you off?"

Klisiewicz seemed to ponder his answer for a moment—a long moment, Leone noted—before replying. "Based on what we know about the Preservers bringing the Tomol to Arethusa, and what we know of the Shedai's methods, it seemed like an avenue worth exploring." He shrugged. "I don't know if it has any merit or not. That's why I'm bringing it to you."

"You should give yourself more credit, Lieutenant," Leone said, genuinely impressed with the science officer's apparent aptitude in a field that usually fell well outside the scope of his duties. "You may be on to something."

Any reply Klisiewicz might have offered was interrupted by the high-pitched boatswain's whistle of the ship's internal communications system, followed by the voice of Captain Khatami. *"Bridge to Lieutenant Klisiewicz."*

Reaching for the intercom on Leone's desk, the science officer pressed the control to activate the unit. "Klisiewicz here, Captain."

"Lieutenant, we need you back up here. That Klingon transponder we've been using to track Nimur and the other Changed just went dead, and we're having trouble tracking their movements. Our last readings indicated they may be moving toward the bird-of-prey crash site."

"That's not good," Leone said. "Our people are still down there, right?"

"We're working on that, Doctor," Khatami replied.

Klisiewicz rose from his seat. "On my way, Captain. Klisiewicz out."

"Hey," Leone said as the science officer headed for the door, "good work, Lieutenant. Let's hope we have a chance to pursue this some more."

Klisiewicz offered a grim, humorless smile. "Yeah, let's hope." He disappeared into the corridor, leaving Leone alone with the computer-generated schematics they had been studying.

"Damn fine work, Lieutenant," he said to himself. "If I'm not careful, you're going to put me out of a job."

13

"*Stand by for transport*," said Captain Khatami, her voice hard with concern as it burst from the speaker grille of Katherine Stano's communicator. "*No arguments, Commander.*"

With Commander Theriault and Lieutenant Lerax guiding the rest of the *Endeavour* landing party along with Kerlo and his fellow Tomol to cover, Stano crouched behind a large boulder situated at the edge of the devastated clearing opposite the direction from which Nimur and her followers should be coming. The oversized rock would provide momentary concealment, but she held no illusions that any protection it offered would be little more than fleeting. Wielding her phaser pistol in her right hand, she raised the communicator in her other.

"Captain, there's no time to get us all out of here before they show up. We can't leave the Tomol here by themselves, and we damned sure can't beam them up to the ship." Just transporting the *Endeavour* personnel and Theriault to safety would take nearly a full minute, given the dozen men and women Lerax had brought with him to the surface at Stano's own insistence.

Not a bad idea by itself, Kate. Too bad it's biting you in the ass right now.

For the first time since taking up her position of concealment, Stano paused to listen to the surrounding jungle. The sounds of teeming wildlife that had returned to the area following the *Endeavour*'s orbital bombardment were gone again, making her own breathing seem unnaturally loud. Whatever creatures called the forest home appeared to have fled, and Stano was certain they were the smart ones.

Looking to either side of her meager protective barrier, Stano saw that Lerax and Theriault had succeeded in moving everyone to places of concealment within the tree line and what scant cover it contained. "Talk to me, Lerax. Where the hell are they?" It had been less than two minutes since the warning from Lieutenant Klisiewicz that the rogue Tomol—or the "Changed," as Kerlo and his companions were calling them—were heading back to the bird-of-prey's crash site, but the *Endeavour*'s science officer also had reported some sort of difficulty tracking Nimur and the others with the ship's sensors.

"Tricorder readings are indistinct, Commander," replied the Edoan security chief from where he crouched behind the trunk of a large tree. He was holding the tricorder in his center hand while his other two limbs brandished phaser pistols. "I did detect transformed Tomol life readings to the north, but they keep fading from my scans."

"Wonderful," Theriault said, kneeling behind another tree to the lieutenant's right.

In the distance, Stano watched what little remained of the Nereus sun continue its slide behind the treetops. Shadows were growing longer, and in the fading light she saw something moving in the sky. "Damn, I think they're already here."

"*Hang on, Commander,*" Khatami snapped. "*I'm getting you out of there right now.*"

Before Stano could reply, a burst of static exploded from her communicator, then the unit's audio port popped from its housing and the indicator lights on its faceplate all went dark.

What the hell?

"Stano to *Endeavour,*" she said, tapping the unit but receiving no response. She repeated the call with the same results.

"Here they come!"

Leaning around her tree, Theriault was pointing to the north, and Stano looked up to see seven objects drawing closer, growing larger with every passing second. They were flying in a wedgelike formation, with one of the figures at the front flanked by its companions, which all seemed slightly smaller than their leader. All of them exhibited dark, wide wings extending from lean bodies that to Stano's eyes looked like the living embodiment of spears or arrows. Their configuration reminded her of the flight exercises she had undertaken as a cadet at Starfleet Academy, maneuvering single-seat training craft around the Jovian moons.

That doesn't sound so bad right about now. The thought taunted Stano as she tightened the grip on her phaser and dropped her useless communicator to the ground. "Stand by weapons!"

"You fools!" Tormog shouted. "Don't you understand? They destroyed your communicator with a simple *thought*! They can kill us with their *minds*! We stand no chance against such power!"

"Don't let them get too close," Theriault said, earning her a quizzical look from Stano. The *Sagittarius*'s first officer added, "From everything we've seen, their telekinetic powers seem to work only if they're in close proximity. In other words, don't let them get a bead on us."

"Easier said than done," Stano said, before instructing Lerax to quickly pass that information to the rest of the landing party. *I'll take whatever edge I can get.*

The flying creatures broke formation, the leader pushing forward while its companions separated and spread out in what to Stano looked like a maneuver to sweep the length of the clearing. Holding her phaser out in front of her and propping her arm against the boulder, she sighted down the weapon's length at the approaching fliers. Her finger was tightening on the firing stud when a harsh whine of harnessed power pierced the air and multiple streaks of brilliant fire sliced through the darkening air, launching from points along the tree line and converging on a single target: the leader of the approaching Changed Tomol. Six beams of energy struck the creature as it was making its descent toward the surface and Stano saw it buckle beneath the onslaught, but only for a moment. Kerlo and his fellow Tomol were bringing their weapons to bear, employing whatever mysterious energy source was used to power them.

"Concentrate fire on that target!" she yelled above the howl of the Tomol lances, aiming her phaser and adding the weapon's discharge to the increasing din. Theriault and the rest of the *Endeavour* landing party followed suit, and within seconds the creature was caught in a web of phaser and lance fire. It tried to dodge and weave around the attacks but continued to be struck no matter in which direction it moved. Finally, the winged demon altered its flight path and shot straight up, vanishing from the clearing into the night sky.

"Look!" Lerax yelled.

Stano turned in the direction the Edoan was pointing and saw more discharges from Tomol lances ripping through the air and catching another of the Changed in a three-way crossfire, and unlike its leader, this creature succumbed to the attack and fell from the sky, disappearing somewhere among the trees to Stano's left.

"Not all of them are as powerful as Nimur," Kerlo shouted. Wielding a lance of his own, the Tomol leaned out from behind the tree he was using for cover and aimed the weapon into the sky before releasing another burst of whatever energy it commanded. Two of his companions and three members of Lerax's security detail joined in the attack, their fire congregating on another of the Changed. Their strikes were only glancing blows as the winged creature was able to avoid the worst of the assault, flying past the clearing and disappearing in the forest somewhere behind Stano.

"Our weapons are having only marginal effect," Lerax called out between shots. "We are already at our maximum settings."

Theriault, gripping her phaser in both hands, took aim at something Stano could not see. "We'll drain our power packs if this drags out much longer." She fired the weapon at another Changed, her shot joining three Tomol lances. The creature's body lurched from the force of the attack and it fell motionless from the sky, crashing through the high branches of a towering tree at the far edge of the clearing, beyond one of the impact craters inflicted on the area during the *Endeavour*'s orbital bombardment.

"Incoming!" someone shouted to Stano's right, and she turned with weapon raised in time to see one of the Changed swooping down and reaching out to snatch one of her security people. Cries of pain and terror split the air as the creature skimmed past the trees and back into the sky. Several phaser beams attempted to track it, but the Changed evaded the attacks, its maneuvers laced with the agonized screams of the hapless *Endeavour* crewman in its grip. Then the creature emitted its own chilling shriek, and a wave of horror and disbelief overcame Stano as the Changed tore the security officer's head and legs from his torso. Blood, bone, and tissue exploded in all directions as pieces of the mutilated corpse fell from the creature's grip before the winged monster flew away.

No!

Were it not for the unchained heat of her rage, Nimur would have collapsed in an exhausted heap and dropped to the forest floor. Her mind was a blur of frenzied and disjointed thought as the attack progressed. What she had assumed would be a quick and devastating strike against the strangers had grown beyond her ability to comprehend. The fire lances wielded by Tomol as well as the strangers' own weapons were proving at least somewhat effective, forcing Nimur and her followers to take defensive action to avoid injury.

There had been no time to relish the form she had

taken, her wings spread out to either side of her body as she held massive claws before her, searching for prey. The wind in her face was intoxicating as she willed her new body to sail among the clouds. In the sky around her, she sensed the uncertain thoughts of Kintaren and the others as they struggled to adapt to the chaotic situation.

Momentary grief seized her as she felt Tane's consciousness fade, the Changed unable to escape the concentration of fire lances that found him in the sky. Nimur saw his limp form falling to the ground as she spread her wings and soared away from the battle, intending to circle the area in search of a new line of attack. Rage flared within her, a shroud of harsh crimson falling across her perceptions. This could not continue, or all would be lost. Like Nimur herself, her fellow Changed were guided more by instinct than experience or skill, relying on the strength flowing through their bodies and their ability to alter their forms as a means of intimidating and overpowering the strangers. So far, the results had been mixed, and for a moment it seemed as though the strangers might have the advantage.

Then she sensed Kintaren claiming a prize. Her mind's eye tracked her sister as she swooped down and snatched the red-garbed stranger and ascended back toward the clouds. Her quarry struggled in her grip, but only until she ripped its head from its body. Nimur felt the surge of gratification rushing through Kintaren, as her sister—now fully in the throes of the Change—screeched in triumph before darting back toward the ground.

The ground.

Yes, Nimur decided. Attacking the strangers from the

air had proved hazardous. Perhaps a new approach was in order.

We must take our fight from the sky. Follow me. She cast the command toward Kintaren and the others, sensing their understanding as they turned and prepared to attack again.

"What the hell are they doing now?" shouted Theriault, and the *Sagittarius*'s first officer took aim with her phaser and fired. Without thinking, Stano turned in the same direction and leveled her weapon, but before she could press its firing stud she gaped at the new nightmare advancing across the clearing. Having dropped from the sky, the Changed had altered their forms again. Their wings were gone, and their humanoid appearance had grown and expanded. Their green skin had darkened and hardened, reminding Stano of the hide of a large reptile, and that resemblance was strengthened by their flattened, elongated heads and facial features. Their mouths now sported long rows of jagged teeth and their arms ended in enlarged hands with long, curled claws. Four of the creatures were crossing the burned, devastated expanse of the crash site, and Stano was certain that their eyes were locked on her.

"Fire!" she shouted, taking aim and firing as Theriault continued to shoot. Along the tree line, members of the *Endeavour* landing party and the Tomol were shifting their fire to engage the new threat, but tracking the advancing Changed was proving harder now that they had taken to the ground. The creatures were jumping and dancing over the obliterated soil, almost taunting the defenders and their weapons. Stano fired her phaser as one ran to her left, catching it in a crossfire with two of her security people and a Tomol lance. Another of the creatures got close enough to the first line of fallen trees and other debris acting as nominal protection for members to reach into the foliage. When it pulled back its massive arm, it had in its grasp one of the Tomol, and Stano watched in horror as the victim was eviscerated in seconds. Still reeling from the loss of one of her own people, this latest casualty further rattled her. The Changed had halted itself, enjoying its dismemberment of its victim long enough to attract weapons fire from the trees, and a moment later it succumbed to the new attack, falling limp to the darkened soil. Someone, one of Stano's people, fired at the motionless Changed as though to ensure it stayed down.

"Commander!" Lerax shouted, snapping Stano from her shock, and she looked over to see the lieutenant tossing something in her direction. The security chief's communicator landed at her feet. "It's the captain!"

She held the device to her lips. "Stano here!" She followed the call with a phaser burst at one of the Changed darting by overhead. "It's getting crazy down here, Captain."

"*Kate,*" Khatami said over the communications frequency, "*we're tracking something heading in your direction. It looks to have been launched from the vicinity of the Preserver artifact and that underground cavern.*"

"It's not Nimur or more of the Changed?"

"*This isn't a life-form. We can't tell what it is, but it's coming at you damned fast, too fast for us to get a weap-*"

ons lock. Get ready for beam-out. I've already got secu-rity teams standing by in the transporter room. We'll deal with the Tomol once you're back aboard."

Had Nimur summoned more followers from the unchanged Tomol, or—worse—found some Preserver weapon or other technology to use against Stano and her people? The idea that Nimur might now have control over something from the subterranean complex was even more frightening to Stano than the scene continuing to unfold around her.

And that's saying something.

"Copy that," she replied. "In fact, tell the transporter room to hurry the hell up."

An enormous dark mass crashed through the trees to her left. She flinched and rolled to her side as something thick and heavy swung through the space her head had occupied only a split second before. She caught a glimpse of the towering creature that had just missed her with the claws of its massive right arm and heard its growl of frus-tration. Pushing herself to her feet, Stano threw herself over a fallen tree and rolled into a small culvert. She ig-nored the dirt in her eyes and mouth, scrambling and crawling over another large rock even as she heard the heavy footfalls of the Changed pursuing her.

"Stay down, Commander!"

The warning came mere heartbeats before multiple beams of energy cut through the growing darkness, each illuminating the menacing creature as it struck. The Changed howled in pain from the ferocious barrage, stag-gering backward toward the clearing. Behind her, Stano heard footsteps coming closer as members of her team and at least two Tomol pressed the attack, pushing the creature farther from the forest and onto the open ground. A final salvo of phaser fire collided with the Changed, and it fell backward, over the lip of an impact crater, and disappeared from sight. Leading a charge forward, Lerax, flanked by two of his security people, verified that the creature was down.

Still holding Lerax's communicator and trying to catch her breath, Stano barked into the unit, "*Endeavour*, what's going on? Why are we still here?"

Khatami replied, "*The transporter room's reporting some kind of interference on the surface that's preventing them from getting a lock.*" After what to Stano felt like an eternity of silence over the open channel, the *Endeavour* captain's voice all but exploded from the communicator, "*We're not going to make it, and we can't track it with phasers or torpedoes. It's coming down right on top of you! Take cover!*"

Shouting warnings to her people and their Tomol charges, Stano dropped to the ground behind the boulder, trying to pull herself into a ball while squirming to keep the clearing within her field of vision. Something in the distant sky was growing larger, arcing over the horizon. A faint, dull rumbling accompanied it, and within seconds Stano could make out a trail of flame and smoke gushing from the object's back end as it altered its trajectory and began a plunging descent. Members of her team were yelling final calls to take cover, but then Stano's attention fixed on one of the Changed.

Still exhibiting its hideous reptilian appearance, the creature had stopped its advance on the tree line fifty or so meters from Stano's position. To her amazement, the thing turned and craned its thick neck so it could look skyward as though transfixed by the approaching object.

What does it know?

It was a silly question, Stano decided, and it would go unanswered. With just enough time to pull herself back behind the boulder, she hunkered on the ground and raised her arms over her head an instant before everything around her flashed white.

14

On the *Endeavour* bridge's main viewscreen, a pale dot appeared on a computer-generated topographical map and began expanding. Atish Khatami stared in open-mouthed horror, certain she was watching the obliteration of more than a dozen of her crew.

"Picking up an energy surge!" shouted Stephen Klisiewicz, lifting his face from the sensor viewer at his station and turning toward the screen, and Khatami saw that the lieutenant's face was a mask of confusion. "But it's not reading like an impact or a detonation." He scowled. "I don't understand."

Khatami watched the pale circle at the center of the viewscreen cease its enlargement at the same time several pinpoints of light began appearing, superimposed over the map representing the Klingon bird-of-prey crash site and the surrounding region of the Suba island. What were they witnessing? The deployment of a force field, or some kind of electromagnetic pulse? Just as long as it meant her people had not been vaporized, Khatami was happy to entertain any and all explanations no matter how bizarre they sounded.

"What the hell is going on, Klisiewicz?" She pushed herself from her chair and crossed the command well to the railing separating her from the science officer.

His attention fixed on his sensor readings, Klisiewicz

replied, "Sensors are showing multiple energy discharges, Captain. I . . ." He paused, and to Khatami he looked as though he might be trying to press his head even farther into the hooded viewer. "Whatever it is, it definitely wasn't an explosive. Judging by these readings, the object is carrying out some sort of automated firing sequence, like a drone weapon, though I can't figure out what's controlling it."

"Get me Commander Stano," Khatami said, glancing toward Lieutenant Estrada, "or any member of the landing party. I want an update on their condition." She knew her first officer's communicator had gone dead moments earlier, but those carried by other members of her team still appeared to be functional.

"Trying to hail anyone, Captain," replied the communications officer, "but I'm not getting any indication that our signal's getting through."

"Keep on it." Looking over her shoulder, Khatami asked, "McCormack, can you get a lock on that thing yet?"

At the navigator's station, the lieutenant shook her head. "No, Captain. The object is emitting some kind of inhibitor that is affecting our sensor and targeting systems."

"What the hell is it?" Utter helplessness was on the verge of seizing Khatami in its viselike grip as she considered the plight of Stano and her team on the surface. What sort of insidious weapon had Nimur found to use against her own people, and what threat did it pose to the *Endeavour* or the *Sagittarius* and their crews?

"Captain," Klisiewicz said, "you're not going to believe this, but the object isn't targeting our people. It's going after the Tomol . . . I mean, the *Changed*."

It took Katherine Stano an extra second or two to verify that she was not, in fact, dead.

The burst of intense white light should have come with a thunderous roar and a shockwave that shredded her body at the subatomic level—assuming they were fortunate enough to be offered instant death by the incoming weapon—but instead all the commander heard was the whine of discharging energy accompanied by an odd rumbling in the ground. Cries of alarm peppered the forest around her, all of them fainter than the chilling shrieks Stano heard coming from the clearing up ahead. Pulling herself from where she lay huddled against the boulder, she peered around the massive rock and got her first look at the latest bit of weirdness this planet had to offer.

Hovering overhead the glade was the newly arrived object, a squat cylinder with rounded ends and featuring a set of what to Stano looked like six stabilizer fins mounted in evenly spaced intervals around its core. The thing emitted a constant low hum, which was accented by rhythmic higher-pitched pulses that were synchronized to the energy discharges bursting forth from a dozen emitters positioned along the object's outer skin. Each of the emitters was releasing a white-blue beam of energy that swept across the desolated expanse of the crash site, and in the beams' wake, Stano could see that what was left behind was . . . *dead*?

Not dead, she told herself. *This is . . . something else.*

"Oh my god," Stano heard Theriault saying, as the *Sagittarius*'s first officer pushed up from where she had thrown herself behind the thick trunk of a fallen tree. "Are you seeing this?"

Stano could only nod. Even with the dim illumination afforded by the dying rays of the Nereus sun as dusk loomed, she was able to see the silhouettes of several trees that had survived the *Endeavour*'s bombardment, only to be caught up in whatever weapon the hovering drone was employing. Moments ago, their towering branches had been swaying in the slight breeze playing over the clearing, but now they stood still, devoid of motion as well as the vibrant orange-green colors of their leaves and their auburn trunks. All the life they once had exuded was gone.

"That damned thing's petrifying everything in its path," she said. It was like a vision spawned from legend, an ancient tale reimagined for the sole purpose of terrifying her. What was the name of that monster from Greek mythology? The repulsive female with a head of snakes rather than hair, with the power to turn to stone anyone who dared gaze upon her?

You can look it up later.

The object's saturation of the clearing lasted for at least another full minute, by Stano's reckoning, at which point its barrage of energy beams ceased, and the area fell to near silence save for the weapon's low hum. Even the wind itself seemed to have faded, as though the very air surrounding the crash site had solidified. Stano raised her phaser and aimed it at the object, even though she suspected that her weapon was feeble if not useless against whatever had been set against her and her people.

Not us, Stano realized. *Them.*

"It was targeting the Changed," she said.

"This is what Ysan, the Tomol priestess, told us about," Theriault replied. "She described the wordstone turning Changed into stone. She called them 'the Endless.' This must be what that meant."

Stano watched as the object rotated in place before lifting from the clearing and arcing back into the sky whence it had come. Only after it had disappeared from sight did the first officer ponder something she probably should have considered when the mysterious drone had arrived.

"Damn it," she said, rising from her crouch and stepping around the boulder. "Did anybody think to scan that thing?"

Emerging from where he had sought cover inside the tree line, Lieutenant Lerax held up his tricorder. "I did, Commander. My scans were able to penetrate the object's outer hull, but the readings I collected are somewhat scrambled. It is possible we may be able to extract something useful from the data I recorded once we have returned to the *Endeavour*."

Stano stepped farther into the clearing, noting that the churned soil and grass were fossilized as a consequence of the drone's actions. Everything in her range of vision had, literally, been turned to ruddy brown stone. Coming abreast of what once had been a squat patch of vegetation, Stano reached out and tentatively brushed her fingers across one of its branches. It, like the leaves it supported, was stiff and unmoving. When she attempted to break off a piece, the bush resisted her effort.

"This is creepy as hell," said Theriault, walking up behind her.

Stano nodded in agreement. "Tell me about it." She stepped away from the petrified vegetation toward one of the numerous large craters littering the clearing. Like everything else around it, the ground that had been pushed aside by the force of what likely had been one of the *Endeavour*'s photon torpedoes also had been converted to a blanket of inert rock.

At the bottom of the depression, posed like a menacing statue, was one of the Changed.

"Holy shit," Stano said, her hand automatically raising her phaser to take aim at the unmoving figure. She halted the motion, holding her position for several seconds as she gazed upon the immobilized monster.

Phaser held in front of her, Theriault maneuvered down into the crater and approached the rigid Tomol. "It's not going anywhere," she concluded after a moment. She rapped on the creature's chest. "Talk about your bad luck."

"Commander," said Lerax. The Edoan was standing before the bush, examining it with his tricorder. Glancing up from the unit's miniature display screen, he gestured toward the object of his scans. "This flora is still alive. It was not actually converted to stone but merely encased in a shell. If I am interpreting these readings correctly, the vegetation is in a state of suspension."

"What about him?" Theriault hooked a thumb over her shoulder at the motionless Changed.

In response to her question, Lerax moved into the crater and scanned the creature with his tricorder. After a moment, the security chief nodded. "I am detecting life readings, though blood circulation and respiration have both been reduced to extremely low levels. As with the plant, this creature has been placed in a state of hibernation."

"Well, that kind of raises more questions than it answers," Stano said, eyeing the entombed Tomol. "If that thing was targeting the Changed, then who sent it?" Hearing footsteps behind her, she turned to see Tormog along with Kerlo and his surviving companions approaching them, escorted by four of Lerax's security team. "Kerlo, do you know anything about this? Do your Wardens have weapons with such power?"

The Tomol's features darkened as he beheld the Changed. "No. Only the Shepherds are capable of such feats, though I have never seen it happen with my own eyes."

"It has to be some kind of . . . *technology*," Theriault said, catching herself before she referred to the Preservers in front of Kerlo and the other Tomol. "Right?"

Stano frowned. "I don't know what else it could be." She had no doubts that the caverns beneath the Tomol village held all manner of interesting artifacts and information left behind by the Preservers. Some of it had been left for the Tomol themselves to use, but the drone represented something else entirely. Was it here to defend the Tomol from outside threats, to protect them from themselves, or to act as a safeguard should the Tomol become a threat to others?

What about all of the above?

"We'll leave that to Lieutenant Klisiewicz to figure out," Stano said.

Theriault smiled. "Maybe we can just seal him in there

with Lieutenant Hesh and let them sort through it all. You know how science officers can get."

"This is amazing," Tormog said, as the Klingon ran his hand along the torso of the statuelike Changed. "The creature is truly in stasis?"

Lerax shook his head. "As I said, the life-forms that have been enveloped by this effect are in a state of hibernation. Their physiological functions do not appear to have been arrested to the degree one might experience when placed into a stasis chamber, but my knowledge of such topics is rudimentary, at best." Looking to Stano, the Edoan added, "Perhaps Commander Yataro or Doctor Leone or Lieutenant Klisiewicz would be better suited to study this phenomenon."

"You're doing fine, Lieutenant." Before Stano could offer further words of encouragement, the communicator Lerax had given her beeped in her hand. "Stano here."

"*Khatami here. Is everybody all right down there?*"

Stano replied, "I have to report one casualty, Captain, but I haven't yet had a chance to identify him." She paused, recalling the ghastly sight of the unfortunate crewman who had been the first victim of the Changed during their attack. "We're still getting a head count now that things have settled down. Did you see what happened?"

"*We caught most of it,*" Khatami said, "*but don't ask me to tell you what that thing was.*"

"As it happens, we've got an idea about that." In rapid fashion, she summarized her observations of the object's actions, including what had been done to the Changed.

"*If that sort of technology is just lying around, then there's no telling what else might be buried in those cav-*"

erns. I don't know that I want our people stumbling around down there until we get a better handle on this situation, Commander."

"What about the Tomol? We can't leave them here on their own."

Khatami replied, *"If what you say is true, there may be a better defense mechanism than anything we've got, save for blowing large holes in the planet, and that's something I'd rather not do, if it can be avoided."*

"What about the Klingons?" Theriault asked. "They're not going to leave this alone."

"You are correct, human," Tormog said. "I have my orders, and Captain Kang has his. We will complete our mission, and you would do well not to interfere."

Stano gestured to the encased Tomol. "If you think you can go up against something that can do this, be my guest. Just give me a few minutes to get some snacks and a good seat."

"Commander Stano!"

She was forced to squint to see one of her people standing out in the open several dozen meters from her, all but lost in the increasing darkness falling over the clearing, waving an arm over his head and gesturing for her to join him. He was standing next to something she could not make out from this distance. After ordering the security team to keep Tormog with them and waiting for Theriault to scramble up from the crater, she along with the *Sagittarius*'s first officer and Lerax jogged across the broken terrain, realizing as they closed the gap that the thing next to the security officer was another of the Changed, trapped like its companion within a stone tomb. Facing away from

her, the figure had been halted in the act of raising muscled arms as though preparing to strike.

"Over here, Commander," said Ensign Joseph Berenato, the young crewman who had called her over. He was
cradling a phaser rifle in the crook of one arm, and with
his free hand he was gesturing for her to follow him past
the frozen Tomol. The expression on his face was one of
dread, and as she proceeded after him toward the lip of
another crater, a sudden knot of unease formed in her gut.

No.

Her worry turned to despair as she gazed upon the petrified form of one of her own people. He had been caught
while running from what likely was the threat of the
Changed readying to attack him. He had dropped to one
knee and his phaser rifle was raised to his shoulder as he
took aim to ward off an attack that would never come.

"Oh, damn," Theriault whispered as she moved to
stand beside her, and when the two women exchanged
looks, each saw the shock in the other's eyes.

"There are others," Berenato said. "Two more that I
know of." He pointed toward the edge of the clearing,
where other members of the landing party were moving
about the stilled figures of another Changed as well as
two *Endeavour* crewmen. "We also count three Tomol
caught up in the effect. Search parties are looking for the
other two, but our tricorders aren't picking up anything.
They may have gotten away, Commander."

Her attention fixed on the unfortunate crewman standing before her, Stano asked, "Who is this?" She moved
closer to get a better look at him, noting that it was a
Vulcan, the distinctive points of his ears still noticeable

even through the stone cocoon in which he had been ensnared.

Lerax replied, "This was Ensign Sotol."

"Is," Theriault said. When both Stano and Lerax looked at her, she jabbed a finger at the fossilized ensign. "You just got through telling us that anything trapped in this stuff is still alive, in a state of hibernation. If it can be done to them, then it can be undone."

"Damn it," Stano said, realizing that—for the briefest of moments—she had allowed herself to forget that very salient point from Lerax's report. "You're right." She placed a hand on the stone façade surrounding Ensign Sotol. "So how do we do it?" Holding up her phaser, she considered the weapon and its possible effect on the unyielding rock trapping her people. "Can we cut through it?"

"No!" a voice shouted, and Stano and she turned to see Ensign Zane sprinting toward them across the field. Holding his tricorder against his hip as he ran, he was waving his free hand to get their attention. His face was flushed from the exertion, and his eyes were wide with near panic. By the time he reached Stano and the others, he was all but out of breath.

"Don't try to cut them free," Zane managed to spit out between breaths.

"Why not?" Stano asked.

The security officer and medic gestured toward the imprisoned Ensign Sotol. "I can't explain it, but the rock isn't just a static shell." He held up his tricorder. "I was adjusting my scans to try to penetrate deeper through the rock and get a better look at the Tomol's life signs, and I started picking up new readings—*from the rock itself.*"

Theriault scowled. "The rock's alive? How is that possible?"

"From what I can tell," Zane replied, "the readings from the rock are connected to the life-forms inside it." He nodded toward Sotol. "The plant life, the Changed, any animals caught up in it during the attack, and our people. If you try to cut through the rock, whatever you're trying to free could die."

15

Even with his face all but pressed against the hooded sensor viewer at his station on the *Endeavour* bridge, Stephen Klisiewicz could feel Captain Khatami's eyes on him as she stood silent, waiting for him to provide her with new information.

Well, perhaps not silent.

"Please tell me you got a tracking lock on that . . . hell . . . you tell me what to call it."

Lifting his face from the viewer, Klisiewicz shook his head. "Whatever it was, Captain, it's gone. Vanished from our scans like it was never there." He had been able to monitor the unidentified object's flight path during the frenetic moments it had spent over the *Sagittarius* crash site, but it had been a struggle to keep up with the drone—or whatever it was—even with the *Endeavour*'s impressive sensor array. "I don't know if it ducked into a hole or ditched in the ocean or even self-destructed." He blew out his breath. "That said, I'm pretty sure I can pin down its point of origin."

"How confident is 'pretty,' Lieutenant?" Khatami asked, and Klisiewicz noted the impatience in her voice.

"I can definitely confirm that it came from the general vicinity of the Preserver pyramid. That entire area is littered with the same mineral deposits that have been fouling our sensors." Reaching for the science console, he input a sequence of commands and in response one of the station's overhead monitors switched its image to display the computer-generated schematic of the Suba island Klisiewicz had instructed the computer to create. "I tried an old-fashioned trick and realigned the navigational deflector to emit a series of low-frequency acoustic waves that I directed toward the ground. As the waves penetrated the surface, they generated minor seismic readings that the sensors could then interpret in order to create a crude imaging of the subsurface areas."

"Like a tomograph," Khatami said, stepping closer so that she could lean against the railing separating her from him. "Basically, you went sounding." She smiled, though she felt anything but happy at the moment. The news of Ensign Sotol and two more members of her crew having been caught up in the drone's bizarre petrification effect was fresh in her thoughts, accompanied by her own doleful ponderings of what, if any, pain or discomfort her people might be enduring. Commander Stano had informed her that the men for all intents and purposes were in a state of deep hibernation, but that did not assuage Khatami's feelings in the slightest.

"That's a nice bit of creative thinking, Mister Klisiewicz," she said after a moment. She looked past him to the rudimentary map. "Can you enhance the imagery you're getting?"

Klisiewicz nodded. "Yes, by increasing the strength of the acoustic signals. We don't want to push too far, of course. We might set off an earthquake."

"That would be bad," Khatami conceded. "Okay, up the power, but just enough to give us a complete picture of that complex. I want to know where those drones are launched and if there are any other surprises waiting for us down there."

Already beginning the process of entering the required instructions to his console, Klisiewicz said, "I'm recalibrating the deflector dish, but this will work better if we can reorient the ship so that I can target the specific coordinates."

"Feed that data to the helm," Khatami said before moving to her command chair and pressing its intercom button. "Bridge to engineering."

"*Engineering. This is Lieutenant Dang, Captain,*" replied the voice of the *Endeavour*'s assistant chief engineer.

"Phu, are you monitoring the output of the nav deflector while Lieutenant Klisiewicz is conducting his little experiment?"

"*Affirmative. So far, we're not picking up anything unusual.*"

"We're about to increase the power. Is that going to give us any problems?"

There was a pause, and Klisiewicz could picture the young Vietnamese engineer consulting various status indicators and other readouts. "*We won't cause any damage to the area being swept, but the harmonics of that beam will cause fluctuations in our deflector shields. We could lower them, but I'm guessing that's not something you want to do.*"

"Probably not a good idea," Klisiewicz said. With the *Voh'tahk* still lurking in nearby space, wounded or not, letting the *Endeavour*'s guard down would not be prudent.

"Exactly," Khatami said. "Thank you, Mister Dang. Bridge out."

"We're ready," Klisiewicz reported.

The captain nodded. "Do it."

After keying the instructions into the ship's computer, Klisiewicz did not have to wait long before results from the sounding and its interpretation by the sensors began to feed to his viewer. The map he already had created began to expand and fill in, the seismic reaction to the enhanced acoustical beam providing information on what he now saw was a vast underground network of caverns and connecting passages.

That's it, he thought, watching the map coalesce. *You just needed a little massage.*

Then the alarms sounded.

"What the hell?" he heard Khatami bark over the Red Alert siren, and he turned from his console to see the captain moving to stand between the helm and navigator positions.

"Something inbound from the planet's surface!" called Lieutenant Neelakanta.

Checking his instruments, it took Klisiewicz only a moment to see what was happening. "Some kind of energy beam, Captain. It's locked onto us!"

"Disengage the deflector!" Khatami ordered. "Helm, get us out . . ."

The deck heaved with enough force for Klisiewicz's knee to slam into the underside of his console. The sensor viewer was his only handhold as the deck continued to pitch, but he lost his grip and spilled to the deck. In his peripheral vision he saw Khatami flopping into her command chair and other members of the bridge crew trying and failing to keep from being thrown from their seats. All the lights flickered at the same time that alarm indicators on every console flared to life, accompanied by a cacophony of harsh tones and whistles demanding attention.

"Evasive!" Khatami shouted above the noise. "Full power to the shields!"

The assault faded after a moment and the deck's movements subsided, leaving everyone on the bridge with the sounds of the various alert indicators. Crew members returned to their stations, silencing the various alarms and already beginning the process of determining the extent of the beam's effects. It took Klisiewicz a moment to realize that the primary lighting had gone out, leaving only emergency illumination around the bridge.

"Damage report!" Khatami ordered. "Klisiewicz, what was that?"

"Still trying to figure that out, Captain," replied the science officer, back at his station and consulting his sensor data. "It looks like the attack tracked right up the deflector beam but stopped just as soon as we disengaged." He flinched as the image in the viewer flashed before his eyes before fading altogether. A cursory check of this console told him what he already suspected. "We've got an overload in the sensor array. I'm blind here."

At the communications station, Hector Estrada said, "Minor casualties reported so far, Captain, but initial damage reports are indicating we took a pretty good punch. Engineering is reporting overloads and cutouts all over the ship. Shields, weapons control, even the transporters." Holding his Feinberg receiver to his ear, he winced, closing his eyes and releasing a grunt of shock as he pulled the device free. "Wow," he said, turning to his console. "Something's up with intraship comm, and ship-to-ship and ship-to-surface communications are already out. I'm seeing an overload in the subspace transceiver as well."

"One hit did all *that*?" Khatami asked. Leaning against the side of her chair, she wiped a lock of hair from where it had fallen across her eyes. "Where are we?"

Having returned to his seat at the helm, Neelakanta reported, "I took us out of orbit. I'm just guessing about a safe distance, Captain. As for our precise location?" He pointed to the astrogator. "Plotting and navigation are down, too."

Grunting in obvious irritation, Khatami activated her chair's intercom. "Bridge to engineering!"

"*Dang here, Captain.*" There was noticeable static on the open channel. "*We're still assessing the extent of the damage down here.*"

"Give me a general overview. How bad?"

"*Scale of one to ten? Range of the problems feels like a nine. Intensity, maybe a three.*"

"Meaning?"

"*We can restore priority systems pretty quickly, but the problems are* everywhere. *Mostly overloads that'll have to be reset or rerouted, but there will be some systems requiring more extensive repairs. I should have a better idea within ten minutes, Captain, but the short version is that we got flash-fried, stem to stern.*"

"That's my fault, Captain," Klisiewicz said, feeling a cold knot of guilt forming in his stomach. "I didn't anticipate that our scans would be interpreted as hostile."

Khatami replied, "None of us did, Lieutenant. Let's not waste time on blame or feeling sorry for ourselves. We've got people on the ground who don't know they're cut off from us. What are our options?"

Neelakanta replied, "We've still got propulsion, Captain. I can maintain a geosynchronous position with the planet even from out here."

"That could help in the event our communications don't get restored to full capacity right away," Khatami said. "Anyone else?"

"We could launch an unmanned survey probe and maybe use it as a communications relay between us and the surface?" Estrada suggested.

Khatami nodded. "Now we're talking. Get on that."

It took the communications officer a few minutes to coordinate his efforts with support personnel belowdecks, during which Klisiewicz and other bridge crew members assisted one another in determining the scope of damage to the different workstations. Klisiewicz had quit counting the number of circuit overloads he came across when Estrada announced that he was ready to proceed with his plan.

"Launching probe," reported Lieutenant McCormack from the navigator's station.

"Mister Estrada," Khatami said, "hail the landing parties and Captain Terrell the moment this thing's operational."

No one said anything else as, on the viewscreen, the bridge crew was treated to the image of a small cylindrical object arcing away from the *Endeavour* and toward the planet, all of which was now displayed thanks to the starship's wider orbit.

A moment later, the probe disappeared in a blinding white flash that obscured Arethusa from view for several seconds, by which time a new round of alarms was triggered. Khatami quickly ordered them silenced.

"The probe's destroyed, Captain. Another beam from the surface."

"Captain," Neelakanta said, "if that weapon can bull's-eye the probe from where it was positioned, we're in range, too."

Khatami gestured toward the screen. "Back us off." She turned to Klisiewicz. "Apparently, the Preservers are pretty protective of their artifacts."

"Looks that way," Klisiewicz said, recalling his comparative analysis of the structure beneath Arethusa's surface with the smaller one found by the *Enterprise*. "Based on what I found from scans of the obelisk, we may not be safe anywhere in the solar system."

"Find me a way back in there, Lieutenant," Khatami said. "Until you do, our people are on their own. Mister Estrada, notify engineering that communications, shields, transporters, and weapons are top priority, in that order. Everything else can take a number. Tell Lieutenant Dang to pull people from wherever he can find them. Until further notice, we're *all* engineers."

16

Stepping down from the shuttlecraft *Masao*'s open crew hatch, Katherine Stano got her first real look at the *U.S.S. Sagittarius*. It had been several months since she had last seen the vessel in person, in the days following the intense battle that had resulted in the destruction of Starbase 47. After the conclusion of that conflict, the compact scout ship, along with the *Endeavour* and the *U.S.S. Enterprise*, had made its way to another Starfleet facility, Starbase 12, for initial damage assessments and critical repairs, before the *Sagittarius* had returned to the Sol system for a more extensive refit at Earth Spacedock.

From the looks of things, the *Sagittarius* might well be making another such journey in the very near future.

"Wow," she said, moving away from the *Masao* and walking toward the larger vessel, which was abuzz with activity as members of its crew along with engineering and other support personnel from the *Endeavour* moved over and about it, all of them focused on some repair task. The *Sagittarius*'s normally smooth hull was marred by all manner of dents and scratches, each of which bore mute testimony to the ship's rough landing. Numerous plates and access panels had been opened or set aside, exposing cavities and compartments beneath the outer hull and within which people were working.

"It's not as bad as it looks," Theriault said, coming up

behind Stano. Pausing, the first officer placed her hands on her hips and regarded her ship. "Well, let me rethink that."

"Take your time," Stano said. "Meanwhile, what can we do to help?" With the *Endeavour* forced to retreat from its orbit above Arethusa following the latest attack from the Preserver pyramid, she and the other members of the landing party who were not engineers suddenly found themselves on the verge of being in the way of the ongoing repair efforts. "If we can't fix anything, maybe we can help with fortifying this place."

"That's a good idea," said Captain Clark Terrell as he moved from where he was standing near the *Sagittarius*'s open main airlock hatch and extended his hand toward Stano in greeting. "Welcome to the party, Commander."

"Glad to be here, sir," Stano said. Then she added, "Not really."

The comment was enough to make Terrell chuckle. "You'll fit right in." His smile fading, he said, "I'm sorry to hear about your people. I hope there's something we can do to help them."

"Thank you, Captain." Stano sighed. "I wish we had Lieutenant Klisiewicz with us but I imagine he's got his hands full up on the *Endeavour*." The fragmented reports received from Captain Khatami in the wake of the attack from the Preserver weapon painted a discouraging picture as far as the starship's current operational status was concerned. There was no estimate on when the *Endeavour* might be in a condition to return to the planet, and there remained the Preserver artifact and whatever threats—known and as yet unrevealed—it might harbor.

"I understand your Lieutenant Hesh is no slouch in the science officer department, either."

Terrell said, "He's on the ship, trying to retune the sensors so we can get a better handle at scanning beneath the planet's surface. Since it looks like Nimur's figured out that's something of a blind spot for us, she's taken to hiding underground on Suba." He paused, looking around the crash site and the surrounding jungle. "As for this little island we're calling home, we haven't found any nearby caves or other entrances to subterranean passages, but that doesn't mean there isn't one we missed. Even though they'll have to swim or fly to get over here, I don't like the idea of Nimur and her friends popping up from a hole somewhere."

"We lost track of her and at least one other Changed on Suba after the Preserver weapon showed up," Stano said. "I figure she's regrouping, using the caverns for cover and maybe trying to turn other Tomol and increase her numbers." Kerlo had described that Nimur, his mate, somehow possessed the ability to initiate and even accelerate the transformation of her people, though Stano suspected this power extended only to those Tomol who were nearing the point in their maturation cycle that the Change would soon happen, anyway.

Let's hope that's the case, she mused, considering the hundreds of Tomol who at this moment were reeling from the massive disruption to their society. *If she can change them all, then we are royally screwed.*

"I'll check in with Commander Sorak," Theriault said, referring to the *Sagittarius*'s second officer, "see how he's doing with prepping our defenses."

Nodding, Terrell gestured toward the ship's stern. "He and Dastin were deploying motion sensors a couple of hundred meters inside the tree line. At last report, they were almost done. If all goes to Sorak's plan, we'll have a complete perimeter within the hour."

"And exactly when does anything *not* go the way Sorak plans?" Theriault asked.

Stano smiled. "I'll send Lerax your way. He can add our people to yours." She looked around the area where the *Sagittarius* had made its less than elegant landing. "The more eyes and warm bodies we have on the line, the better off we'll be."

"Amen to that," Terrell said. "Master Chief Ilucci's trying to see if he can coax a little more magic out of our deflector shield generators and maybe buy us some extra protection if we're still stuck here on the ground. Without the *Endeavour* to provide support, this could end up being one very nasty place to be, if and when Nimur and her people decide to pay us a visit." It was not far from anyone's mind that the *Sagittarius*, even in its compromised state, still represented a valuable prize to Nimur and the other Changed in their quest to find a way off Arethusa.

As Theriault moved off in search of Sorak, Stano sighed. "I have to be honest, Captain. I'm wondering if anything we do to get ready is worth it. Based on what I saw, that thing the Preservers sent after the Changed, we're pretty much just in the way down here."

Terrell shrugged. "From what you said, that drone or whatever the hell it was took its sweet time getting to the scene. If we get attacked, we may have to hold our own until it or another like it gets here, and that's if one shows up at all. We're talking about an ancient technology that's been buried underground for thousands of years, with no one to look after it or take care of it. There's no way in hell I'm relying on something like that to save my ass."

"Can't argue with that, sir."

Heavy footfalls echoed from the corridor leading away from the *Sagittarius*'s airlock, and Stano looked up to see a tall, thin Arkenite male emerging through the open hatch, dressed like his crewmates in an olive drab Starfleet jumpsuit that looked to be in severe need of laundering. His bronze skin contrasted with his clothing, and his height was enough that he had to duck in order to avoid hitting his oversized, hairless head on the hatch's frame. Stano recognized him as Lieutenant Sengar Hesh, Captain Terrell's science officer. He was moving at a rapid pace, giving Stano the impression that he had something on his mind and was ready to talk about it to the first person he could find.

I'm doubting that's a good thing, considering our current situation.

"Captain," Hesh said as he drew closer, indicating Terrell with a nod before turning to Stano. "Commander. It is a pleasure to make your acquaintance." His eyes, bright green orbs possessing no pupils, were wide as he regarded her with an air of inquisitiveness.

Stano nodded. "Same here."

"Forgive me, Commander, but I have only just been informed as to the details of your encounter with the evolved Tomol. After a cursory review of the tricorder readings you and your landing party collected, I realize that you have shed new light on something that was recorded by our own ship's scans during our initial reconnoiter of the planet." To Terrell, he said, "Captain, I think this is something you both need to see."

Trees, some towering into the air from the floor of the wide, shallow valley, provided a canopy that all but blocked out the rays and warmth of the Nereus star. To Stano, the scene above her almost resembled the curved ceiling of an underground cavern, with holes punched through the rock and allowing the merest pinpoints of sunlight to peek through the gaps. Looking skyward, Stano saw the trees' thick branches and their lush foliage, none of it moving the slightest millimeter in response to the gentle breeze she felt on her exposed skin. The petrified crust encasing everything flowed down the trunks of the trees and to the ground, forming what looked to be one single piece of artfully carved stone. Conspicuous by its absence was any hint of animal or insect life. There was not the single sound of something moving among the trees or above their heads in the arcing branches. No insects sang or chirped. This place was completely inert.

Standing at the center of it all, covered in the same stone cocoon as everything else for dozens of meters in every direction, were six humanoids—Tomol.

"I don't know that I can ever get used to looking at anything—or anyone—subjected to this," Stano said, swallowing a nervous lump that had formed in her throat. Seeing the trapped Tomol reminded her of the three members of her landing party she had been forced to leave behind at the bird-of-prey crash site on Suba.

You're not leaving them, she rebuked herself. *We're going to find a way to free them.*

"When did you find these?" asked Captain Terrell, who had accompanied her and Lieutenant Hesh aboard the shuttlecraft *Masao* after leaving Commander Theriault to oversee the ongoing *Sagittarius* repair efforts and promising his first officer that they would not be gone long.

Stepping closer to one of the petrified Tomol, Hesh said, "I only became aware of this area while reviewing the scan data we collected during our initial survey of the planet. Since the rock shields life signs unless our sensors are tuned to account for its natural scattering properties, this region was not flagged for further study before our landing party was dispatched to investigate the Tomol. When I gave the data further scrutiny and discovered the presence of these life-forms, the connection to what you encountered became obvious."

"Now I have to wonder if there aren't more spots like this," Terrell said. "On Suba or any of the other outlying islands."

"I have not yet had the opportunity to conduct scans to make such a determination, Captain," replied the science officer. "Once we get past our current crisis, I hope to do just that. Of course, there is also the matter of determining whether this process can be reversed."

"Right," Stano said, thinking once more of Ensign Sotol and the others standing immobile and insensate to the world around them. How long would they remain there?

Until we figure out how to help them.

Moving in a circle as he examined one of the statues, Terrell asked, "What do your scans show about these Tomol? Had they undergone the Change?"

"It appears at least three of them had begun the transformation, sir." Hesh held up his tricorder and studied its miniaturized display screen. "According to my readings, they are suspended in the same manner as the other Changed and Commander Stano's people. Their life functions have been arrested such that they have not aged, and neither are they aware of the passage of time."

Stano asked, "It doesn't look that much different from what we observed at the crash site." She looked around the valley, noting that the surrounding vegetation had not encroached upon the stone covering the ground all around them. "How long have they been here?"

"My scans indicate that these Tomol were imprisoned more than three thousand years ago." Lowering his tricorder, the Arkenite shook his head. "It is, in a word, amazing."

"Three thousand years?" Terrell blew out his breath. "That's not amazing. It's damned incredible." He reached out to touch the arm of the Tomol he was studying. "All this time, and they're still alive. How does a technology like this work without someone to look after it? How much longer will it keep working before somebody has to come and fix it?"

Stano knelt and ran her hand over the rock plate covering the ground, marveling at the silhouettes of grass, leaves, and other vegetation and terrain features that had been trapped within the neutralizing effect. If Hesh was right, and the stone had been cast all those centuries ago, then the life trapped within its confines dated back to Earth's late Iron Age, the time of Plato and Confucius. And what of the Tomol? What was their society like in the distant past? Indications were that this planet and the people living on it was a classic example of an arrested culture, trapped in limbo by design and for reasons known to none but the mysterious benefactors who had brought the Tomol to this world.

"Makes you wonder if the Preservers are really dead, doesn't it?" she asked.

"No kidding." Terrell smiled again. "It's those sorts of questions that made me join Starfleet in the first place."

"I, too, was so motivated," Hesh said.

"Why not kill them?" asked Stano after a moment. Continuing to inspect the unmoving figures, she crossed her arms. "I mean, if we're to believe what the Tomol have told us, the Preservers went to an awful lot of trouble to set up this society. They instituted the rituals that see to it that the Tomol sacrifice themselves before they undergo the Change, and they provided weapons and other tools for the Wardens to enforce the laws or beliefs or whatever you want to call them." She gestured to the statue. "And then there's this. If Hesh's scans are right, these Tomol have been standing here, suspended, for three millennia. Why? Wouldn't it be easier to just eliminate a perceived threat, particularly if it represents the kind of power we've seen demonstrated by Nimur and her followers?"

"All good questions," Terrell said. "I'm betting the answers are buried somewhere down in that pyramid, or with some other artifacts or whatever else the Preservers left here."

Hesh said, "Perhaps the answer is quite simple. We know this race as 'the Preservers,' so perhaps it stands to reason that they are described in this manner because their desire was to preserve life at all costs, rather than destroy even those life-forms that present a threat. Considering what we know of them and the extraordinary lengths to which they are believed to have gone in order to relocate segments of endangered species or representatives of other, larger civilizations, it seems uncharacteristic of them to then destroy that which they have safeguarded."

"Has anyone told you you're sounding more like Sorak every day?" Terrell asked.

The Arkenite offered a small, thin smile. "Master Chief Ilucci has made a similar observation. I shall tell him that it is not—as he put it—just him."

There was a familiar beep, and Terrell reached into a pocket of his drab green jumpsuit to retrieve his communicator. Flipping open the unit's antenna cover, the captain said, "Terrell here."

"Commander Theriault, sir," replied the voice of the Sagittarius's first officer. "Sorak's been fiddling with the sensors, and he's got some faint readings on the Tomol. That is, Nimur and her group. They look like they might be on the move again. They're still on Suba, but he can't verify if they're heading our way. You should probably get back here, Skipper, just to be safe."

"Copy that," Terrell said. "We're on our way." Closing the communicator, he turned to the group. "Well, you heard the lady. Let's get back to the shuttle."

Stano nodded. "Aye, sir." As the trio made their way

back to the *Masao*, she could not help a long, lingering final look at the trapped Tomol. Why had the Preservers expended such effort to contain their charges? Further, what if Nimur and her fellow Changed evolved to the point where such measures proved ineffective?

Then we're all probably screwed.

17

"Gentlemen, I've made a decision," Khatami said by way of greeting as she entered the briefing room to find Klisiewicz and Doctor Leone waiting for her. "I've appointed myself morale officer, and as morale officer I have one rule: our meeting will begin with good news. So who's first?"

"If that's the rule," said Leone without missing a step, "then why am I even here?"

Beaten at her own small game, Khatami smiled, conceding the point to her friend. "Nicely played, Doctor." She paused, eyeing both men. "Well? I'm waiting."

Klisiewicz cleared his throat. "Lieutenant Dang reports that repairs are under way. The astrogator and other bridge systems are already back online."

"See?" Leone said. "Phu fixed the astrogator. You didn't need me, after all."

"Actually, it was Lieutenant Estrada who made the repair," Klisiewicz replied. "Lieutenant Dang has people all over the ship diagnosing and repairing minor tasks. Estrada took charge of the bridge and has that pretty well under control."

"That's to be expected," Khatami said. Hector Estrada had more time in Starfleet than her and Klisiewicz combined, and a length and breadth of experience to go with it.

The science officer continued, "Shield generators are

back online, and sensors should be up and running within the hour. Communications and weapons, too. Transporters are a different story. The energy beam damaged the energizing coil, and the pattern buffer is off-line. Dang has people on it, but it'll be several hours, at least." He paused, grimacing. "That's really the sort of work for a starbase, but he's making do."

"He's the best we've got, for right now, anyway." Khatami reminded herself to make a note of commendation in the assistant chief engineer's service record at her next opportunity. The younger officer had distinguished himself with poise and resolve while standing in for Commander Yataro, who remained on the planet surface with the rest of the *Endeavour* landing party. Looking to Leone, she asked, "What have you learned from our guest?"

"She doesn't like it when the ship shakes," replied the doctor, earning him a glare from Khatami. Leaning back in his seat, he added, "Okay, how's this? I think I may be able to reconstruct the Tomol genome and repair their DNA so that they can do . . . whatever it is they're supposed to do."

That caught Khatami by surprise. "Really? Well, keep going. You've got my complete attention."

Leone gestured to Klisiewicz. "A lot of the credit goes to our science officer here. He's the one who pointed me down the path of sorting out just what kind of genetic damage was dealt to these people." He looked to the other man. "I think you missed your calling, kid. You're a natural geneticist."

As though uncomfortable with the praise, Klisiewicz shifted in his seat. "It was just a theory, Captain. Shooting in the dark, if you will. Doctor Leone is the closest thing we have to a xenobiological expert."

"Are you kidding?" Khatami asked, happy to lighten the mood if only for a moment. "Do you know how hard it is to get any sort of compliment from this man? Consider yourself appropriately honored, Lieutenant."

"Just don't let it get around," Leone said. "I've got a reputation to protect." His tone growing more serious, he continued, "It was Klisiewicz who got us thinking that maybe the whole process of the Change, or at least its aspects of psychosis and rage, is a problem of omission rather than addition to their natural genetic state. If we consider the Tomol as a victimized race, perhaps one subjugated to genetic experimentation and deliberate mutation, it casts information from our scans in a whole new light."

Khatami nodded. "I'll pretend I understood some of that."

"It's not really that complicated," Klisiewicz countered. "In fact, it's almost deceptive in its simplicity. At least, if what we're getting from our analysis of the glyphs on that obelisk is accurate, this theory might be closer to the money than we first thought. In comparing the symbols on this obelisk to the one the *Enterprise* found, and assuming the folklore passed along to us by Seta wasn't being misrepresented and thus makes a reliable benchmark for translation, I think I may have pieced together an origin story for the Tomol."

Leone said, "Do I have time to make popcorn?"

Smiling at the comment, Klisiewicz shook his head. "I'll stick to the highlights. From what I can determine, the Tomol at some point in their early evolution endured a radical physiological change, which now manifests itself as what we've seen from Nimur and her followers. I'd be guessing as to the cause, but the more important part is that well after this change was introduced, they were found by the Shedai."

"Wait," Khatami said, "found by the Shedai? Not *created* by the Shedai?"

"No, Captain," replied the science officer. "The first translations from the *Sagittarius* crew got that wrong. I wouldn't hold it against them, though. The Preserver glyphs are very hard to interpret correctly, even after you have a key to work from and some context to go with it."

Khatami considered this. "So, what? The Shedai attempted to subjugate the Tomol?"

"It appears so," Klisiewicz said. "According to the glyphs, the Tomol referred to the Shedai as 'the Dark Gods,' and their plan was to exploit the Tomol's natural powers and abilities as a result of their Change, and use them against their enemies like the Tkon and whoever else they were pissing off hundreds of thousands of years ago. This wasn't a case of uplifting a civilization, as we know they did with the Tholians and perhaps other races as well. The Tomol already had the natural means to fight back, and that's what they did despite the Shedai's efforts to control them through selective genetic manipulation."

"I'll bet that went well," Leone said, tapping his fingers on the table.

Klisiewicz nodded. "Exactly. Needless to say, the Tomol didn't take too kindly to being forced into servitude. They began to rebel, and things became even more complicated when the Shedai realized their efforts to control the Tomol through genetic engineering were beginning to have disastrous side effects. Something had gone wrong, so that when the Tomol experienced a Change, their intellect began to devolve, to the point that they were little more than wild animals, uncontrollable beasts harnessing great strength and telekinetic abilities."

"The Shedai made a mistake?" Khatami asked.

"In a nutshell, yes," replied the science officer. "By this point, the Tomol had been spread out to worlds across the Taurus Reach to serve the Shedai, and once the Change took hold they were destroying anything and everything in their path. The glyphs describe groups of Shedai sent to hunt the Tomol, as much for sport as to contain and control them."

Leone held up a hand, and Khatami saw the doubt in her friend's eyes. "Wait. We're talking about the Shedai here. Master genetic builders of the first order and all that, right? The same ones who built entire worlds out of their own special brand of genetic goop? You told me earlier that you thought they tried to fix whatever it was they'd done. Did they screw that up, too?"

"The glyphs describe the Shedai's efforts to undo the damage they caused, but by then the situation was unraveling faster than they could control it." Klisiewicz sighed. "At some point, they just decided to cut their losses. Their solution was to isolate all of the Tomol to their home planet and let them obliterate each other."

"Dear god," Khatami said. "Self-inflicted genocide."

"That's essentially it," replied Klisiewicz. "The Tomol came within a hairsbreadth of wiping themselves completely from existence, except that someone else took an interest: the Preservers. They found the Tomol on the brink of extinction, collected several hundred specimens, and relocated them to Arethusa." He shrugged. "I'm still looking for something to support my theory, but I'm guessing this planet has a biosphere similar to that of the Tomol homeworld. In fact, there's no mention of the original planet anywhere that I can find."

Leone said, "So it could still be out there, somewhere, with legions of frothing Tomol rampaging all over it?"

"More likely they would find the uninhabited husk of whatever's left of that world," Khatami said. Though remote, the possibility of the *Endeavour* or another vessel happening across the Tomol homeworld was still there.

Won't that be fun.

Shifting in his seat, Leone leaned so far from his chair that Khatami thought he might lay his upper body across the conference table. "Okay, so the Preservers set up the Tomol on this planet, lay down a bunch of laws and rituals for them to follow in order keep them from being taken over by the Change, and then install one of their gizmos to babysit the whole brood and make sure they all jump into the fire pit when the time's right. Is that where you're going with all of this?"

Klisiewicz replied, "I am."

"You have to wonder why they didn't try to fix whatever genetic anomalies the Shedai introduced before leaving the Tomol to be fruitful and multiply or whatever," Klisiewicz said. "Was it because the Preservers didn't have technology on the Shedai's level? That doesn't really make sense when you consider everything else they've apparently done on at least two planets we know of."

Klisiewicz replied, "Making such alterations to a species doesn't really fit with what little we know of the Preservers." His expression turned sheepish. "They preserve what they find. If they fixed things, then we'd call them . . ."

Holding up a hand, Leone said, "Stop. I think maybe you and I are spending too much time together, because that sounds like the kind of smart-assed answer I'd have given. If you're going to do that, you need to work on your delivery."

"Gentlemen." Khatami tapped her finger several times on the table, her signal that it was time for her companions to rein themselves in. "All right, so the Preservers set up the Tomol society we found on Arethusa, but they also left them with the tools and knowledge to take matters into their own hands in the event any of their people succumbed to the Change. And we've seen a couple of different backup protocols in case things get out of hand, and for all we know, there are a dozen more such measures waiting to be triggered. Also, don't forget what Commander Theriault reported about her conversation with Seta in the caverns: the obelisk itself may be some kind of fail-safe device meant as a last resort. She called it a possible 'doomsday weapon,' and even though she indicated it was only a theory, I'm not ruling it out for now. Making sure these people didn't fall victim to their own biology was obviously of prime importance to the Preservers."

Klisiewicz replied, "Exactly. The Preservers were uncertain of what might happen if a Tomol who had undergone the Change was allowed to continue evolving unimpeded. There are notations about speculations that they might eventually transform beyond the need for a physical form."

"Because there's not enough of *those* running around the galaxy," Leone offered.

"As I said, it's speculation, but there was a very real fear of the Changed somehow finding their way off Arethusa and to other worlds. So they put in these various safety measures to keep them here."

Sighing, Khatami rubbed her eyes. How long had it been since she had last slept, or eaten a decent meal? Even as she asked herself those questions, she could feel Leone studying her with his practiced eyes. "I know what you're going to say, Doctor."

"Then save me the trouble of saying it," Leone countered.

"Later." Drawing a deep breath, Khatami shifted to a more comfortable position in her seat. "This fossilization process Commander Stano described. Is there anything pertaining to that among the Preserver glyphs? Can it be reversed?"

Klisiewicz's expression turned glum. "I haven't found anything yet, Captain, but there's still more to translate, both along the obelisk's shell and almost certainly inside it."

"And you think there might be instructions on how to deal with the Changed, perhaps even to save them and the rest of the Tomol?"

"There has to be," the science officer said. "Otherwise, what's the point behind everything the Preservers did?"

Khatami could not argue with that line of thinking. "I agree, and as much as I'd like to wait until the circumstances were better on the surface, I don't think that's going to happen until we do something. I want you to give that obelisk a thorough going-over. Once we get most of the repairs addressed, I'll be sending you down. If the transporters aren't ready, then we'll use a shuttlecraft."

"Are we sure that obelisk won't shoot at anything coming toward the planet?" Leone asked.

"I've been thinking about that," Klisiewicz said, "and I wonder if the defensive measures it took were because it perceived a threat. After all, it didn't shoot at us when we made orbit, or when we sent landing parties or the first shuttle down to the surface. Only when we started our intensive scans did it seem to take notice. It's possible we can move back into orbit and the obelisk won't care."

It was a valid point, Khatami thought, and worth considering. "One thing at a time. Prepare a shuttlecraft in the event we don't have the transporters, and assemble a landing party of whomever you need, including a full security detachment. Take Seta with you. If anyone's going to help us get inside that thing, it's her. Do what you can, but at the first sign of trouble, I want you out of there."

"Understood." Klisiewicz rose from his chair and looked to Leone. "Doctor, when the time comes, I'd really like to have you along. If you've made any progress with your treatment experiments, maybe we can test whatever you've managed to come up with."

Leone drew a deep breath and released a heavy, melodramatic sigh. "I should've seen that coming. I'm still conducting tests, Lieutenant, but I'm at your disposal."

After the science officer had departed, Khatami relaxed into her chair and ignored the signals her brain was sending her that it was past due for some rest.

"I hate to be the one to say this," Leone offered after a moment, "but it's entirely possible we won't be able to stop any of this."

"So either these Changed run around, lording over the planet until others change, and then they go to war like they did on their own world and destroy each other. Or something from the Preservers' ancient bag of tricks comes along and somehow puts a stop to the whole thing. I don't know that I want to see what that might be, Tony."

"Hard to say," Leone said. "Even Klisiewicz doesn't know. At least, not yet. Still, you've got to give the kid credit. He did his homework. I know he's been busting his ass since this started, but I have to say I'm damned impressed with how much progress he was able to make."

"We'll need more of that from him before this is over." Khatami pushed herself from her chair and headed for the door. Then she stopped, turning to face her friend. "And you, too, Tony. I don't want to just sit back and let whatever happens happen down there. It's our fault—ours and the Klingons'—that the Tomol are dealing with this now, and it's up to us to put things right. I'm going to need every resourceful officer I've got if we're going to figure this out."

Leone smirked. "Great. I'll let you know if one comes along."

18

Bare chested and bathed in sweat, Kang dodged and weaved, ducking beneath the swinging arm of the combat drill mannequin. The figure's other arm was spinning around, timed with the arms of a second trainer. Like its companion, the model had been made to resemble the arms, torso, and head of a muscled Klingon, and one of his crew had taken the liberty of dressing the simulations in an officer's heavy dress tunics complete with baldrics and other decorations. Raising his hands to block the attack, Kang pushed away the arm and forced the training model to begin turning in the opposite direction, which afforded him the opportunity to strike at its torso. His fist slammed into the unyielding material and he heard the satisfying tone signaling that he had landed another hit. There was no time for rest, as the first mannequin's arms came around again. Though he parried the first swing, the second arm caught him in the left shoulder, sending forth a measured yet still severe jolt of electricity as its pressure-sensitive hand made contact with his body.

Grunting more from irritation than any real pain, Kang stepped to the side, distracted only for a moment by the strike, but it was enough for the second trainer to come about, and its arm swung into his back and delivered another shock. Now truly angry, the Klingon captain howled as he kicked at the mannequin's torso. He planted the heel of his boot squarely in the center of the trainer's chest with enough force to snap the figure from its swivel base, and it crashed with a heavy thud onto the metal deck. A few telltale sparks from severed electrical connections spat from the base, and an alarm tone sounded in the room. Kang was sure the ship's computer shortly would notify his chief engineer that yet another item had been added to his already long list of things requiring attention and repair.

From behind him, a familiar voice asked in a gently mocking tone, "I trust you feel the rush of victory coursing through your veins as it sets your very blood aflame?"

Kang released a deep, bellowing laugh as he turned to face his wife, who stood with crossed arms in the doorway leading from the *Voh'tahk*'s physical-training chamber, regarding him with a small, wry smile. She was dressed in the female equivalent of standard shipboard exercise attire, which consisted of a close-fitting dark gray bodysuit that conformed to her alluring figure. Engrossed as he had been in his own exercise regimen, Kang had not even heard the parting of the doors and Mara's stealthy entrance into the room. "Were you of a mind to do so, you could have easily taken my life."

"The thought has occurred to me, on occasion," Mara replied, her expression flat. Then, continuing their game, she added, "On more than one occasion, actually. Usually when you are sleeping. And you know I would not even need a blade." Her comments elicited another laugh from Kang, and it was only then that the frustration he had been feeling began to lift. He noted that she wore no shoes, leading him to surmise that she either was coming from or on her way to her usual *Mok'bara* training interval. Already an accomplished student of the unarmed combat discipline when he had first met her, Mara had continued to hone her skills in the time they had been mated. With the possible but by no means certain exception of Kang himself, there was no one aboard the *Voh'tahk* able to best her in the crew's regular shipboard competitions.

"I understand there have been some delays with the repairs," she said.

Kang nodded, reaching out to push the remaining training mannequin's left arm so that it began to swivel in a counterclockwise motion. As it turned around toward him, he made a halfhearted attempt to parry its swing, sending it spinning in the opposite direction. "Konvraq has informed me that he has found additional damage in our propulsion systems as well as our forward weapons array. The engineers who overlooked the faults during their initial inspections have been punished, of course, but I cannot afford to kill them at the moment." The error, in Kang's mind, at least, had been egregious, given the *Voh'tahk*'s current tactical situation and its vulnerability to the Starfleet vessel still lurking nearby. "We have an opportunity to gain an advantage over the Earther ship, but it is being squandered by sloppiness and inattention to vital detail." The *Voh'tahk*'s sensors had observed the unexplained very powerful energy beam fired from somewhere on the Tomol planet as it struck the Starfleet cruiser, and the ship's feeble attempts to combat the assault before its retreat from orbit. From what Kang had been told by his tactical officer, the *Endeavour* had sustained some damage but nothing debilitating, and he suspected that its repairs would be completed before Konvrag and his engineers finished their own work. This, of course, added to Kang's mounting frustration.

As always, Mara could sense what he might be thinking just from studying his face and body language. "You feel useless at the moment, do you not? With all the repairs that still need to be completed, you think your time is better spent helping with that work."

"You know me too well, my wife," Kang said, crossing the exercise floor to a metal bench affixed to the wall. He had placed a rough-hewn towel there, and he began wiping at the perspiration on his chest and arms. "In situations like these, a captain is little more than an impediment, an obstacle his crew must negotiate while seeing to their tasks. Despite all the time I have spent commanding ships of the empire, I have never grown comfortable sitting idle as others work around me." As captain of a battle cruiser that remained compromised and in need of repair, there was little for him to do while his crew worked to return the *Voh'tahk* to operational capability.

Stepping farther into the room, Mara allowed the doors to shut behind her. "It is not proper for you to attend to such matters, my husband. Your place is one of leadership, above and apart from those you command."

Kang was aware of this, of course. While he certainly possessed the necessary technical expertise and experience to assist in any or all of the damage control efforts currently under way across the *Voh'tahk*, protocol demanded that he remain above such menial tasks. An opportunistic subordinate might see any move on Kang's part to contribute to the physical labor as lowering himself from his position of leadership and disrespect for the title he held. As far as Kang was concerned, such thinking was nonsense, and he would gladly kill anyone who challenged him on such a ridiculous point. He also had to remain mindful of his crew's morale, which might be disrupted in the face of any threats to his authority, perceived or real.

"Protocol does not require me to be happy about such things," Kang said, wiping his face with the towel as he stepped back toward the room's center and the training mannequins. "But rather than allow the crew to see my discontent, I take refuge down here and purge my frustrations on inanimate objects." He approached the model that still stood upright, waiting for him to begin another exercise interval, but instead of activating the unit, Kang kicked at it, toppling it as he had done to its companion and watching as it broke from its base and tumbled to the deck.

Mara asked, "Do you feel better now?"

The sound of metal impacting against metal should have placated him, if only a small bit, but Kang felt no satisfaction. He grunted this displeasure rather than giving it voice, and he heard his wife chuckle behind him. Saying nothing further, he watched as she moved to the door and engaged its lock before turning to face him. She reached for the closure at the neck of her bodysuit and pulled it down past her waist, revealing that she was wearing no other clothing. Pulling the suit down past her shoulders, Mara freed her arms and allowed the garment to drop into a pile around her feet.

"Perhaps what is required is some other means of easing your stress and frustration," she said, walking naked across the floor toward him.

Kang smiled. "I am, of course, open to exploring all possibilities." He embraced her, his fingers tracing her familiar curves, and she responded in kind, and within moments he felt the pressures of command slipping away, helpless against his wife's raw, unbridled sensual energy. She pressed her body against his, lifting her head so that her eyes met his.

A loud, electronic tone echoed in the exercise room, followed by the voice of his communications officer, Kyris, filtered through the ship's intercom system. *"Bridge to Captain Kang."*

Growling in annoyance at the untimely interruption, Kang crossed to the intercom panel mounted to the bulkhead near the door and smacked the activation control with the heel of his hand. "This is Kang," he snapped, making no effort to hide his displeasure. "What do you want?"

"I apologize for disturbing you, Captain, but we are being hailed by the Federation cruiser. Its captain wishes to speak with you and says it is urgent."

Still naked, Mara moved to stand beside him, and Kang exchanged doubting glances with her before replying, "Very well. Transfer the communication to this station."

Kyris acknowledged the order and a moment later Kang heard the snap and buzz of frequencies being shifted before a new voice said, *"Captain Kang, this is Captain Khatami of the* Endeavour. *Thank you for agreeing to speak with me."*

"What do you want, human?"

"To put it bluntly, I need your help, but you're no good to me with your ship all but dead in space. So I'm proposing an exchange: I'll help you complete your ship's repairs if you'll agree to help me rescue my people from the planet's surface."

Kang's eyes widened in surprise. "Why would assisting a human to aid other humans be of interest to me?"

"My landing party has your doctor, Tormog, in custody. His wounds have been treated and he is being handled with respect. Helping me to retrieve my people would allow us to return him to you."

Though Khatami could not see him do so, Kang shrugged. "You may keep him, or kill him. It is of no difference to me."

The human did not hesitate with her response. *"Are you sure about that? He's collected quite a bit of information pertaining to your mission here. Aren't you supposed to be gathering data and specimens for your superiors? My suggestion is that you forget about the latter, but the former may still be of some value."*

"My mission is of no concern to you," Kang replied. "And I have no need for any advice you might care to offer."

"Listen to me, Kang. The beings who relocated the Tomol to this planet have put in all sorts of protective measures to make sure they don't go through this transformation you want to exploit so badly. It's already cost you one ship and the lives of its crew. As the Tomol who've changed keep growing more powerful, these countermeasures have been escalating, and that includes react-

ing to any perceived threats from orbiting ships. We have to assume that there's some kind of protocol designed to keep the Tomol from leaving the planet."

Despite himself, Kang once again found himself admiring—if only a small bit—the human woman's guile for talking to him in this manner. As for her claims, he suspected what she was saying was true, at least in some respects. The readings collected by the *Voh'tahk*'s sensors confirmed Khatami's report about the energy weapon coming from some sort of apparatus buried in the ground on that cursed planet, utilizing a technology far too advanced for the primitive Tomol to have created.

"If what you say is true, Captain, then your ship is in danger if you return to the planet. So what do you suggest?"

"As I said, my people can assist you with finalizing the repairs to your ship. Tell us what you need, and my engineers will supply it. After that, I think that if we work together, your ship could provide a diversion while mine moves close enough to beam up my people, and your Doctor Tormog. If necessary, we combine our forces to destroy the weapons being used against our ships and our people on the surface. Once everyone's clear, I'll transfer Tormog—and whatever data he's collected—to you."

"You seem rather trusting of me, Captain," Kang said. "Most atypical of a human."

Khatami replied, *"I can't very well ask you to trust me if I'm not willing to reciprocate. I don't think either of our ships working alone is enough to combat whatever weapons are being used, but together I believe we have a chance. Also, we both know I'm not asking you to do any-*

thing you haven't already done before. I read Captain Kirk's report of your previous meeting, and he wrote that you are a Klingon who values honor and kept to your word when circumstances required you two to work together."

"Kirk," Kang said, exchanging another knowing look with Mara as he recalled the odd encounter he, along with his wife and a handful of survivors from his previous ship, had when they found themselves trapped aboard the *U.S.S. Enterprise* and at the mercy of a strange noncorporeal energy being who was manipulating the emotions of everyone aboard the starship for its own benefit. The *Enterprise* crew discovered what was happening, and Kirk in turn convinced Kang of their situation and how to free themselves. Though the *Enterprise* captain had used subterfuge in the beginning to gain an upper hand, in the end he had comported himself with integrity and decency, earning from Kang a measure of grudging respect.

"You would allow us to return to the empire with knowledge of these people?" Kang asked, still harboring doubts. "And if I wish to take specimens with me as well?"

"*I think we both know I can't allow that,*" Khatami replied. "*But I've already seen what happened when your other ship tried to beam up some of the Tomol. If you think you can do better, I'll be happy to sit back and watch.*"

The bold statement evoked a hearty laugh from Kang, loud enough to echo off the exercise chamber's metal bulkheads. "I begin to take a liking to you, human."

"*What does that mean, exactly?*"

Kang laughed again. "That I'm not as eager to kill you as I was earlier today. You took even less time to change my mind than Kirk did." Taking note of Mara's skeptical expression, he said, "Very well, Captain. I accept your proposal. My engineer will prepare a list of components we require to complete our repairs, and I commit on my honor this vessel's assistance in retrieving your officers."

"Thank you, Captain," Khatami replied, and Kang heard the small air of relief in her voice. *"For whatever it's worth to you, I'm in your debt."*

"I may well collect on that pledge one day." Kang pressed the control to end the communication before turning to Mara, who still regarded him with obvious skepticism.

"Allying yourself with her?" she asked, folding her arms across her bare chest. "What will your crew think?"

"They will do as they are commanded," Kang replied. "The truth is that if we stay out here, she will find some way to exploit the knowledge we seek for the Federation's use. Taking advantage of whatever generosity she offers gives us an opportunity to keep her and her ship close until such time as we are ready to acquire the data and the specimens we need."

"What of her claims about this odd weapon that's being used?" Mara asked. "Do you believe her?"

Kang nodded. "I do, which is why I intend to use the Starfleet ship as a diversion of my own, even as I help its captain to rescue her subordinates." His mission still foremost in his mind, Kang already was pondering scenarios whereby the *Endeavour* could be offered up as fodder for the mysterious weapon on the planet's surface, even as the *Voh'tahk* secured the Tomol specimens he had been ordered to collect. As for the threat Khatami had theorized if Kang succeeded in capturing any of the Tomol, it would just have to be an acceptable risk.

Until he could find a way to offer the *Endeavour* to the weapon, of course.

19

"All hands to your positions! Let's move, people! Move move move!"

Clark Terrell's voice exploded from Katherine Stano's open communicator, the volume of his shouted commands enough to make her flinch. She stepped up onto the small cargo crate and peered over the larger container that had been set into the ground before her, giving herself a better view of the area around the *Sagittarius*. Defensive positions similar to her own had been prepared at intervals in a circle around the crashed scout ship, consisting of cargo containers, the trunks of felled trees, and even duranium plates Master Chief Ilucci and his engineers had pulled from the ship's hull. The components had been set into the ground, behind which were holes, excavated using phaser rifles from the vessel's armory, which were shallow enough for a person to stand upright while using the crates and other items for cover.

"Here we go again," Stano said, looking to either side of her hole as stragglers moved toward their positions on the hastily constructed perimeter. Terrell had reported moments earlier that the *Sagittarius* sensors had picked up the approach of airborne Tomol life-forms, heading away from Suba and toward this island. Repair tasks on the ship had been suspended as the entire crew scrambled to complete final preparations for what everyone was sure was another attack. Based on the sensor scans, Nimur and her fellow Changed would be here in minutes.

And here we are, stuck.

The *Endeavour* had been out of communications for an extended period, with the exception of a single burst transmission containing a brief summary of the starship's present condition following an attack from a ground-based energy weapon. Repairs currently were under way or being finalized on systems across the ship, which meant it still was vulnerable to attack from not only the ground but also the Klingon warship that remained in the Nereus system. Even delivering this update had proved to be a challenge, as the ship had been forced to attempt a high-speed flyby of the planet and stay within communications range just long enough to transmit the message. The short version of the story was that Stano and everyone else here on the ground would be without support from the *Endeavour* until further notice.

"Showtime, people!" shouted Vanessa Theriault, calling out to those *Sagittarius* and *Endeavour* personnel within earshot. Standing several meters to Stano's right, the first officer had taken up position in the adjacent hole, her left hand resting on the stock of the phaser rifle she had laid across the edge of the hull plate barrier. Behind her, Lieutenant Lerax was talking into his communicator, no doubt working with Senior Chief Petty Officer Razka, the *Sagittarius*'s lead field scout and security head, to coordinate final placements of the scout ship's crew as well as the *Endeavour* personnel, along with Kerlo and his fellow Tomol who had survived the fight with Nimur at the bird-of-prey crash site. Even Tormog had volunteered to take up a position on the line, the Klingon scientist currently occupying a hole with the *Sagittarius*'s medical officer, Doctor Babitz. Looking to her left, she nodded to Stano while indicating her hole with a wave of her free hand. "Be it ever so humble. Something tells me the locals won't like what we've done with the place."

"Moving into a new neighborhood is always a challenge," Stano said, attempting to join Theriault in the first officer's feeble attempt to lessen their mutual tension. Using her sleeve, she wiped perspiration from her forehead, the result of time spent out in the midday sun. Though the temperature was not oppressive, there was no breeze. The air was still and the ground here was dry, so anyone running past kicked small clouds of dust into the air, which in turn settled into the defensive positions and onto their occupants. Having experienced the grit in her mouth more than once, Stano had already consumed half the contents of the water canteen given to her by Theriault from the *Sagittarius*'s cache of field supplies.

Looking past their own holes, she saw that people were moving about the *Sagittarius*, handing out power packs for weapons and other equipment or supplies she could not identify. She shifted her attention to the crate she had placed near her feet to act as a table, regarding the canteen as well as the five power packs, four for her phaser rifle and one for the pistol on her hip. The *Sagittarius*'s armory along with the much smaller cache aboard the *Masao* had been raided and everything distributed in as equal a manner as possible to everyone taking up positions around the ship. Stano had taken advantage of the dispersal to acquire another communicator as well as a tricorder.

Each position was manned by members of the *Sagittarius* crew, Commander Yataro's team of engineers, or her own landing party. The group had been divided into pairs, and Lieutenant Lerax had seen to it that each position was numbered and assigned a field of fire for which it would be responsible, and each position's sector overlapped with the ones to its left and right. The shuttlecraft *Masao* sat on the ground just behind the scout ship's saucer section, tucked between the nacelles. Atop the *Sagittarius* itself was another pair of defensive positions, with Ilucci and Commander Yataro overseeing that effort. Their placement near the maintenance hatch along the rear of the saucer section's dorsal hull afforded the engineers access to control consoles they had set up within easy reach so that they could monitor the ship's deflector shield generators, which had been modified to act with greater efficiency to protect the vessel while it remained on the ground. Stano's hole, which she would shortly be sharing with Captain Terrell, had been designated Station 1. Theriault and Lerax were manning Station 2, and the numbers increased in clockwise fashion around the *Sagittarius*.

"Kate," Theriault called out, and Stano saw her colleague examining her tricorder. "I'm picking up something. Indistinct life-form readings." She pointed into the forest beyond the clearing where the *Sagittarius* rested. "They're on the ground, now. Two thousand meters, that way."

Stano turned to her own tricorder, which was propped up on the narrow parapet she had fashioned from the heavy earth surrounding her hole. Like everyone else, she had set the device to make continuous scans of the area Lerax had designated as her position's field of fire and increased its scanning range to maximum, keeping watch for any life-forms that might enter her sector of responsibility. The tricorder's readings remained fixed.

"I don't have anything here," she said.

To Stano's left, standing in what had been designated Station 14, Commander Sorak said, "Our tricorder readings also are negative." Next to the *Sagittarius*'s second officer, Lieutenant Sengar Hesh held up the unit he shared with Sorak, as though to emphasize the Vulcan's statement.

Next to Theriault, Lerax reported, "I am getting reports from other positions, picking up Tomol life readings and movement. There's no pattern, but it is obvious that they are attempting to advance on us from multiple directions."

"Do we have any idea how many we might be dealing with?" Stano asked.

"At least ten, possibly twelve." The Edoan security officer's pronounced brow furrowed as he adjusted a control on his tricorder. "Or more. Their life signs are fluctuating, much like they did when they transformed from flying creatures to the larger bipeds that attacked us."

Stano altered her tricorder's settings to expand its scan vector, and now she saw the life readings. From what she could tell, two or perhaps three individual life-forms were approaching from somewhere ahead of Lerax's position.

"They're going to try to envelop us," she said, setting aside the tricorder and retrieving her phaser rifle. She checked the weapon's power level, verifying for the third or fourth time that it contained a full charge and was set to maximum. With sustained use, the rifle's power pack would drain within ten to fifteen minutes, but a gnawing feeling in the pit of her stomach told her that the impending skirmish, regardless of its outcome, would take only a fraction of that time.

She heard running footsteps behind her and looked over her shoulder to see Captain Terrell carrying a phaser rifle and sprinting across the open ground separating the fighting hole from the *Sagittarius*'s main airlock. Behind him, the heavy hatch cycled shut, and she could see a handful of other personnel scrambling for their own positions. Terrell covered the remaining ground between them and hopped over the parapet, dropping into the hole beside her.

"Welcome aboard," Stano quipped.

Terrell nodded. "Happy to be here." Reaching into a pocket of his rumpled jumpsuit, he extracted a communicator and opened it, then pressed one of the unit's controls. Immediately, Stano's own communicator—still open per the captain's earlier instructions—emitted the familiar tone alerting her of an incoming message. "Terrell to all hands. Maintain this open frequency until further notice. If you need assistance, call out, and let's keep tabs on each other, in case any of those bastards slip through, somehow. Good luck, people." Setting the active communicator on the parapet, he turned to Stano. "I was never much for inspirational speeches. We usually end up not having time for that sort of thing."

"I know the feeling," Stano replied.

After checking his phaser rifle as though verifying it had not been damaged, Terrell laid the weapon's barrel on the edge of the section of hull plate forming his end of the hole's fortification. Shifting his stance so that he leaned against the hole's forward wall, he looked up to where Ilucci and Yataro sat atop the *Sagittarius*'s primary hull. "What's the story with the shields, Master Chief?"

"About as good as it's going to get, Skipper," replied Ilucci, not quite shouting. "I've extended the range out to one hundred meters in each direction, but that could stress the generators if we start taking any kind of concentrated assault. I know these guys aren't supposed to have any weapons, but I still don't like it. If the shields go, we may not be able to get them back up."

"Understood," Terrell said. "Do the best you can." He sighed before looking to Stano. "We've done all we can to keep them away from us. Here's hoping we can drive them off before they find a way to get through the shields." It had been at Theriault's recommendation that Ilucci retuned the *Sagittarius*'s shields to extend their reach beyond the ship, in a bid to keep Nimur and the other evolved Tomol from getting close enough to employ their telekinetic abilities. Of course, there was no real way to know how far the Changed's mental powers could reach; Theriault had been making an educated guess based on what she and Tormog had witnessed. Stano had wondered about their defenses and whether they might be up to the formidable task of shielding the Starfleet personnel from Nimur and her followers.

There's really only one way to find out, isn't there?

An energy discharge echoed across the clearing from

her left, near the rear of the *Sagittarius*'s port nacelle and the defensive position designated Station 11. Stano turned to see something impacting against the deflector shield that had been extended almost to the tree line in that direction, ending just before reaching several trees that had been ripped from their roots and toppled from the scout ship's crash landing.

"Here they come!" Stano heard a voice shout from above and behind her, and saw Master Chief Ilucci and Commander Yataro waving aft as something crashed into the deflector shield a second time. Another surge of crimson-hued energy flared at that point, and Stano saw the muzzles of two phaser rifles moving to aim in that direction from the firing position closest to the impact.

"Over here!" came another yell, this time from Stano's right, and she jerked around to see a new burst of light in the distance ahead of the ship's bow. The spark repeated twice in rapid succession, and this time Stano spotted a dark, hulking figure dashing back toward the tree line. Mere seconds later, something hit the shields at the edge of the trees in front of Theriault's hole, and again Stano noted something moving away from the point of contact and disappearing into the forest. The flashes were repeated twice more, each at different points along the perimeter.

Terrell grunted as he lifted his phaser rifle. "Bastards are probing us, looking for a weak spot." Looking over his shoulder and up to the *Sagittarius*, he shouted, "Master Chief! How are the shields?"

"They're hitting different spots, Skipper," replied Ilucci, "and we're reading minor fluctuations at those points of impact, but so far everything's holding."

"Uh-oh." Theriault pointed toward the tree line just as another, much larger flash of crackling reddish-white light erupted at the forest's edge. Stano counted at least five figures—large, dark-skinned reptilian creatures just like the ones into which Nimur and her followers had transformed during their previous skirmish. All of the Changed had slammed as a single projectile into one area of the deflector shield, and even from this distance Stano could hear the crackle of energy, which lasted for several seconds longer than the other strikes.

"Okay, that's different," Ilucci called out from above and behind her. "We've got a power spike here. If they keep that up, we might have a problem!"

Propelled by her own unbound wrath, Nimur threw herself against the barrier she could not see. What was this madness? Some new trick of the Shepherds, brought forth to throw yet another obstacle into her path? Or perhaps the sky people had conjured this feat.

No matter its origins, the invisible wall stood between her and those who threatened her people, inflaming her rage as she lashed out at it. Every strike against the barrier sent lightning strikes of energy blasting into her body, further stoking her fury such that she began to feel the grip on her awareness beginning to ebb. Madness flared in her consciousness, her every thought surrendering to savagery and carnage. She wanted to run and smash and kill, with no regard for her fellow Changed or any Tomol. Her followers registered in her mind, their aggression and violence melding with hers as they too attacked the unseen barricade, but their presence was masked by the bloodlust driving her forward, beyond which Nimur felt nothing save the lone, all-consuming desire to unleash death.

And yet it was Kintaren and the others who offered the merest spark of hope. She felt them gathering near her, using their own bodies to hammer at the barrier, energy flaring with every impact.

There!

Amid the cacophony of light and noise assaulting her heightened senses, she felt it.

Weakness!

The wall had buckled, ever so slightly. She was sure of it.

With renewed verve, Nimur threw herself again at the barrier, allowing its power to wash over her. It inundated every last sliver of her being, as though setting her ablaze from within, but even as she felt the barricade's resistance she also sensed her own body responding in kind, growing stronger the longer she waged this battle. Kintaren's thoughts merged with hers, along with those of Jorn and Bhar and Ayan, offering Nimur reassurance that her followers were channeling their own strength to the fight.

And again, the barrier moved. More, this time.

Fight! her mind screamed. *Fight!* The power drenching her body howled in her ears and blinded her eyes. Her flesh and bones rippled as it defied her.

And then Nimur fell forward and the maelstrom was gone.

Another large strike flashed against the shield, this time at the edge of the forest line just to Stano's left. To her surprise, it was even larger and louder than the previous attack, and this time she could see the deflector shield wavering at the point of contact. As the flare-up began to fade, there was new movement and it took her an additional moment to realize the figure moving across the open ground was coming closer.

Damn.

"We've got a breach!" she shouted, shifting the barrel of her phaser rifle so that she could take aim at the oncoming Tomol. Like its companions, this Changed had taken the form of the hulking, muscled creatures that had attacked them earlier, and with long strides it was eating up the distance separating it from the line of defensive positions.

Beside her, Terrell raised his own weapon to his shoulder. "Fire!" His was the first salvo unleashed at the approaching enemy, a blue-white beam of energy spitting forth and accompanied by the phaser rifle's familiar high-pitched whine. It was followed by three others, Stano's as well as those fired by Theriault and Lerax. The four beams converged on their common target, striking the Changed in its broad chest and stopping the creature in its tracks. It released a piercing howl of pain, stumbling backward several steps before tripping over a fallen tree and crashing to the ground behind it.

Lowering the barrel of his phaser rifle, Terrell blew out his breath. "Tough sons of bitches." Behind them, other flashes against the *Sagittarius*'s extended deflector shields were popping up, but Stano heard no new reports of any Tomol somehow finding a way through the energy barrier.

"That's a neat trick they pulled," she said. "Ganging up on the shields and overloading it at the point of impact? They couldn't have known how to do that."

Terrell frowned. "No, but they don't seem to have any problem learning new things."

From his position in the hole to Stano's left, Lieutenant Hesh called out, "Captain, I am sensing something." Stano saw that the Arkenite's eyes were closed and he was holding one hand to the side of his head, his expression indicating he was experiencing some form of discomfort. "It is as though another consciousness is . . ." The rest of his report faded as the science officer released an agonized grunt and gripped his head in both hands, sinking to his knees and almost out of sight below his hole's parapet. Next to him, Commander Sorak reached out to support his companion, and Stano noticed that the Vulcan also appeared uneasy.

"Sorak?" Terrell said. "Are you all right?"

The tactical officer replied, "I believe Lieutenant Hesh and I are experiencing a psionic assault." He paused, and for the first time his stern façade wavered as his pain became evident. "It does not appear to be a focused attack, but rather a broad sweep. I believe it may be one of the Tomol."

"Damn it," Stano said. "If they get a bead on any of us, they can kill us all."

Behind them, Lieutenant Lerax shouted, "Captain Terrell! My tricorder is picking up two new signals approaching this location. Distance less than two kilometers and moving at a rapid pace. Whatever they are, they appear to be airborne." The Edoan security officer looked up from his tricorder. "I believe they are aerial weapons similar to the ones we encountered before."

As if in response to Lerax's report, Sorak cried out in pain. So startled was Stano by the unexpected outburst that she flinched. "Commander! Are you all right?" She began scrambling from her hole, but the Vulcan held up a hand, gesturing for her to maintain her position.

"I am uninjured."

Still studying his tricorder, Lerax said, "The drones are emitting some kind of signal. It is not a communications frequency, at least as far as I am able to determine."

"I sense it," Sorak reported. He paused, his gaze shifting skyward as though looking for the source of a sound only he could hear. Leaning against the side of his hole as if attempting to steady himself, he added, "I believe the signal is creating a form of psionic dampening effect. The only way to describe it is that areas of my mind seem to have been blocked."

"We've got incoming!" shouted Master Chief Ilucci, and Stano saw the *Sagittarius*'s engineer pointing at something in the distance forward of the ship. In the bright midday sun it was easy to spot the pair of dark shapes moving against the backdrop of clouds and blue-green sky.

Grabbing his communicator, Terrell snapped, "Heads up, people! We've got inbound. Hunker down and be ready for anything."

The drones grew larger and closer with every heartbeat pounding in Stano's ears, along with the cries of alarm and warning coming from the other positions all around the ship. The drones separated, continuing their approach while altering their trajectory to arrive at different sections of the clearing. As they passed the last line of trees at the glade's far edge, Stano saw that they looked identical to the device from their earlier encounter with the Changed, only this time the drones had arrived with their weapons emitters already glowing with harnessed energy. That power was unleashed just as both objects slowed their advance and began hovering over the clearing, with both drones' set of twelve emitters firing continuous streams of intense white light. Even from this stance and behind what she hoped was the hardy protection offered by the *Sagittarius*'s deflector shields, Stano recognized the familiar, and terrifying, results of the beams' fossilization process. Everything in the drones' sights—trees, grass, and soil—was swathed by the fresh layer of rock, which formed in seconds. Like a wave moving across a lake, the hardening effect washed over the clearing until it came into contact with the deflector shields. Visible ripples rolled across the shields' curvature, the supposedly immovable barrier now quivering beneath the onslaught of a possibly unstoppable force.

"Dear god," Terrell said, gripping his phaser rifle though aiming it at nothing, as no targets presented themselves. Ahead of them, an uneven wall of rock was growing, tracing the exterior curvature of the deflector shields and now beginning—at least in some areas—to block out the forest behind it. Looking to either side of her position, Stano beheld the effect in the first stages of crawling up other sections of the shield bubble. The crescendo of colliding energies was increasing, and she was certain she heard a low rumbling or cracking sound as the drones' weapons continued to fuel the petrification effect.

"Skipper!" yelled Ilucci. "There's no way our shields can take much more of this!"

20

Nimur rose from the soil, her body already shaking off the effects of the fire lances. She had barely managed to force her way through their unseen obstacle before their weapons found her, uniting in their quest to defeat her. Despite her rapid recovery, there could be no denying that the sky people's weapons were formidable. It was only through chance and her strengthening body that she had not been left helpless and at their mercy long enough for them to kill her, but the moment was past, and she was whole once more.

Her efforts, along with those of her fellow Changed, had not been wasted. Nimur was now within the barrier, and without its interference she was better able to sense the thoughts of those who hid behind its protection. Sky people and Tomol alike were here, and seeing her own people aligning themselves with these insolent strangers ignited her anger anew.

You will pay.

But now there was something else demanding to be heard, a rush of sound permeating the air and even the ground beneath her feet. What dark magic might this be? All around her, beyond the confines of the barrier that had tested her, Nimur saw a wall of stone growing as if from nothing at all, encircling the clearing in which the sky-ship rested. It reminded her of what she had seen at the crater where the other ship had fallen from the stars. The searing fires of the Endless had come again, dispatched by the wordstone that continued in its mission to keep the Tomol servile and stagnant for reasons only the Shepherds understood. Nimur realized that if she remained here, she would be trapped within the stone, in the eternal grasp of the Endless. But could she escape? It had taken the combined efforts of Kintaren and the others to help push her through the sky people's invisible wall. How could she get back without that aid?

Wait. Of course!

What of the Tomol she had detected here, those who had allied themselves with the sky people? She pushed her thoughts outward, searching for the familiar sensations that had caught her attention at the start of the attack. Yes, they were here, and within two of them she felt the spark she now knew so well. It lay within each of them, all but dormant yet perceptible to her. Reaching into their minds, she found that small shard of warmth and drew it outward, basking in the glow they offered as they grew stronger.

Accept the gift that has been kept from you.

Then, one of the minds reached out to touch hers, and Nimur was startled to discover that the probing carried with it wisps of intimate association. The consciousness extending itself toward her carried with it all the closeness of hands on her bare skin, hands she knew as well as her own.

Kerlo?

Nimur? No! What have you done?

What is necessary. Soon you will understand.

She felt his resistance as well as his fear, but by now it

was too late. The ember she had found within him had grown to the point that extinguishing it was impossible. It already was flowing through him, and she sensed him growing stronger, but so too was something else. Even as Kerlo submitted himself to the Change, the wrath of the Endless was continuing its unrelenting advance, pushing inward on the sky people and their ship. It seemed as though the Shepherds and their metal birds were determined to claim victory today. She heard their incessant buzzing as they attempted to cast her into the clutches of the Endless.

I will not yield.

Movement in the distance caught her eye, and Nimur saw Kintaren leaping over the stone wall and landing on the grass well within the boundary of the unseen wall. Had it fallen? Whatever the cause, Nimur was buoyed by the arrival of her sister. Now inside the shield they thought would protect them, the sky people would be at their mercy.

Kintaren, running across the open expanse of broken terrain, was caught by the beams of four fire lances, all joining to strike her chest. She staggered in the face of the attack before falling just as Nimur herself had done, sagging to the ground.

No!

Leaping into the air, Nimur felt her body transforming again. The wings returned, sprouting from her back as bone and muscle stretched and twisted to assume the new shapes. Beneath her feet the ground fell away as she took to flight, extending her newly formed claws as she darted to where Kintaren lay. Even if they failed to destroy the sky people today, Nimur would not leave her sister behind.

All around her, the shriek of the metal birds filled the air, and she felt them drawing closer, hunting her.

I will not yield!

All around the *Sagittarius*, the wall of rock continued to grow, layering itself atop the curved barrier of the ship's deflector shields. The field cracked and flashed in protest from the force of whatever was being thrown against it by the Preserver drones, and the clash of energies was thunderous even where Stano hunkered next to Terrell in their hole. Stano guessed that the petrification effect had risen at least ten meters above the ground on all sides, forming a solid dome around the ship.

"Those damned things are going to bury us," snapped Terrell. Then he flinched as the area of deflector shield twenty meters above their heads cracked and popped. "Some days, I really miss ships that can't land." Into his communicator, he said, "Master Chief! Can the ship's phasers punch through this stuff?"

His voice sounding harried, Ilucci replied, *"It's taking everything we've got just to keep the shields up! One crisis at a time, please!"*

An earsplitting buzz pierced the air, loud enough to make Stano wince, and she heard Ilucci unleashing a string of profanity celebrating at least a half dozen languages from his position atop the *Sagittarius*'s primary hull. All around them, intense bursts of harsh white energy heralded the loss of the deflector shields, and Stano looked up to see the chief engineer waving his arms.

"That's it!" he shouted. "The generators reset to prevent an overload. Two minutes to get the shields back."

Terrell, dividing his attention between Ilucci and their now exposed perimeter, grunted in irritation. "Shit. This'll be over in two minutes."

"Look!" shouted Theriault.

Stano was still wondering how the fossilization effect had not already washed over them but instead seemed to have halted, but she pushed aside such thoughts at the sight of a single figure leaping over the edge of the rock barrier. It dropped to the ground inside the shield perimeter, landing on the grass with a grace that in almost any other circumstance she might find beautiful. It pushed off from its touchdown point and lunged forward, aiming for the *Sagittarius*.

"Get it!" Terrell snapped as he and Stano maneuvered their phaser rifles into position to take a shot. All of Lerax's planning with respect to fields of fire was abandoned as everyone with a sight line on the approaching creature took aim at it. Stano and Terrell fired at the same time, with Lerax and Theriault joining in as four phaser beams struck the Changed in the upper torso. It remained standing for several seconds before collapsing backward onto the ground.

"That's how we do that," Terrell said, but his victory was short-lived as Stano detected other movement in the area. Bringing her phaser rifle back to her shoulder, she turned and searched for the new threat.

"There!" she shouted, in time for Terrell, Lerax, and Theriault to see another Changed, this one sprouting wings as it transformed into one of the flying creatures that had attacked them earlier. With a great leap, it left the ground, wings stretched out and back as it rose into the air, only to be caught in the sweep of the drone's energy beam. The creature's body halted in flight, encased in a calcified cocoon and suspended three or four meters above the ground atop a column of rock.

"Son of a bitch," Stano said, scarcely daring to believe what had just transpired.

"Better him than us," Terrell countered. He said nothing else, and the only thing Stano could hear was the sound of the captain's accelerated breathing. Then it dawned on her that no other sounds seemed to be intruding on her. After the cacophony that had dominated the previous several minutes, the near silence was startling.

Theriault said, "I'll be damned. It stopped. Another couple of minutes, and we'd have been trapped beneath that stuff."

"Small favors," Terrell replied, raising his phaser rifle as though taking aim at the drone.

"Don't!" Stano warned, waving her free hand. "Everything we've seen says they don't care about us, but that doesn't mean you want to piss them off."

Terrell nodded, lowering his weapon. "Good point." He reached for his communicator. "Terrell to all hands. Do not fire on the drone. I repeat: *Do not fire on the drone*. Stay alert in case any of the Tomol managed to slip through." He and Stano watched the device hovering just beyond the highest point of the wall its weapons had created. After a moment, it banked and fell out of sight, the hum of its engine or whatever powered it fading to nothingness.

"Okay, now what?" Terrell asked, though Stano got the sense he was talking to no one in particular. "Did they get all of the Changed this time? Lerax, what's the story?"

Still with Theriault in their defensive position to Stano's right, the Edoan said, "Scanning now, Captain. The Changed life signs we detected earlier are stationary. I believe all but one of them were caught by the preservation effect. As for the remaining Changed, it appears to be making a hasty retreat."

"I'll want visual confirmation on the ones that got caught, and keep your eyes on that last one, in case it decides to double back," Terrell replied, scrambling out of the hole and making his way toward the one occupied by Sorak and Hesh. "Commander? How are you two?"

The Vulcan replied, "The effects I was feeling have dissipated, Captain. I no longer sense whatever dampening signal the drones were broadcasting, and the psionic assault we experienced earlier also has ceased."

"Thank the drones for that," Stano said as she moved to stand beside Terrell.

The captain added, "I want Babitz to give you both a once-over as soon as possible, just to be on the safe side."

"Understood," Sorak replied. "It was, however, a most interesting sensation. I would be curious to learn how the drones were able to combat the Changed Tomol's telepathic attacks, and whether it means they also have the power to counter the other telekinetic abilities we have witnessed."

Stano said, "He's got a point. It'd be nice to know what other tricks the Preservers have—or had—up their sleeves."

"We can worry about all of that after we get the ship fixed and out of here." Terrell gestured toward the rock barrier that had sprung up around the *Sagittarius*. "I don't want to be here if any more Changed decide to attack us again, particularly if the drones come back and finish what they started. Vanessa, keep a security detail watching the perimeter just in case, but everybody else is on working detail until we're airborne." He eyed Stano. "That means your people, too, Commander. We're stuck with each other for the time being."

Offering identical crisp nods, Stano and Theriault responded in unison, "Aye, sir."

"Master Chief!" Terrell shouted, directing his attention to Ilucci and Commander Yataro atop the ship's saucer section. "Let's get on the rest of the repairs. I think it's safe to say we've overstayed our welcome."

Ilucci looked up from the work he and Yataro were doing. "On it, Skipper!"

Weapons fire from somewhere close interrupted the exchange, making Stano cringe as she whirled toward the sound and raised her phaser rifle. Searching for whatever new threat might be nearby, she saw two members of Lerax's security detail firing their phasers at a running figure she recognized as Kerlo. The Tomol had dropped his lance and was sprinting away from the ship across the open ground, dodging and weaving as though anticipating the phaser beams approaching him from behind.

"What the hell?" Stano shouted. She started to move toward the security officers only to hear additional phaser fire from elsewhere around the perimeter. Members of her landing party and the *Sagittarius* crew were calling out warnings or pleas for help, all of it emphasized by the whine of weapons discharges.

Behind her, she heard Lerax say, "Kerlo! He's undergone the initial stages of the Change."

"We've got to stop him," Terrell snapped. "The drones might sense him in here and come back. If that happens, we're screwed."

Dropping to one knee, Stano sighted down the length of her phaser rifle and took aim at the fleeing Kerlo, but before she could fire, the Tomol had reached the newly formed rock barrier surrounding the *Sagittarius*. The wall at this point had risen only a few meters, which Kerlo cleared with an effortless leap, dropping out of sight. It took Terrell an additional minute to verify that another of his companions had likewise made a similar escape.

"It looks like two of them made the change," said the voice of Ensign Zane, one of Lerax's security officers, over Stano's communicator. *"They killed the others. It happened so fast, Commander. I don't get it."*

"What the hell was that about?" Terrell asked, turning to Stano and Theriault. "They flipped at the same damned time?"

Theriault said, "It had to be Nimur, Skipper. Tormog told us he saw her trigger the Change in other Tomol."

"Neat trick," Terrell said.

Stano gestured toward the stone barrier. "If Nimur's somewhere out there, buried in the rock, that might be enough to throw off the rest of the Tomol who've Changed, at least for a little while. It could be a chance for us to regroup." It was not much of a plan, she knew, but at the moment it was all they had, and she was certain that whatever reprieve she and her companions had been granted would at best be fleeting. "We could use the *Masao* to track Kerlo and the others. If we could get to them quickly, we might be able to subdue them before they get too powerful or—worse—trigger the Change in other Tomol." There were hundreds of Tomol in the village, many of them perhaps still oblivious to the most recent developments involving Nimur and her followers.

"We don't even know how many Changed there might be now," Terrell said. "Besides, anybody willing to bet that any of them can't do what Nimur was able to do? Or maybe they can't right now, but what about after they continue to evolve?"

Theriault asked, "So what's the plan, Skipper?"

"Same as before," Terrell replied. "Patch up the ship and get the hell out of here."

21

"Nurse Amos, a moment, please?"

The young lieutenant had returned to her desk in the examination room of the *Endeavour* sickbay, and Leone waved her over to where he was working at the medical section's lab table. He tried not to shake his head in bemusement as Amos smiled before setting aside her work and walking—no, bounding—across the office space separating the lab from the patient treatment area.

Where the hell does she get all that energy?

Not for the first time, he pondered the unassailable fact that Holly Amos, regardless of the situation or even the time of day, seemed to have no shortage of enthusiasm or spring in her step. Upon her arrival aboard ship during its recent extensive repairs, resupply, and crew rotation at Starbase 12 prior to setting out on its new mission into the Taurus Reach, the nurse had demonstrated the usual overflowing eagerness befitting young Starfleet personnel embarking on their first assignment. At first, Leone had taken it in stride, chalking up her personality to youthful exuberance that would temper in time. Even Captain Khatami had mentioned it, teasing him that she would be a good influence in sickbay, a counter to his usual somber and even sardonic demeanor.

Because I'm just not cheerful enough all by myself.

"Hi!" Amos said as she approached the lab table, her

smile wide and her teeth almost bright enough to act as an independent light source. Then, as though realizing that she might be overdoing things even by her standards, her expression turned serious. "I mean, yes, Doctor? You wanted to see me?"

"Um, hi," Leone said, unable to completely suppress a reflexive sneer. He nodded in the general direction of the sickbay's patient ward. "How's our guest?"

Turning her head fast enough that the dark locks of her regulation bob hairstyle looked as though they might separate from her head, the nurse looked at their young Tomol charge, resting quietly. "Seta? I think she's holding up well enough. She's a really tough kid. Between what's happened on her planet and everything she's trying to understand up here, she seems to be handling it." She frowned. "A lot better than I would've been able to do at her age."

"Now, *that* I find hard to believe," Leone said.

Amos smiled. "I had a pretty hectic childhood, Doctor. Starfleet brat, getting dragged to eleven different starbases and planet-based duty assignments before I graduated high school, but that's nothing compared to what she's dealing with."

Tapping a control on the terminal interface, Leone instructed the computer to carry out the next step in the testing he was conducting. "You've been talking?" he asked, moving away from the workstation.

The nurse nodded. "Absolutely. She likes me."

Leone was happy to hear that his plan—somewhat sneaky but not at all sinister—was beginning to have a positive effect. Having Amos talk with Seta in the hopes of the young Tomol girl becoming comfortable around her and by extension the rest of the *Endeavour* crew would go a long way toward earning her trust as they worked together to understand not only her role as leader of her people but also what he and the rest of the crew could do to help her. "What have you been talking about?"

"Everything," Amos replied. "Her life here, her training to be Holy Sister and eventually take over as priestess from her mentor, the laws and rituals surrounding her people, including their commitment to sacrificing themselves when the time came—all of it. The Tomol pretty much live their lives in a perpetual fast-forward mode, Doctor. They take in a lot at a young age, far more than anything you or I had to deal with as teenagers."

"I don't remember that far back," Leone said. "How's she *doing*, though? I mean, since we brought her aboard?" Exposing someone from a primitive culture to the wonder that was a starship orbiting the planet they called home would be a shock for anyone, regardless of her age, and while the doctor had of course been concerned about Seta's reaction, his gut instinct told him that the girl would adapt in short order to her new surroundings. She exuded an inner strength that belied her handful of years, he decided, even more so than what she had been required to demonstrate just as a matter of course for a Tomol and after being tossed into the proverbial deep end so far as her new leadership role.

"Aside from that one incident, she's been fine." Amos shrugged. "Kids adapt."

Leone grunted. "I appreciate your helping her through that. Adolescent emotional outbursts never were my strong suit." He paused, realizing his off-the-cuff comment had given him something new to consider. "When you think about it, this is probably the first real crisis that any of them have experienced in their lives, I mean *ever*." When Amos frowned, obviously uncertain where he was going with this, he added, "Think about it. With no one on that planet who's older than . . . what? Twenty? They have no one from a previous generation to tell them how tough things were in the old days, or that a crisis is survivable. They can't look to older relatives or friends for help or advice when there's a problem, and as problems go down there, someone deciding not to jump into that fire pit is a big damned deal."

Amos nodded. "That makes perfect sense, and it has to be unthinkable that someone would bring such pain to his or her own village. Seta knows her people must be lost down there trying to figure things out, and the one person they look to for answers is the Holy Sister, and where is she? Eating ice cream."

Scowling, Leone looked through the window separating the lab from sickbay's front office but could not see the young Tomol. "Really? Ice cream?"

"Hey, it was your idea, remember?" Amos hooked a thumb over her shoulder, toward the patient ward. "It blew her mind. She's a fiend for the stuff."

"Better than french fries, anyway." It had been Leone's suggestion to let Seta try the dessert, which was one of his few real vices. As silly as it might sound for a man of his years to admit, a bowl of ice cream was one of his preferred methods of relaxing at the end of a long day. It also had fewer detrimental side effects than bourbon. "Let's not tell the captain about that, all right? For all we know, introducing french fries and ice cream to a prewarp civilization is a Prime Directive violation."

His workstation, silent for the past few moments, beeped to alert him that the program he had been running had completed. "Hey, come look at this. I want a second set of eyes on something." As Amos stepped toward the lab table, he pivoted the computer terminal so that she could see its display.

"Are you looking at the Tomol helix?" Amos leaned closer, her eyes narrowing as she studied the image on the computer screen, which depicted a strand of Tomol DNA.

"Yeah. Now watch this." Leone reached for the terminal's keypad and entered a sequence. "This is a computer simulation of the tests I've been running." On the screen, a flood of small blue particles swept across the image of the slowly twirling DNA helix. In short order the particles began attaching themselves to the helix, concentrating on a single section of the strand before beginning to disassemble.

"Those look like virions," Amos said, to which Leone replied with a silent nod. "Are you infecting the Tomol with a virus?"

Leone made a show of holding one finger to his lips. "Just watch," he said in a deliberate stage whisper.

The computer screen depicted the severed ends of the helix as they started to lengthen, carrying the virions along the new segments that had formed, before reattaching themselves to the point of the original split.

"It's replicating code and repairing the genome," Amos said. "You're creating new genetic material."

Impressed with her summation, Leone replied, "In theory, yes, based on the existing material and gaps of information that predictably should be there, and letting the new sequences fill in the blanks. I've run this model over and over, and I think it'll reset the Tomol's genetic profile back to the way it was before it was first altered."

Amos frowned. "So this won't eliminate the Change?"

"No, we don't want to take that away," Leone said. "The Tomol were always supposed to evolve in that manner, but without turning into destructive psychopaths along the way. I'm basically trying to cancel out the errant genetic coding introduced by the Shedai and allow whatever's left to carry on without the extra piece. It was Klisiewicz who pointed me in this direction. Once we started thinking of this from the standpoint of how the Shedai likely would've tried to correct the problem, some things started to make sense."

He pointed to the helix on the screen and indicated sections of the simulation that were highlighted in yellow. "See these areas? These are parts of the sequencing that—as far as the computer's able to determine—don't belong there. They're not part of the Tomol's natural DNA. I mean, they are in a sense, since every Tomol's born with them, and we're talking about genetic manipulation that would've happened hundreds of thousands of years ago and passed on from generation to generation. Still, even after all this time, these markers have Shedai fingerprints all over them. Klisiewicz made the point that whatever the Shedai did would've been motivated by their desire to control the Tomol rather than trying to cure or help them, so anything they did would still show in the genetic code as something that's not supposed to be there in the first place." He tapped the computer monitor. "So we basically built a synthetic virus designed to seek out, hunt down, and rewrite anything within a genetic sequence that's determined to be not part of the whole, using existing information to fill in the resulting gaps."

"I don't understand," Amos said. "I read the report Doctor Babitz sent from her own analysis of the Tomol. According to her, entire sequences of their DNA had been replaced by the Shedai with their own genome segments, and there was no way to know what had been taken out of the original code, and to attempt a resequencing like this would be hazardous if not fatal to the Tomol."

"Oh, ye of little faith," Leone said. Again, he indicated the computer model. "We have Mister Klisiewicz to thank for this bright idea, too. Instead of looking at this like a geneticist, he took a different approach and came at it like someone writing a computer program. It was his idea to create what I'm calling a 'generic marker,' or basically an 'adapter.' He says he stole the idea from the Shedai themselves, based on some research he did back when we were involved with Vanguard." He paused. "By the way, you know the first rule of Vanguard is that we don't talk about Vanguard, right? I mean, ever? As in, once we're done here, you flush it from your brain and forget we ever had this talk?"

Her eyes widening, Amos nodded. "Yes, Doctor."

Satisfied, Leone continued, "Good. I'd hate to see Admiral Nogura fly all the way out here from Earth just to kick both our asses." He rapped his hands on the lab table. "Okay, back to work. Klisiewicz's idea seems to have paid off. It took us a while to work out all the particulars, since there are no examples of the Shedai metagenome to work from, but the kid was a champ. He helped me work out the genetic sequencing models with the computer, and we even managed to conceptualize in pretty crude fashion the missing segments of the original Tomol genetic segments. Once we did that, we had everything we needed to let our new generic marker go and do its seek-and-find thing. If all goes according to plan, the Tomol will still change, but now that cycle won't be interrupted or hijacked by the Shedai elements of their genetic code."

"What about those who are already Changed?"

There's the rub, Leone mused. "Good question. I don't have a sample of that DNA, so I can't run any tests to determine if this will work the same way for them. Besides, we may never even get close enough to one to take a sample, let alone administer any cure we come up with."

Nodding in understanding, Amos said, "There are nearly fifteen hundred Tomol down there." She shook her head. "I guess we'd better get started synthesizing the compound."

"Yeah." Leone ran a hand through his hair. "And we'll also need equal doses of a general antibiotic and antipyretic that works with Tomol physiology." He gestured toward the computer. "According to the computer model, the patient appears at risk of developing a pretty nasty fever while undergoing the genetic resequencing. The scenarios show the febrile neutropenia kicking in anywhere from two minutes to six hours after the viral agent is introduced. In English, that means every patient's going to be different, but we knew that already, because that's the way it always is."

"I can start searching the pharmaceutical database for something compatible with Tomol physiology," Amos said.

Waving toward the computer again, Leone replied, "I've worked out the basics already. We just need to refine it."

Amos smiled. "Sounds easy enough. I'll get started."

"Great," Leone said, stifling a sudden yawn. "Now if you don't mind, I think I'd like to get something to eat before slipping into a coma." The evening plans were shaping up nicely, but he put that thought on hold as the intercom beeped.

"Bridge to sickbay," said the voice of Lieutenant Klisiewicz.

Keying the companel on the wall behind the table, the doctor said, "Sickbay, Leone here."

"Just letting you know that the captain's cleared us for the landing party, Doctor," replied the *Endeavour*'s science officer. *"Our shuttlecraft departs in ninety minutes."*

Leone scowled. "And we're still going with the idea that something on the planet won't want to shoot us down when we try to land?"

"Doesn't seem to be an issue, at least for the moment. We've reentered orbit and there's been no reaction. We're keeping sensors away from the underground caverns, and the captain figures there's really only one way to find out how the obelisk might react to a shuttlecraft."

"I suppose you're right," Leone said, trying to sound more confident than he felt. "Anything new from Commander Stano?" He had been told by Khatami about the attack on the *Sagittarius*, and that unlike their first skirmish with the Changed, this encounter thankfully had not yielded any casualties from the scout ship's crew or the *Endeavour*'s landing party.

"They're finalizing repairs to the Sagittarius *and getting ready to move. There's not much we can do for them at the moment, but maybe the Preservers can show us some other way to help. See you on the hangar deck, Doctor. Klisiewicz out."*

The connection terminated and Leone leaned against the lab table, drawing a long, deep breath. "I guess that's that, then." Looking to Amos, he said, "Feel like another excursion?"

Amos nodded. "Of course!"

Was there no crushing this woman's enthusiasm?

"Let Seta know we'll be leaving soon," Leone said, "and let's work up some doses of the viral agent and our accompanying antibiotic. We may as well give that a shot, too."

"Right away, Doctor." Amos departed the lab area, leaving Leone to talk to no one but himself.

He sighed, shaking his head. "So much for dinner and a coma."

22

Advancing through the forest, Kerlo felt his mental abilities growing stronger with every step. Trees bent or broke at his approach, falling away and clearing a path through the undergrowth as he pressed forward. Though he was certain he did not yet command the level of power exhibited by Nimur, there was no mistaking the heat growing within him, along with an increasing awareness of the world around him and even his place in it.

This was the clarity of which Nimur had spoken with such conviction, the implicit, instinctive understanding of the potential he harbored and that all Tomol possessed.

Kerlo had been a fool to deny what his wife had tried to show him. The energy radiating from his body and from his mind was rightfully his, just as it had been the birthright of every Tomol. That it had been denied to him and his people for uncounted generations infuriated him, though there remained a part of him that could not believe that the Shepherds, who had taken such steps to safeguard them here on this world, had done so for malevolent purposes.

Questions lingered, and while instinct told him he and his people were meant to evolve in this manner, he could not deny the swelling sensation that the Tomol somehow had been betrayed, whether by the Shepherds or another party.

And what of the sky people and their allegiances?

They already had demonstrated their willingness to fight and even kill Nimur and any of the other Changed who threatened them, but Kerlo knew that any danger they posed was limited, and growing weaker with every moment. Soon they would be helpless before the unfettered power he and his people wielded, but the sky people must not be destroyed. To that end, he had instructed his followers not to kill them but instead to capture and bring them to him. He did not need all of them, of course, but there was no way to know who among the group of intruders would provide the most value, for despite their collective weakness before the Changed, they still held one thing of value: their sky-ships. At least one or two of the interlopers would be of use in obtaining access to the ships, and with those at their disposal, Kerlo and his people did not need to remain confined to this one world. Perhaps there were Tomol living elsewhere among the stars, waiting to be reunited with others of their kind and to have their true potential revealed to them.

We need the sky-ships.

Cries of alarm and the sounds of movement echoed through the forest, and Kerlo could discern through the trees the silhouettes of numerous Tomol running along the winding trail that connected the village with the Caves of the Shepherds. He suspected that his fellow Tomol would seek shelter in the caverns, and it was likely that a significant number of his people had already found their way into the subterranean passages.

Would the wordstone protect them?

It had failed to do so when Nimur had entered that sacred realm, but Kerlo did not discount the possibility of Seta, the new priestess, having found some new weapon to use against him and his fellow Changed. Was it she who had unleashed upon them the flying weapons that had doomed Nimur and other Changed to the fate shared by the other Endless? Kerlo's thoughts still were haunted by the image of his wife, imprisoned within the stone shroud, perhaps for eternity. Might Seta be able to turn those weapons upon Kerlo and his followers?

There also were the sky people, who wielded their own versions of the fire lances carried by the Wardens, but even those had proved to be of only limited effectiveness. Still, Kerlo knew that he did not yet possess the strength exhibited by Nimur, so there remained a tangible risk to him and those he led. Therefore, the best course of action now was to attack with speed and ferocity, in the hopes of overcoming the sky people before they could assert any kind of advantage.

We also are outnumbered, and there is only one way to address that disparity.

23

As the shuttlecraft *Simone*'s personnel hatch depressurized and slid open, Leone was the first one to disembark from the compact vessel, and as his boots touched the ground he gave serious thought to kneeling and kissing the soil.

"I want to thank you for that ride, Ensign Gaulke," he said, looking back into the shuttle's passenger cabin as Klisiewicz stepped through the hatch.

"Anytime, Doctor," replied Adam Gaulke, the security officer charged with piloting the *Simone*. "All part of the service. Sorry about the bumps, though."

The flight down from the *Endeavour* had been anything but dull, thanks to the Preservers and their unpredictable planetary defense system. Though the ancient, inanimate artifact had taken no apparent notice of the starship's return to geosynchronous orbit over Suba, it had exhibited a keen interest in the *Simone*'s passage through the atmosphere and down to the ground, despite Ensign Gaulke's best efforts to give a wide berth to the mountain containing the Preserver complex, at least until whatever monitoring systems that were tracking the shuttlecraft determined that it was unarmed or otherwise posed no discernible threat. Those few moments had been harrowing, to say the least, though Gaulke had executed a series of impressive evasive maneuvers to avoid the two attempts by the defense system to bring down the tiny vessel. Following that bit of momentary excitement, the ensign had brought the *Simone* to an uneventful landing in a clearing near the Tomol village.

"If you find my stomach in there, let me know, all right?" Leone said as he waited for Seta and Nurse Amos to exit the shuttlecraft, followed by security officers Carlton McMurray and Derek Zapien.

"Looks like we've got a bit of a hike ahead of us," Klisiewicz said, nodding toward the trail that Leone knew connected the village with the entrance to the caverns containing the Preserver pyramid. "Guess that's my own fault, though. I'm the one who suggested not landing too close to the caves." He gestured toward the security guards. "Ensign McMurray, you're with me. Zapien, you'll go with the doctor, and Gaulke will stay with the shuttle." Turning to the pilot, he added, "Keep the sensors active and your eyes open. If we get any unwanted company, get the shuttle out of here and back to the *Endeavour*. We can always call you back, but we don't want any of the Changed getting their hands on it." That was just another part of the plan that bothered Leone, as the starship's transporters still were under repair.

Gaulke nodded. "Aye, sir."

With everyone taking charge of the equipment they had brought with them, Klisiewicz and McMurray set off up the trail. Shouldering a satchel containing—among other items—doses of the viral agent he and Amos had synthesized, Leone began walking the short distance to the village. Sensing movement to his right, he saw Seta hurrying her pace in order to walk alongside him.

"Are you sure you want to go through with this?" he asked. "I don't think anyone would think less of you if you changed your mind." When he had explained to her how his viral agent was intended to work—how it would allow the Tomol to undergo the Change as their ancestors originally had experienced it, but without the debilitating psychological effects that were an outgrowth of the Shedai's tampering uncounted millennia ago—Seta at first had been wary, but the girl's uncertainty was quickly replaced by the resolve of the leader she had become. She had accepted his explanation and conveyed her trust in him, and then surprised him by taking his idea one step further with her suggestion of explaining to her people the bold decision she had made.

"I am the leader of my people," Seta said. "Who better to show them that your desire to help us is genuine? Also, how can I expect them to trust me if I do not demonstrate my willingness to accept your treatment?"

Pretty sharp, kid.

The path turned and bent through the woods, widening as they approached the outskirts of the village. Even now Leone saw some of the same structures he had encountered during their first visit, along with larger buildings and huts in the distance toward the village square. Though she said nothing, Seta increased her pace and now was walking in front of Leone, leading the small party. Tomol who observed their approach began gathering along their path.

"Gather everyone!" Seta shouted, holding out her hands. "Tell them that we will meet at the village square." There were murmurs from the crowd as Seta's instructions were passed on, and as the priestess continued walking, many of the Tomol fell in behind Leone and the others. In short order there were dozens of villagers walking with them, and more were adding themselves to the procession. To either side of the main thoroughfare, Leone saw still more Tomol moving between huts and other structures, but everyone seemed to be heading in the same general direction.

Everybody loves a party.

The village square was, as far as he could tell, exactly what its name implied: a mostly rectangular expanse of open space bounded on all sides by several of the settlement's larger and more ornate structures. Its sole feature was a raised dais at its center, and villagers already were gathering around the platform, leaving a path to it clear for Seta.

Two Tomol women, whom Leone thought he recognized from his previous visit to the village, emerged from the crowd, carrying the feathered ceremonial garb Seta had worn during his first encounter with the priestess. They helped her drape the elaborate garment across her shoulders, which reminded Leone that despite her young age, she carried a weighty responsibility well beyond her years. Now suitably attired, Seta ascended the dais and stood at its center, waiting in silence as villagers continued to stream into the square. According to the chronometer on Leone's tricorder, it took nearly twenty minutes for what he guessed was the balance of the village's population to make their way to the gathering place. From where he, Amos, and Zapien stood next to the dais, the doctor looked out upon the hundreds of faces looking toward their priestess, and he could hear the rumbling of numerous conversations taking place throughout the crowd. On the stage, Seta stood silent, waiting, and Leone could not help but be impressed by her poise at being the focus of so many expectant people.

"Kid's got guts," Zapien said.

Amos nodded. "You better believe it."

A group of four Tomol, two females and two males, dressed in ceremonial garb that was similar to Seta's robes but less adorned with colorful feathers, moved through the crowd and stepped onto the dais, each taking a position at one of the platform's corners. This seemed to be an understood signal of some sort, as Leone noticed an immediate cessation of chatter among the gathered Tomol. Within moments, the entire square fell quiet, the silence so complete that the doctor was able to hear Seta draw a long breath before raising her arms as though to embrace the audience.

"Thank you for joining me. I know that this is a time of difficulty for all of us. One of our own has embraced the Change, and as it has been told to us for generations, you have seen the destruction she has wrought. You have felt the fear she brings. We have lost many friends and loved ones, both to death and to Nimur's influence.

"But I am here to tell you that I have seen a way for us to emerge from this trial. The Shepherds have given us the tools so that we might see ourselves through these troublesome times, but we cannot do it alone." For the first time, she gestured toward Leone, Amos, and Zapien. "These are friends, who have traveled a great distance and who now stand ready to help us. With Priestess Ysan's tragic passing, they have helped me to understand what I must do as your Holy Sister. I trust them with my life, just as you have pledged your trust to me."

"What can they do to help us against the Changed?" a voice called from the audience. Several shouts of support accompanied the question, and a renewed murmuring swept over the crowd.

"That is but one of the things they have pledged to help us understand. As you all know from the stories given to us by the Shepherds and the wordstone, each of us will embrace the Change if we do not commit to the Cleansing. What we have not understood—what has never been explained to us—are the true reasons for the lives we lead here on Suba. Nimur was right when she tried to tell us that the Change is not a scourge or a punishment! We were always meant to ascend in this way, to achieve a higher form of existence, but the Dark Gods who once enslaved our ancestors perverted that destiny. They twisted our people ages ago, using us to secure their own selfish desires."

The mumbles of confusion were getting louder, but to her credit Seta ignored them. She moved about the dais, making sure to look in each direction so that she made contact with all her fellow Tomol. Tapping her chest, she said, "Here, inside each of us, deep within our blood and bone, is the truth." She pointed to Leone with one hand while holding up her other arm. "This man and his friends showed me that when the Shepherds brought our forebears here from our world far away among the most distant of stars, it was to protect us from what the Dark Gods had done to us. They did not know how to help our people, so they left us here to live in peace. We can still do that, but without the need for the Cleansing, and without a need to fear the Change!"

"How is that possible?" another voice shouted.

"We are to become like Nimur?"

"The Shepherds will see us cast for all time among the Endless!"

For the first time, Seta appeared nervous, and Leone could see that the young priestess was beginning to fear that she was losing the support of her followers. She looked to Leone, who nodded and offered what he hoped was a smile of encouragement. After a moment, she seemed to regain her bearing and straightened her posture. Around her on the dais, the four robed Tomol were raising their arms, attempting to reestablish order among the assembled villagers. Only when the crowd returned to silence did Seta speak again.

"I understand your doubts. I understand your fear. I have only been a priestess for a short time, but many of you know me from my apprenticeship under Ysan. You know that I am not rash or given to pretense." Once more, she gestured to Leone. "These friends of mine are healers, and they are ready to help us cast off the madness that grips us when the Change comes. They will help us take back the very birthright that has been withheld from us."

"What will they do to us?" asked one of the villagers standing just a few meters from Leone, his wide, golden eyes studying the doctor with obvious distrust. It required physical effort for the doctor not to reach for the phaser on his hip, and he cast a glance at Zapien, shaking his head to tell the ensign not to draw his weapon either.

"He has brought a medicine," Seta said, "a medicine he

made for us. Once given, it will allow us to welcome the Change as we were meant to, without the curse placed upon us so long ago by the Dark Gods. We will be free to live in peace and to explore the destiny denied us for countless generations."

"How do we know this is not a deception?" cried another doubter. "How can we be sure?"

"There is but one way to be sure," Seta said, moving back toward Leone and the others. "The medicine must be given to us. I shall be the first. I will take it to prove to you that it is not a threat. However, as the time of my Change will not come for several sun-turns, we will not know if this will work on me for some time. There are those among us whose time is coming much sooner. If you are willing, you too can take the medicine after you see that it does not harm me. Only when the time of Change comes to you will we know for certain."

She paused, staring out at the hundreds of faces looking back at her, and Leone noted the varying expressions of the Tomol nearest to them. Indecision, skepticism, fear, and worry, of course, but he also saw . . . anticipation? He could not be sure.

Seta, on the other hand, seemed confident. Turning to Leone, she smiled once again. "Are you ready, Leone?"

"Wait!"

The sharp voice was loud enough to make Leone turn to look for the source, and his eyes widened. Two Tomol males, strapping specimens, to say the least, were making their way through the crowd, and the doctor again stopped his hand's movement toward his phaser. Zapien stepped forward, his hand dropping to his hip, and Amos moved back a step until she bumped into the dais. Before Leone or Zapien could brandish his weapon, the two villagers stopped before the platform.

"We choose to stand with the Holy Sister," said one of the Tomol. Looking to Leone, he added, "Give us your medicine as you would Seta."

Leone felt his eyebrows rising as though they might try to hide themselves under his hair. "Really?" Then he realized that other Tomol, males and females, were emerging from the crowd. Each of them in turn made a similar pledge to Seta.

"I'll be damned," Amos said.

"Okay," Leone replied. "Me, too, I guess." As he spoke, he heard new rumblings from the crowd, but the tone now was noticeably different. The villagers, a portion of them, at least, seemed to be favoring what was happening at the dais.

Beaming with pride in the confidence and trust bestowed upon her, Seta stepped down from the dais, touching each of the Tomol volunteers on the arm before moving to stand before Leone. "Shall we begin?"

The obelisk was a gold mine. Of this, Stephen Klisiewicz held no doubts whatsoever.

"I can hear your jaw hitting the ground even up here, Lieutenant," said Captain Khatami over the speaker of his open communicator. *"What have you found?"*

Standing before the polished bronzelike artifact situated in the middle of the massive underground cavern, Klisiewicz's first instinct as he beheld the ancient construct was to shout, "Everything!" He managed to maintain his composure and instead replied, "With Seta's help, we were able to enter the cavern. From what I can tell, we found the pyramid in the same position and configuration as the last time Commander Theriault and her team saw it." The Tomol priestess had come to assist him following her audience back in the village. "So far, Doctor Leone's viral agent seems to be causing no ill effects."

"We're able to pick up the pyramid's power readings, even without an intense sensor scan," Khatami said. *"Any idea what it might be doing?"*

"Nothing yet, Captain," Klisiewicz replied. A low, omnipresent reverberation was audible, though he had no idea from where it might be coming. It seemed to be all around him, in the cavern's floor, walls, and ceiling. As for the structure itself, although it featured no light sources or other illumination, Klisiewicz could not shake the sensation that the thing oozed power. "Whatever Seta did when she was here with the *Sagittarius* team, the obelisk is still showing significant signs of energy usage, drawing from the geothermal power source deep in the bedrock."

"Have you found a way inside, or made any progress translating more of the glyphs?"

"Yes to both questions, Captain." Klisiewicz moved down one side of the pyramid toward his recent discovery. "There is an entrance leading into the obelisk that Seta says wasn't here before. She thinks it must've opened when she spoke the commands she thought would give her access. As for the glyphs, everything I've been able to translate so far relates to the Preservers and some of the measures meant to protect the Tomol if any of them becomes Changed."

"That sounds promising."

Klisiewicz replied, "I don't know if I'd go that far. From what I can tell, the defense system—for lack of a better term—went operational the moment Nimur's genetic transformation had progressed to a point of divergence from the Tomol and she started exhibiting signs of her superior strength, telekinetic powers, and so on. As far as I can determine, these protocols have two basic purposes: protect the Tomol and contain the Changed. Not kill them, just contain them."

"That would explain why that petrification process keeps alive anyone or anything it traps. Can it be reversed?"

Klisiewicz blew out his breath. "I haven't found that yet, Captain, but I'm working on it. However, it might end up not mattering. From what I'm able to gather, the defense system is one of increasing escalation. The lances carried by the Wardens in the village are among the first, immediate responses, then it grows from there, and the petrification process isn't the top end of that scale."

"So what is?"

"I don't have the first damned idea, Captain. At least, not yet. We've found what's basically an armory containing weapons that operate in similar fashion, but they look to pack a lot more punch. There are enough of them here to arm a whole squadron of soldiers. Seta didn't know anything about them, but a cache of this size might explain why the obelisk was off-limits to all but a trusted few. They didn't want just anyone to have access to it."

"You'll be securing some of those weapons, Lieutenant?"

"Already done it, Captain," Klisiewicz said. Once the Changed surmised that he and his people were here, aiding Seta and the rest of the Tomol, they would be coming. The science officer had no doubt about that. "There's something else you should know. Some of the symbols I've read indicate that if the upper echelon of these protocols is deployed, the Preservers will come to investigate."

"I don't think waiting for them is an option, Lieutenant," Khatami said, *"so that means it's up to you. I'm not leaving any of our people behind. Finding a way to reverse that process is your first priority. Understood?"*

"Understood, Captain," Klisiewicz said. As the communication ended, the science officer felt the weight of responsibility pressing down on his shoulders. Before him, the obelisk stood in silence, waiting. For what, he had no idea. Maybe it waited so that it could help him find the answers he sought, or perhaps it stood ready to thwart him at every turn.

"Decipher a dead language, and figure out how to use an ancient pyramid to stop a band of homicidal monsters. Oh, and find a way to reverse a process that should take hundreds of years and instead make it happen in minutes." Klisiewicz shook his head as he pondered the herculean tasks that lay before him. "Yeah, no pressure."

24

"Everybody stop looking at me," Katherine Stano joked, glancing at the thirteen people who had crammed themselves into the shuttlecraft *Masao*'s seating area, behind her and Lieutenant Lerax. "And stop sweating. And breathing. This place stinks worse than my first apartment."

Chuckles answered her mock order as those passengers not occupying the five seats behind her steadied themselves in response to the shuttlecraft's lifting from the ground. Stano glanced over her shoulder and saw the Klingon, Tormog, glowering at her from where he sat in the rear seat on the cabin's starboard side. From the look on his face, he had not appreciated her attempt at humor, or perhaps he thought it more a verbal jab directed at him.

He does have that lived-in smell about him.

The shuttle swayed a bit until Stano activated maneuvering thrusters to keep the *Masao* stable. She tapped a series of controls on the forward control console, and the craft's nose lifted as she guided the *Masao* up and away from the *Sagittarius*. With repairs to the scout ship completed, or as complete as they were going to get for the time being, she had opted to take as many members of her landing party as possible with her aboard the *Masao*, if for no other reason than to keep them out of the way. However, Commander Yataro and a select few members of his engineering team remained aboard the scout in order to render any needed assistance. The onboard computer had calculated transit time to the Tomol village at less than ten minutes, but that was at the speed on which Captain Terrell had decided for his compromised ship, and assuming the vessel even managed to make it out of the clearing.

Here's hoping.

"This is your quarter-hour deodorant check," remarked Kerry Zane. The ensign pointed at another junior officer, Ensign David Hewitt. "You fail." The comments elicited more small laughter, and even Stano smiled at the banter, which had continued off and on throughout the afternoon and helped to lighten the heavy mood that had hung over everyone since the group's last encounter with the Tomol. The pace of activity in the aftermath of that attack had kept them all busy for hours. Fatigue was beginning to set in and tempers in a few cases had grown short, necessitating several quick bouts of conflict resolution on the parts of Stano and Vanessa Theriault. Despite those obstacles, repairs to the *Sagittarius* had progressed to the point that Captain Terrell was satisfied that the vessel was able to operate and maneuver, and perhaps even do so without breaking apart the instant it reached orbit above Arethusa.

Tormog spoke up, "I've never been in such a contained space with so many Earthers before." He made a show of sniffing the air and scowling. "I cannot say it is an experience I wish to repeat."

"You can always walk," Zane replied, then gestured toward the sealed hatch on the cabin's port bulkhead. "Or fly."

"That's enough," Stano snapped. "We'll all be back in the fresh air soon enough."

Transporting Tormog was a matter of practicality but not one she particularly enjoyed. After hearing from Captain Khatami that the commander of the Klingon battle cruiser, Kang, had pledged the assistance of his ship toward protecting the Tomol villagers and the *Endeavour* and *Sagittarius* personnel still on the planet's surface, Tormog also had volunteered to aid in the effort. Stano suspected both he and Kang still had ulterior motives, not the least of which was capturing one or more Tomol specimens to be returned to the Klingon Empire for study. However, with the battle that likely was coming, she had enough to worry about without keeping an eye on one lone Klingon scientist. Once he was on the ground and under the supervision of the *Endeavour* landing party's security detail, Stano would direct Klisiewicz to take any action he deemed necessary if Tormog tried anything. It certainly was not the ideal situation, but for the moment another pair of hands and eyes on the ground would be helpful.

Using both the shuttle's instruments and her own eyes as she divided her attention between the controls and the forward view ports, Stano guided the craft up and out of the stone ring created by the Preserver drones. Satisfied that the shuttle was clear of the crash site, she keyed the console's communications panel. "*Masao* to *Sagittarius.* We're out of your way, if you're ready to give it a try."

The cabin's internal speakers crackled with the voice of Captain Clark Terrell. "*We read you, Commander. Stand by. We're engaging thrusters now. Here goes nothing.*"

Adjusting the *Masao*'s orientation so that she could observe the *Sagittarius* through the shuttlecraft's forward viewing ports, Stano watched as the *Archer*-class scout's thrusters came online, blasting plumes of dirt and grass into the air in multiple directions as the vessel pushed itself from the ground. Even through the shuttle's thick duranium hull plating, she felt the reverberations from the force of the other ship's engines as it began lifting toward the sky.

"Looking good, *Sagittarius*," she said. "Nothing's falling off. At least, not that I can see." She noted that the ship's navigational deflector dish, though battered and dulled as a consequence of the crash landing, remained in place as the ship rose. Terrell and Ilucci had been particularly concerned about the dish, as it was necessary for the *Sagittarius* to travel at warp speeds. For her part, Stano still was not entirely certain the vital component would function properly once the ship was back in space and under way, but for the moment the fact that the dish remained attached was a victory worth celebrating.

"Ilucci will be happy to hear that," Terrell replied. *"So far, everything's still green. We're powering up."*

The whine of the *Sagittarius*'s thrusters increased as the ship continued to ascend, and it took only a moment for it to emerge from the band of rock encircling its former resting place. Stano adjusted the *Masao*'s controls and the shuttle retreated, giving the larger vessel greater room to maneuver. For the first time, she had an unimpeded view at the landscape below her, transformed as it had been by both the *Sagittarius*'s crash landing and the tremendous power of the Preserver drones.

"That is amazing," Lerax said, his attention riveted on the scene from where he sat in the shuttlecraft's copilot seat. The petrification effect had covered a lopsided circular area of the ground more than two hundred meters in diameter, the rock converging toward the center of what now was a misshapen oval, from which both the *Masao* and now the *Sagittarius* had emerged. From this height it was easy to see that the aperture was nowhere near small enough to have prevented either ship from escaping. Still, there was no denying the immense power held by the Preserver technology present on this world, even if its creators had been dead for millennia.

"*Okay, Masao,*" Terrell said a moment later, "*we're clear. There's a few things rattling around in here, but so far Ilucci's work with all that emergency tape seems to be paying off. We'll keep our fingers crossed.*"

"Are you able to achieve orbit if necessary?" Stano asked. As she spoke, she watched the *Sagittarius* shudder from port to starboard and back again before once more leveling its attitude.

"*We think so, but I don't know if I'm ready to go to warp until we get a chance to give everything another once-over, or six. But everything should hold together if we don't bounce around too much.*"

Stano nodded in satisfaction, impressed with the amount of work the repair teams, operating under the watchful eyes and relentless supervision of Master Chief Ilucci and Commander Yataro, had been able to accomplish in such a short amount of time. "If nothing else, the *Endeavour* can tow you to Starbase 71." The relatively new, planet-bound facility located in the Benecia system near the Federation boundary of the Taurus Reach still had large areas under construction, but a maintenance depot was already up and running and would be more than sufficient to tackle the repairs to a ship like the *Sagittarius*. Orbital repair docks soon would come online, allowing for maintenance and repair of larger vessels like the *Endeavour*. Another *Watchtower*-class station, similar to the late Starbase 47, was supposed to be established sometime in the coming year, but for now the *Endeavour*, like the *Sagittarius*, would call the new base its home port.

"*Wonderful. Your captain will never let me live that down, but it'll be worth it if I can sleep all the way there.*" Stano heard Terrell making inquiries and requesting updates from his bridge officers before he returned to the communications link. "*I think we're as good as we're going to get for the time being. Ready to get out of here?*"

Stano replied, "Yes, sir. Do you want to take point?" Outside the *Masao*'s viewing ports, she watched as the *Sagittarius* banked to starboard and began climbing higher into the sky, heading away from the clearing.

"*Not a bad idea. That way, you can pick up anything that falls off us on the way there.*"

"Acknowledged." Tapping controls on the console, Stano guided the shuttlecraft to follow the *Sagittarius* before settling back into her seat.

"Commander," Lerax said, "I know that Captain Khatami hopes to provide support for us with the *Endeavour* and the Klingon ship, but what if the Preserver weapons prevent that? If and when the Changed attack, how can we possibly hope to defend the entire Tomol village on our own?"

Stano replied, "Good questions, Lieutenant. At least

we know the Changed can be stopped." She had seen with her own eyes the fossilized form of Nimur, the female Tomol who had forsaken generations of ritual and societal obligation when her transformation had gripped her. Nimur had been caught up by the drones dispatched from the subterranean complex, and now she stood on the outskirts of the clearing from which the *Sagittarius* had just risen. It seemed somehow an ignominious fate for someone who had caused such strife and suffering. How long was Nimur fated to remain there, isolated from the rest of existence?

At least long enough for us to be long gone, I hope.

Lerax said, "Do you think Lieutenant Klisiewicz and Doctor Leone can find a way to help the Tomol, or at least something we can use to fight the Changed?"

"If anyone can," Stano replied, "it's those two." According to the last report she had received from Khatami, the *Endeavour*'s science officer and chief medical officer had taken another landing party via shuttlecraft to the Tomol village on the far side of the larger, neighboring Suba island. It seemed that Leone was on the cusp of finding a means of countering or preventing the Change, while Klisiewicz was still attempting to understand the true nature of the Preserver presence on Arethusa and their guardianship over the Tomol in the hopes of finding a way to combat Kerlo and the other Changed, whose numbers appeared to be growing. Even with Nimur immobilized by the Preserver containment protocol, Kerlo and others looked to be stepping up in order to fill the leadership void she had left. Their ranks would continue to swell, Stano knew, as there were hundreds of new foot soldiers in the Tomol village, helpless against forced enlistment by Kerlo and his followers.

So we find a way to stop them. Piece of cake, right?

Perched atop the curved railing to the left of the *Endeavour* bridge's main viewscreen, Atish Khatami regarded the computer-generated map of Suba and the two blue dots now moving across the island's green expanse after making the transit over the stretch of ocean separating the landmass from a smaller, neighboring island. The icons represented the *Masao* and the *Sagittarius,* the latter not having yet exploded in flight.

"Glad to see you're up and about, Captain," she said, raising her voice for the benefit of the bridge's communications system.

Over the speaker, Clark Terrell replied, *"Ilucci's one talented sorcerer. It's really the only reason I haven't had him court-martialed. That said, we couldn't have done it without your people, Atish. Commander Yataro and his team are first-rate, and don't even get me started on the rest of what we've been dealing with down here. Drinks are on me the next time we all find ourselves in the same bar."*

"Let's hope that's sooner rather than later. Contact us when you've arrived at the village. We're maintaining station for the time being, just to be on the safe side. *Endeavour* out." Khatami allowed herself a sigh of relief. With the worst of the damage inflicted upon the *Sagittarius* repaired or at least mitigated, its crew as well as her landing party could now safely depart the planet and avoid any further attacks by the Changed. This was a huge weight off her shoulders, given the *Endeavour's* own problems with repairs and only partially functional transporters. Other shuttlecraft were available, of course, but she was reluctant to use them for fear of giving the Changed more targets to capture and perhaps use to escape Arethusa. This threat likely brought with it further fear that the Preserver pyramid beneath Arethusa's surface, which so far had seemed willing to leave her ship alone, might react in a hostile manner if it detected any of the Change attempting to make a getaway.

Of course, much of this was irrelevant. Despite their previous skirmishes and the very real threat to their own safety, neither the *Sagittarius* nor her landing party was leaving the planet, not while the Tomol were endangered by the Changed. It was why the scout ship and her own people now were on their way to the village, and why Lieutenant Klisiewicz and Doctor Leone had gone to the Preserver pyramid in the hopes of finding some way to combat the rapidly evolving Tomol. Klisiewicz was continuing to investigate the ancient race's technology, and Leone was closing in on some form of cure for the Tomol's affliction. How much time did they have to pursue their goals? Khatami knew it almost certainly would not be enough, which was why she and the *Endeavour* and her crew—along with the unlikely assistance of Captain Kang and his ship—would be on hand to provide support for operations on the ground

Once more unto the breach, and so on and so forth.

Pushing herself from the railing, she made her way around the starboard side of the bridge's upper deck toward the science and communications stations. "Mister Estrada, I take it our communications are holding steady?"

The veteran lieutenant replied, "That's affirmative, Captain. The relays we've deployed around the planet to boost our signal throughput don't seem to be attracting any unwanted attention." It had been Estrada's idea to launch a trio of subspace relay buoys, which the *Endeavour* carried in storage. Though intended for use in extending Starfleet's communications reach into newly charted territory—which at present included much of the Taurus Reach—Estrada, working with the *Endeavour*'s assistant chief engineer, Lieutenant Commander Phu Dang, had recalibrated the devices to operate at a lower power and more limited range of frequencies. It was hoped that the relays' reduced capacity might enable them to escape notice by whatever sensors were active within the Preserver artifact, and so far Estrada's plan seemed to be working.

"Nice work, Lieutenant," Khatami said. "Let me know the instant you detect even the slightest change."

Estrada nodded. "Aye, Captain."

"Iacovino," Khatami said, turning to the science station, "any signs that the pyramid cares what we're up to?"

Standing at her console, one hand resting on the station's sensor viewer, Ensign Kayla Iacovino replied, "So far, it seems content to leave us alone, Captain. Just to be on the safe side, I haven't subjected the pyramid site to a full sensor scan using the modifications made by Lieutenant Klisiewicz, but I figure we've given it plenty of reasons to be angry with us by now."

Khatami crossed her arms. "You've had time to analyze the sensor data we've collected to this point. What's your take on all of this?"

"My take, Captain?"

"What's your gut feeling, Ensign? Does the pyramid consider us a threat?"

The junior science officer shrugged. "Based on what we've been able to determine about the structure, we could destroy it via orbital bombardment, but we obviously don't want to if that can be avoided. I don't know if its own scans have convinced it of that or not, but I'll take what I can get."

"Agreed," Khatami said. "Whatever automated defense protocol was triggered by our first attempts to scan the pyramid seems to be able to examine and adapt to evolving situations. That said, I'm not willing to push our luck until we have to."

"And it doesn't seem to have raised any issues with our people studying it on the ground." Iacovino tapped several controls and one of the larger display screens above her console activated, displaying a computer-generated schematic of what Khatami recognized as the Preserver pyramid. "He's been poking around in there for a couple of hours and hasn't reported anything troublesome. I suspect that as long as we don't damage anything stored there, the pyramid will not register our activities as threatening." She shrugged again. "After all, they called themselves 'Preservers,' right? It seems reasonable to think they wouldn't harm or kill others unless they had no other choice."

"It's a nice theory, at any rate," Khatami conceded. Despite the Preserver pyramid's earlier defensive action in response to the *Endeavour*'s initial sensor sweep, the ancient artifact had taken no overt notice of the starship's subsequent activities. Following the deployment of the communications relay buoys, Khatami had ordered the ship's orbit around Arethusa contracted, with an emphasis on maintaining sensor contact with her landing party and the *Sagittarius* while studiously avoiding the pyramid. She very much wanted to employ her ship's full spectrum of sensor capabilities on the artifact buried within that mountain hideaway in the hopes of learning as much about the Preservers as possible. However, she knew that using the enhancements Klisiewicz had made to the sensor arrays likely would invite unwanted scrutiny, or worse. Therefore, Khatami had prohibited the use of such tactics against that area of the Suba landmass until further notice. So far, the *Endeavour*'s movements appeared to be attracting no attention from the Preserver complex.

For now, anyway.

"What about Kang?" Khatami asked. "Is he behaving himself?"

Iacovino nodded. "Seems to be, Captain. The *Voh'tahk* is holding station near Arethusa's inner moon, and sensors show their propulsion and weapons systems are back online."

"Good." Following the deal she had struck with Kang, Khatami had seen to it that replacement components and other requested items—including a few that had required fabrication—had been transported to the Klingon battle cruiser. Kang, true to his word, had incited no provocative action and even had thanked her for the assistance. Though she was confident the Klingon captain would honor their agreement, Khatami held no illusions that he was not planning some final move once the current situation was resolved.

Assuming we can *resolve it, that is.*

An alert tone sounded from the science station, and Iacovino turned to investigate. "Captain, you asked me to keep sensors trained on the surface near the Changed Tomol's last known location. I'm picking up Changed life signs where I wasn't before." She paused, tapping several controls on the console, each eliciting a melodic beep. Moving to the sensor viewer, the science officer bent over to peer into the unit, pale blue light playing across her face. "Sensors are detecting several Changed bio readings. They may be airborne."

Khatami frowned, recalling Katherine Stano's report of the ability of the Changed to transform into other lifeforms capable of flight and even—according to Captain Terrell—maneuvering underwater. "Let me guess. They're on their way to the Tomol village."

"Affirmative, Captain. At their present speed, they should be there within half an hour."

Sighing, Khatami shook her head.

"Time's up, people."

25

Standing alone at the center of the control room, Stephen Klisiewicz continued to marvel at the chamber's array of consoles and panels.

"This place is incredible," he said to no one, just as he had uttered similar comments and observations throughout the brief time he had been working here. The workstations—as he chose to call them—were covered with all manner of switches and indicators, arranged in multicolored clusters of varying size and number. Everything was accented by the familiar yet still largely unintelligible glyphs exhibiting the language of the Preservers.

The glyphs themselves were as much works of art as articles of communication, but it was their latter properties that concerned him at the moment. After being granted continued permission by Seta to enter the Caves of the Shepherds and ultimately this hallowed space, Klisiewicz had benefited from her ability to read the symbols adorning the pyramid's exterior surfaces as well as much of the walls and consoles inside the structure the Preservers had left here at some point in the distant past. Like the rest of those personnel from the *Endeavour* and the *Sagittarius*, he had refrained from revealing the identities of the "Shepherds," not willing to risk further cultural contamination of the Tomol beyond what circumstances already had forced upon them. Despite the best efforts of the two Starfleet crews, the damage to the people of this world had been done. While the case could be made that Nimur's rebellion against her people likely would have happened regardless of outside interference, the matter had been rendered moot by encounters with the Klingons and the *Sagittarius* landing party. The only option available was to help Seta, Kerlo, and the rest of the Tomol to mitigate the effects of that inadvertent meddling by any means necessary, which included understanding and exploiting whatever technology the Preservers had seen fit to leave there.

I just wish we had time to truly study this place, he mused. *Maybe later. Assuming we survive, that is.*

"You want to wipe that drool off your chin?" asked a voice from behind him, which Klisiewicz recognized as that of Doctor Leone. "It's embarrassing. Besides, you don't want to make a mess of the nice ancient alien cave, do you?"

Despite the seriousness of the situation, Klisiewicz could not help laughing at the physician's dry wit as Leone stepped farther into the room. How had he not heard the other man enter the chamber? "How are things outside?"

"Commander Stano and the *Masao* showed up and dropped off most of her security detail," Leone replied. "They also left Tormog. He says he's here to help, and Captain Khatami says Kang will vouch for him, but Stano said you're supposed to put a boot up his ass if he gets out of line."

Klisiewicz grinned. "She really said that?"

Leone shrugged. "She may have said something about stunning him into next week, or whatever else you think you need to do if he starts going off script, but my idea sounds better."

"Have a couple of security people bring Tormog down here," Klisiewicz said. "He can't cause too much trouble if he's stuck in here with the rest of us." Though he doubted it, there remained the possibility that Tormog had information of value about the Preserver artifacts, or something else he had seen during his encounters with Nimur and the other Changed. Right now, Klisiewicz would take any advantage he could find. "What about the Tomol?"

"Seta and some of the Wardens or whatever they're called are overseeing the evacuation." Leone shrugged, and there was no mistaking the worry on his face. "I don't know how the hell they're going to get everyone down here, but it's the only thing that even remotely resembles a safe place."

It had been Seta's suggestion to evacuate the village and move all of the Tomol into the Caves of the Shepherds, in the hopes of protecting them from Kerlo and those handful of Changed who followed him now that his mate, Nimur, had been rendered inert by the bizarre countermeasures deployed by the automated Preserver drones. It would be a tight fit down here, Klisiewicz guessed, with nearly fifteen hundred people requiring relocation, but they would be all but defenseless in the village. Even now, with the transfer under way, there remained hundreds of Tomol out in the open on the trail connecting the village and the caves, and while the effort was proceeding apace, it still was too slow for Klisiewicz's comfort. Wardens and others from the village who had volunteered to act as defenders had been armed from the weapons cache discovered by the landing party.

Assuming they work, Klisiewicz reminded himself. After all, the weapons had been stored down here for uncounted thousands of years. On the other hand, the drones had performed admirably during the Changed's two previous encounters with *Endeavour* and *Sagittarius* personnel. The problem was that there was no predicting how or even if the weapons would appear again, even with Kerlo and his followers poised to strike. *I guess we'll find out soon enough.*

"Speaking of Seta," Klisiewicz said, moving back to what the Tomol priestess had identified as the room's primary control console, "how is she? Any signs of possible side effects, in her or the others?"

Leone shook his head. "Nothing so far. I'm up to twelve test subjects, all of them believing they were getting close to their own time for jumping into that fire pit, and because they trust Seta. Based on what I've been able to learn about their physiology and from my tricorder readings, each of them could reach that point within four to six months, with the closest one happening within a week to ten days." He sighed. "Give or take, that is. It could happen a month from now . . . or tomorrow. Even with all the scans I took of Seta up on the *Endeavour,* there's just not enough information on their particular physiology for me to pin it down any better than that. I couldn't find anything in the medical database about a similar species, so there's nothing to compare them against." He waved his hand in the air as if to indicate the control room. "I don't suppose you can tell me if there's anything useful about the Tomol stored somewhere down here, can you?"

"Not yet, I can't," Klisiewicz replied, "but I'm still looking." Despite the time crunch under which the crews of the *Endeavour* and the *Sagittarius* had been working since their arrivals at Arethusa, he was impressed by how much progress Leone had made in his own research into the Tomol and how quickly he had formulated the synthesized compound he had administered to Seta and her fellow volunteers in the hopes of neutralizing the Shedai's genetic manipulation. Even with the assistance Klisiewicz had provided thanks to the Operation Vanguard files he possessed, the doctor had made several intuitive leaps of his own, covering some of the same ground addressed in the information Klisiewicz himself had mined from the metagenome data so meticulously cataloged by his late friend, Ming Xiong.

Standing next to Klisiewicz, Leone leaned against an adjacent console, glancing behind him as though to ensure he was not inadvertently moving or otherwise activating any of the controls. "Assuming we don't want to wait around here any longer than we have to—and I really don't, in case you're wondering—the only thing I can think to do is administer the treatment to a Tomol who's already undergone the Change." Klisiewicz cast a questioning expression at the doctor, who shrugged and admitted, "Yeah, I think that's a pretty damned crazy idea, too."

"Maybe not," Klisiewicz said, realizing too late that he had spoken the words aloud. When it was Leone's turn to eye him with open skepticism, the lieutenant added, "Obviously I don't mean trying to chase down one of the

Changed that are running around out there." He gestured toward the room's entrance. "But we have several specimens just standing about in the woods, waiting for something to happen."

"You mean one of the frozen guys?" Leone crossed his arms, frowning as he considered the notion. "But that would mean drilling through the rock encasing them, right? Didn't Stano and the others tell us that could be dangerous, even fatal to the person trapped inside that shell?"

Stepping back from the console, Klisiewicz shook his head. "Not necessarily. Even though I think trying to break one of them free could be life-threatening, it might be possible to drill a small hole through the rock shell, just enough to let you administer your serum. That shouldn't have too drastic an effect on the rock itself."

"Shouldn't?" Leone's eyes narrowed. "You're not sure?"

"No. It's an educated guess." Despite the progress he had made deciphering the glyphs and other script left behind by the Preservers, there still was much he had not yet translated, let alone understood. Thanks to Seta and information collected by Commander Theriault and the *Sagittarius* landing party, he had read and translated several sections of the glyphs inscribed on the pyramid's exterior containing information about the Endless and how they were turned into stone by an unknown power source located somewhere within or near the obelisk. What he had not yet found was anything about reversing the process, but to Klisiewicz it simply made no sense for there not to be such an ability. Surely the Preservers, with their apparent penchant for safeguarding representatives of endangered or doomed civilizations, would not consign their charges to eternal imprisonment with no hope of reprieve?

What about the Tomol who've been standing in that valley for thousands of years?

No, Klisiewicz decided. There had to be a logical reason for that as well. Was rescinding the interment effect a duty to be performed by a priestess such as Seta? Perhaps it was knowledge that had been lost over the generations, or the technology for overseeing such things was malfunctioning. That certainly was not out of the question, given the untold millennia for which the obelisk had sat here, buried beneath the planet's surface. The answers to the questions the Tomol posed were here, embedded somewhere in the perplexing script of the wordstone left by the Preservers. Klisiewicz simply had not found it.

Yet.

Shouts of alarm from outside the control room echoed through the open portal leading from the obelisk. Moving to the entry, Leone peered out before looking over his shoulder to Klisiewicz. "Something's happening. Tomol are running all over the place."

"Kerlo and the others," Klisiewicz said. "They're here." His communicator beeped, and he flipped open its cover. "Klisiewicz here."

"Hewitt here," replied Ensign David Hewitt, the *Endeavour* security officer who had been placed in charge of the relocation effort. *"We've got trouble out here, Lieutenant. Company's coming, and there's no way we can get everyone inside the caves before they get here."*

"Aw, hell," Leone said. "They'll be sitting ducks out there." Klisiewicz could only nod in agreement, already imagining what Kerlo and the other Changed might do once they arrived to see so many defenseless Tomol for the taking.

Hewitt continued, *"We've got our people and the Tomol Wardens deployed all along the side of the mountain leading to the caves, but if they attack us the way the other Changed went after the* Sagittarius . . ."

Klisiewicz heard the unspoken worry in the young officer's voice. "We only have to hold on for a few minutes." Feeling a knot of anxiety growing in his gut, he scanned the consoles around him, searching for some sign that his nagging suspicions were correct. "If I'm right, the obelisk should deploy some kind of countermeasure once it detects the Changed threat."

"Do we want to be here when that happens?" Leone asked.

It was a good question, Klisiewicz conceded. As for the answer?

"There's only one way to find out."

From the forest flanking the trail leading to the Caves of the Shepherds, Kerlo saw two villagers emerge into the open, each wielding what he at first thought to be a Warden's fire lance. The implements they carried were at once recognizable as weapons and yet unfamiliar in form or function. He had no idea if they might be more powerful than the lances and he would not wait to see them tested. Lunging toward the new arrivals even as they raised their weapons in their direction, Kerlo slammed a fist into the first Tomol's chest. The villager was thrown off his feet and back toward the trees, crashing to the ground and sliding into a depression on the far side of the trail. His companion, as though shocked by the speed and ferocity of the attack, froze in the act of aiming his lance, and that brief hesitation was all Kerlo needed to close the distance and swat the weapon from his grip. It sailed into the trees and the Tomol turned to flee. Kerlo was faster and grabbed the man by his neck and flung him into the forest. He heard the impact of the Tomol's body against a tree, but by then Kerlo had all but forgotten about him, relishing in the wave of power and increasing strength surging within him.

Whatever drove him now that he had accepted the Change was asserting itself with unexpected force. Every breath he drew brought with it heightened vigor and awareness. Further, he could sense a similar progression in those who had been Changed by Nimur during the battle at the crashed sky-ship. Like him, they were advancing toward the throngs of Tomol frantically seeking shelter, or simply plunging into the forest and away from the caves. Kerlo knew he could not waste time pursuing those who fled, but he would find them in due course. For now, though, there remained others in need of the guidance and truth they had been denied all of their brief lives.

Turning his attention farther up the trail to the clearing near the caves, Kerlo saw dozens of villagers running toward the entrance. One of them, a young female, caught sight of him and pointed, yelling out in fear. Kerlo saw the bluish-purple aura emanating from her, communicating her dread, but he also sensed in her another energy—a flicker of untapped strength waiting to be summoned.

Though he did not know her, Kerlo intuitively realized that he was seeing the first sparks of the Change beginning to spread through the female's body. Had life here on Suba not been upended by Nimur's rebellion and spurning of village law and tradition, the female would be giving herself over to the Cleansing before the next cycle of Arethusa's moons.

No. Your fate, as with mine and that of our people, lies elsewhere.

Kerlo focused his mind on the ember he felt growing within her, reaching out and pulling at it, coaxing it forth to join with him. He sensed the female's initial resistance, but by now there was no stopping him. The spark erupted into flames, which Kerlo saw reflected in the female's eyes. Her expression was at first one of shock, replaced quickly by uncertainty, but already Kerlo could see her aura shifting as the Change took hold within her.

She was only the first, with others following in short order. Marching up the trail on his way to the caves, he saw the glint of power radiating from other villagers. Most of them were not old enough that the Change could be convinced to spring forth, but others awaited him. For those whose Change was not imminent, enticing the transformation taxed Kerlo, but the results were the same. Within moments he had recruited five Tomol to the cause. The number was small, but it was a start.

Others will follow.

A high-pitched whine from somewhere above and behind him filled the air beyond the trees, and Kerlo looked up to see what he recognized as the smaller, boxlike skyship that had come to the aid of its larger companion craft.

Arriving at incredible speed, it had slowed to hover above the tops of the tallest trees, its nose pointed slightly downward. This craft lacked the artistic beauty of the vessel that had crashed on Suba's far side, but that did not concern him now.

Instead, he fixed his gaze on the vessel's open portal and the sky person who appeared to be leaning out of that aperture. She was aiming the newcomers' version of a fire lance toward the ground, as though searching for targets.

They had come to defend the Tomol against him. While part of him remembered that the sky people presented themselves as peaceful strangers, he saw now that they were obstructing the path his people were destined to travel.

Though they still possessed some limited value in the larger goal of claiming one of the sky-ships, their presence and interference could no longer be tolerated.

26

"Keep her steady," said Katherine Stano, kneeling on the *Masao*'s deck plating and bracing herself as best she could against the shuttlecraft's port-side interior bulkhead. Wind whipped through the open hatch, pushing at her as she steadied her phaser rifle against the edge of the portal. Having taken over the cockpit controls, Lieutenant Lerax was doing a commendable job maintaining the *Masao*'s attitude, bringing the shuttlecraft to a hover just above the tops of the trees encircling the small clearing near the cave entrance. From her vantage point, Stano could see dozens of Tomol scattering in all directions. Some were racing for the cave and whatever shelter might exist in the subterranean caverns, while others ran for the feeble protection offered by the surrounding forest.

"You sure this is a good idea, Commander?" asked Ensign Kerry Zane from where he crouched against the bulkhead on the hatch's opposite side. The junior security officer's own phaser rifle extended through the open doorway, beneath Stano's and covering angles she could not see.

Stano shrugged. "We can't risk leaving the shuttle on the ground, and there's no way I'm leaving people behind down there." It had been Lerax's idea to utilize the *Masao* as air cover, maneuvering above the trees in a bid to target and subdue any of the Changed before they could get to the cave or cause harm to any of the other Tomol villagers. Agreeing with the security chief's evaluation, she had landed the shuttle long enough to offload Tormog and the bulk of her landing party, transferring her security detail to the one that had accompanied Klisiewicz and Doctor Leone.

One virtue of Lerax's plan was that it would serve to keep the shuttle away from the Changed, who doubtless would seize any opportunity to get their hands on it as a means of making their way into orbit in an attempt to attack and commandeer the *Endeavour*. It was because of this that Stano had ordered the *Masao*'s sister shuttlecraft, the *Simone*, back to the *Endeavour*. As neither the *Simone* nor the *Masao* had armaments of its own, any defensive usefulness came from one or more people positioning themselves at the open hatch and firing at targets on the ground, hopefully without falling to their own deaths.

Nice positive thinking you've got there, Commander.

Shifting his kneeling position, Zane said, "Remind me to ask Commander Yataro when we get back about installing tie-downs or something in these shuttles."

"Noted," Stano said. Designed primarily as personnel transports rather than tactical vehicles, standard shuttlecraft of the sort carried by most Starfleet vessels lacked many of the uninteresting yet very useful features found aboard vessels intended for more martial purposes. Small things like tie straps or foot- and handholds, taken for granted aboard military craft, were conspicuous by their absence here aboard the *Masao*. Stano and Zane had adapted to the situation as best they could, taking lengths of cord from a survival kit in the shuttle's aft storage compartment, tying them around their waists, and securing their makeshift harnesses to two empty passenger seats. The cord supposedly was rated to support a weight of four hundred kilograms, but that did little to ease Stano's anxiety as she peered through the open hatch to the ground below.

From the cockpit, Lerax called out, "Sensors are picking up fluctuating bio readings, similar to what Commander Theriault warned us about. Several of the Tomol are undergoing the Change."

"How many?" Stano had expected this to happen once Kerlo and the handful of followers who had escaped with him from the *Sagittarius* crash site made their way to the Tomol village.

Lerax replied, "Sensors show eleven Tomol exhibiting the altered readings." A moment later, he added, "Twelve."

"At least we know Kerlo can't change them all," Stano said. According to Doctors Leone and Babitz, Kerlo and Nimur before her had been able to trigger the Change only in those individuals already naturally presenting the first symptoms of the cycle. Therefore, the vast majority of the villagers would not fall victim to Kerlo's telekinetic manipulations of their peculiar body chemistry.

Next to her, Zane grunted. "Small favors."

"Yeah, but the Changed can still kill anyone who gets in their way," Stano countered. "Including us." Raising her voice, she asked, "Where's the *Sagittarius*?"

"Holding station starboard aft," Lerax answered. The Edoan's body movements were a flurry of activity as he oversaw the shuttlecraft's maneuvering and sensor controls at the same time, making full use of his third arm.

"What about our people on the ground?" Stano asked. "Any sign of them?"

Lerax shook his head. "Negative, Commander, but sensor scans are inconclusive for areas below the surface. At last report, Lieutenant Klisiewicz and the *Endeavour* landing party were still inside the caves, having been joined by my security team. It's likely that they are still there."

"Probably the safest place to be, for the moment, anyway." Stano knew that with the *Sagittarius*'s single transporter pad still off-line, the only way to evacuate *Endeavour* personnel from the surface was either to land or for the *Endeavour* itself to get close enough to use its own transporters. Leaving the Tomol defenseless against the Changed was not an option, which is what had led to Stano sending in the balance of her landing party to bolster Klisiewicz and his group. As for Klisiewicz, he had ventured into the underground complex to try to translate enough of the Preserver obelisk's glyphs and other systems to be able to deactivate whatever defensive protocols had damaged the starship. If the science officer could not accomplish that feat, then Stano knew she might be forced to land once again, in defiance of her own desire to keep the *Masao* away from Kerlo and the other Changed.

"Somebody's checking us out," Zane said, pointing through the open hatchway. "Look."

Returning her attention to the scene below, Stano saw three figures giving chase to other Tomol, while another stood alone on the trail leading to the caves, his gaze turned up toward the shuttlecraft. Even from the *Masao*'s position above the treetops and dozens of meters away,

Stano could see the crimson glow in the Tomol's eyes. It was Kerlo, she realized, now fully gripped by the effects of the Change. He was beyond rescuing and had turned from being an ally to an enemy.

Balancing herself against the bulkhead, Stano aimed her phaser rifle and fired, unleashing a beam of blue-white energy toward Kerlo. The beam struck the Changed in the torso and he staggered back several steps, bending at the waist and reaching for his chest at the point of impact. He stumbled and dropped to one knee but did not fall, and he was still conscious. Stano was increasing the phaser rifle's power setting when Kerlo looked up again, and this time he smiled.

"Uh-oh," Zane said, raising his own phaser rifle.

"Lerax!" Stano shouted. "Get us the hell out of here. *Now!*"

She issued the order just as she saw Kerlo raise his arms, the palms of his hands toward the sky. Then the *Masao* bucked and pitched as something she could not see slammed into the shuttlecraft, and everyone crammed into the tight quarters cried out in alarm at the sudden attitude change. Stano and Zane tumbled away from the open hatch to the cabin's starboard side, rolling into one of the empty passenger seats. Alert tones wailed in the confined space and Stano heard the whine of the maneuvering thrusters as they fought against whatever unseen force pushed against the shuttle.

"Hold on!" the Edoan shouted. "Initiating evasive maneuvers." Lerax's three arms were almost a blur as he worked the controls, fighting to keep the *Masao* airborne.

Stano felt a hand on her shoulder and looked up to see

Zane staring down at her, the junior security officer's anxiety evident on his face. "You okay, Commander?"

Before she even could nod an acknowledgment, the shuttlecraft rocked again as it weathered a second assault, and this time Stano bounced on the deck plating as the ship shuddered around her. She already had lost count at the number of warning lights and other status indicators that had flared to life on the cockpit console, and a glance through the open hatch revealed a heaving view of sky and forest as Lerax continued to wrestle with the controls.

"Starboard stabilizer is out," the lieutenant reported. "Aft maneuvering thrusters are failing." His focus remained on the console. "We need to land, Commander."

"Do it!" Stano said. "But put some distance between us and the caves." Kerlo attempting to commandeer the shuttlecraft remained a valid concern, after all. Pulling herself to her knees, Stano reached for the cockpit's other seat, noting as she did so from the console's status monitors that the *Masao* was in a rapid descent.

Outside the hatch, the trees were getting closer.

Leaning forward in her command chair with her arms resting on her thighs was doing nothing to alleviate the knot at the small of Atish Khatami's back. She ignored her discomfort, instead directing her attention and energies to the tactical schematic displayed on the *Endeavour* bridge's main viewscreen. In place of the customary plot of the starship's position in space relative to allied or enemy vessels, the graphic offered a computer-generated view of Suba, in particular an enhanced view of the terrain surrounding the mountains near the Tomol village and the entrance to the caves leading to the Preserver artifact. Superimposed over the green-and-brown mass were two bright blue dots representing the *U.S.S. Sagittarius* and the shuttlecraft *Masao*. Both vessels were moving about the cave entrance and the surrounding area, near which glowed dozens of smaller red dots—far too many to count—indicating life signs in the vicinity. Other red markers were moving in all directions away from the caves, and Khatami guessed these were Tomol retreating to the relative safety of the surrounding forest.

"Sensors," Khatami snapped. "Any signs the pyramid's taking an interest in us?"

Ensign Kayla Iacovino turned from the science station. "I'm seeing no such indications, Captain. I'm picking up new power sources coming online, but without probing deeper I'm not able to investigate what those might be for." She paused, then asked, "Should I increase our scan intensity?"

"Not yet." Khatami had already undertaken a risk just by ordering the *Endeavour* to move within transporter range and altering its course so that it now was in geosynchronous orbit over the Tomol village and the caverns. So far, the Preserver pyramid had taken no overt acknowledgment of those actions, and Khatami wanted to keep things that way. "Where are our people on the ground?"

"Other than those aboard the shuttlecraft and the *Sagittarius*," Iacovino said, "I'm not seeing any of our people on the surface. It's possible Lieutenant Klisiewicz's landing party is with him belowground." The junior science officer did not need to elaborate; Khatami was well aware that the *Endeavour*'s sensors remained incapable of penetrating the mineral-rich rock and soil obscuring the Preservers' subterranean complex from prying eyes. While the passages and caverns might provide some degree of protection from the Changed, they also would prevent Khatami from beaming those people back to the ship.

She asked, "What about Changed life signs? Can you distinguish them from the other Tomol from up here?"

"Yes, Captain," Iacovino responded. "There's a definite difference in bio readings that we can detect even from this distance."

"Feed that information to McCormack." Rising from her chair, Khatami placed one hand on the navigator's shoulder. "Lieutenant, start tracking the Changed life signs and be ready to target them with heavy stun."

McCormack looked over her shoulder. "From this altitude, targeting individuals could prove problematic, Captain."

"Understood. If necessary, we'll blanket an area, but I want to be ready to back up the *Sagittarius* any way we can."

From the communications station, Lieutenant Hector Estrada called out, "Captain! Receiving an urgent message from Commander Stano on the *Masao*."

"On speakers," Khatami ordered, moving to the rail separating her from Estrada. A second later, Katherine Stano's voice exploded from the bridge intercom system.

"*Masao to* Endeavour*! We've been attacked by the Changed and have suffered damage that's forcing us to land. I'm putting her down two kilometers southwest of the cave entrance. Stand by to beam us up!*"

Waving toward the communications console, Khatami told Estrada, "Notify the transporter room." She turned back to the viewscreen, where the blue dot representing the *Masao* was moving away from the cave entrance and toward a small clearing. "Commander," she called out, "do you have any injuries on board?"

"*Negative,*" Stano replied, "*and I'll be requesting permission to lead a team back to the surface to help our people down there.*"

Despite the danger it entailed, Khatami had expected her first officer to make that request. She did not like the idea of sending her people back into harm's way, but at the moment it was among the least objectionable options available to her as far as getting assistance to Klisiewicz and his landing party. "Understood, but it's you and trained security people only. We'll have fresh phaser rifles ready for you when you get up here."

"*Acknowledged,*" Stano replied, the tension in her voice obvious. "*We're setting down now.*"

From behind her, Estrada said, "Captain, the *Sagittarius* is hailing us. They're under attack, too."

Khatami gestured for the communications officer to switch frequencies. A moment later, the image on the main viewscreen changed from the tactical plot to the face of Captain Clark Terrell. Sweat shone on the man's forehead, and his expression was tense as he leaned forward in his chair. All around him, alarm indicators flashed across the scout ship's compact bridge, and the overhead lighting was flickering.

"Clark? What's your status?"

"*We're getting hammered down here. We tried coming*

*in low to target some of the Changed, but they turned and
hit us with . . . something. Sensors never saw it coming,
but it was like running into a concrete wall. We were in
bad shape to begin with, but now I've got system failures
all over the ship. Even with full shields, they managed to
hurt us pretty good."*

"Can you stay on station?"

Terrell nodded. *"For now, you bet."* His features softened. *"We're not going anywhere, Atish. Our transporter
pad's operational, but we could use some bigger guns."*

"We're on that," Khatami said. She knew that Terrell
was taking a tremendous risk with his wounded vessel
and its battered crew, but she had no doubts that the *Sagittarius* would remain on the scene until it was pulled from
the sky. "You concentrate on avoiding the Changed and
evacuating any of our people who make it to the surface.
We'll cover you."

"Got it." Terrell offered a mock salute. "Sagittarius
out."

As the image on the screen shifted back to the tactical
schematic, Estrada reported, "Captain, the transporter
room just notified me that Commander Stano and the others are aboard, and she's readying her team to beam back
down."

"Good." Khatami allowed herself a small sigh of relief
as she moved to stand between the helm and navigator's
stations. "That only leaves us with an even million things
to worry about."

27

Emerging from the Preserver obelisk, Stephen Klisiewicz was taken aback at the number of Tomol who had relocated into the immense cavern surrounding the ancient artifact. Hundreds of villagers, almost all of whom had never set foot in or laid eyes upon this hallowed place, were moving about the chamber. Loud voices echoed off the cave's high, arched ceiling, bellowing instructions for people to keep moving deeper into the subterranean passages rather than clogging the area near the great cavern's primary entrance.

"This is getting out of hand," he said, noting how the pace of the proceedings was nearly frantic, in response to what Klisiewicz knew was a rapidly deteriorating situation on the surface. Tomol were running into the caves, some carrying young children in their arms, and while most heeded the instructions of those villagers who had been tapped to serve as stand-ins for those Wardens already killed by Nimur and her followers, there were some whose fear had all but blinded and deafened them to such direction. In those cases, the newly deputized Wardens took direct action, pulling aside the more troublesome refugees and calming them before sending them deeper into the cavern.

"Damn," said Leone as he stepped from the obelisk's

opening and moved to stand beside Klisiewicz. "This doesn't look good, does it?"

"Tell me about it," Klisiewicz said. The entrance remained open, its rectangular shape and smooth lines at odds with the rest of the cavern that retained much of its natural beauty. Through the entrance Klisiewicz could see still more Tomol, waiting in the anteroom as they were ushered into the cavern, and standing at the opening were four members of the *Endeavour*'s security detail, each armed with one of the weapons from the cache he and Leone had found within the obelisk. Additional security officers were deployed at the other entrances and tunnels leading to and from the cavern, all of which had been sealed to limit access to the vast chamber. Klisiewicz suspected that neither Kerlo nor any of the other Changed knew much if anything about the underground complex and would be limited to following the main passageway from the surface if they wanted access.

In other words, they'll be coming right at us.

He and the rest of his people did not appear to be the only ones taking notice of the new developments. Moments earlier, a low thrum had begun from somewhere deep within the obelisk, or perhaps the rock beneath the artifact, the source of which Klisiewicz had been unable to pinpoint. His tricorder had registered two new energy sources from somewhere deep in the complex's bowels, readings that had been confirmed in cursory fashion by Ensign Iacovino aboard the *Endeavour*. His studies of the glyphs inside the obelisk had not given him sufficient insight into the mechanism to determine the purpose of the new energy readings, but Klisiewicz guessed the Preserver artifact was enabling protocols similar to what it already had done during prior skirmishes with the Changed.

At least, I hope that's what it's doing.

His communicator beeped. "Klisiewicz here."

"Ensign Hewitt, sir!" Anxiety laced the junior security officer's words. *"Our tricorders are picking up Changed in the tunnels, coming this way. We're still getting interference from the surrounding rock, so they have to be close."*

Klisiewicz recalled that Hewitt and a team of three security officers, part of the group deployed by the recently arrived Commander Stano to reinforce his own landing party, were positioned at one of the tunnel junctions nearly one hundred meters from the cavern entrance. If they encountered no significant resistance, the Changed could be at the massive door protecting this chamber in two minutes or less.

"How many are you picking up?" As he asked the question, Klisiewicz kept his attention on the number of Tomol still entering the cavern and being directed away from the entrance. Someone obviously had communicated the threat of the approaching Changed, as the villagers were proceeding at a desperate pace farther into the smaller rooms and the tunnels leading deeper into the belly of the mountain protecting the Preserver complex.

"Two, at least. But there's a third reading I'm not sure about."

Leone said, "The first two could have triggered the Change in one of the other villagers. I tried to give the serum to everyone we thought was close enough to the Change to pose a threat, but it would've been easy to miss one . . . or more."

And none of that, Klisiewicz reminded himself, took into consideration the doctor's lingering concern that his unorthodox treatment might end up not working, anyway.

"Hewitt, what's the situation with the evacuees?"

"They've pretty much scattered, sir," replied the ensign. *"Most of those who were making their way down here are already in the anteroom, or else they've taken off down some of the other tunnels. I don't think very many of them know where they're going. Commander Stano reports that no more Tomol are attempting to enter the caves from the surface. They've taken off up the mountain or into the forest. There are some stragglers down here, and we're sending them your way."*

"Don't stay there any longer than you have to," Klisiewicz warned. "Get back here so we can seal the entrance."

"We're not making a run for the surface for beam-out?"

"We will, but we'll find another way out of here. Get here as fast as you can."

"Aye, sir. Hewitt out."

Behind him, a deep, gruff voice said, "We should retreat to a secure and defensible position." Turning, Klisiewicz saw Tormog glowering at him from where he stood before a pair of *Endeavour* security officers, Ensigns Leandro Weinreich and Javokbi. Weinreich, a human male, was carrying a standard-issue phaser rifle, whereas his female Rigellian companion carried one of the weapons found in the storage chamber. To Klisiewicz, Javokbi seemed as comfortable with the alien "fire lance" as she would with any Starfleet weapon.

"Where do you suggest we go, Doctor?" Klisiewicz asked.

Leone added, "Yeah, it's pretty much all up from here, no matter which way we go." He gestured toward the main entrance. "Lead the way."

Weapons fire from the anteroom or somewhere farther up the passageway echoed across the cavern, and the dozens of Tomol who still were in the vicinity of the entrance renewed their flight deeper into the mammoth chamber. Six newly appointed Wardens and the four *Endeavour* security officers were backing away from the opening.

"Here we go," Leone said, and for the first time Klisiewicz noted that the doctor had brandished his own phaser. Then he pointed. "Look!"

More security people were plunging through the entry. Klisiewicz saw Seta standing near it, holding out her arms, and he could tell she was saying something he could not hear. Seconds later, the section of stone wall serving as the door began sliding from its pocket, narrowing the gap just as the one last *Endeavour* security officer leaped into the cavern. The wall slid shut, and something clicked loud enough to cast its own echo across the room. Moving from the obelisk, Klisiewicz jogged toward the entrance and recognized Ensign Hewitt as the man who had been the last to enter.

"They're right behind us!" Hewitt shouted.

As if in response to his warning, a large thud slammed against the wall panel, and Klisiewicz was certain he saw it tremble in its mounting.

"That wall's three meters thick," Leone said. "It's strong enough, right?"

Standing behind Hewitt, Seta said, "I do not know how long we will be protected. I suspect the Changed will find another way inside."

"Always the optimist," Leone quipped.

Tormog said, "Perhaps my proposal to find a more secure position to await our attackers has merit after all."

Before Klisiewicz could say anything, a deep rumbling reverberated through the chamber, emanating from the rock beneath their feet and coursing through the walls around them.

"Okay," said Leone. "This is different."

Holding up his hand, Klisiewicz snapped, "Listen! Hear that? That's artificial. It's something new coming online."

Leone grunted. "Something pretty damned big, by the sound of it."

"Seta," Klisiewicz said, even as he was reaching for the tricorder slung over his shoulder, "do you know what that might be?"

The young Tomol priestess shook her head. "I do not."

Adjusting the scan settings on his tricorder, Klisiewicz frowned. "I think I might. These energy readings are a lot like the energy spikes the *Endeavour*'s sensors picked up when those drones were launched, but they're a lot more powerful."

"Of course they are," Leone said. "I think this is the obelisk's way of telling us it's time to haul ass."

From the readings he was seeing, Klisiewicz nodded. "Yeah, I think you might be right, but that means leaving this nice sealed room and going out to see our friends."

Neither option was particularly appealing at the moment. Though he had recorded a map of the underground passageways leading here from the surface cave entrance, he was not thrilled with attempting to navigate the subterranean maze while trying to avoid the Changed. "I'm open to suggestions."

"I will go outside," Seta replied. "I will face Kerlo."

Leone said, "That's crazy. She's a kid, for crying out loud. What the hell can she possibly do against Kerlo or any of the Changed?"

"He'll kill you with a single thought," Tormog said, sneering at the adolescent Tomol, "assuming he doesn't just turn you into one of his followers."

Seta shook her head. "He cannot do that. I am not yet of age. Also, I am the priestess. I believe he will talk to me. I do not believe he wants to kill any of us, but instead help us all through the Change."

"Your predecessor might not agree with that evaluation," Tormog said. "Nimur killed her and relished doing it. I saw it with my own eyes."

"As did I, only I did so while standing before Nimur, rather than cowering in the shadows."

"Ouch," Leone said, noting the irritated expression clouding the Klingon's features. "I've got a salve for that burn, if you want it."

Ignoring the verbal jousting, Klisiewicz looked to Seta. "You're serious about this? Do you think you can confront Kerlo peacefully?"

Seta appeared to Klisiewicz to have summoned a maturity and poise far beyond her handful of years. Her expression was one of quiet confidence as she offered a single nod.

"There is only one way to know."

This was an incredibly bad idea.

The errant thought mocked Katherine Stano as she fired her phaser rifle, its power setting pushed almost to maximum. She loosed the torrent of energy at near point-blank range, blasting into the chest of the oncoming Changed who had taken on the form of an immense, hulking brute. The force of the beam should have been sufficient to punch a hole the size of Stano's fist through the center of the creature's torso, but instead the transformed Tomol howled in response to the devastating attack as it was blown off its feet and sent sailing a dozen meters across the small clearing. It landed on its back atop the packed soil and bounced to a halt. Tracking its movements with her phaser rifle, Stano watched the Changed raise one feeble arm before the limb fell across its torso and the creature lay still.

"Nice shooting," said Ensign Kerry Zane. The broad-chested security officer wielded his own phaser rifle as he moved toward the fallen Changed. Stano stepped closer, noting how the transformed Tomol's dark oily skin was reminiscent of a snake's hide as it reflected the light of the midday sun. She probed its chest with her rifle's muzzle, noting that the skin did not yield. It was thick, perhaps possessing qualities that might explain how the creature had been able to withstand her weapon's effects. The Changed's face had elongated and narrowed, giving it a distinctly predatory appearance, and Stano saw that its muscles rippled beneath its dense skin.

Zane indicated the unconscious Tomol with his weapon's barrel. "He's still alive."

"Lucky us," Stano replied. Upon beaming up from the *Masao*'s landing site to the *Endeavour*, she had wasted no time grabbing a fully charged phaser rifle and extra power packs from the selection of arms waiting for her in the starship's transporter room. Along with Zane, Ensign Hewitt, and three other security officers, she had transported back to the surface, in the forest near the clearing that fronted the entrance to what the Tomol called the Caves of the Shepherds. There, they had witnessed the near chaos as Tomol villagers and some few Changed ran about. While most of the Tomol obviously were intent on seeking shelter, a small cadre had taken up defensive positions at or near the cave entrance, using weapons from a storehouse somewhere in the caverns in a bid to prevent any of the Changed from getting into the subterranean complex.

Despite those valiant efforts, at least two of the renegade Tomol had made it past the protective line and now were somewhere deep underground, heading for the positions Ensign Hewitt and his team had taken up near the entrance to the cavern holding the Preserver obelisk. It would be up to them and the other *Endeavour* personnel accompanying Klisiewicz to protect the ancient artifact from attack, all while the science officer worked to find some weapon or technology that might be of use in defending against the Changed.

"Incoming!" Zane shouted, dropping to one knee and

aiming at a target somewhere behind Stano. She heard running footsteps approaching at a rapid clip, and instinct made her throw herself to one side as the ensign fired his weapon. Lying on the ground, Stano heard the high whine of the phaser rifle and then the impact of the strike as well as the growl of pain from the Tomol who took the full force of the energy beam from a distance of less than ten meters. She saw the Changed—a female—staggering in reaction to the attack. Unlike the Changed Stano had just dispatched, this one had not altered her Tomol form, and when she did not fall, Zane fired again, this time keeping his finger on the weapon's firing stud and maintaining the onslaught until the Changed lurched backward before tripping over a rock and crashing to the ground. Still conscious, she attempted to raise herself to a sitting position only to be met by a third shot from Zane's phaser. This time, she stayed down.

"I'm down to less than thirty percent power," the ensign said, before pointing to the spare power packs attached to either side of the phaser rifle's stock. "Even with extras, these things will be dry in no time."

Stano nodded. "Let's find our people and go home."

Though the original plan to defend the Tomol villagers from Kerlo and his small yet growing band of renegade Changed was still the primary mission, Stano could see the writing on the wall. Kerlo's numbers were increasing every few minutes, and tricorder readings as well as sensor scans from the *Sagittarius* and the *Endeavour* told her that she and her people already were facing at least two dozen Changed. It was entirely possible that more were roaming the tunnels leading into the depths of the mountain and the cavern containing the Preserver obelisk. As much as it pained her to face the possibility of retreating from the skirmish, there were larger concerns. She had heard the shouts of the Changed who had attacked her moments earlier calling out to its companions to capture any or all of the "sky people" they encountered. This likely was part of a larger plan to use her or other members of the landing party as leverage to force Captain Khatami or Terrell to allow access to either or both of the Starfleet vessels. Stano had no intention of letting herself or any of her people be used in that way.

A loud rumbling hum from above preceded a long shadow sweeping across the clearing, and Stano looked up to see the *Sagittarius* flying past overhead. It was low enough to the ground for her to make out hull seams as well as the damage the scout ship had suffered on its ventral hull. As tough as it was, the *Sagittarius* still was looking at repair time once it made its way back to the nearest starbase. The ship banked to its left, the port phaser emitter on the top of its primary hull firing a harsh blue-white beam of energy toward a target on the ground Stano could not see. A blast in the distance among the trees made her flinch, and she tightened her grip on her phaser rifle in anticipation of one or more of the Changed plunging headlong from the forest. Moving away from the clearing, the ship fired twice more toward the ground.

"This is getting a little crazy," Zane said.

"More than a little." Stano activated her communicator. "Stano to *Sagittarius*. What's the story up there?"

A moment later, the voice of Captain Clark Terrell replied, *"We're keeping busy, Commander. Our sensors are tracking twenty-six Changed. We've incapacitated eight of them. If there are more below the surface, we're not seeing them, so watch your backs down there. Are you ready for us to try beaming up people?"*

Quelling her first instinct, Stano said, "Negative. Since you can only beam up one at a time, I don't want to run the risk of someone being left alone down here. I'm going to call in the *Endeavour* and hope that doesn't piss off whatever's underground."

"Understood. Be advised that we're picking up what look to be pretty powerful scanning beams, tracking us as well as the Endeavour *and the Klingon ship, so be ready for things to go bad in a hurry. We'll cover you as best we can, but we've already taken a pretty good pounding from those things. They overloaded our shield generators again, but Ilucci's working on a fix."*

Stano imagined the burly master chief toiling in the depths of the *Sagittarius*, sweating and cursing as he fought with his ship's damaged systems in an effort to get them to behave. "We appreciate the help, Captain. I . . ."

The rest of her words died in her throat as she caught sight of the scout ship turning in the distance to head back toward the clearing just as a pair of dark objects lunged upward from the forest. Looking like twins to the Changed Stano had just put down, the figures rose into the sky, arms spread wide and transforming before her eyes into long angled wings as they sailed toward the *Sagittarius*.

Stano shouted into her communicator, "Captain Terrell! You've got incoming!"

Now creatures of flight, the Changed pursued the ship as it banked away from the clearing and its nose tilted upward, and Stano heard the whine of its maneuvering thrusters as it pushed itself higher into the sky.

"*Hold steady, Commander,*" Terrell's voice snapped over her communicator. "*These things are trying to latch on to us!*"

"Damn," Zane said, his voice low. The single word was heavy with disbelief.

Watching the *Sagittarius* pull away, Stano realized that as Captain Terrell and his crew dealt with the new and very immediate threat, she and her people on the ground were for the time being without air support. The sensation of being exposed out here in the open was impossible to deny. With that in mind, she reached once more for her communicator and activated the frequency designated for her team.

"Stano to landing party. The *Sagittarius* is out of the picture until further notice. Continue protective measures and stand by for transport to the *Endeavour.*" Returning the communicator to her waist, she raised her phaser rifle. "Come on, Zane," she said, setting off toward the caves, "let's go find our people."

28

Since he was not a member of the *Sagittarius* bridge crew, or even part of the ship's total complement, there was no place for Lieutenant Commander Yataro to sit. The Lirin engineer could do nothing except grip one of the handholds situated near the command center's aft control stations and watch the careening, spinning image on the main viewscreen. Sky and ground rotated clockwise and then back, switching places with utter frenzy as the ship's helm officer, Ensign Nizsk, guided the *Sagittarius* through the latest in a series of frantic evasive maneuvers. The Kaferian's fingers were almost a blur on her console, but despite her best efforts, there seemed to be no shaking their pursuers.

"Sensors are detecting two life-forms on the outer hull," reported Lieutenant Commander Sorak, the ship's tactical officer, from where he sat at the station to Terrell's left. "I am also reading a series of breaches in those sections."

"Let me see," ordered Captain Clark Terrell. In response to his commands, the viewscreen shifted to show two dark figures crouching on the *Sagittarius*'s polished duranium skin. Yataro could see that both Changed had reverted from the flying forms they had used to chase the ship and now appeared as large, muscular behemoths with dark reptilian skin and long, flat heads. Rows of sharp teeth accented their long mouths, and their hands featured extended, multijointed claws. Each of the Changed was holding on to the hull with one hand, and Yataro realized that their claws had penetrated the thick plating.

"You've got to be kidding me," said Lieutenant Commander Vanessa Theriault, the ship's first officer. Everyone watched as one of the Changed balled the fist of its free arm and drove it straight down, punching through the duranium shell as though it were paper. Its face twisting into an expression of rage and exertion, the rogue Tomol pulled at the edges of the hole it had created, and Yataro saw that section of plating begin to curl upward.

"It's going to tear its way inside," Terrell said.

A new alarm sounded on the bridge, and Sorak reported, "Another Changed has affixed itself to the underside of the primary hull, and it just tore away part of the navigational deflector. All the telemetry feeds to the dish are now offline."

"That'll piss off the master chief," said Theriault.

Terrell replied, "We'll worry about it if we survive the next five minutes. Nizsk, do whatever you have to do to get those damned things off my ship."

"Acknowledged," replied the helm officer, her attention focused on her console. Under her guidance, the viewscreen changed to a tactical plot of the ship's course as the *Sagittarius* began another series of aerial acrobatics that Yataro was certain were pushing the vessel's internal gravity and inertial dampening systems to their limit.

That much was obvious from the warbling whine of the maneuvering thrusters, which still were hampered from the earlier crash landing. Nearly every major component on the entire ship had been compromised to one degree or another, and the present strain would make matters worse. Yataro was not sure which would doom the *Sagittarius* to another unwanted landing on the planet surface first: the Changed, or the ship simply buckling under the stresses being inflicted upon it.

A chirp from the intercom system preceded the agitated voice of the ship's chief engineer, Master Chief Petty Officer Michael Ilucci. *"What the hell are you people doing up there?"*

"We've got at least three Changed traipsing about the outer hull, Master Chief," Terrell replied. "They're punching holes in the ship. Want to go outside and tell them to knock it off?"

"Not really, but we're in no shape for this sort of maneuvering, at least not down here in the atmosphere. Inertial dampeners are going nuts, so whatever you're going to do, do it quick. Otherwise, we're all walking home!"

"Master Chief," Yataro said, stepping toward Terrell's command chair and gripping its headrest with both hands, "are you able to channel an electrical charge through the outer hull?"

"Sure. Hell, right now I'm amazed all of us haven't been electrocuted, already. Why do you . . . Oh! Now I get you. Nice thinking, Commander. Why the hell didn't I think of that?"

"You're a little busy?" Terrell offered.

"Hang tight. I'm on this."

A moment later, every console and light on the bridge flickered, and Yataro heard the unmistakable shift as power distribution was rerouted from nearly every shipboard system. All of this was accompanied by a low, resonating hum lasting several seconds.

"Please don't let there be an overload," Theriault said in a low voice. "Please don't let there be an overload. Please don't let there be a *damned* overload."

"I think it's working," reported Sorak. "I have lost one of the Changed life signs." Ilucci, doing whatever he was doing down in the engineering section, triggered another electrical charge across the ship's outer hull. This time, three of the auxiliary consoles along the bridge's bulkhead blinked in chaotic fashion before shutting down, their banks of display monitors and status indicators all going dark.

Overloads, Yataro realized. His idea, if nothing else, was having an adverse effect on the ship's already compromised systems.

His gaze still fixed on his instruments, Sorak said, "The other two life signs have fallen away, and I am not detecting any others. I believe we are clear, Captain."

"Right in the nick of time, too," replied Ilucci over the open intercom. *"We've got about a billion overloads and burned-out circuits all across the ship. I hate to say this, Skipper, but I'm pretty sure we voided the warranty this time."*

Despite the obvious tension permeating the bridge, Yataro saw Terrell bow his head for the briefest moment and emit a low, soft chuckle. Shaking his head, the captain straightened in his seat. "All right, Master Chief. Do what you can to hold things together, but we've still got a job to finish. Ensign Nizsk, take us back, and let's try to avoid picking up any more hitchhikers." Terrell regarded Yataro. "Nice thinking, Commander."

The Lirin nodded. "Happy to be of service, Captain."

Gesturing with a thumb over his shoulder, Terrell said, "I'm betting Ilucci could use some extra help back there."

"Agreed, sir," Yataro said, already moving for the hatch at the rear of the bridge in search of the *Sagittarius*'s distressed engineering section.

"It's getting a bit too exciting down here, Captain," said Katherine Stano over the *Endeavour*'s bridge speakers. *"I don't know how much longer we can hold them off. Also, our tricorders are picking up increased energy readings from somewhere below the surface. Are you getting that?"*

"What about that, Ensign?" asked Khatami, swiveling her command chair to face the science station.

"Affirmative, Commander," replied Ensign Iacovino. "We don't know what to make of it. The energy signature is similar to what we've seen in conjunction with the deployment of the drones you encountered on the surface, but this reading has a much higher intensity. Whatever it is, it's big."

Stano said, *"I'm thinking it's time for us to be elsewhere, Captain."*

"Agreed." Pushing herself out of her seat, Khatami

stepped around the helm console, her attention directed to the computer-generated tactical schematic displayed on the main viewscreen. Ensign Iacovino had enhanced the readout to show the positions of all *Endeavour* personnel on the surface, as well as the locations of all Tomol, Changed or otherwise. "We've got fixes on all but six of our people, but we're at least still in contact with them. The transporter room's standing by to start hauling everyone else back." It certainly was not the most desirable action to take, given the threat the Changed still posed to the rest of the Tomol villagers.

However, if what Klisiewicz had relayed to her was true as far as Priestess Seta's beliefs regarding Kerlo and his followers, it was entirely possible that removing the landing party from the equation might end or at least severely curtail the violence taking place on the surface. If Kerlo and the other Changed were struggling to show the rest of the villagers whatever "truth" existed with respect to the origins of the Tomol and the evolutionary course this people was supposed to take, then both the Starfleet and Klingon presence on this world was superfluous at best, and hazardous at worst. That the first Tomol to undergo the Change and forsake her society's rituals and rules did so without interference from the Klingons was a moot point, as were the attempts by the crew of the *Sagittarius* and her own people to mitigate the damage caused by that meddling. The simple truth was that, either by direct action on the part of the Klingons or accidental intrusion by Starfleet personnel, the Prime Directive had been violated here on Arethusa. Khatami was sure that the report she filed to Starfleet

Command—assuming she and the *Endeavour* survived the next few minutes—would provide fodder for all manner of debates over Starfleet's General Order Number One for some time to come.

And if that's not incentive enough to want to survive this mess, nothing is.

"Mister Estrada," Khatami said as she moved to stand at the railing in front of the main viewscreen, "notify the transporter room to begin beaming up our people."

"Captain," Stano said, *"request permission for me and Ensign Zane to remain here until we get Klisiewicz and the others out of the caves."*

"I'm not liking that idea very much, Commander."

"They may need backup getting past any Changed who've made their way into the tunnels. We can't let Kerlo or the others get their hands on even one of our people."

Considering the precious few options available to her, Khatami knew there was no time to wait for conditions to improve on the surface. "Permission granted, but we're going to give you some help." She looked to the science station. "Iacovino, full sensor sweep of that underground area. I want the rest of the landing party pinpointed."

The junior science officer replied, "Even if I can do that, Captain, our transporters still won't be able to lock on to them."

"No, but we'll know where they are, and we can guide them to Commander Stano. Mister Estrada, tell Lieutenant Klisiewicz that his captain is ordering him and the others to tie it up and get out of there." She sighed, pondering the ramifications of evacuating her people. "The Preservers left that thing down there who knows how many millennia ago. It'll still be waiting for us when we figure out how to get back to it."

At the communications station, Hector Estrada called out, "Captain, transporter room reports all but eight of our people are back aboard."

Khatami nodded in acknowledgment. Stano and Zane, along with Klisiewicz, Leone, and the four-person security detail accompanying the latter two, were belowground. Eight people was a lot to track in a situation as fluid and chaotic as their present circumstances, even if they were within a known, contained area.

"I've got them, Captain," said Iacovino. "Commander Stano and Ensign Zane are making their way to the main cavern, and I've got Lieutenant Klisiewicz and Doctor Leone thanks to Mister Estrada contacting them. I also have four other readings for our security team. Everyone's accounted for."

"Tell them their time's up," Khatami said. "Mister Estrada, use our sensor data to get everyone guided back to the surface, and I want the transporter room to yank them up the second they hit fresh air."

"Captain!" Iacovino shouted, turning from her sensor readings. "We're being scanned, and I'm picking up indications of a new power surge, beneath the surface. It's what preceded the weapons used against us before."

Recalling that the deflectors had been of only marginal use the previous time the Preservers' energy weapon was used against them, Khatami was of no mind to wait around to be hit again. She turned from the screen, point-ing to Lieutenant Neelakanta at the helm. "Evasive! Get us out of here. Full power to the shields!"

The order was barely out of her mouth before a new alarm wailed for attention and the Red Alert indicators scattered across the bridge began flashing in unison.

"Incoming fire!" Iacovino warned an instant before the energy beam slammed into the defensive barrier sur-rounding the *Endeavour*. Every light and indicator on every bridge station blinked in response to the strike, and Khatami heard the telltale groan of protest from the ship's main power plant as it worked to answer the renewed de-mands placed upon it.

"Our shields are weakening," reported Neelakanta, as he wrestled with the helm controls and attempted to guide the ship from danger. "Another hit like that and they'll go altogether."

"Break orbit," Khatami ordered. "Where's Kang's ship?"

Iacovino replied, "Still holding geosynchronous posi-tion. They're being fired at as well, but sensors aren't picking up any damage."

Of course not, Khatami mused. Then again, the *Voh'tahk* likely had not employed the full power of its sen-sors against the Preserver complex, so it had not irritated whatever automated systems beneath the surface were tracking the two orbiting vessels. Whatever the pyramid was doing, it did not like being disturbed while it made its preparations.

"To hell with this," she said. "Iacovino, find me the source of that weapon. We're taking it out of the game." It was unfortunate that she was being forced to damage or possibly destroy at least a portion of the treasure trove of knowledge contained within the Preserver artifact, but given a choice between protecting the site or her people, there truly was no choice, at least in her mind. "Estrada, notify Commander Stano that we're having to pull back and regroup, and that evacuation might be delayed for a few minutes."

Hang on, Kate. We're coming.

29

Stephen Klisiewicz had at first been unsure about wielding the heavy, cumbersome alien weapon, but such feelings of uncertainty vanished as he targeted his first opponent and fired.

The weapon, a larger, bulkier version of the lance carried by the Tomol village's Wardens, bucked in his hands as it belched harsh orange energy that lit up the entire anteroom. Its report was deafening in the confined chamber, but Klisiewicz ignored that as the beam punched the advancing Changed in its chest and sent it flying backward. The transformed Tomol's head struck the stone ceiling before its body fell back to the unyielding floor, skidding on the well-trod rock before coming to rest against the room's far wall.

"That's going to hurt in the morning," said Doctor Leone, standing with Tormog behind Klisiewicz.

"Indeed," said the Klingon. "A most impressive weapon." Both he and Leone also carried lances, and the ancient weapon seemed a natural fit for the Klingon both in terms of design and size. Though Klisiewicz had been reluctant to arm Tormog, the simple truth was that, for the moment at least, he and the landing party were allies against the Changed. However, seeing the look of satisfaction on the Klingon's face, Klisiewicz was certain the scientist likely was considering how he might be able to abscond with the lance when they all made it back to the surface for evacuation to the *Endeavour*. Even if he was unable to secure a Tomol specimen for study once he returned to the empire, Tormog might be able to preserve some sense of dignity and honor if he was able to present a representative sample of the Preservers' millennia-old yet still remarkable technology. Klisiewicz knew that was something to be prevented if at all possible, but right now he was concerned more about surviving the next few minutes, after which he would worry about possible repercussions from any mistakes made during this mission.

At this point, I honestly don't give a damn.

"Come on," he said, using the lance's bulbous head to gesture up the gently sloping passage. "Let's get out of here." Despite his own order, Klisiewicz paused for one last look at the Preserver obelisk standing at the center of the great cavern. The hundreds of Tomol who had sought refuge had gone deeper into the subterranean complex, and the artifact was alone in the vast chamber. Using the command sequence he had recorded Seta employing to open the ancient artifact, Klisiewicz had managed once again to seal the pyramid. At first he had been worried that the Changed might succeed in forcing their way into the mysterious structure, but then he was struck by the thought that if the Preservers were to do anything to protect against the Tomol or the life-forms into which they might evolve if left unchecked, it would be to prevent unwanted intrusion into their own creation. If that were the case, then the obelisk likely would be secure even from the power of a Changed.

It's a good theory, anyway.

"Are you sure this is the right way?" Leone asked, eyeing the various passages leading from the anteroom. "All these tunnels look alike."

Klisiewicz held up his tricorder. "I'm sure." Not for the first time, he patted himself on the back for his foresight in recording the route from the surface to the great cavern. Even without Seta to guide the way, the map he had created would be enough to lead them out.

Hearing sounds in a nearby tunnel, Klisiewicz raised his lance and braced himself to fire at any new targets. But a wave of relief washed over him when he saw that the four figures emerging from the passageway wore Starfleet uniforms. Ensign David Hewitt was leading the small group, with each member of the detail carrying a phaser rifle.

"Lieutenant," Hewitt said as he drew closer, and Klisiewicz noted that the ensign was slightly out of breath. Seeing the unmoving body of the Changed lying against the far wall, he looked to Klisiewicz. "Are you all right?"

"As good as I'm liable to get," replied the science officer. "You?"

Hewitt held up his phaser rifle. "Well enough, but these things are all but useless against the Changed. They've grown too strong. I blew through two power packs keeping a few of them off our backs out in the tunnels. If we're going to make a run for the surface, now's the time, sir."

He studied his tricorder's compact display screen. "That power reading is still increasing. It's much bigger than what we recorded when those drones were deployed."

Leone said, "But similar, right? That doesn't sound good. *At all.*"

"Could it be an explosive?" Tormog asked. "A form of self-destruct protocol?"

That made no sense to Klisiewicz. "It'd run counter to everything we know about the Preservers, including the things we've seen happen here in response to threats perceived by systems within the obelisk." It would not be the first time he had witnessed a version of some ancient race's last-ditch fail-safe protocol in action. The Shedai had employed such technology on uncounted worlds throughout the Taurus Reach, and several of those planets had been destroyed during Operation Vanguard as a consequence of unwittingly triggering those processes. As far as could be determined, the destruction of the Shedai had resulted in the obliteration of all their remaining technology in the region of space they once had ruled, but that certainly did not discount the possibility of another race possessing comparable resources and the willingness to employ them.

There's a happy thought.

"Sir," Hewitt said, "the *Sagittarius* will be waiting for us, but I don't know how long they'll be able to hang on. They're banged up pretty good."

The entire group turned at the sound of something moving and saw the massive stone door to the great cavern sliding back into place, seemingly of its own volition, sealing off the chamber and the Preserver obelisk. Within seconds, the other doorways leading from the anteroom closed in similar fashion, save one: the path leading to the surface.

"What the hell?" Klisiewicz asked of no one in particular as he reached for his tricorder. "Why would it do that?"

"Maybe it knows something we don't," Leone offered. He gestured toward the remaining accessible tunnel. "And I think they're trying to tell us something. I'm not a universal translator, but I think the message is pretty clear: get your asses out of my house."

Studying his tricorder's display, Klisiewicz frowned. "Yeah, you may be right, Doctor. These new power readings are spiking. Whatever's getting ready to happen, I think we want to be someplace else. Let's go; we're out of here."

Something big and solid slammed into one of the wall panels blocking the other exits, loud enough to make Klisiewicz flinch. Dropping his tricorder, he fumbled for the lance and readied it to fire as a second object hit the wall from outside, and this time the panel shuddered, though it remained in place.

"There seems to be very little on this world that can stop these infernal creatures," Tormog said, hefting his lance and aiming it at the wall.

"Go!" Klisiewicz gestured for Hewitt and his team to head for the only unblocked tunnel. "Head for the surface."

Raising his phaser rifle as a third collision rocked the thick wall panel, Hewitt said in protest, "I can't leave you here, sir."

"Your weapons aren't any good against these things, remember?" The security team would be sitting ducks once the Changed—however many there might be—came crashing through the wall. Again, Klisiewicz pointed to the tunnel. "Go. Get up there and let the *Sagittarius* beam you up. That's an order, Ensign!" His command was punctuated by another strike against the wall, and this time a crack formed, spreading across the middle of the dense panel.

"Holy shit," Leone said, bringing up his lance. "Run now, argue later, people!"

"Go!" Klisiewicz shouted, backstepping toward the tunnel as Hewitt and his team evacuated the anteroom. The science officer allowed himself a brief sigh of relief, satisfied that—for the moment, at least—the security officers were out of immediate danger.

Guiding Leone and Tormog toward the tunnel, Klisiewicz was the first to see the crack in the wall widen, then another resounding clap of thunder echoed in the chamber as the barrier was attacked yet again, and this time the wall came apart. Chunks of stone, breaking away from the wall itself, flew outward, and it was all Klisiewicz could do to avoid being struck by the airborne debris. Behind him, he heard Leone cry out, and a grunt of surprise made him turn to see Tormog's legs giving out and his toppling to the floor. A piece of the demolished wall fell beside him, and the Klingon howled in obvious pain, dropping his lance and gripping his right thigh with both hands. From the knee down, his leg was bent at an unnatural angle.

As Leone rushed to Tormog's side, Klisiewicz backpedaled to the mouth of the narrow tunnel as the rest of the wall fell apart, revealing another passage and two Changed pushing their way through the widening gap. The first creature was tearing at the crumbling door, ripping free pieces of stone and enlarging the hole.

Klisiewicz waited until one of the creatures showed its

face in the newly formed aperture before firing his lance.

The weapon again kicked in his grip as its energy beam spat forth, the full force of the salvo catching the Changed in its face. The creature's tortured howl echoing in the anteroom was enough to make Klisiewicz flinch, but he pushed aside his fear and fired again, his beam this time striking the second Changed in the chest and pushing the renegade Tomol back and away from the hole.

A second beam added to the chorus of energy permeating the anteroom. Leone had fired his own lance, though not at the Changed or the gap through which they were trying to force themselves. Instead, the doctor had taken aim on the upper edges of the wall and surrounding frame, blasting loose chunks of stone. Rubble began piling up, blocking the opening until a large slab of rock tumbled atop the growing heap, sealing it.

"Cute toy," Leone said. "Now, can we please go home?" Both men turned to the injured Tormog, still lying on the floor and gripping his broken leg and gritting his teeth against obvious pain.

"Leave me," the Klingon hissed, his eyes wide. "I cannot walk."

Mirroring Leone's movements as both men slid a free hand under one of Tormog's armpits, Klisiewicz said, "We'll help you."

"Why?" Tormog asked, grunting his discomfort as the two men helped him to stand.

Klisiewicz shifted his stance to accommodate their charge's unexpected weight. "My captain promised your captain that we'd return you to him."

"Kang is not my captain," Tormog countered.

Leone said, "Fine. Want to stay here?"

Pausing only a brief moment, the Klingon shook his head. "No."

"Good answer." Klisiewicz cradled the lance in the crook of his right arm and tried to position the weapon so that he could fire it while assisting Tormog. "Let's haul ass."

Rounding yet another bend in the tunnel, Stano and Zane came to a larger chamber. Despite its rough walls, floor, and ceiling, Stano could tell that both the passages and this room had been cut from the rock by someone or something. The walls were too straight and the ground too flat, and there were grooves and ridges in the stone, which suggested some kind of drilling apparatus. It reminded Stano of the tunnels created by dilithium miners in the Rigel colonies, or when Starfleet's Corps of Engineers assisted in the construction of planet-based starbases, or the outposts built on asteroids along the Neutral Zone. The tunnel leading to this modest-sized cavern continued on through its far side, but there also were three more passages heading off in different directions, each like the one they had been traversing illuminated by lamps set into the walls and fueled by oil or some other flammable substance her tricorder could not identify. Checking the unit's readings, Stano was able to confirm the intersection's location using the map created by the unit's scans of the mountain's interior.

"You should be meeting up with each other in a minute or two," said the voice of Captain Clark Terrell over her open communicator. *"But our sensors are also picking up Changed life-forms in the area, so stay frosty."*

"I don't suppose this is a good time to mention that I'm claustrophobic?" Zane asked, and when Stano looked to her, the ensign offered a sardonic grin.

"That's my joke," said Doctor Leone over the open channel. *"Write your own material, Ensign."*

Ignoring the banter, Stano said into her communicator, "Thanks, Captain. Any report on our other people?"

"Beaming up the last one now," Terrell replied. *"It was hairy there for a minute, but we're good. That defensive beam or whatever the hell it is took a shot at us at first, but we managed to avoid being hit. After we beamed up the second man, it seemed to lose interest. We were able to grab Ensign Hewitt and the last man without incident."*

"That's good to hear," said Lieutenant Stephen Klisiewicz. *"One . . . no, make that four fewer things to worry about."*

Stano agreed and released a small, relieved sigh, grateful that four more members of her landing party were safe, or at least safer aboard the *Sagittarius* than they were on the ground. Terrell and his crew had undertaken enormous risk by continuing to provide cover for her and the rest of her team, as well as using their sensors to penetrate the mountain and aggressively search for stragglers supposedly making their way to the surface. For whatever reason, the Preserver obelisk, which currently was taking shots at both the *Endeavour* and the

Klingon battle cruiser in orbit above Arethusa and which also had attempted to engage the *Sagittarius*, had turned its attentions away from the small scout ship. Stano did not begin to understand what was motivating the ancient mechanism one way or the other, and at the moment she did not care. All that mattered now was for her and Zane to find Klisiewicz and Leone, and the four of them could call it a day.

Amen to that.

"Captain, anything new on those power readings you're watching?"

Terrell said, *"Only that they're continuing to increase. I don't like it, Commander."*

"We definitely don't want to hang around here any longer than necessary," added Klisiewicz. *"We don't know for sure, but we think it could be some kind of self-destruct protocol."*

Before Stano could respond to that unsettling theory, her tricorder's scan readings began to fluctuate. Rather than a crisp display of data, the unit's small screen was filled with static. "We must be entering a larger concentration of mineral deposits or something. My tricorder's gone screwy."

"According to our sensors, that area is almost a blind spot," Terrell said. *"We're making adjustments to see if we can push through the interference, but it might take a minute. I'd keep moving, if I were you."* A moment later, he added, *"Hold on. We're getting indications of other life-forms in your vicinity, but we can't lock them down."*

Klisiewicz said, *"Is it us? My tricorder's acting up, too."*

"I don't think so," Terrell replied. *"We're trying to pinpoint a location."*

"I am here."

The voice came from behind her and Stano froze, feeling a chill course down her spine as she recognized the speaker: Kerlo. Closing her communicator, she gripped her phaser rifle, although she knew that she would never be able to turn and fire before the Changed killed her where she stood. With that in mind, she removed her left hand from the weapon's barrel and held it up to show that it was empty. She then allowed the rifle's muzzle to drop toward the ground before turning slowly. It was a struggle to maintain her bearing as she beheld Kerlo for the first time since Nimur had triggered his Change, standing at the mouth of a tunnel that cut deeper into the mountain. Though he had retained his normal form, there was no mistaking the iridescent glow of his eyes as he regarded her. Had he tracked them, sensing their presence with whatever abilities he now possessed?

"You would be wise to surrender to me," Kerlo said, raising his arm and pointing at her. "Obey me, and I will spare your lives. Defy me, and die, here and now."

Stano, despite the knot of fear growing in her gut, held the Changed's gaze and forced her voice to remain level. "You can't kill us. You need us to get to our ship." Though she expected some form of sharp rebuke, Kerlo smiled.

"I don't need all of you to get to your sky-ship. Some of you are more valuable than others." He pointed at Zane, and in that horrible instant Stano understood that Kerlo meant to kill the ensign right in front of her.

"No!" she said, raising her hands in protest, but Kerlo seemed to ignore her as his attention focused on Zane. It took Stano an extra second to realize that based on what he had seen Nimur do with her own telekinetic powers, the security officer should already be dead. Instead, Kerlo grimaced in abrupt shock, his other hand reaching for his head. The Changed emitted a low grunt, his discomfort obvious as he staggered backward and bumped into the unyielding tunnel wall.

The psionic dampener. She recalled the odd inhibiting effect it had produced in Commander Sorak and Lieutenant Hesh back at the *Sagittarius* crash site. That ploy supposedly had been emitted by the Preserver drones, so it made sense that similar resources could be brought to bear here within that very same underground complex from which those weapons had been dispatched.

As Kerlo dealt with the unexpected mental assault, Ensign Zane, reaching his own conclusion that he was still alive for reasons not yet explained, reacted in the only way he likely thought appropriate: he raised his phaser rifle and opened fire. The blue-white beam struck Kerlo in his left shoulder and sent him spinning back into the tunnel from which he had come, but he did not fall. Stano added her weapon to the attack, her strike slamming into the Changed's back and causing him to stagger until he fell against the passage's rock wall.

Otherwise the phasers had no meaningful effect.

"Damn," Stano hissed, adjusting her rifle's power output to its maximum setting. At that intensity, the phaser should be sufficient to disintegrate Kerlo along with a substantial portion of the surrounding mountain in the blink of an eye, and for a brief instant she worried that firing again might trigger a cave-in.

We're likely dead either way.

As Kerlo regained his footing and turned to face her, Stano raised her rifle to her shoulder and took aim at his chest. Zane followed suit, and their actions seemed not to faze the Changed, as he once more stepped from the tunnel into the larger chamber.

"Enough of this," Kerlo said. "Your weapons are useless against us now. There is nothing and no one to save you from your fate."

"I will save them."

Stano was stunned to behold Seta standing at the entrance to another of the tunnels. For one so young, the Tomol priestess impressed Stano with her composure.

"They do not understand our people, Kerlo," she said, stepping farther into the small cavern, "but that is not a criminal offense."

Sneering, Kerlo replied, "They are outsiders. They care not for us but for what they can learn or take from us. We are better than that. After uncounted generations spent doing the Shepherds' bidding and living the perpetual lie they foisted upon us, it is long past our time to assume total control of our own destiny."

"We can still do that, and without further bloodshed." Seta held out her hands. "Please, Kerlo. You have always been one of the most gentle, caring people in the village. I know that part of you still exists. Do not let it be consumed by the Change."

Kerlo shook his head. "If you will not join us, Seta, then

you are no better than the sky people, and you will share their fate, as will any Tomol who seeks to oppose us."

"I will not join you," Seta said, her voice firm.

"So be it." Kerlo stepped toward her. "Let you be the first example to all who would stand in our way."

30

Alert klaxons clamored for attention, inundating the bridge of the *Voh'tahk* with their incessant wailing like infants who yearned for feeding, but Kang ignored them. Gripping the arms of his chair, he held himself steady as the battle cruiser trembled around him, absorbing another salvo from the mysterious planet-based weapon.

"Evasive!" Kang shouted over the din. "Turn our weakened shields away from our enemy! And silence that alarm!" Once more, he cursed the adversary he could not see. The strike was the third inflicted upon the *Voh'tahk*, which still had not been returned to full operational status following its encounter with the planetary defenses. "Where does it hide?" he asked. He had gleaned enough information from previous sensor scans to understand that whatever technology was being employed against his ship likely was automated, its builders either having long since died out or fled the planet. That it still operated with such efficiency even after a protracted period of neglect was a testament to its construction, and Kang wished he could convey his admiration to those who had created it . . . before carving out their hearts with his *d'k tahg*.

"Captain!" called Mahzh, the *Voh'tahk*'s weapons officer. "I believe I've found the source of the attacks."

"Target that location and prepare a full barrage," Kang ordered. "Where is the *Endeavour*?"

Mahzh replied, "The Federation ship is continuing its own evasive maneuvers, but they also are locking weapons at the same point on the planet's surface."

"Captain," said Mara, in a low voice as she leaned in close to his left ear, "why do you continue this fight? Let the Earth ship deal with this. When they have departed or been destroyed, this planet will still be here."

Kang was forced to admit that while he had entertained that very thought, there was a simple reason he had not acted upon the notion. "I gave Khatami my word."

"What does Klingon honor mean to an Earther?" His hard glare caused her to glance about the bridge, and when she spoke again her voice was softer still. "How do you know you can trust her?"

"Earthers have their own form of honor," Kang said. "You have seen it with your own eyes. I believe this ship captain to be of similar character."

"What makes you so certain?"

"My instincts." Honed in battle, they rarely failed him, and he trusted them now. Kang waved her away. "Attend your station."

Nodding, Mara stepped back from his chair. "Yes, Captain."

As she returned to her science console, a new alarm sounded on the bridge, and Mahzh announced, "We have been targeted again. Incoming enemy fire!"

There was no time to call for any maneuver that might guide the *Voh'tahk* out of danger before the deck heaved beneath Kang's feet and he felt himself lifting from his seat. Only his grip on the chair's arms kept him from being thrown to the deck, and he noted that his bridge officers were faring in varying degrees to the attack. Mahzh and Mara were holding on to their consoles, but his communications officer, Kyris, tumbled to the metal floor grates.

"Move us away!" Kang bellowed over the sound of the new alarms. All around the bridge, alert indicators were flashing their different warnings from different consoles. This latest attack had caused even more damage, he surmised, perhaps more than even Konvraq, his loyal friend and engineer, might be able to repair.

"Maneuvering thrusters are off-line!" shouted his helm officer, Ortok. "Impulse engines are slow to respond. Our shields are down to critical levels, Captain!"

From her station, Mara said, "If they strike us again, we will be defenseless."

"We are defenseless *now*!" Kang barked. As though mocking his mounting frustration, the *Voh'tahk*'s primary power generators chose that moment to fail, their omnipresent drone fading as lights and displays across the bridge dimmed, their operations continuing only because of the battle cruiser's backup power sources.

"We have lost all propulsion!" Ortok reported.

Mahzh added, "Weapons and shields are inactive."

"Life support is holding," Mara said, "though our sensors are on reduced power."

Snorting, Kang pounded the arm of his chair. "Excellent. At least we will be alive, breathing and warm, when death deals its final blow upon us." His gaze fixed on the main viewscreen and the lush world displayed upon it, and Kang all but jumped from his chair when he observed several beams of energy following what he recognized as a barrage of eight Starfleet photon torpedoes dropping toward the planet's surface. "What is this? The *Endeavour*?"

"Affirmative, Captain," Mara answered. "They are firing on the source of the weapons attacking us." A moment later, she said, "I am detecting explosions on the surface and at points belowground. Their counterattack appears to have been successful!"

Behind him, Kyris said, "Captain, we are receiving a hail from the Starfleet ship."

"Open the frequency." He pushed himself from his chair as the image on the viewscreen changed from Arethusa to the Earther captain, Khatami.

"Captain," she said, *"we think we've neutralized the weapon. Our sensors aren't picking up activity from that area anymore."*

Kang moved toward the screen, nodding in admiration. "Well done, Captain. You have slain my enemy."

"We're also reading the damage to your ship. Do you require assistance?" The question was presented without the slightest hint of arrogance or superiority, and Kang knew that she was reaching out, ship master to ship master, with a genuine desire to render aid.

"I may well accept your offer, Captain, but in due course. I know you have more pressing matters to attend to." He glanced about the bridge of his wounded ship. "We shall be here." As the communication faded, Kang shook his head and released an irritated sigh.

Where else are we to go?

* * *

Fueled by determination and a clarity he had not known before giving himself over to the Change, Kerlo crossed the chamber toward Seta. There was no denying the bravery exhibited by the young priestess, who had found herself unceremoniously thrown into her position as leader of the Tomol following the death of her mentor, Ysan, at Nimur's hands.

"I see it in your eyes," Seta said, holding herself straight and meeting his gaze. "You will kill me just as Nimur murdered Ysan."

The statement, delivered in such a blunt manner, gave Kerlo pause. It was unfortunate that his mate had deemed it necessary to kill the high priestess, and he remained troubled that Nimur seemed to have taken satisfaction from her actions, but even that regret was colored by the growing realization that not all of his fellow Tomol would understand or accept the truth of their existence, and that they were destined for things far greater than what the Shepherds would have them believe. The time had come to cast off the shackles holding them prisoner on this world, and Kerlo suspected that with sufficient opportunity to acclimate to their new reality, most of his people would make the transition without great difficulty. Of course, there would be those, like Seta, who would resist, and the longer this battle continued, the less inclined Kerlo was to entertain such defiance.

And why must it be this way? Why can we not simply show them the truth behind the Change and allow them to accept it on their own terms? Is this confrontation truly necessary?

Those and so many more questions had plagued him almost from the moment he had surrendered to the Change, but he was finding the effort to seek the answers growing more difficult as time passed. They were being replaced by a persistent need to carry on, as though survival depended on prompt, decisive action. Kerlo could not summon a reason for why he was gripped by such feelings, only that he must follow them.

These thoughts dissolved in an eruption of pain as flames from the sky people's fire lances once more reached out for him. Though his body recoiled at the assault, Kerlo realized the sensations were duller than before. The flames held less power over him now, and with effort he remained standing in the face of the renewed attack. Behind him, the two sky people, Stano and her male companion, continued to fire their lances, then one of the weapons stopped firing.

"Damn it," said the male. "Power pack's drained."

Kerlo did not understand the words, but he comprehended that the man's lance no longer carried a flame. They obviously did not channel the energy provided to the village Wardens by the Shepherds, which meant they soon would be helpless against his people.

In time, he reminded himself.

"Seta!" shouted the female sky person, Stano. "Get away from him!"

"There is nowhere for her to run," Kerlo said, his attention fixed on the young priestess, who looked to the sky people as if hoping for them to come to her aid. Though the assault on his thoughts continued and he knew he could not influence her or the sky people with his mind, he still possessed the vision provided by the Change to see the aura surrounding Seta, and it was this that intrigued him. Though he knew her to be of an age where the fires would not burn within her for some time, there still was something in her that he did not recognize, a new quality to her deepest self that he had not seen in the other Tomol, even those approaching the time of their own Change. He could not identify this new ember radiating from within Seta, but on some level Kerlo grasped what it represented.

"Seta!" Stano warned again, but this time the girl's attention did not waver from Kerlo. She stood still, as though prepared to embrace whatever fate might bring her. Kerlo ignored the sky people, reaching out with one hand to caress Seta's face. The spark was there! It was faint, but present nonetheless. Pushing through whatever veils the Shepherds' wordstone was using to cloud his thoughts, Kerlo reached across the void to touch the girl's mind, taking hold of the feeble fire he sensed there and coaxing it forward. It took only a moment before he felt his efforts being rewarded and Seta's aura began to shift. The Change blossomed, swelling within her, and unlike others he had transformed, the girl did not seem overcome by fear or uncertainty. Like the leader she was destined to be, Seta was accepting this transition with courage and grace, and Kerlo smiled with an almost paternal pride.

"Soon you will understand."

"I already understand," Seta replied. "It is you who requires enlightenment."

Moving with a speed he had not anticipated, the girl reached forward with something in her hand and pressed it against his arm. Kerlo heard an odd hiss and immediately realized that she had used some device to introduce something into his body. It was not a weapon, but the shock of the abrupt action still caught him by surprise. He stepped backward, feeling no pain but rather sensing something foreign now working within him. Looking down at his hands, he already could detect minute changes in his aura, and the shift was growing both in intensity and velocity.

"What have you done?"

Seta regarded him with an expression of confidence, though her features betrayed her concern. "I am saving my people, Kerlo, and you are going to help me."

Helpless to do anything except watch the confrontation between Seta and Kerlo, Stano grabbed Zane's arm and pulled him with her into the tunnel, holding in her free hand her all but useless phaser rifle. Eyeing the weapon's charge, she guessed she had one or perhaps two shots at its maximum intensity setting before the power pack was exhausted. Not that it mattered, as it had proved to be increasingly ineffective against Kerlo, who appeared to be growing stronger with every fleeting moment.

"What the hell did she just do?" Zane asked, still holding his drained phaser rifle.

Stano said, "Some kind of injection from a hypospray, one of ours. It must be the treatment Doctor Leone came up with." Thanks to an update from Captain Khatami, she knew that the *Endeavour*'s chief medical officer had arrived at what he thought might address the anomalies introduced millennia ago by the Shedai into the Tomol's genetic makeup, and that Leone already had administered his potential solution to Seta and several of her people who were approaching that period of their development where the Change could take place. As far as she knew, the treatment had not been given to any Tomol who already had undergone the Change, until now.

"Look." Zane pointed to Seta. "He's done it to her. She's changing, too."

Pulling again at his arm, Stano retreated farther into the tunnel, watching as Kerlo reacted to whatever Seta had injected into him. He staggered away from her, but as he regained his balance his expression darkened, and Stano was certain the glow in his eyes intensified.

"Your potions or poisons will not stop me," he said, growling the words at her as he closed the distance separating them.

Seta stepped away and to her left to avoid being trapped with a wall to her back. "I am not trying to stop you, Kerlo. I want to help you, so that we both can work to help all of our people."

The words seemed to fuel Kerlo's growing anger, and he lunged forward, raising one arm to strike. Seta, smaller than her opponent, deftly sidestepped the attack, and as he dashed past she reached out and hit him in the back of his head. Not expecting her to defend herself, Kerlo staggered forward and fell into the rock wall, the force of his punch enough to gouge out a section of stone and send it crashing to the uneven floor.

"This is getting ready to get totally out of hand," Zane said.

Stano nodded, mesmerized as the two Changed faced off, realizing that this was the first time she had witnessed such a confrontation between two Tomol so transformed. "Between them, they could probably bring half this mountain down around our ears."

"Then it sounds like a good time to find the way out."

Startled by the new voice, Stano and Zane whirled about, phaser rifles up and ready, to see Klisiewicz and Leone, helping to support an obviously wounded Tormog.

Leone, his face flushed with exertion, said, "That means let's get the hell out of here."

"Are you all right?" Stano asked, trying to divide her attention between the new arrivals and the two Changed. Seta, still maneuvering much faster than Kerlo, was evading his attacks, which seemed to deepen Kerlo's fury.

"What the hell . . . ?" Klisiewicz asked, watching the proceedings. "Seta?"

"Kerlo changed her," Stano said.

The young priestess feinted to her right before ducking the other way and coming in low, up and under Kerlo's right arm. She lashed out with what Stano recognized as some form of practiced self-defense technique, striking Kerlo in his right armpit. The blow must have hit something sensitive, because Kerlo dropped his arm and howled in pained surprise, reaching for the wounded area with his other hand and moving away from the small but feisty Seta.

"We need to help her," Zane said.

Stano shook her head. "There's nothing we can do."

"What about this?" Klisiewicz asked, and the science officer held up a weapon she did not recognize; it appeared to be related to the lances wielded by the Wardens of the Tomol village. Taking it from Klisiewicz, she tested its heft before deciding to aim it at Kerlo.

Then her communicator beeped. Stano was unable even to utter a greeting before Captain Clark Terrell's voice bellowed, "*Sagittarius to Stano! You need to get out of there right now!*"

Frowning as she watched Kerlo and Seta dancing around each other, Stano said, "Captain? What is it?"

"*Another treat from the Preservers,*" Terrell barked. "*Some kind of fail-safe contingency, maybe. It's the same fossilization effect the drones deployed, but this looks designed to blanket an area. We've isolated its origin at several points in a ten-kilometer radius around the mountain, and it's spreading in all directions and picking up speed, with no signs of stopping. Nothing in its path is being spared. For all we know, it's going to cover the whole damned island. Based on our readings, you've got about six minutes to get to the surface or you'll be cut off when it washes over that mountain. Our transporter's down, but the* Endeavour's *waiting for you to get clear of the underground interference. Get moving, Commander! Now!*"

"Six minutes?" Leone said, his words wrapped in disbelief. "We'll never make it."

"Well, I'm damn sure not staying here," Stano said, gesturing up the tunnel. "Move out." Still holding the lance Klisiewicz had given her as her people began hurriedly shuffling their way toward the surface, she turned for one last look at Kerlo and Seta, who now saw only each other as they continued their fight. They were oblivious of the lesser creatures watching them battle, just as they knew nothing about whatever was coming in the next six minutes.

Less, Stano reminded herself before turning to run.

31

Kerlo's rage was mounting with every passing heartbeat. How dare this impudent whelp defy him? How could she not understand the gift he had given her, and what it meant not only for her but also for the continued existence of all their people?

At long last, he swung at her and his fist impacted against the side of her head. Seta tumbled to one side, trying and failing to maintain her footing on the uneven ground. Kerlo moved closer, raising both hands with the intention of delivering a blow to the top of the girl's head, but he realized too late that her stumbling and struggling to regain her footing was a ruse. As he stepped in and began bringing his arms down, she rose to meet him, clasping her hands together and slamming them into the underside of his chin. The force of the attack was uncanny, doubtless owing to her own increasing strength as a result of her Change. Light exploded in Kerlo's vision and a wave of dizziness washed over him as he crashed to the ground. His stomach heaved and for an instant he thought he might retch, but then hands closed around his ankles.

To his utter astonishment, he felt himself lifted from the stone floor and flung away, discarded like refuse. There was no time to prepare and he hit the wall. Rock cracked and gave way in the face of the assault, and as he slid to the floor, debris rained down upon him.

"Impressive," Kerlo said, noting his uneasiness as he pushed himself to his feet. To her credit, or perhaps naïveté, Seta did not press her own attack but instead allowed him an opportunity to collect himself.

"Do you not understand?" Seta asked, exertion evident in her words. "We cannot keep fighting like this. The Shepherds did not intend this for us."

Kerlo released a derisive grunt. "The Shepherds. We are their playthings. Worse, we are like pets in a cage. They brought us to this world to amuse them, to live in a vacuum and fated to die with no hope of reaching our true potential. That is the crime the Shepherds perpetrated against all our people."

"They also will not allow this to continue," Seta said. "You have seen what the wordstone has done. Do you wish to become one with the Endless?"

"The Shepherds and their infernal devices have cowed us for too long," Kerlo said. Without warning, he launched himself toward Seta, but the girl had anticipated his attack and managed to sidestep him. He thrust out one arm and caught her about the ankles, tripping her and dropping her to the floor. Rolling through his fall, Kerlo was able to regain his feet, but as he turned to face her, Seta was already charging him, her small hands lifting a large piece of rock, which she rammed into his face. Kerlo felt his jaw and nose cracking and several of his teeth loosening, and he tasted the thick, oily tang of his own blood. Seta did not rest, following with a second strike and pummeling the side of his head with the stone. In blind rage he swiped at her with his hand, but she was moving again, dancing away out of his reach.

She's beating you, his pain-racked mind taunted him. *A child is beating you!* For a brief moment, he pondered the irony in his internal rebuke, as he was but a small handful of sun-turns older than Seta, but then the anger reasserted itself, and his thoughts began to clear. What was this?

"I can sense it within you," Seta said, again moving to a safe distance rather than pressing her attack or lashing out in defense. "Your thoughts are becoming yours once more. Do you not feel it?"

This is wrong.

The musing came unbidden, erupting from the depths of his troubled mind and fixing itself at the forefront of his consciousness. "This is your doing?"

"Yes," Seta said, "with the help of the sky people. Without their assistance, we are doomed, Kerlo. The Shepherds will permit nothing else."

Something new was intruding on his thoughts. There was no intelligence or emotion; he saw only the manifestation of a great force, unyielding and unrelenting, growing more powerful as it drew closer. He tried to see into it and came away with nothing but darkness, deep, impenetrable blackness from which there was no escape.

"The Endless," he said, but as he spoke the words he realized he was alone. Where had Seta gone? He reached out with his thoughts and found her, moving deeper into the mountain. She was fleeing toward the great cavern, to the wordstone.

"The Shepherds will not protect you." Even as he spoke the words, Kerlo perceived something new, something heretofore unknown even with the heightened awareness granted to him by the Change. All of this, everything for which he now fought, and for which his mate Nimur had fought, and for which they both had come to believe was necessary in order to secure freedom for the Tomol from their faceless oppressors, was wrong.

Seta's reply echoed in his mind: *The Shepherds will not protect any of us now.*

"What have we done?" Why had this clearness of mind been denied to him all this time? Why had his mate not benefited from such insight? Had the sky people been right all along and sincerely worked to help his people? If so, what then was the true destiny of the Tomol? Was there a life to be lived while having accepted the Change, but without the violence that had so characterized the supposed freedom and autonomy Nimur believed to be their birthright?

You were wrong, Nimur. We all were.

Was it too late to correct the grievous mistakes they had committed?

Plunging headlong down the tunnel, he pushed himself as fast as his legs would carry him, tuning his thoughts to Seta's and letting them lead him to her. She was in the great cavern now, close to the wordstone. What could she hope to do before he caught her?

The approaching darkness and cacophony rang in his ears, and Kerlo realized it was more than simply a manifestation of a force clouding his thoughts. All around him the very stone of the mountain itself trembled, and there was a new energy filling the air. It played across his exposed skin and he sensed heat and cold waging war for supremacy over his body. Instinct made him look back the way he had come, and Kerlo found himself staring into . . .

. . . *endlessness.*

"Come on! We have to keep moving!"

The trail was narrow and steep, cutting a swath across the face of the mountain, but not so extreme that it could not be navigated. Stano, still wielding the lance weapon Klisiewicz had bestowed upon her, led the way up the path, keeping her eyes on the loose, uneven ground while trying to remain alert for threats.

"Are you okay?" she asked, halting her advance and turning to check on her charges. Ensign Zane was assisting Lieutenant Klisiewicz in carrying the wounded Tormog, scrambling for every foothold as they pushed themselves up the trail. The Klingon was hobbling on one foot, his wounded leg having been set in a makeshift splint fashioned by Zane from two inert torches the security officer and medic had found at the entrance to the caves. Doctor Leone was bringing up the rear, ready to help Klisiewicz or Zane if either man stumbled, all while keeping an eye out for threats trying to chase them down.

"We're okay," Klisiewicz said. "We only have to hang on for another minute."

Neither Stano nor the rest of her group had seen any Changed since emerging from the caves, and the reason for that had become obvious when she got her first look at what was happening all around them. The surrounding terrain—the forest, clearings, bodies of water, everything for as far as they could see—was succumbing to the effects of the petrification. Looking back the way they had come, Stano saw the wave of energy washing over the entire area, leaving behind a blanket of pale brown stone covering everything from the base of the mountain to the horizon. A constant low rumble accompanied the effect, sounding like a mix of rushing water and the steady ebb of a starship's warp engines. Stano found the sound not even remotely pleasant. As for the mountain itself, it was the epicenter of this newest tactic from the Preservers and their ancient yet seemingly omniscient technology, with a tightening ring of energy pulsing up from the base and rushing to cover the slope. The effect was accelerating as the circle drew tighter, leaving her group precious little time.

"Are we clear yet?" Zane asked.

Consulting the tricorder slung from her left shoulder, which she had left open and active in order to provide constant updates on their progress, Stano shook her head. According to her scans, which were little more than a muddled mess of incoherent data, they still were too close to the mineral deposits that clouded sensors and transporters. "I can't tell. My tricorder's still screwed up. There's a shelf about fifty meters ahead. If we can get there, the *Sagittarius* may be able to get close enough for us to hop aboard."

"*Transporters have a lock on you,*" said the voice of Captain Khatami over her open communicator, "*but it's still iffy. Keep moving.*"

Stano saw the *Sagittarius* hovering near the shelf. The scout ship was definitely the worse for wear, but right now she was the most beautiful thing she had ever seen. Even from this distance she could see that its rear cargo ramp had been lowered, and someone was standing near its edge, waiting for her and the others to close the gap between them and the ship. The distance to the *Sagittarius*, Stano realized, was greater than the area of mountainside separating the landing party from the wave of materializing stone rising toward them. So close was the effect now that she could hear it moving over grass and rock on the slope, covering everything in its path. There was nowhere to go but up.

"You know how you sometimes imagine the different ways you might die?" Leone asked, his breathing labored as they continued to climb. "This one's never come up."

"*Sorry to disappoint you, Doctor*," Khatami said.

Then Stano smiled as she felt the first familiar tingle of a transporter beam forming around her body.

Khatami stood spellbound as she watched the flood of stone sweep over the sides of the mountain, coming to a halt perhaps one hundred meters from its peak. The image provided by the *Endeavour* bridge's main viewscreen was from almost directly above the Suba island, with the mountain and surrounding area enlarged and enhanced and sparing no detail as the Preserver fail-safe protocol continued unimpeded. Aside from the mountain's summit, the rest of the landmass was now covered by a blanket of red-brown stone. Grooves and ridges reminded her of rock canyons and formations she had hiked while on vacation in the desert regions of North America. That it had sprung up before her eyes, and not because of millions of years of erosion, uplift, or other tectonic activity, actually was the least disturbing aspect of what she beheld.

"Readings are stabilizing, Captain," reported Ensign Iacovino. "The field is . . . it's not really inert. I've never seen anything like it, but I'm registering indistinct bio readings from within the rock. Tomol, indigenous wildlife, flora—it's all there. The entire island's been perfectly preserved, just as if it had been put into stasis."

At the rear of the bridge, the turbolift doors parted to admit Commander Stano and Lieutenant Klisiewicz, exhausted in their dirty and torn uniforms, but Khatami was relieved to see them. Stano made eye contact with her and nodded.

"Thanks for the pickup, Captain."

"Remember that when you sign for the tip. Status?"

Already moving toward the science station, Klisiewicz hooked a thumb over his shoulder. "Doctor Leone and Ensign Zane took Tormog to sickbay."

"Tormog has a broken leg," Stano added, "but the doc thinks he'll be okay." She pointed to the viewscreen. "That's *insane*."

Still marveling at the effect herself, Khatami replied, "We're monitoring the end of the process now. Ensign Iacovino says everything caught up in it is still alive, just locked in whatever the Preservers call hibernation."

"The whole damned island?" Klisiewicz asked, shaking his head in obvious disbelief. "Any Tomol life signs outside that area?"

Iacovino replied, "Nothing I can find, sir." Bending over the science console, she adjusted a handful of controls and peered into her hooded sensor viewer. "There are several hundred Tomol within the mountain who haven't been caught up in the effect. All of them are in the cavern with the Preserver obelisk."

"Are any of them Changed?"

"I can't tell, Captain." Iacovino frowned. "We're already pretty much at the limit for our sensors penetrating the interference from all the mineral deposits."

"So all of those people are trapped?" asked Lieutenant McCormack from the navigator's station.

Klisiewicz tapped a series of controls on the console next to Iacovino, and one of the station's overhead monitors activated, transferring data from the sensor viewer to its display. "It doesn't look that way. According to these readings, the cavern containing the obelisk wasn't included in the wave, and there's at least one open passage leading from the cavern to the top of the mountain."

"So you're saying the Tomol could just walk out of there?" Khatami asked.

Shrugging, Klisiewicz replied, "More like someone could walk down there. The Preservers, for example."

"That would make sense," added Iacovino. "You said from your study of the pyramid that the Preservers would send someone to investigate if the failsafe protocol was triggered, and maybe even reverse the process once it was determined it was safe to do so."

"Too bad they all died out," Stano said.

"Exactly." Klisiewicz returned his attention to the monitor. "We're still detecting the energy sources from the caverns, including the obelisk. They definitely meant for it to remain unaffected by any last-ditch effort to contain the Tomol."

At the communications station, Lieutenant Estrada announced, "We're being hailed by the *Voh'tahk*, Captain."

"Tell them to stand by," Khatami said. She knew that the Klingon battle cruiser had suffered significant damage during the final moments of it and the *Endeavour*'s standoff with the Preserver planet-based defenses, and that Kang would be wanting an update on any assistance she would be providing. "They can wait, at least for a few minutes."

Returning her attention to the main viewscreen, Khatami studied the mountain and its adjacent terrain, all of it surrendered to the whims of a race believed to be long dead. That the Preservers had planned for this, even after all of their effort to bring the Tomol to this idyllic world and establish their self-policing society rather than simply snuffing out the remnants of their species on their homeworld, how great was the true threat embodied by this people? What secrets had the Preservers taken with them on their path to eventual extinction? Of those, which ones remained to be discovered?

The obelisk, of course, was the key. There was no other logical conclusion.

"Get yourself cleaned up, Mister Klisiewicz," Khatami said, shaking her head in wonder at the Preservers' handiwork. "And tell Doctor Leone to do the same. Our job's not finished here just yet."

32

There had been infrequent occasions during her life when Atish Khatami had wished for nothing more than a fleeting respite from the demands of duty and obligation, whether to her uniform or even her family and friends. She always imagined a quiet refuge—a garden, a small mountain lake, or even a cabin with a fireplace before which she might curl up on a sofa with a favorite book— that offered escape, if only for a few precious moments, from such pressures.

As she walked through the quiet environs of the Tomol village, Khatami felt herself wanting both to flee to that illusory safe harbor and yet unwavering in her desire not to leave this place, at least not until she could find some way to restore to it the life that had been taken from it.

The sound her boots made with every step over the rough, unyielding stone material covering the entire village and everything for kilometers in every direction drove home the enormity of what had happened here. The huts and other structures, sculptures and other freestanding decorative pieces, furniture, trees and other vegetation and, yes, even those Tomol who had not evacuated to the relative safety of the caverns all stood silent and still, bereft of anything that indicated that this place mere hours earlier had been home to hundreds of people. Now all of it, along with the rest of the Suba island, was still, arrested by the unyielding stone shroud.

Some Tomol—far too few of them—walked about the village just as she did, their expressions all conveying the same horror and disbelief at what had been visited upon them. These were the fortunate ones who had been inside the cavern containing the Preserver obelisk, which had been sealed to prevent entry by Kerlo or any of his Changed followers. As such, they had been insulated from the effects of the Preserver's final protective measures against the Changed, but Khatami knew their relief—if they even felt such an emotion—was at best bittersweet.

Far more prevalent was the sadness gripping those spared the Preservers' last strike against the Changed, as villagers returned aboveground to try to locate friends or loved ones who had not made the flight to safety. Khatami herself had seen several Tomol caught up in the effect, immobilized with the same cold yet ruthless efficiency as that visited upon the Changed and indeed everything else within the targeted area. Still lingering in her mind was the image of the young female she had seen after peering into one hut's open window, huddled on the floor with her arms hugging her legs and her chin pressed against her knees and enveloped in the same reddish-brown crust that coated everything else. The ghastly scene had hammered home the point that three members of her own crew also had been so imprisoned. Khatami had visited the area where her people were targeted by the Preserver drone, and the sight had filled her with sorrow and a grave sense of utter helplessness. Being forced to leave them behind was a decision she dreaded. Likewise, she knew she would be forever haunted if she were forced to depart this place after failing to do anything to restore it to what it once had been.

So let's do something about it.

Her communicator beeped, and she flipped open its cover. "Khatami here."

"Captain, this is Commander Yataro," said the voice of the *Endeavour*'s chief engineer. *"You asked to be notified when we were finished assisting the Klingons with their repairs. Our tasks are complete and we have returned to the ship."*

"I trust everything went well?"

"It did. The Klingons exhibited their usual displays of effrontery, as well as making no effort to hide their chagrin at being forced to accept our assistance, but Captain Kang saw to it that our efforts were not wasted."

Khatami nodded, satisfied with the report. "Excellent news, Commander. My compliments to you and your team. You've had a pretty busy last couple of days, but you came through in fine fashion. I appreciate it."

"You are quite welcome, Captain. Yataro out."

As she closed her communicator, Khatami heard footsteps approaching from the path leading out of the village. It was Leone, walking alone. The doctor's face was grim, which by itself did not communicate a great deal as that tended to be his default expression. Now, though, she thought she saw a definite sadness in her friend's eyes.

"Tony? What is it?"

"A big bunch of nothing," Leone replied, shaking his

head. "I just talked to Klisiewicz, and they're coming up empty back at the obelisk." He let his gaze drop to the ground, which like everything else was encased in the same stonelike material. "It's like we said earlier—this stuff, whatever it is, is a living thing with a single purpose: keep whatever it holds within it *alive*." Dropping to one knee, he ran a hand across the stone veneer's rough surface. "I could spend the rest of my life here studying it and never find all the answers."

"And we're sure that trying to cut through it could kill anyone trapped inside it?"

The doctor frowned. "I don't think cutting into it will kill everyone across the whole zone, if that's what you're asking, but it could certainly be detrimental to anyone in close proximity."

"But you're not sure?"

"Hell, no, I'm not sure." Leone rose to his feet, eyeing her. "Why, what are you thinking?"

Khatami blew out her breath. "Ensign Sotol and the others. I'm not willing to leave them here. If we can't find a way to reverse the process, then . . . then I want you and Klisiewicz to attempt removing them from the rock."

She saw the struggle playing out across her friend's features, his oath to do no harm to a patient weighing against his obligations to her, along with the realization that trying to free the captive officers and failing might somehow be a preferable fate than eternal imprisonment. "Atish, I don't know."

"Captain? Doctor?"

Lieutenant Klisiewicz and Seta were entering the village from what had been the path leading to the mountain, followed by a small band of Tomol. Scanning the crowd, Khatami noted the range of expressions on the faces of the survivors and the emotions they conveyed. Despair was present, of course, but there also was something else.

Hope?

"Seta," Khatami said, smiling at the sight of the young priestess. "It's good to see you again." Their previous meeting had been a rushed affair on the *Endeavour*'s hangar deck prior to her leaving with Leone and Klisiewicz to return here to Arethusa. "At first I'd thought you were caught up in all of this." It was only after she had sent people back to the surface to survey the results of the Preserver obelisk's actions that Khatami learned that Seta was among those Tomol who had been protected inside the cavern.

Smiling, Seta extended her hands and Khatami took them in her own. Was it her imagination, or did she sense a warmth and energy radiating from the young Tomol leader? There was no mistaking the glow in the girl's eyes, indicating that the Change had taken place within her as a result of her encounter with Kerlo, but there was no sign of the rage or madness that had characterized Nimur and the others who had fallen victim to the transformation.

"I am happy to see you as well," Seta said. "I wish to thank you for everything you have done for my people. We owe you a debt we can never repay."

Uncertain such a sentiment was deserved, Khatami felt a pang of remorse gripping her. "I don't know what to say, Seta." She looked away from the priestess, her eyes once more taking in the lifeless village. *No, not lifeless*, she reminded herself, *but it might as well be*. "I look around, and all I see is an enormous testament to our total failure here. All of this is our fault. If we had chosen not to visit your world, if our enemies had left you in peace, you . . ."

"Nimur would still have embraced the Changed," Seta said. "We would still have attempted to reclaim her, and we might well have ended up just as we are now. For all I know, I too would be with the Endless, forever unable to help my people." She squeezed Khatami's hands. "But you are here, and because of that, I stand before you, apart from the Endless." Looking to Leone, she added, "And if not for you, I would not be able to help my people as I now am prepared to do."

"I don't understand," Khatami replied, then looked to Klisiewicz. "Wait. Did you find something in the obelisk?"

The science officer indicated Seta with a nod. "Not exactly."

Releasing Khatami's hands, Seta held her arms away from her body in a gesture of embrace. "Kerlo changed me, but not before Leone provided me with his medicine. Though I now am one with the Change, it is not like it was for Nimur and the others. This is something . . . quite different."

"Different how?" Leone asked, reaching for his tricorder and retrieving the scanner from its storage compartment. He activated both devices and waved the scanner over Seta's head and down across her body. "This is . . . I don't know what the hell this is. Elevated heart rate and blood circulation, but no sign of stress or pressure. Brain activity is off the charts. It's like she's got ten or twelve of them in her skull. Neurological activity is . . . this is *unreal*."

"It is very real, Leone," Seta said, "and it is just the

beginning. My eyes see everything. My ears hear everything. My mind understands. The wordstone has finally shown me the way."

"You were able to read the symbols?" Khatami asked.

Klisiewicz said, "I think the best way to describe it is that it spoke to her, Captain. I didn't hear anything, but she certainly seemed to. When she emerged from the obelisk, she asked to come here."

"I want to share with you what I have learned. Without the haze of fury that has clouded the minds of all Tomol since the time of our enslavement by the Dark Gods, my people possess a potential far beyond anything we could possibly have imagined."

Stepping back from Khatami, Seta knelt on the stone shell encasing the village and everything else for kilometers in all directions, placing her hands flat atop its surface. "The pulse of life flows through this, the Shroud of the Endless. I touch it, just as it touches me." As she spoke, her hands began to emit a soft, golden glow that seemed to enter the rock and expand across the stone.

"Dear lord," Leone said, looking at first as though he wanted to run from the effect, but then it reached where he stood and continued past him, washing over the rock without regard for the doctor or Khatami herself, as well as everyone else moving about the village.

Hearing the whistle of a tricorder, Khatami saw that Klisiewicz was conducting a scan, and when he looked away from the device, it was to stare at her with wide eyes and a half-open mouth.

"Captain, this is incredible. My tricorder's showing this as an energy field, but it contains . . . it contains elements of the viral agent Doctor Leone created and administered to Seta and the other volunteers. It's reacting with the rock at an astronomical rate." The science officer paused, his brow furrowing as he continued to consult his tricorder. "It's as though it's rewriting its molecular structure, and the effect is accelerating. It's like wildfire."

"He's right," Leone said, now working with his own tricorder. "The agent's not just being absorbed by the rock; it's being transmitted along with the wave as it expands." Looking up from the readings, he shook his head. "Son of a bitch. The stone's actually acting like an inoculating infuser. I'm scanning some of the nearby Tomol who were caught up in the effect, and I'm seeing signs of the agent entering their bloodstreams." Stepping past Khatami, he was immersed in his tricorder readings. "This is the damnedest thing I've ever seen."

"Look!" Klisiewicz pointed to the ground. "It's starting to break down!"

Beneath their feet, the red-brown stone was dissolving before their eyes. Its color was fading and Khatami felt it compressing under her boots. Within moments, soil and grass were visible, everything still saturated by the sparkling glow of the golden energy wave.

And at the center of the miracle unfolding before their eyes was Seta, silent and unmoving, perhaps not even breathing. The glowing energy was continuing to emanate from within her, but the girl showed no sign of strain or discomfort. It was as though she had been destined for this moment.

Perhaps she was?

"The closest comparison I can come up with is that the

rock is sublimating," said Klisiewicz, "and at a staggering rate. In a couple of hours it will have swept across the entire island." He looked to Leone. "Did you count on something like this?"

"Hell, no," replied the doctor. "If I thought I was that good, you think I'd still be working for Starfleet?"

The science officer's expression was one of utter disbelief as he waved his tricorder. "I can't even begin to explain this."

"That's medicine for you, Lieutenant," Leone offered. "Sometimes shit happens, and you just roll with it."

Life had returned to the village.

The Tomol moved about, crowding the paths winding through the settlement or gathering at the village square. Hundreds of people, each of them appearing—to Khatami, at least—to embody the renewed promise and joy that now seemed to permeate the restored community. Khatami knew that was wishful thinking, of course, and that even with the incredible events of the past days as well as what Seta had accomplished, there would remain distrust and fear from many of the Tomol as they struggled to adapt to the new paradigm that was reshaping not just their lives but also their very reason for living.

Nearly two hours had passed since Seta's remarkable demonstration, and as far as Khatami could tell, there remained no evidence of the Preservers' petrification effect. As the process had continued to unfold, sweeping across the ten-kilometer area that had been encased in the astounding living rock, she had received reports from the

Endeavour detailing the progress of the energy wave Seta had set into motion. The village was as it had appeared from orbit, as idyllic, alive, and full of warmth and beauty as it had been before outsiders had seen fit to encroach upon its unfettered tranquillity.

"*I've just given Sotol and the others a quick once-over,*" said Doctor Leone over the open communicator frequency, "*and I'm not seeing any detrimental effects of the hibernation, but I'm taking them back to the ship for a complete physical just to be on the safe side.*"

"Excellent news, Tony. Keep me informed."

As she closed her communicator, Khatami saw Seta at the front of a small group of Tomol, walking up the path leading from the village square. A male and female were flanked by two males who were dressed in what Khatami recognized as the vestments worn by village Wardens, and each wielded a lance. The female Tomol was cradling a swaddled infant in her arms. As they drew closer, Seta offered one of her wide, contagious smiles, which forced Khatami to do the same.

"Captain," said the priestess, stopping before her and gesturing to her two charges. "These are Nimur and Kerlo."

Despite knowing that none of the Changed posed a threat, thanks to Doctor Leone's viral agent, Khatami still tensed at Seta's mention of the names. A nervous lump formed in her throat as she regarded the new arrivals before focusing her gaze on the priestess, and she now realized that, like Seta's, their eyes burned with the heat of the Change. "I see." She gestured to the infant. "You have a child."

Nimur smiled. "Yes. This is Tahna."

"She's beautiful," Khatami said, "like her mother."

The compliment seemed to make Nimur uncomfortable, and she shifted her feet while casting her gaze toward the ground. "I wish to apologize to you, Captain. I am told I brought pain and suffering to you and your people, and that I also brought death to my own people."

Khatami was surprised. "You don't remember what happened?"

"No. The Change robbed me of my memories, just as it took my body." She adjusted the child in her arms. "I cannot ever atone for the crimes I committed, or the pain I caused."

"Nor can I," added Kerlo. His features were clouded by sadness. "Our regrets are many, Captain, and we will spend the rest of our days attempting to redress the grief we have caused."

"I understand that your actions were not your own." Looking to Seta, she asked, "What will happen to them, and the other surviving Changed?"

"That is a matter for our forum to decide," the priestess replied. "There will be much to discuss. Though the crimes committed by the Changed are numerous and severe, Nimur was an instrument of our long-overdue transformation, rather than a cause. This, too, must be considered if we are to justly resolve this matter."

Khatami smiled, impressed by how much Seta seemed to have grown not only in the short time since she had assumed the mantle of priestess but also in the hours that had passed since the liberation of the Tomol from their stone prison. "You speak wise words, Holy Sister. I hope they will be heard by all who need to hear them."

Instructing the Wardens to escort Nimur and Kerlo back to the village, Seta waited until they were out of earshot before turning back to Khatami. "Before, we did not concern ourselves with the past to any great degree, as our lives were short and without the luxury of dwelling upon past transgressions. Things are different now, of course, so this demands a new way of thinking. Nimur and Kerlo will be treated with all fairness. The forum almost certainly will recommend some penalty, but I suspect that they will be lenient. After all, Nimur and Kerlo did not ask for what happened to them, and neither did the others."

"You're going to be a wonderful leader to your people, Seta," Khatami offered, placing a hand on her shoulder.

Seta attempted a small smile. "It is difficult."

"You'll manage. Great leaders always do."

"That is not what I mean." The priestess held up a hand. "My Change continues. I find my thoughts are so great that they feel as though they wish to escape my mind. My senses are aware of everything. I am . . . growing in so many ways, but I do not yet grasp it all, and I feel that I will soon find it difficult to be . . . of this life."

Alarmed, Khatami said, "I don't know what you mean. Are you . . . ?"

Seta, her face as calm and bright as it had been the first time Khatami met her, reached out to touch the captain's hand. "No, I am well. Please do not worry. I am becoming more than I was, as are we all."

"The Change?" Khatami asked.

"Yes. I can feel it flowing through me, yearning to grow, longing for release. I do not know what the future holds for me, but I know that we will strive to live in peace, as our ancestors did before the Dark Gods came for us."

Khatami nodded. "I think I understand. Is there anything more we can do?"

"You have already done so much," Seta replied. "Please know how grateful we are, and always will be, but I believe it is time for you to leave us. You are our friends, and we would welcome your return, but we must find our own path toward our new lives."

"Of course," Khatami replied. After contacting the *Endeavour* to stand by for transport, she let her gaze rest once more on the extraordinary young woman standing before her. "We will leave you in peace. I can't speak for other parties, but I can promise that my people will not return to your world without your permission."

Seta smiled. "You will always be welcome." She paused, her gaze turning away from Khatami for the briefest moment as though studying something only she could see. "Though I cannot promise that we will be here when you return, at least not as you now know us."

The young Tomol's final words, along with all the promise and even wonder they carried, rang in Khatami's ears as the transporter beam whisked her away.

33

"Thank you for your assistance, Captain. I truly appreciate it."

Standing before the viewscreen on the wall of her office, Atish Khatami regarded the visage of Captain Kang, who glowered at her as she spoke. Then, to her surprise, his features softened and he almost smiled.

"The honor was mine, Captain." The Klingon appeared to be seated in some sort of private office or other room that most certainly was not the bridge of the *Voh'tahk.* Hanging behind him on the stark gray metal bulkhead was a painting depicting dozens of Klingon warriors engaged in fierce combat, each wielding what Khatami recognized as *bat'leths* and *mek'leths,* traditional bladed weapons of the empire. The uniforms and armor worn by the soldiers suggested an ancient battle, doubtless one of the many campaigns peppered liberally throughout Klingon history as well as being of some particular significance to Kang, but Khatami reasoned that her relationship with her fellow captain had not yet progressed to the point where she could ask him about such things.

Someday. Maybe.

"And thank you as well for your assistance with our repairs. They will be sufficient for us to travel to a support base." Kang paused, as though studying her for a

moment, before continuing. *"You are the second human to defy my preconceptions regarding your people. Your science officer and doctor did so, as well. That they were willing to risk their own lives in order to save that of a Klingon—even one such as Tormog—earns them my respect."*

Smiling, Khatami repressed an urge to chuckle. "I'll be sure to convey your message." She paused, clearing her throat before reminding him, "Of course, there still remains one other matter of importance."

"The Tomol. Rest assured, Captain, that my interest in these people is concluded. Now that your doctor has restored the Tomol the gift of their advanced evolution and abilities while retaining their intellect, it is obvious that they are a people who will not so easily be . . . enlisted to serve the empire."

"That's an interesting way of putting it, Captain," Khatami said.

Kang shrugged. *"I see no reason to deny the empire's interest in the Tomol."* He leaned closer to the screen. *"However, I gave you my word that I would leave them in peace. I will honor that promise, but I cannot speak for my superiors. They may well decide to revisit this planet, and either conquer or destroy it as they see fit."*

"The Tomol will probably have something to say about that. After all, this race was at one time powerful enough to stand toe-to-toe with . . . well . . . some former inhabitants of this region." Khatami was certain that Kang knew she was referring to the Shedai, but neither captain was going to say that on an open communications frequency. There also could be no denying that the Tomol, now free of the madness that had consumed them upon the onset of the Change, would continue to grow stronger as their abilities developed. Even without a ship, they might one day find a way of leaving their planet, though she suspected their peaceful nature would compel them to remain on the world that they now truly could call "home."

For the first time since the start of their exchange, Kang's ominous expression softened and he almost smiled. *"I suspect that you are correct, Captain, and I will convey that observation to my superiors. What they decide to do with that information is beyond my control."*

After explaining the situation with Seta, she had convinced the young priestess to request her world be granted Federation protectorate status. As a side benefit of such an arrangement, Federation and Starfleet science teams would be allowed to return to the planet in order to further study the Tomol and the Preserver pyramid. A formal request was already on its way to the Federation Council, who in turn would inform the Klingon High Council of the Tomol's desire to be so recognized. Would that be sufficient to convince the Klingons to leave Arethusa and its people well enough alone? Only time would tell.

I guess it'll have to do, Khatami mused. *For now, anyway.* Besides, if Seta's predictions were true, she and the rest of the Tomol who underwent the Change might well be gone from the planet by the time anyone decided to return for a visit. How far would their evolution take them? Khatami had no idea, though she was certain it was something she would want to see for herself.

One day, hopefully.

Sensing that the conversation had served its purpose,

she said, "I don't wish to keep you from your duties any longer, Captain. Thank you again, and safe travels to you and your crew."

Kang seemed to ponder this, and for a moment Khatami wondered if she may have given inadvertent offense by not wishing the Klingon captain glorious victory or heroic death or some such thing. She relaxed when he laughed.

"*Safe travels to you and your crew, Captain. Perhaps we will meet again one day, in honorable battle.*"

"Let's hope not," Khatami said, offering a wry grin. "*Endeavour* out."

The viewscreen's image of Kang faded, replaced by a view of space as the ship continued on its journey away from Arethusa and toward Starbase 71. With the communication ended, Khatami allowed herself a small sigh of relief. She suspected that the Klingon Empire's interest in this world and the Tomol would not soon fade, as Kang had warned, but she was certain they at least would think twice before attempting any further "research" here. There were other worlds in the Taurus Reach that could be claimed—or conquered, in the empire's case—with far less trouble. Khatami held little doubt that this would not be her last run-in with the Klingons, or even Kang himself.

Won't that *be fun.*

She turned from the viewscreen as her office intercom beeped for attention, followed by the voice of Anthony Leone. "*Sickbay to Captain.*"

She keyed the control to open the channel. "Khatami here. What can I do for you, Doctor?"

"Just an update on Ensign Sotol and the others. I found no indications of any long-term effects from their ordeal, and I'm releasing them back to full duty."

"Excellent news, Tony. Thank you." She paused a moment before adding, "And thank you again for the work you did on the planet. If not for you and Lieutenant Klisiewicz, all of this would've turned out quite differently."

"So that means I'm due for a promotion or something, right?"

Chuckling, Khatami said, "Duly noted." Then her tone turned serious. "Even with everything you and Klisiewicz accomplished, we only just scratched the surface of the technology the Preservers left down there. It's too bad we might not get a chance to study that complex any further." Seta and Nimur had made plain their people's wish to be left undisturbed as they worked to restore—and in some cases restart—their society.

"They didn't rule out inviting us back, one day," Leone said. *"And even if they do, that'll likely be someone else's problem. You've done your duty, Captain. There's not much else for you to deal with until we drag the Sagittarius back for repairs, so how about you call it a day, skip whatever horrible sludge you're about to order from the garbage recycler you call that food slot in your office, and join me for a drink? I promise I won't mention your overdue physical even once."*

Leone's comments elicited another laugh as she eyed the food slot on her office's far wall. It had been her intention to eat her evening meal here while working on one of the backlogged reports for Starfleet Command, but the offer by her ship's doctor held much greater appeal. He was right that the journey to Starbase 71 with the *Sagittarius* in tow via tractor beam likely would prove uneventful. The repairs to the scout ship would take at least a couple of weeks, and Captain Terrell and his crew were looking forward to a well-earned shore leave.

Her door chime sounded, making Khatami glance at the chronometer on her desk to confirm that her next appointment was right on time. "Thanks for the offer, Tony, but I'm not quite done with the day's duties. I'll get back to you." Severing the communication, she called out, "Come in."

The door slid aside to reveal Stephen Klisiewicz, his arms clasped behind his back and his expression passive, though Khatami detected in his eyes any number of unspoken questions.

"You wanted to see me, Captain?"

Waving him in, Khatami gestured to the two chairs situated before her desk. "Have a seat, Lieutenant." As Klisiewicz lowered himself into one of the chairs, she said, "As I was just telling Doctor Leone, I wanted you to know how impressed I am with the work you did, both here and on the planet. That you were able to accomplish what you did under such pressure is incredible, and that's exactly what I'll be saying in my report to Starfleet Command when I submit you both for commendations."

Klisiewicz blinked a few times as he processed her remarks, then nodded. "Thank you, Captain. I appreciate that."

Moving to her own chair behind the desk, Khatami sat and crossed her arms. "That you were able to make the connections between the Tomol's condition and the changes made to them by the Shedai was remarkable all by itself, but that you also were able to assist Doctor Leone in creating his cure was something else entirely." She had been considering how best to broach this subject, coming to the conclusion that there was only one way to confront her suspicions.

"As I recall, your studies and research regarding the Shedai during Operation Vanguard focused on their technology and the various artifacts and structures we found. Your role in those missions had no real need to focus on Shedai biology or any medical applications of the metagenome, and assisting Leone as you did would require such knowledge, or at the very least access to research data and other materials from the Vanguard project." Khatami leaned forward in her chair, resting her forearms on her desk. "But since all of that information was purged from the ship's memory banks and anything pertaining to the project has been classified and archived under Starfleet's tightest security protocols, I'm curious how you were able to reach some of the conclusions you made."

Though he was making an admirable effort to control his facial features and body language, Khatami saw through the façade, her hunch strengthened when he shifted in his seat and attempted to swallow.

"I've never lied to you, Captain," he said after a moment, "and I'm not about to start. Ming Xiong gave me a complete copy of all the Project Vanguard data he collected." As he spoke, Klisiewicz's gaze dropped to his hands, which were clasped in his lap. "It happened the last time I saw him, before the Tholians' final assault on Starbase 47. We'd just conducted our experiment with the

Shedai array on that planetoid, Ursanis Two." He shook his head. "We destroyed it, Captain, as easily as I might delete a file from the computer's memory banks. The power we were holding in the palm of our hand was staggering, and all Ming and I could think about was what could happen if that power fell into the wrong hands. Can you imagine that thing under Klingon or Romulan control? I break out into a cold sweat just thinking about it."

Khatami recalled the experiment, which had involved Lieutenant Ming Xiong constructing an array consisting of thousands of crystalline artifacts created millennia ago by a long-extinct race, the Tkon, who at one point in the distant past had been rivals of the Shedai. The crystals had been built for the purpose of containing the Shedai in noncorporeal form, and once trapped, each crystal was capable of producing immense energy that could be directed at the whim of its wielder. The Tkon had used Shedai in this manner to create weapons of unimaginable destructive power as well as to power data and transportation networks spanning the Taurus Reach. Ming Xiong, more than anyone else involved with Operation Vanguard, had learned enough about both ancient races and their technology to cobble together the array of crystals and interface it with the interdimensional conduits used by the Shedai to move through space. This had resulted in the capture of every surviving Shedai life-form. With the Shedai now harnessed in the array's individual crystals, Xiong was able to experiment with channeling the power they produced, and the target of his test was the remote, uninhabited planetoid Ursanis II. Nearly one hundred light-years from Starbase 47, the small, insignificant world had been crushed from existence without the slightest lingering trace, leaving Xiong and everyone else who knew about the experiment to wonder what would happen if such a weapon were used against a populated planet.

"Ming knew that the higher-ups in Starfleet were watching us," Klisiewicz continued. "He knew that the potential for abuse of the array was a legitimate concern."

Khatami shook her head. "Admiral Nogura would never have allowed that."

"Admiral Nogura doesn't outrank everyone, Captain. Someone somewhere had plans for that thing, and that's before we get back to the idea of the Klingons or Romulans or someone else ever getting their hands on it. Ming knew that, too, and he wanted someone to safeguard everything we'd learned in the event something happened to him."

Reaching behind his back and under his blue uniform tunic, Klisiewicz produced what Khatami recognized as an old-style Starfleet scanning device, the twenty-second-century ancestor to modern tricorders. Opening the unit, the lieutenant held it up for her to see, and Khatami noted that the scanner's innards were in fact a compact, self-contained data storage and access device.

"It's all in here," Klisiewicz said. "Everything Ming recorded during his time on the project."

Unable to take her eyes from the scanner, Khatami felt her throat tighten. "You understand that just having that, let alone accessing its contents, is a violation of more Starfleet regulations than either of us can count? Tell me none of the data's in the main computer."

Klisiewicz shook his head. "I can review it without

linking to the memory banks, so there's no record of it anywhere."

"You've put me in a bind here, Lieutenant," Khatami snapped, rising from her chair. "I should throw you in the brig and destroy that thing, then contact Admiral Nogura and beg him not to bury us both in whatever hole he stashed what's left of Vanguard." She knew that the admiral, following the loss of Starbase 47 and as one of his first official duties after being posted to Starfleet Headquarters on Earth, had assembled all remaining records and artifacts related to Operation Vanguard and secreted them at one of Starfleet's classified archive installations. While she hoped the data collected by Ming Xiong and others might eventually serve to benefit the Federation, its allies, and perhaps even adversaries that might one day be friends, that time was not now. Wounds inflicted while acquiring that knowledge had not yet healed. Buried under uncounted layers of security and bureaucracy, the chances of that information resurfacing in Khatami's lifetime were slim at best.

"I understand," Klisiewicz said, again holding up the scanner. "But without it, we might never have figured out how to help the Tomol." He paused, shrugging. "I mean, Doctor Leone and I might have eventually stumbled onto the cure, but I doubt we'd have done it in time to do any good."

"I'm aware of that," Khatami countered, "and it's the only reason you're not in the brig." She held out her hand. "Give it to me."

Without hesitation, Klisiewicz surrendered the scanner. "And before you ask, there are no copies. Everything Ming gave me is in there."

Pausing, Khatami drew a deep breath as she contemplated the situation she now faced. "Your initiative was commendable, Lieutenant, as is your desire to be some sort of defender of truth and ethics in Ming Xiong's stead. For what it's worth, I agreed with him about how we should treat the Shedai technology." She held up the scanner. "But rules such as those surrounding this material are there for a reason. If I find out you've circumvented them again, regardless of your intentions, you're through. Do I make myself clear, mister?"

Klisiewicz straightened in his chair. "You do, Captain."

"Good." Khatami waved toward her door. "Dismissed."

As the door slid open at his approach, the science officer turned to face her. "Captain, may I ask what you're going to do with that?"

"I don't have the first damned idea. Go away, Lieutenant." She waited until Klisiewicz departed and the door slid shut behind him to release an exasperated sigh. "I should've resigned and gone home when I had the chance."

Khatami swiveled her chair to the section of bulkhead positioned to her left and below her desk. There, a small access door and a recessed keypad had been installed, and she entered a private security code into the pad. The panel slid aside, revealing several computer data cards and a small binder containing an old-fashioned journal—a book of bound paper—in which she recorded by hand whatever information or thoughts she did not want entered even into the personal log maintained for her by the ship's computer. She placed Klisiewicz's scanner at the rear of the compartment, then moved the stack of data cards in front of it before placing the journal atop the pile.

After entering the code to close and lock the secure alcove, she leaned back in her chair and closed her eyes.

What the hell am I supposed to do now?

Her first instinct was to follow her initial gut decision to destroy the device and the data it held. On the other hand, Klisiewicz was correct: it was the knowledge she now held that had allowed him and Leone to save the Tomol from an eternity of imprisonment on Arethusa. How many other planets or races were out there, enduring some long-term effect or injury as a consequence of past subjugation or exploitation at the hands of the Shedai? It stood to reason that in the course of their mission to further explore the Taurus Reach, the *Endeavour* or some other starship might encounter such a civilization. Did Khatami hold a key toward helping them as well?

And is keeping it worth the risk?

She had to believe that Starfleet and the Federation, as a collective, would never allow worst-case scenarios such as those envisioned by Ming Xiong and Admiral Nogura. Still, she knew that there always would be someone who thought such heinous acts were acceptable in the name of security or some such damned thing. It was why Xiong had taken steps to safeguard what he had learned, and why Nogura had done his level best to sweep away any vestiges of Vanguard and most of those who knew the whole story. How long could a secret of such magnitude stay hidden?

However long that might be, Khatami decided it likely would not be long enough.

"To hell with this," she said, pushing herself from her chair. She would have to give the matter serious thought, but it would wait for a short while, at least until after she found Doctor Leone.

Because that drink sounds damned good right about now.

ACKNOWLEDGMENTS

We offer our sincere thanks to our editors at Pocket Books, for daring to take a chance on this new series. They'd already given us a lot of leeway with the *Star Trek Vanguard* novels, and no sooner were the last words of those books committed to the page than we were thinking, "Okay, now what?"

Thanks as well to David Mack, our co-conspirator. Working with him on the *Vanguard* novels was tremendous fun, made all the more so by our friendship and our joint passion for the work. *Star Trek: Seekers* was born out of a desire to find something new and shiny so that we might once again harness some of that aforementioned fun.

We tip our hats to Rob Caswell, whose fanciful imagery depicting a ship not at all unlike the *U.S.S. Sagittarius* provided us with our inspiration. It's not unreasonable to think that *Seekers* would not have come about if we hadn't stumbled upon his work. So blame him if you end up not liking any of this stuff.

Finally, we thank you, our readers who followed us during our first adventures into the Taurus Reach and who now have opted to journey with us once again. Or maybe you've never read the *Vanguard* novels and you're checking us out for the first time. No matter your reasons for being here, we're thrilled you're along for the ride.

ABOUT THE AUTHORS

Dayton Ward has been modified to fit this medium, to write in the space allotted, and has been edited for content. Reader discretion is advised. Visit Dayton on the web at www.daytonward.com.

Kevin Dilmore is universally specific and easily sendable. If you have questions about postage rates, contact your local post office. Should you need him, he's usually goofing off on Facebook.